THOUSAND EYES

Book 2 of
The Deep Wide Black

JCH Rigby

Cover Art by Duncan Halleck
Cover Design by The Gilded Quill (thegildedquill.co.uk)

JCH Rigby
Visit my author page at www.castrumpress.com /jch-rigby

Printed in the United Kingdom

First Printing: Aug 2018
Castrum Press

ISBN-13 978-1-9123273-3-1

THOUSANDEYES

Contents

PROLOGUE

Villages I Cannot Name

A scrimmage in a Border Station –
A canter down some dark defile
Two thousand pounds of education
Drops to a ten-rupee *jezail.*

"ARITHMETIC ON THE FRONTIER," RUDYARD KIPLING (1886)

Date Redacted

As far as I can tell, my name is Rifleman Sushant Rai. I think I am twenty-nine years old. When I concentrate long enough to recollect who I am and why I'm here, I remember floating in this reconnaissance ship on counter-penetration duty, watching the galaxies turn for fifty-two standard years. But that's nonsense, isn't it?

Through my sensors, far-off dust motes resolve into spiral arms, radiating across the spectrum as my craft bobs on gravitational tides. A million suns are pouring into a black hole in Virgo; I've listened to them shrieking as they die, bleeding gouts of elementary particles. In this eye-blink instant of the universe's life, I have seen two supernovae. Pulsars flicker on my sensors; stars blaze in colors that I once could not have seen. Radiations wash me, gravities pull me, particles breathe their momentary existences out against the hull.

My life has slowed to a crawl, in man-time.

Once, long ago above Lhasa, I lay awake for three days, twitchy from stimulants, camouflaged and motionless, my face pressed against my rifle's stock. It tested me; I found it hard to lie so still. But I must have been good at it. The Chinese clearance patrol hunting for us went right through our position twice, and they never knew it.

The second and fatal time, they settled down to administer themselves inside the ring of our close observation platoon, right on top of my section. On a word from our naik, we leapt from the rocks and slew them all. Well, most of us leapt. My legs were so stiff that I lost my balance and nearly fell on my own kukri. My target almost got away. Almost. Soon my friends mocked me as we stood among the corpses.

Now, three months might pass in my three days. I lie still for years. Like the others, I sit among the stars, dreaming decades away as my instruments watch and listen. Music, books, mind games distract me. Machines tend to me; they feed me, maintain my systems, and repair me at need. My little friends, I call them; tiny servants which scuttle around the ship, clambering about me in cozy intimacy. Their minute tentacles drip nutrients, whisk away stray hairs and nails; they analyze my wastes, adjust my diet, exercise my muscles and tenderly investigate every particle of me, organic or artefact.

I snuggle in to the sheltering planetoids of this system and smile indulgently as they hum about their parent sun. I have given them silly names and made pets of them. Showers of rocks tumble, endlessly chasing out into the black and then scuttling back to the comfort of the light. There, a little moon loops and dashes about a gas giant, swooping in and out of its rings. Here a pair of planets perform figures of eight in a shared atmosphere as if they hold hands; they are like lovers dancing, always facing each other.

I dream of my home, of my family, of smoke rising above the stupas of Pashupatinath Temple, of mountain streams and villages which now I cannot name, of cold beer, even of my old battalion – all long dead, long forgotten, our battles meaningless now. Can anyone else still remember them? What would my naik make of a solitary, barely-human creature drifting among these ageless stars and musing on ancient wars? They are all as lost as Bharatpur, Fatehgarh, Tunisia, Borneo, Bluff Cove.

We wait, so few of us; we wait for signs of the enemy.

△ △ △

There is a picture on the screen in front of me. A smiling man is holding a Bren gun, and he is my ancestor. There are too many great-greats for me to be sure what he is to me. His name is also Rai, but I can't recall the rest. Sometimes I don't know what I'm called either.

The picture is very old, and has no color. How do I know that the weapon is called a Bren gun? How do I know that he is my ancestor?

His steel helmet is pushed back and he is smiling at the camera. The picture is unusual. Many pictures of that time are stiff and formal. Was this one taken by a friend?

He sits on a rock in a jungle clearing, the unloaded Bren across his knees. A water canteen rests by his feet. He is cleaning the light machine gun; its working parts are exposed. A magazine lies beside him on top of a small pack, next to his unsheathed kukri. I can just see the top round inside the mag, so I know he can reassemble the weapon and open fire if he needs to.

Pictures of what time?

△ △ △

I am abruptly awake. My craft has seen something, and has alerted me. I have no more time for dreaming. The sensors are pawing through the black in response to the alarm.

They direct my attention to the fourth planet of this system. I study their data for a few moments and then spot the anomaly. Something is rising from behind a moon. The signal matches nothing of human make.

My smiling ancestor encourages me. *"Lie still, be quiet, be patient. The least snap of a twig will tell the enemy that you are there. His eyes, ears, nose are seeking you, but you can feel him approach. He moves like a snake, but you can see him. The jungle is silent, but you can hear him.*

"Let his scouts walk into your killing zone, onto the sights of your weapon. Then let his rear guard pass your cut-offs and your stops. When all are inside the reach of your weapons, he is yours. Ayo Gorkhali!"

He is called Tulbah Rai.

Thank you, Tulbah.

I am called Sushant Rai, and I serve on Operation ThousandEyes.

△ △ △

A faint vibration runs through the ship as the nose swings onto a new heading. The engines begin to push. The thrust feels as if heavy gravity has returned. My head sags rearwards and a loose cup tumbles aft; how careless of me. Acceleration builds as the cabin fills with protective gel. I feel the facial pressure which the pilots called "eyeballs-in." These metal eyeballs barely move.

My seat straps tighten; I hope that I haven't snagged the umbilical leads. An opaque tube runs from my throat to the air handling system. A pair of clear hoses, running between my arm and the medical unit, are full of my blood. They become heavy and sag into a curve. Lighter tubes and cables tether me to other units; I can't remember what each one does, but I'm sure I would know in a second if I needed to. They all trace loops through the protective gel and across the cabin.

I check the thousands of sensors I have scattered across this system. The intruder is lifting away from the moon's orbit, on a course which will intercept the fifth planet in seventy-three days. I shall be waiting for the trespasser in sixty-eight days.

My arm feels cold as fluids flow into my veins. Through the screens I see the stars accelerate. The dreamtime always feels like this. I do not slow down; instead, the rest of the universe speeds up.

I think about a .303-inch light machine gun, of 22.8 pounds weight, an effective range of 600 yards from the bipod, and mounting a curved thirty-round box magazine on top of the body. Because of this, the iron sights are offset to the left.

I'm sure that there was a picture of someone on the control screen, or was that my imagination? I cannot recall.

I will be in position in thirty-four days.

Chapter 1

I slew them

My little friends brought me back from the dreaming and speeded me up to man-time, and on again into neural overdrive. Before the enemy vessel could fight or flee, I reached out from my lair and struck; then I ran. Ran like a thief; ran like a peasant who has killed a prince; ran, scattering drones and sensors to watch my back. Ran from retribution and hid light-months away, trembling with reaction after the kill. Skulked and watched, slowing myself back down little by little as no retaliation came. Then I crept back to my post, every sense and sensor straining to detect ambush, but finally burying myself safely amongst the planets and giving myself up to guilt.

Why should I feel guilty? We stood and laughed above Lhasa, surrounded by Chinese bodies. "He's a fat one! Lucky he didn't trip up and land on you, Rai!" The naik was laughing.

"Limbu! Stop groping him! He's sound asleep!" shouted my friend Thapa. Limbu was searching one of the bodies. His hands were bloody.

They were men like us. They had families who wondered how Dad or brother Li was doing, and worried about them away in the war. We had just made orphans and widows. This meant grief, loneliness, hardship. Somewhere, children would be sobbing, wives staring wide-eyed and silent, bereaved parents struck dumb. But we felt no guilt. Brother Li would have killed me in a moment, if he had known I was there. If I had moved, he would have laughed over *my* corpse. They were men exactly like us.

But I didn't know this enemy. I knew that they weren't men. They could have been anything – tigers, demons, spirits.

I sprang from the dark into the heavens to slay my enemies. Am I a demon?

△ △ △

They are out there, whoever they are. *Whatever* they are; I don't know. I have forgotten much, and there is much more that I don't know right now, but that I could remember if I needed to. But this ignorance is different.

I am called Sushant Rai, and I serve the ARTOK Company on Operation ThousandEyes. I must remember these things. We – my brothers and sisters and I – are searching for signs of the enemy. Scattered across humanity's stub-end of the galaxy, we wait for the unknown.

Who have I killed? *What* have I killed?

I know that I *don't* know the enemy, and that I never have done. No one ever has; no one human, at any rate. I'm not sure if the craft that I destroyed belonged to the enemy, but the wreck certainly wasn't a human ship.

I remember my training. We have not met the enemy. The octomorphs met the enemy, and the octomorphs lost their planets. And the fang-gliders met them, and the fang-gliders lost their minds.

The enemy are out there, and they are unknown, and they extinguish species which dare to travel between the stars.

Species like us.

△ △ △

It has been twenty-three years since I killed that craft, years in which its people must have wondered what became of their ship – was this just an inexplicable loss on a wild frontier? But today I found the body of a victim, a being drifting in a ripped suit amidst a cloud of wreckage.

Perhaps a maintenance worker, attending to the needs of the ship when my missiles swooped in? Or perhaps a soldier like me, like Limbu, like dead brother Li, moving out in a patrol to secure their perimeter. I'll never know. Nothing else survives from its vessel.

I don't think that this was the enemy.

△ △ △

I pull the little body into the airlock, and I search it like Limbu did. There is no risk, for it is certainly dead. The little creature has strangely articulated arms and legs, and a long tail. Under the suit, the body is furry. The creature may have been a mammal. Yet the jaws seem to operate sideways, under insect's eyes; it would have stood no more than a meter tall. The torn EVA suit was a single-piece garment, containing some small tools that I don't understand.

There is nowhere on my tiny ship to store the corpse, so I record as much data as I can. The havildar will want to see everything.

But there is no havildar, and I find that while I have been studying the body, I have forgotten my name once more. I salute brother Li, and I ask his forgiveness before sending him on a long path sunwards.

A man stares at me from the screen. He is holding an ancient weapon, and he is smiling at me. I have no idea who he is.

Chapter 2
Mexican Stand-Off

"Congratulations, dear boy. You really do deserve this role; the work you've been doing in Business Development has been terribly exciting. Quite splendid, in fact. You'll bring such a wonderful range of experience to the Executive Board. We're looking forward to your simply marvelous insight. Smashing." The avatar of Andy Gregory smiled benignly at his younger colleague.

Floridly English mannerisms were once again fashionable in the higher echelons of ARTOK. Such trends had an almost predictable life. The company was the *Anglo-Russian Trading and Operations Konglomerat*, after all – the spelling was traditional – and from time to time a rising generation of corporate stars rediscovered the drawling speech patterns and tweedy dress sense of their predecessors and aped them. The stylized affectations followed them up the company ladder, and eventually became identified with the class of senior executives whom some nameless junior wag had dubbed "the weather people." They were so high up that you couldn't influence them; like weather, they just happened to you. In time, however, the currently influential and powerful Anglos would retire or move out, and Anglicization would be replaced by whatever now-trendily-Russian fashion defined the next wave of future leaders.

Gregory, born Andrei Konstantinovich Grigoriev, was the outgoing operations director who had the pleasant task of handing over this poisoned chalice. Operations was the highest-profile role in the company, demanding commercial aggression, compulsive attention to detail, and endless watchfulness; his baby for seventeen exhausting years. Now he was looking forward to retirement, crown green bowls and watching cricket, and if this blasted Ivan Alexandrovich Lavarev couldn't speak English like a gentleman, then that was his lookout.

△ △ △

Lavarev tiptoed around the office as if he expected to be found out. This had been his breakthrough moment, but he still couldn't quite believe his luck – or that good luck could be so tainted with bad.

The hotbed of sales mania that was Business Development had one saving grace – you could always shift the blame for any performance failure onto the Operations guys. You prostituted yourself to sell a brilliant service to the customer, bled your budget dry to give them the best terms, struck a deal which had the Sales guys cheering you and buying you drinks – and then these grubby Operations dolts screwed up the service delivery for you.

But be careful what you wish for, and try not to do *too* well. His success in the last job had won him a seat at the top table, but his new post was the worst one possible – Operations. And now he had to deliver on the wild promises made by those idiots in Business Development.

He looked out of the window at Red Square. On the other hand, coming back to Moscow in person had advantages, and this fabulous view was one of them. So never mind whining about the downside – here he was with a seat on the executive board of one of the largest corporations in human history. Something this big was never going to be easy. Now, how soon could he get shot of this old Anglophile fool and start kicking out at NipponDeutsch?

Gregory wasn't going quietly, though. He spent the next two hours battering Lavarev's ears with the minutiae of every damn shuttle, every pathetic habitat, every petty mining operation. Tea and biscuits came, and Lavarev consumed them. Then Gregory went on to the Out Systems, and clattered on and on about the company's activity in every colony where humanity had ever been.

Lavarev began to pray that the damned man's avatar would somehow lose connection with its principal's character map and simply fizzle out. Where was the crusty old idiot, anyhow? Somewhere on Earth, or out in the System? Surely he wasn't further away than that.

He snapped back to the here and now when his attention was caught by something interesting. The last time he'd paid attention, Gregory had been talking about the ruinously expensive licensing arrangements into which ARTOK had been locked, an arrangement made to get access to the opposition's FTL space drive technology. Lavarev had stopped listening, relying on his own avatar to track the conversation covertly and notify him if anything more considered than "Yes, I see, interesting" was required. The Anglophiles regarded that as very poor manners, so he had the thing in a state of high readiness.

His avatar duly alerted him to something in Gregory's tone, and replayed him the last few seconds while he tried to look wise and thoughtful. His mouth dropped open. "I'm sorry, Andy, I think I missed something there. Did you just mention *aliens*?"

The older man stared at him, evidently aware that he hadn't been listening. "I was saying that, yes. I'll just recap, shall I? Righty-oh. This bit is very need-to-know, and you do, now. On one of NipponDeutsch's earliest FTL test missions, back in 2310, a vessel called *Amaterasu Ōmikami* encountered a derelict fleet of eleven non-human starships in orbit around a Jupiter-like planet. Inside the hulls, they discovered hundreds of dead bodies of one alien species, and – in one of the ships – a single huge carnivore of a different species.

"The alien ships had a device which vectored gravity, and this somehow caused the death of one member of the NipponDeutsch exploration team. Rotten luck, that. Then all the alien starships began to move at once. The exploration team fled, leaving the chap's body aboard. NipponDeutsch's *Amaterasu* went one way; the alien fleet went the other, left the system and accelerated for several years.

"The system itself was rather interesting: a suite of planets which are a very close match for our own, but orbiting one member of a binary star. The details are all in the catalogue. Anyhow, we've not been back there since, and neither have they, we believe. And we know that the alien fleet hasn't.

"That's what I said, old boy. Any questions on that so far?"

Lavarev hardly knew where to begin. After a few seconds of spinning his wheels, he thought he'd spotted a flaw. "How do we know about all this, but the public doesn't?"

"We were brought this by a NipponDeutsch defector, a German soldier who had been on the *Amaterasu* mission and was running for dear life. He told us that the rest of the test crew had disappeared. Our predecessors speculated that NipponDeutsch had killed them to preserve operational security.

"The German's former employers evidently weren't prepared to reveal their shiny new FTL technology just yet, so they could hardly mention stumbling across two lots of aliens in orbit around a theoretically inaccessible star, could they? So they kept it private."

"Hmm." Lavarev thought that killing corporate traitors was a perfectly reasonable precaution. He got up and started pacing once more. "Aliens... and a vectored-gravity device. What does that do – point gravity in a different direction?"

The avatar smiled, marking the point with a thumbs-up. "It seems that it does, perhaps purely locally. Handy on a spacecraft. But it might do even more. You'll understand there's very little information about it. But consider the implications: these creatures have technologies which we don't understand, and which we can't yet reproduce. Think of the opportunities for a trading advantage!"

Lavarev drew a breath. He was sure that his heart was beating faster. "That would be spectacularly valuable. Where did the *Amatera*-whatsit encounter these aliens? Where were the aliens headed – and where are they now?"

Gregory pursed his lips. "*Amaterasu Ōmikami.* Japanese, of course. The Shinto religion's sun goddess, I gather. It took us a long time to find out where the aliens were going. For all that we had the defector, filling in the gaps in what we knew was extremely costly, in both treasure and lives.

"And what we found out is that the aliens are still moving. Look here, old boy."

The avatar gestured into existence a black sphere filled with constellations. Deep inside it, points of colored light flashed in time with his words. "Here we are in the home system. Here is Epsilon Indi, and here are Centauri and Cygni. Let's move further out, shall we?" The twisted orb representing human space shrank until the colored points merged into one; new star systems and constellations swam in from the periphery as the black globe expanded. More highlighted points flickered into existence, one of them far outside the human region.

"Here is where the *Amaterasu* found the eleven derelicts. Well, a few years after they left, the alien ships stopped accelerating, and they've carried on at a very high sub-light speed ever since. This is the current approximate location of that fleet. They're now around thirty-five light years from where they were first encountered." A section of the globe glowed crimson. "We think they may be heading for somewhere in this area."

Lavarev's mouth had dried, and he struggled to speak. He forced himself to drink some of the stone-cold tea. "That's an enormous distance. Presumably we're going after them, aren't we? Whoever these people are, we'll meet them again sooner or later. We'll have to get our hands on that kind of technology. We need to trade with them." He stared at the globe. How the hell had this stayed secret for well over a century?

△ △ △

Gregory's avatar smiled. "Of course you're right, Ivan. But going after them is rather the problem. Our technologies are mismatched. Travelling faster than light could put us ahead of them, if we knew where they were going, but we can't just catch up with them and then slow down as we hurtle past. You know that the Waldschmidt drive doesn't permit such maneuvers. Their high conventional speed means that we can't easily catch them in a sub-light speed tail chase, either.

"The NipponDeutsch *Amaterasu* left a small remote behind when they fled, and we sent an unmanned probe ship to the system some ten years later, once we had the FTL tech. That's how we know about this; of necessity, our first information was quite old. Now we regularly jump an FTL probe out on their trail to get an update."

Lavarev seemed out of his depth, Gregory thought. He knew how the younger man felt; seventeen years ago, he had received a very similar brief. Extraordinary how little the situation had changed in that time.

"But there's even more to it than that," he went on. Lavarev's mouth was ajar. "The *Amaterasu* operations team spent their entire return trip talking it over, modelling the options, game-playing some alternatives. Their best call was that there were *three* sets of aliens, not two. They felt it was likely that the carnivore used no technology, which meant that something else had to have brought it there.

"The then-executive board went over all this, as you'd expect. They decided to track the alien ships, and to see where they went. Remember, these are derelict ships, moving automatically. Their crews are long dead. It's not them we want, it's access to their home systems. So we pop up and look at their current position, year after year. And of course, the Euro-Japanese opposition are doing the same."

Gregory's avatar watched Lavarev's face for a reaction. The youngster was annoying and cocky, but that didn't mean he was stupid.

Lavarev seemed to get hold of himself. "But this was, oh, 130 something years ago. We started using NipponDeutsch's FTL technology around then, soon after they did. In these circumstances, how the hell did we manage to persuade them to license it to us? Why did they give away that huge lead?"

The avatar chuckled like an elderly uncle. "My dear fellow, once the defector told us what they had, we simply put the Euro-Japanese under a great deal of pressure. We threatened to leak that NipponDeutsch's *Amaterasu* had attacked the aliens and put us all in danger of an interstellar war, and that we had a witness who had been there and was willing to say so. All high-risk nonsense, of course, but the Euro-Japanese didn't want to jeopardize their new toy starships by linking them with bad publicity and nasty politics.

"They denied it, of course, but our directors of the day were able to persuade them. Taking soldiers with them on those missions was a huge mistake, and killing their own staff was another. It wouldn't have helped their public image at all if it had got out, and back then they weren't quite as independent of the European and Japanese governments as they are now.

"But it would have hurt us too. The thing is, however poorly the other chap's behaved, people tend to disapprove of blackmail. So we privately agreed that state intervention – by any state – would be very bad news." Lavarev nodded repeatedly, as if he was trying to assimilate too much at once.

The avatar went on. "They eventually gave us access to their FTL tech. Still cost a bloody great deal, though. Our silence was part of the price; not a word to anyone about aliens. Now we're keeping an eye on the alien ships, and so are they, and neither of us are talking about it. And not a word about dead soldiers or dead aliens.

"However, it's fair to say that NipponDeutsch took rather a dim view of us leaning on them. It's likely they'll try to make us pay for it eventually. One day the alien fleet will start to decelerate, and we'll have a proper idea of where they're going. And then there'll be a race to get there first, with the likelihood of significant fisticuffs between us and NipponDeutsch, whatever these aliens may turn out to be. Until then, it's Mexican stand-off. Modest and deniable violence only. We know it, NipponDeutsch know it, and now you do too."

Δ Δ Δ

Lavarev poured himself a glass of water, and called for more tea. He needed the thinking time while he processed this series of revelations. Whichever company won the race for this alien technology would be handed a massive advantage. He'd heard a lot this morning, and he had a great deal to do if he wanted to improve on Gregory's undoubted achievements, but this was the most important news by far. No wonder it had been kept very quiet indeed.

He thought of a loose end. "And what happened to the German defector from the *Amaterasu*?"

The avatar sat, plucked at its semi-visible trouser legs and then smoothed its clipped moustache. "Our predecessors set him up in the operations security organization for a few years, and he did a decent job for us here and there. We've got some jolly well-armed chaps who make life nasty and short for anyone who tries attacking us. You'll need to spend some time with that crowd – real little terriers; they bite your legs and they won't let go."

"And then what became of him? He must be long dead by now."

Gregory smiled. "Actually, no; at least, I shouldn't think so. What do you know about the Human Enhancement Program?"

"What, the cyborgs and so on? Wasn't that shut down last century?" Lavarev couldn't see where this was leading.

"That's what the Company would like people to think. It became politically unacceptable to use those cyborgs on Earth. But you'll understand, old boy, that the military human enhancement program soaked up massive amounts of ARTOK time and money, so the Company wasn't just going to throw it all away."

The answer came to Lavarev in a flash. "They're far out in the deep wide black somewhere? And the German is with them? He's now a cyborg?"

The avatar's expression was a combination of smugness and cunning. "Best thing to do with him. Too knowledgeable to be turned loose, too useful to kill. We've got quite a lot of special forces soldiers, but the skills can't just be implanted. Human enhancement meant that we could access his knowledge and control his memories. We could even extend his life, if it became necessary."

"And he agreed to that?"

"I doubt it, but does it matter? As I say, his memories can be controlled. Anyway, think back to the *Amaterasu,* and the dead aliens which the Euro-Japanese discovered. Hundreds of them. Little creatures about the size of a ten-year-old child. Long arms, a tail. Insect eyes. Jaws worked sideways. Maybe hostile, maybe not. The ships were probably their colony vessels. Slower than light, big enough to carry several generations for decades, if not longer.

"And remember the huge creature they found? Six limbs – arms and legs like a centaur, but teeth and claws like some sort of lizard. Skin like armor. A real nightmare. Clearly a carnivore. No clothes or tools, although it did have opposable thumbs about the size of your forearm, with massive talons. Maybe it was intelligent, maybe not."

Lavarev felt they were getting close to another revelation. "If it wasn't intelligent, how did it get there? Was it a pet or something?"

"If it was a pet, what the hell was its owner like? You know how I said that there might be *three* sets of aliens? Perhaps something else put the carnivore aboard the alien ship. Something smart enough to travel in space, powerful and hostile enough to attack a fleet of starships, and genocidal enough to massacre the occupants.

"The Euro-Japanese didn't seem to be very interested in that, but we are. We've been keeping a very quiet eye out for that 'something else' ever since. There's a mission called Operation ThousandEyes, which you also need to know about."

Lavarev felt a grin split his face. "You've got the cyborgs keeping an eye out for hostile aliens?"

"Exactly. The perfect mission for them. They've got all the necessary skills, and we can leave them out there for decades, slowed down to tick over. If anything hostile does appear, they'll be extremely useful. You never know; we might need them again."

Lavarev thought of a problem. "What if the story gets out? It'll be tricky to portray the cyborgs as saviors of the human race. They're not going to be popular hero material."

"Vladimir Filippovich Semyonov himself is very interested in making this work. The Chairman has had our senior public relations people thinking about how to manage the story. They think it might be possible to shift public opinion over time, if the tale is pitched sympathetically. But it may need a – shall we say? – more independent voice.

"Have you ever heard of a journalist called David Chambers? Vladimir Filippovich wishes to cultivate the gentleman."

SANCTUARY
2445 – 2447

Chapter 3
To The Zoroastrian Republic

"This war, like the next war, is a war to end war."
— DAVID LLOYD GEORGE

For David Chambers, and only for him, it started on Orchard, like everything in his life. Later, when he put the story together, he needed a place to focus it. Orchard was too personal; Sanctuary was the answer. So for everybody else, it started on Sanctuary.

Before he took the job on Sanctuary, Chambers had made his name reporting wars. He'd covered everything from minor insurgencies to major conflicts, getting up close and personal with the action, filing reports from the very center of the battle. He became famous by showing the exhilaration and the terror, the ferocity and the boredom. He walked the streets of the wrecked cities, he depicted the shattered lives, he teased the individual stories out of the lines of refugees. A David Chambers story took the viewer right into the heart of the action. Chambers laid his life on the line so his readers could know the reality of war.

He told himself that he was following important news, but he knew that he was chasing after the adrenalin high, and running away from what he'd left behind on Orchard. His home had become unendurable. One day he'd have to face it, but for now there were conflicts to report and stories to file.

The wars brought him those moments of elation, but there were revulsion and horror as well. He'd seen too many columns of displaced people, too many burning towns, too many mass graves, too many armed and unstable idiots holding power they weren't capable of handling. One day he realized that the smell of the dead bodies had lingered, and he couldn't face it any more. Corpses walked through his dreams. Sudden noises made him flinch. Cooked food reeked of rotting flesh. Distant aircraft made him anxious. In the street, he hugged the edges of buildings, in case snipers watched the pavements. Whenever the traffic slowed, he feared an ambush. War wouldn't leave him alone.

This was no good. Conflict had been his comfort blanket for a while. If he couldn't face war zones any longer, it was time to tackle something different, something more investigative and less explosive.

When he saw the advert, he considered it carefully for at least a minute. Now that the civil war had ended, Sanctuary's new government had created a public relations department. Their image needed to improve if they were going to attract foreign investment. He read, and he applied. A week later, he was a valued employee of the Zoroastrian Republic of Sanctuary.

Chapter 4
The Ghillie Suit

"You may not be interested in war, but war is interested in you."

– LEON TROTSKY

2445

The cloud base began at around 1500 meters, and likely climbed another four or 5,000 after that, giving the moors a steely grey sky which offered little contrast to the muted tones of the heather. Rocky streams cut through the peaty soil on their way to a deeper watercourse.

Overhead a bird hung in the breeze, no more than a speck in the grey sky. From time to time its head turned, looking for movement in the empty landscape. The sniper had been watching it for an hour, factoring in the bird's movements and reactions, and adding it to everything he knew of what was happening across the moor.

For most of that hour the bird had been looking for prey, the sniper thought, but so far it had told him nothing to add to his own picture of the landscape. Now it dipped a wing and banked, letting the wind carry it several hundred meters away before it turned again and took up a new station. Something on the moor below had disturbed it.

"You lose, birdie boy."

The sniper smiled fractionally. He'd been watching the two figures for twenty minutes, the last ten with the naked eye. The bird had plainly been unaware of them.

He'd first seen the cam-suited pair through his remote mini-cams, and had followed them since they had rounded the rocky outcrop 1200 meters away. They were obviously trying hard, all the same, and they had done well, considering who they were and who he was.

Beating the bird had been a nice tribute to his professionalism.

Now he shifted position minutely, tracking the nearer of the two with his cross hairs. They were oh-so-easily in range – had been for ages – but he'd been asked for a little drama, to play it a bit flashy. It was a touch embarrassing letting them get this close, but he knew the major would realize how vulnerable they were. As for the journalist – well, who gave a toss what a civilian thought?

He tightened his trigger finger minutely. Had to be around 600 meters, falling ground, light breeze from right to left; dampish air, so the chamber pressure and muzzle velocity would be a fraction higher than when he'd zeroed the sight. *Easy peasy. Aim point is... about... there...*

Just for the fun of it, doing it the old way. Now he touched the button under the rifle's handguard, smiling as the sight's green dot popped into existence exactly where he'd put the cross-hairs. The god had provided.

A faint steady tone started in his earpiece. A second touch of the button, and the sight tracked the target as it moved. Now, of course, he could even put the rifle to autonomous mode and relax. *Have a coffee, maybe. As if.*

Ah well, what a waste of a perfect shot. He keyed the radio send button.

"Bang, sir. You're dead."

Δ Δ Δ

Major Erich Jorgensen glanced down at the red dot on his chest. He grinned and turned to the journalist.

"That's me gone, Mr. Chambers. You'd be on your own now. Oh, look: you too."

A red dot had also appeared on David Chambers' chest. He glanced at the infantry major, smiled ruefully, then stared across the drab moor.

"Okay, so your boys and girls can shoot. Where is he, then? Er – she?"

"I don't know where, exactly. Two Three Charlie, what's your location?"

The sniper's voice fizzed faintly in the major's earpiece. "Keep coming the way you're headed, sir. You've another five eighty to go."

The pair set off again, making faster time now that they had abandoned their attempts at concealment. A little later the journalist, sweating heavily, stopped next to the officer in another nondescript patch of moor.

"We're here, Mr. Chambers. He's within three meters of us."

"You've got to be kidding. There's nothing here. Are you sure?" Chambers was breathing hard, but Jorgensen was as relaxed as if he'd just strolled out for a pint. *Bloody man.*

A figure erupted from the ground at their feet, and Chambers leapt back, then laughed. The sniper was probably a man, and probably of average build and height, but it was hard to distinguish him as human at all. His outline was lost under a ragged suit covered in living vegetation. What the journalist could see of his skin seemed to be painted from the same palette of colors that the moor itself had used. His rifle looked more like a tree branch than a weapon.

"Nicely done, Private Takahashi. You see, Mr. Chambers, he's insulated against any thermal trace, and he's got chemical protection, air filtration and the ability to blend visually into any environment in this outfit – it's called a ghillie suit. The longer he's going to stay out, the more he'll integrate himself into his surroundings."

"That was just extraordinary, Mr. – Takahashi? But how long can you stay in a place like this?" Chambers, his heart still pounding from the exercise and the fright, looked around them at the barren moor, kicked at the heather for emphasis and then – glancing at the soldier for permission – fingered the material of the strange woven suit. The outfit felt weirdly animate, and its colors squirmed in response to his touch. In the space of a few seconds, it was starting to match the color of Chambers' skin where his finger was touching it.

"Longest I've been in place was a week, sir. It's no sweat."

"But what about food? Sleep? Toilet?"

"Cold rations, proximity alarms and some rather unpleasant chemical arrangements, in that order," smiled the major. "I'll let Takahashi talk you through the communications, sensors and weapons while I get our transport in a bit closer." He pulled a key pad out of his pocket.

"Of course, this is doing it the hard way. First off, I don't need to be right here. There's four more auto-rifles slaved to this one, and I can set each one to operate autonomously." Takahashi was tapping the rifle sight. Chambers studied him. The soldier spoke with an accent that Chambers couldn't quite place, and his manner suggested education and intelligence.

The long plait of hair which draped over his shoulder in a tight cam-net identified him as devout, Chambers knew; what fed that devotion was more of a mystery. He'd seen a few of those plaits in the last week, neatly tucked into uniforms in one way or another. None of them worn by women, come to think of it. Just another thing he'd have to figure out if he wanted this story to come good.

"When I designate you as a target, I'll upload the information to my local commander, and he'll set the rules of engagement for that kill," the sniper was saying. He stared at the journalist. "Come into my kill zone after that, sir, and if you come up as a green-to-kill, well – you're toast."

Chambers found the man's matter-of-fact way of discussing his theoretical death quite unnerving. "Look, I know this is going to sound stupid, but – why do all this live-in-a-swamp, look-like-a-hedge stuff, and put yourself to the risk of firing the shot yourself, if the equipment's able to do it all for you?" He had learned early on that the technical details were no use to a story if they didn't reveal the person behind them.

"Because it's only a machine, and machines go wrong. However smart the programmers are, if I'm here I can make my own decisions, and the god will guide. I don't want some digital idiot getting me into something I can't get out of."

There it was again. *The god.* It didn't feel right to ask directly; he'd have to get to know them better, first. Best stick to non-contentious stuff. "So you'd sooner not use the technology?"

△ △ △

Takahashi wanted the journalist to get it. He'd grafted to set up this demonstration, and he knew his own worth. He didn't want to come across like some sort of throwback. "No, that's not it, either. There's a time and place for high-tech soldiering, but I don't feel that the kit's flexible enough to replace someone's brain. On some jobs it's great, but the day I rely solely on it...

"Look. I was trained to shoot, and I'm pretty good at it. So I'll get into place, I'll lie up for as long as it takes, and I'll take the shot. But this kit's fine for intelligence and backup. That's all. Some guys use it differently, but in this unit we like to keep the people in charge, not the machines. That's just the way we are, I guess. I'm a man, not a bloody cyborg." He tapped his plait. "And that suits me fine."

The major was looking back across the moor. "Where the hell is that... oh, of course. Turn off the bloody cam. Stupid." He stabbed angrily at the key pad. Takahashi smirked.

A couple of hundred meters away a spot on the moor shimmered, and now a transport sled was visible, picking its way towards them across the heather. The sniper waited while the major and the journalist climbed onto the vehicle.

"Thanks, Takahashi; good demonstration. Pack your stuff up and be ready to head on to the training camp; I'll send the wagon back for you."

Takahashi watched them go. *Thanks for the helping hand, boss.*

In the distance, the bird shrieked and dived. The sniper turned his head and snorted. "Found your tea at last? Second place, first loser."

Chapter 5
Tone All The Way

"Firing!" Sergeant Farzana Carmalette needed this one to work. Her crew had been getting a little slack, and the simulation results hadn't been great.

The weapon carrier rocked on its suspension, the air falling back into the missile's vortex with a flat hollow boom. 300 meters down-range the main motor ignited, winglets deployed, and the stubby canister curved upwards, vanishing high into the atmosphere. Reopening their hatches, the crew watched it go. Small pieces of packaging were bouncing around the launch rail and on top of the upper armor; some were still fluttering down to the concrete.

The gunner was jubilant. "Got to be a good one. I had tone all the way. Dead-Eye Drovan nails it again."

"Drovan, you couldn't hit your own arse if you had homing bog paper." The sardonic voice came from the driver's hatch.

"Harvetz, you're a typical bloody wagon driver. *You've* hit everything between the hangar doors and the range hut. There's not a fence left standing anywhere in the county."

"God, that bloody exhaust stinks." Carmalette, a slender dark-skinned woman, climbed stiffly out of her commander's hatch. Muttering, she jumped awkwardly down from the decks and began a series of martial arts stretches. "Someone get a brew on before the boss brings that damn journalist along to see how wonderful we are."

Drovan jumped down behind her, pulling off his gunner's sighting goggles and headset. "What's the crack with the journalist? What's he up to?"

"He's here to tell the worlds that the Army's made up of fine, upstanding, professionally skilled clean-living patriots who are driven by the single goal of giving their lives to defend freedom," said the voice inside the vehicle.

"Hope to fuck he never meets you, then, Harvetz." The gunner's response suggested a longstanding mutual irritation.

An arm came out of the driver's hatch, brandishing a steaming mug. "Brew up!"

The commander spun round. "How the hell did you do it that fast?"

"Being a mere man, I recognize my limitations with regards to simultaneous multi-tasking, holding down a top-flight career, nurturing, asking directions, and putting the bog seat down. Thus, I do one thing at a time, but I do it brilliantly."

"You're full of shit, you know." She took the mug. "Ahh, that's good."

"Also, I plan ahead. You always want a brew when we pop the lids. While Robin Hood here was mincing around getting tone-all-the-way and playing with his sights and stuff, I put the brakes on, turned off the engines, assessed the situation and established that the wagon wasn't going to drive itself off.

"Being on a training range, there also seemed to be little danger of a counter-attack that might call for rapid movement. Thus, I read the news and made you a cup of tea." Another mug came up from inside the vehicle. "And cheff for Dead-Eye Dick, the finest marksman in – well, within a few hundred meters." A last mug was balanced on the cupola, as Harvetz pulled himself out of the driver's hatch. "And proper coffee for me, which you two degenerates are utterly unable to make, my gorgeous leader."

The commander sighed. "Harvetz – do you ever, even for a wee moment, actually *stop bloody talking?*"

"You wouldn't appreciate me as much if I did. You'd be stuck with Robin Hood's riveting conversation about trajectories and launch velocities and fire-and-forget widgets. Recognize when you're well off and stick with grace under pressure, culture, education, bonhomie and repartee. Forget the smartarse shooting stuff and go for quality, and one day you'll climb into my sleeping bag, my beautiful commander. You know my motto – be the best that you can be."

The gunner sipped at the fragrant cheff. "Not that superstitious shit again. If the bloody god does guide and provide, why the hell didn't he provide you and that screwball priest of yours with a bleeding off switch and guide me to find it?"

The hatch fell back with a clang; steaming coffee spilled across ceramic armor plate. In two seconds of scuffling, the gunner was pinned against the vehicle's hull with a combat knife at his throat. Dropping her tea, Carmalette grabbed for the two cursing men.

"Pack it in, Harvetz. Put the bloody knife away. Drovan – apologize!"

Harvetz released his grip. "Listen, you half-machine lackwit. The god in his generosity provided you with a brain, which I know you can use. Think on this. You can mock me for my failings, and you can envy me for my strengths. I'll answer for those.

"But if you mock the god, you'll answer to him for it, because you'll be seeing him straight afterwards. And right now, *I'm* the weapon that he has to hand." The driver sheathed his knife. "So, Drovan, the next time you blaspheme just might be the chance you get to find out if he's everything that I believe he is. Do you want to take that chance?"

Chapter 6

Schwerpunkt

*"No plan ever survives contact with the enemy.
Even fewer survive contact with the Treasury."*

– ANONYMOUS SENIOR BRITISH OFFICER, 2006

"So, what can you do for us that we can't do for ourselves? Why do we need a spin doctor?" The artillery colonel, a little drunk, was toying with his huge moustache. He also sported a tightly woven plait. Complicated hair seemed to be required in this army. Dogs, too – the officers' mess was full of them. Right now, a black Labrador was sniffing David Chambers' beer. "What's wrong with being seen just as we are?"

There was a rumble of polite agreement from the others. Chambers nodded and waited for the silence that he knew would follow. It was a fair question, and he knew that despite the evening's surface friendliness, this was the key moment. A major in the armored unit had used the word *schwerpunkt* that afternoon; he'd had to explain it to the journalist. "It's the focus, the pivot; the moment on which the outcome of the whole battle hinges." This seemed like the *schwerpunkt* for Chambers, at least for this new contract.

Despite his hosts' forceful hospitality through the long and noisy dinner in the officers' mess, Chambers had tried to regulate his drinking. Spirits had now been served, but apart from this last beer, he'd stayed with several cups of the strong and bitter coffee. He concentrated, trying to clear the fog from his brain.

The Labrador nudged his foot amiably. Chambers shifted in his chair, stifling a belch. Alienating his hosts wouldn't help. "Here's how I think of it, ladies and gentlemen. You know this better than I do. Sanctuary needs investment, but money won't flow in automatically. You must show that your society is stable, and a stable society can't pretend that it has no need for a military. However painful the past, it's time for Sanctuary to put the war behind itself, and to recognize that you've moved on. We must accept each other, and integrate civil society and the military together into one body. The government feels I can help with that."

Silence had fallen on the group, and it was spreading out across the mess. A couple of others had joined the fringes, perching on chair arms or leaning on the wood-paneled walls, listening. They weren't hostile, but apparently weren't yet ready to open up to him, either. Just reserving judgement.

"I can't pretend to know much more yet. A couple of days with Erich has taught me that your troopers are a lot more than I might have thought they were, if – to be honest – I'd ever thought about them at all. I would have guessed that they were tough. Now I know they're smart as well. They do what they're told, but they think for themselves. And when they talk to you, you listen."

Usually true, if not always, from what he'd seen in the past two days, but a little flattery could only help at this stage. "And I know that Erich can talk quite well himself – I'm just not sure about his jokes. And as for his singing!" He grinned at the lanky infantry officer who'd been his principal host and escort. That gained him a few appreciative chuckles, and Jorgensen returned a rueful smile.

"We're gaining acceptance steadily enough. People are coming to see that they need a professional army. And a navy, and airspace forces." It was the moustache-wearing gunner colonel again – this last comment with a nod towards a group of blue-clad officers at the neighboring table. They too were listening to the exchange. "It may take generations, but the god will guide and provide."

He tugged briefly at his plait, a lot less drunk than he'd seemed earlier. The gesture was copied by several others, but there were a couple of stony faces, and somebody snorted derisively.

"I think you're right, Colonel. That's why I'm happy to take on this job. The times are a-changing, and people are changing with them. But I'm not sure it'll take generations; I think we can get acceptance quicker than that. Let people understand what you do, and show them that the military are highly skilled professionals, just like they are. I can help with that.

"Your job and your skill is to defend us. It's my job to tell stories – not made-up ones, but stories that tell people the things they'd want to know if they were able to ask about them. And it's my skill to tell those stories the right way, to present them in the most positive light that I can.

"But you said 'spin doctor', and I can understand why." Now Chambers took a calculated gamble, and went on the offensive. "You're my clients, and I'll do my honest best by you. But please understand me, ladies and gentlemen: I don't tell lies to my readers. To me, that's the first rule of journalism. If you tell lies to me and I find out, I'm gone. Then I'll want to know why you've been lying. Then I'll have to decide what to do about it.

"So if there's stuff you don't want me to know, don't tell me anything. I'm not talking about classified military secrets, you understand; just don't mislead me about your attitudes and behaviors and cultures. Because in my own way, I'm a bad enemy. But I'm also a bloody good friend. You can trust me, because I'm trusting you."

Another silence fell on the tables. Then one of the older men chuckled. "I think that's the first time I've ever heard an unarmed man threaten an army. You're not short of bottle, are you? Nice one, Mr. Chambers." The tension dissolved into laughter, and Chambers found he had earned himself some hearty slaps on the shoulder, and a whisky was pushed into his hand. A tail thumped beneath the table. The artilleryman's neighbors nudged the officer and laughed, but Chambers was struck by the sober calculation in the man's eyes.

The group began to break up, some heading to the bar, others to card tables or the dance floor. Chambers realized he'd been hearing music for a little while; now, as a group of men and women pushed out of the anteroom, the volume rose and fell in time with the swinging of the doors.

He moved across to the artilleryman and took an empty seat next to him. Only three remained from the original group; this gunner colonel, Jorgensen, and a tough-looking captain in a sand-colored dress uniform that Chambers didn't yet recognize. The captain was another man who wore his hair in a plait.

A huge mastiff lay at his feet, its head held high, watching every move Chambers made. Another dog, but quite a bit less amiable. He looked around for the friendly Labrador, and saw it slinking away through an open door.

"I'm sorry, Colonel, Captain; I missed your names in the wave of introductions. I apologize."

The colonel toyed with his drink, and paused for so long that Chambers doubted he'd get any answer. Then: "It's Davidson, Mr. Chambers; William Davidson," he answered, without raising his eyes. The body language said consideration; contained and confident, rather than evasive. Then the captain reached across the table, stretching out his hand. "Andrew Macdonald." A friendly gesture and manner, but the eyes were intense and probing.

Chambers took the hand, nodding acknowledgement. "Call me David, please, Colonel Davidson, Captain Macdonald." There was a story here, and this story had legs. Now if the man would only talk to him...

"Colonel, I was interested when you mentioned your faith. It's not familiar to me, but I've met several men whose hair is worn similarly to yours, and I've heard that phrase about 'the god providing' a few times since I've been a guest here. No women using the phrase that I recall, though. This may seem impertinent, and I mean no offence, but can you tell me about the god?"

Davidson raised his eyes, and took a breath. Before he could speak, Macdonald coughed, and the colonel glanced across the table at the other officer. The captain's curious gaze had intensified.

Now Davidson turned his gaze on Chambers for several seconds, as if preparing a different response to the one he had been about to deliver. What was happening here? Had he just seen a colonel take an order from a captain?

"No. That I won't." Davidson took a breath. "I'd have to know you a whole lot better for that. But as to what you were saying just now – if you're prepared to play straight with us, I'll take your offer and play straight with you. Let's talk about your assignment, if that's the right expression. What are you going to need from us?"

Chapter 7
Children of Cincinnatus

*"They shall beat their swords into ploughshares,
and their spears into pruninghooks: nation shall
not lift up sword against nation, neither shall they
learn war any more."*

– ISAIAH 2:4

At first, Chambers thought of the Sanctuary job as a potboiler, a routine assignment while he rested up and searched for the next big idea. But the place got its hooks into him. He hadn't expected that.

Civil wars took generations to heal, but Sanctuary couldn't wait that long. The planet was poor, and they had to get industry and agriculture restarted. That meant foreign money, and it wouldn't come in if investors were scared off. Sanctuary had a tale to tell, so Chambers had to get to know the place. Learning about national recovery meant talking to politicians, community and business leaders, teachers, farmers and technicians. Along the way, he found out that most people had also been soldiers, at some point; civil wars had that effect. What other societies regarded as a separate profession was the background reality of many Sanctuary lives.

He interviewed everyone who would talk to him, recording the *vox populi* as they told him what they thought about the way society was rebuilding itself. After some weeks, he realized that the government line was a little simplistic. He wasn't surprised; he'd been hired to spin a story. But the so-called civil war was starting to seem more complicated.

He decided to dig deeper, so he asked broader questions. The stories he heard went back generations.

#

A CIVIL SERVANT - 'NipponDeutsch financed the entire Sanctuary colony project. Ship time, transportation, construction, terraforming, the whole thing. The deal was pretty good. Sign up, and you had a free trip to a brand-new world. Accommodation, food, healthcare, education, a job. I think you had to show that you had a skill set they needed and that you were willing to leave home for at least twenty years, and you had to have no pending criminal charges and be healthy. Look at the mess Earth was in back then. No wonder people jumped at it."

A TEACHER - "They came here on the slowboats, at first. They called them slow, but they weren't. Just slower than the speed of light. Imagine it – hundreds and hundreds of frozen people on each one. A string of colony ships launched six months apart, every ship taking decades to get here. I think there were six or seven of them."

A MECHANIC – "It must have been a bit crazy in those days. One of my great-greats set off in the slow liners. She spent decades on the journey, frozen to sleep. Then NipponDeutsch got the Waldschmidt faster-than-light process to work, and suddenly it all got a lot quicker and a bit easier. When she arrived, her own grandchildren were already here. They hadn't been born when she left Earth. They came out on the FTL fast liners, and they had the colony well under way by the time granny arrived. Physically, she'd have been the same age as them! Weird."

A FARMER – 'Many of the First Settlers just wanted to find a place with a steady job, decent prospects, and a chance to practice their religion

#

So NipponDeutsch had just lost interest in the place, and then ARTOK got involved? Was that when this "Zoroastrian Republic of Sanctuary" stuff had started?

A politician's aide – "The government took out a bloody great mortgage on the colony, and we brought in ARTOK to develop the infrastructure, since NipponDeutsch weren't interested any more. There wasn't any other company big enough to handle the contract, and ARTOK had got into FTL ships as well by then. I guess ARTOK did a decent enough job at first, but then they started trying to push us around. They wanted to run the whole planet. Eventually the pushing and shoving got serious."

Chambers knew how that felt. He was starting to see similarities with Orchard's history. A pattern was emerging, if you looked at it in the right light. The corporations had put human outposts across the nearer stars. They arrived in a solar system, built the basics of a colony, and then moved on, leaving the settlements only barely viable. Orchard was dirt poor, but at least it had avoided a civil war, unlike Sanctuary.

What the political aide told him was strictly deniable, non-attributable, background only. "Civil war? There was no civil war. When NipponDeutsch dropped us in it, we refinanced the whole thing. It's cost us, but this is *our* world. These are our farms, our seas, our cities, our communities. ARTOK were just the contractors we brought in to put up more buildings, lay more roads, dig in the pipework and finish the terraforming. A civil war is a fight within your own family. The people you pay to build you a house don't become a part of your family. These builders refused to move out once the job was finished. What you call a civil war was the nation repossessing its own territory. This place is ours."

Chambers needed to understand the economy as well, so he spent a lot of time with businesspeople, logistics geeks, food growers and power generation people. "My grandmother and grandfather fought them. She was half a mile away when he was killed by an ARTOK cyborg. He was a comms techie, a godly man, running a satellite set in the village guardhouse. They didn't have much on the way of weapons – shotguns, rifles, even a few bloody halberds! But the cyborgs came for them anyway, blowing the doors in at the dead of night, killing my granddad and his mates before they even knew they were there. She heard the dogs barking, all the way from the village fish farm where she was a manager, and she knew something was wrong. Then she heard the shooting. They'd wanted a baby. It was a war, and they'd known what could happen, so they'd planned ahead. My dad was born eight years later, courtesy of stored semen, once she'd laid down her rifle and got back to the fish."

A technician, a woman who maintained power and lighting systems – "At least NipponDeutsch didn't start shooting when they pulled out – they just dumped us and left. But the ARTOK people claimed that they lived here, and they had a right to remain. This is our world! Not one of them was a follower of the god. Our ancestors came here to be free. But the ARTOK people fought us to take control of our own planet."

Another teacher, this one a military reservist – "ARTOK denied it all, like you'd expect. The Anglo-Russians pull some huge military stunt and everyone knows it's them, but they just face you down and deny it. All those Russian-speaking soldiers? Concerned citizens, taking spontaneous action in defense of their communities. All that equipment? Military surplus items, legally obtained. ARTOK were just providing them with a legal resupply service. Lying bastards."

Another farm worker – "It cost a lot of lives before we were finished with ARTOK. It wasn't just the cyborgs, but they were the worst. Killing machines disguised as people. Even thinking about them gives me the creeps. I tell you, man: the god despises them."

△ △ △

After that, he'd wanted to know more about the cyborgs. Once he finished this government spin doctor job, this could be his next story – still military, but a bit safer than following the sound of shot and shell. He'd give Sanctuary a couple of years, tops, and then perhaps...

It wasn't the entire population, but many Sanctuary men were followers of the god. That's what they called themselves, nothing more, as if "the god" was enough explanation. And it seemed be only men; he couldn't find out what role women played in this religion. Nobody was willing to explain any further. There was a sort of overt privacy about it. *I want you to know that there's a higher purpose, but I'll tell you no more than that.* This didn't seem like Judaism, Christianity, or Islam. What was this faith? Chambers began to feel that there were subtexts within subtexts here. They were decent people, by and large, friendly and welcoming; but even more than Sanctuary's non-religious citizens, the followers of the god loathed the cyborgs.

There were dozens of insulting nicknames. *Robot Nazis*, people said. *Metal eyes. Half breeds. Auto-grunts.* Over a century had passed since they had disappeared, yet still people despised the cyborgs.

Why the passion? Weren't ARTOK's pets little more than a scary memory to frighten kids with now? He'd probed at the hatred, and found that the attitude was common across Sanctuary, particularly among soldiers. Back on Orchard, the cyborgs were an irrelevance – weird enough, but they'd played no part in the habitat's brief history. It was different here.

Regular soldiers were proud of their toughness, their endurance, their skill – and of the determination it had taken to acquire these strengths. Perhaps they were contemptuous of anyone whose abilities were designed into them. And if soldiers felt like that, how much stronger would their contempt be if it was supported by religious faith? All the main religions had denounced artificial intelligences; they still did, whenever some innovative technology tested the boundary. Back then, how had the other churches reacted to cyborgs? He should find out.

Meanwhile, where had the cyborgs gone? Were there any still around? No one seemed to know. He took the obvious route of trying the company which had made them, without any real hope that ARTOK would even acknowledge him.

They didn't. Eighteen standard months passed while Chambers wrote Sanctuary government spin stories, coaxing investors to pour money into the planet. On this cyborg-hating world, he learned to keep his interest to himself. But discreetly, every now and then, he tried again, firing off a request for an interview, comments, a press pack. Nothing.

Then one afternoon, out of a clear blue Sanctuary sky, he got a message that ARTOK's elusive Chairman, Vladimir Filippovich Semyonov himself, would like to talk to him. David Chambers couldn't believe his luck.

Chapter 8
Trepanning the Planet

*"I have never made but one prayer to God, a very
short one: Oh Lord, make my enemies ridiculous.
And God granted it."*

– VOLTAIRE

"Ahh, it's good to be back in here. I don't know how long it's been since we could relax and just talk." Captain Andrew Macdonald pushed away the remnants of the meal, snuffed the little candle, and settled himself on the reclining bench. Colonel William Davidson thought his priest seemed calm in the shadows' embrace; less highly-strung, perhaps.

"Guess who I heard from the other day." The mastiff raised its head at the sound of Macdonald's voice.

"I hate people saying that, Andrew. Haven't a clue." Davidson finished a mouthful and fastidiously wiped his moustache. The silence and near-darkness of the cave-like room wrapped around them soothingly. He remembered being a child, ten or eleven, at home with his parents and brothers. Contentedly self-aware, thinking of the future as a wonderful prospect. He'd be a soldier, or perhaps a pilot, or go to space and roam the deep wide black. But meanwhile, this was home, safe and warm. His. Belonging. But on top of that, far more than that, was the awe. The holiness. The spirit, open to the cosmos. Naked before the eyes of the god.

"Do you remember Richie Belyakov?" Macdonald was staring up at the dim ceiling of the cave, but the casual tone didn't fool Davidson. He thought for a moment.

"Combat Engineer major, tall guy – is that the one? Russian family originally, I think, but I gather they integrated well. Not a great attender at temple, as I recall, but you know – I always thought he was quite a strong believer."

"That's him. And you're right about the attendance. He'd be very observant for a while, but somehow he just kept lapsing."

"Stuck at *Corax*, didn't he?"

"No, actually made it to *Nymphus*. Well, he was back then. Don't know about now. Anyhow, he's out now. Been retired a few years, went out to Rheparion as a security guy for the mines. Said he fancied a quiet life."

"*Rheparion?* He wanted *quiet?*" Davidson started chuckling. This should be good.

"I suppose it seemed like a promising idea at the time. The Fundi and ProEx stuff went sleepy around ten years back, didn't it, once everyone and his granddad among the radicals was either dead, jailed or mindwiped? The Worlds had to step in to provide government. That left a few thousand unemployed former squaddies looking for stuff to do and a living to make."

"So it started up again with a touch of freelancing in the woods and hills, then?" Davidson knew how that went. Their own war was a vivid and painful memory.

"You've got it."

"I guess it can't have taken long for someone to think of the mines."

"Long enough for Richie to have read the ad, got the interview, and turned up for day one in the new job." Macdonald's tone was neutral, but Davidson recognized that there was a message in this story.

"Which was?"

"The very day they hit the mines, demanding some nonsense along the lines of turning them over 'to the exploited people'. With a pile of cash on one side for the liberators, of course. Demonstration nuclear weapon down a shaft on one of the volcanic island sites, just to make a point. Caused some major seismic events. Broke a dam, flooded two valleys and the island capital. Wrote off forty square kilometers of what little fertile land the island had, just before the harvest. The flood lifted the crop, topsoil and all, right out to sea. The dust and filth took around half a year to settle out of the atmosphere.

"The irony was that the mine was almost completely worked out. But the nuke hit a major fault line, and the idiots bloody near trepanned the planet. Around 35,000 of the famously exploited people either drowned straight away, or starved over the next few months. Good to know it was in the name of liberation."

It was coming back to Davidson now. Rheparion had been a byword for chaos. Sanctuary's own problems had seemed minor against the bloody turmoil that Rheparion had suffered for years. But although the populations of several worlds had sickened of the place, the nuclear weapon catastrophe had forced the issue back into prominence.

"Richie's boat touched down just as the tsunami was settling, and they went ashore through a sea of corpses, to hear him tell it. He found what was left of his new employers and spent the first few weeks alternating between disaster response, hands-on civil engineering, riot control, and leading counter-attacks against the freelancers."

"Hell of a first day." It wasn't even remotely funny, now that he heard it.

"Put that on your CV." Macdonald stood, and walked away into the darkness.

Davidson sat forward on the stone bench and leaned his elbows on the table. The dog studied him disconcertingly. "So what's Richie saying now?" He knew they hadn't got to the real point yet.

"Interesting," Macdonald's voice emerged from the gloom. "He's been on Rheparion for about five years, and the weather since then has screwed up most of the harvests, though it seems that they're feeding themselves again. But the armed groups there are still throwing their weight around, and there's only an apology for a government. The Worlds run damn near everything.

"Well, Richie was out on a hearts and minds job a few months back, somewhere a bit up-country, trying to build some credit with the locals. He and his men blundered into a biggish contact between the local army guys – you remember, the crowd that the Worlds recruited and financed – and some thug's group of bandits." There was a thump in the darkness.

"The army were on a search-and-destroy against the bad guys' base somewhere in a network of canyons. Remember that these bandits are always ex-regular, so they're quite disciplined and damn well armed. Richie and his lads did the sensible thing and holed up in their own cave to wait it out. But he could see that the bandits were well-positioned on the key ground, and the army guys weren't up for the fight. So they called in some help."

"Who was the help?" It sounded like Macdonald was getting to the nub of this story. But what the hell was he fiddling about with back there?

Davidson's question was ignored. "That was where Richie should have bugged right out," Macdonald continued. "He wasn't in contact himself, and he had a fairly clear route away. He had ten blokes with him – few enough that he wouldn't attract very much attention if he moved, but enough to look after themselves if they ran into any opposition on the way home. But he decided to sit tight. Says he wanted to see what the outcome was, now he knew he had a major bandit presence in his own back yard. See his point, I suppose."

There was another thump. A faint mechanical sound. A hiss of air. "Anyhow. They watched the army and the bandits swapping rounds and lasing each other for a while. Both sides were sitting on their arses, the canyons were too steep and narrow for indirect fire to be much use, and there weren't any aircraft or satellites anywhere useful for directing SmArtillery, if anyone had any." This was intriguing stuff, but Davidson wanted to see what Macdonald was doing. He peered into the shadows.

"The bandits were cracking mortars and dumb artillery around, just bouncing stone chips everywhere. Nobody was brave enough to have a proper go at dislodging the other side. The army boys had a few sallies but got knocked back each time. What it needed was someone with a bit of zip."

He heard a grunt, then the voice again. "After a couple of hours of hostile stalemate, Richie had spotted a route up a side canyon that the bandits hadn't covered properly – just a light machine gun or two. If the army commander had seen it, he'd bottled out of trying it. Richie was beside himself with frustration, and he was just getting ready to go down there, shove his way in and tell the chap what to do. Typical Richie, if you remember.

"Then a couple of personnel carriers arrived. And what was in them completely changed the battle. A section of light infantry – just eight strong – came out of the carriers and took that canyon apart in under five minutes. They moved so fast that he could hardly see them. They broke straight through the bandit lines and killed several of them, then they let the army take it from there." Footsteps sounded in the gloom.

"When Richie got eyes on one of them through his binos, he could see it wasn't a human face. Cam skin, mesh-covered ears, nose filters. Metal eyes, he said."

Macdonald emerged from the shadows. He was carrying something.

It took a moment for the words to register. *"Cyborgs?* I didn't think there were any of those things left. Weren't the last ones killed about forty years ago?"

The dog got to its feet, and lifted its huge head. It gave a deep coughing growl.

"Settle, Enkidu. A bit less, I think, William. But they died hard." He dropped the thing on the table. Davidson sprang back, sudden vomit rising in his throat. His chair crashed over. The dog was snarling, hackles erect. "This one died particularly hard. And six of the faithful died with it."

The head had been frozen. He could feel it drawing the heat from the room. Silver lines traced its leathery skin. Buzz-cut hair, warped and twisted ears. Hard black artificial eyes, lenses at their centers, stared sightlessly at Davidson.

He was gasping, struggling to breathe. "What – where did you get this thing, Andrew? Is this one of them?"

Macdonald shrugged. He prodded at the severed head, waving his hand in front of it. "Look at this, William." The eyes snapped into focus, and swiveled to follow his moving fingers. "Do you see? This particular beast was killed nearly sixty years ago, and it still holds a little power. I almost admire the perverts who made it. It's a superb device.

"There's a kind of supplementary brain in there, a processor busy doing the god knows what. The creature receives radio. Its hearing is augmented. There may be other vile contraptions as well. It hardly matters.

"This one has been kept as a warning. The things were hateful to the god, and they merited his wrath. They had to be destroyed. It was a holy duty. But either a few of the things escaped, or else someone has started making more. Probably the ARTOK people again, may the god destroy them.

"The abominations are back. How can I ignore this? I am Leo, and if that title means anything, then it means that I must act. *We* must act. They're an offence to the god. It's our sacred duty to act.

"William, we must raise battalions of true believers to seek out and destroy this evil filth."

Davidson tore his gaze away from the head and looked up at him, startled by Macdonald's tone. The man's eyes were fixed on some distant vision, something only he could see, an image of the divine will revealed uniquely to him.

In military terms, Colonel William Davidson outranked his Leo; in the hierarchy of their shared belief, he had to defer to the other man's greater learning and spiritual development. Captain Andrew Macdonald was an Adept, purified by the ordeals of heat, cold, and fasting, sanctified with honey. He had the understanding necessary to grasp the cosmic implications of the water miracle. When the Leo spoke of the revealed mysteries of the universe, initiates had to listen and learn their true path. Davidson was awestruck and troubled. He slipped down from the bench and knelt.

Macdonald knelt alongside him. The priest reached out both hands, fingers spread in imitation of the rays of the rising sun. The dog dropped to its belly. Staring up and out as if through the roof of the cave, through the rock over their heads, through the planet's atmosphere and far out into space, the Leo delivered his judgement.

"We must find these creatures, and we must destroy them all. We shall raise a force of holy warriors. Your god requires you, William, to soldier in his name. As the god slew the bull, so we must slay these demons. The Invincible God – the Undefeated Sun!"

The mechanical eyes contracted in the frozen skull.

Chapter 9

Nice People To Be Invaded By

*"God doesn't want you for a sunbeam – he wants
you for a soldier."*
– FATHER NICK GOSNELL, CHAPLAIN TO BRITISH 16TH AIR ASSAULT
BRIGADE, IRAQ 2003

2446

I t had taken him months to arrange this meeting. The listeners were a mixture of financiers and military contract managers. Specialists and sceptics all.

Captain Andrew Macdonald, Adept of the god, Leo of his faith, studied his audience. How they reacted to this would be critical to his plans. He checked that he had everyone's attention, and launched the presentation.

△ △ △

Against the deep wide black, the spacecraft is initially no more than an inconsequential speck, less noticeable than the moons, far less interesting than the cloud formations on the planet. The craft is following a gradual curve. Its motion is only fractional at first, then some trick of perspective flings it forward.

The spacecraft is a lightly armed military or police machine, covered with stern authoritarian markings, complex weaponry and antennae. One emblem resembles a stylized bull's head. It closes steadily, something about its movement suggesting imminent purpose. A larger craft comes into view: a heavier, slower and older vessel with a travel-stained air of weary industriousness about it. The police vessel converges on it, docking with an upper-deck port some distance aft of the bridge.

Now our eyes turn to the planet, tracing the storms building over the southern hemisphere, following the growth of a hurricane in the tropics, watching the outline of the massive southern island continent unveil itself from the clouds. It dominates more and more of the visual field. As the hurricane grows, the coupled freighter-police vessels pass to one side. Absurdly, a deep bass throb can be felt as our center of awareness passes over the freighter's huge and ancient engines. As the craft passes out of view behind us, something in the noise suggests a history of erratic maintenance.

A communications satellite flashes past as we fall; it is beeping and warbling as it handles data. More absurdity. Atmosphere arrives, at first in traces, then thickening enough to be felt as heat and buffeting. Dropping now through the clouds, the view hazes and shifts. Moisture can be felt; whiteness turns to grey and then to black. This is no picture postcard fluffiness; thunderstorms breed in this region. A sudden flash of retina-searing white gold, then the stink of ozone. An electric tension can be felt on exposed skin; hair stands on end with a crackle. A blast that is more vibration in the bones than noise in the ears follows within seconds. Rain floods planetward. The light returns and the view clears. The clouds thin, then part. Thousands of meters below, crumpled mountains divide the continent into jungle, savannah and cultivation. Some hints of industry and a few urban areas can be seen. It is plain that this is Rheparion.

With a roar, three fighter jets appear below, flying in an arrowhead formation. We fall into place alongside them. Each white and silver aircraft carries a full load of missile cassettes, comms fit, ground-attack smart bombs and gunpods. One has a massive sat-killer missile under its fuselage. All carry that same bull's-head marking. The lead pilot turns his head and looks straight at us; his face mask dangles loosely from one side of his helmet, revealing a handlebar moustache and twinkling eyes. His devotional plait is clipped neatly over one shoulder. With a roguish smile, he twirls his moustache and flips the plane away in a wingover. His wingmen follow; we briefly see that one is a pretty blonde woman, then we feel the heat from her plane's jet pipes. She winks at us as she follows her leader. The planes' camouflage shifts color to show as matte earth tones. As they dive, we follow them, but they bank and accelerate away from us.

Now we are falling faster across the mountains, dropping towards the savannah. Below us a battle is taking place. We come to a halt in mid-air, as if waiting. Something invisible whoops past us, then another and another and another. The air ripples. This is artillery fire at the apex of its trajectory. We rush on again after the falling shells.

100 meters above the ground, they burst into bomblets that track individual vehicles in the armored wave below us.

These tanks and personnel carriers are black and filthy, no two alike, each decorated with garish death's-heads and crossed bones, snarling monster faces, cutlasses. Most of the vehicles have extravagant additional weapons lashed onto their hulls and turrets. Some have steel fence posts welded on to their hulls; the barbed wire and blades slung between them form a crudely effective protection against an infantry attack. The vehicles' exhausts belch black smoke, their tracks squeak and rattle, their side skirts hang loose. Some machines have decaying corpses strapped to their upper decks. It is ridiculously obvious that these are the bad guys. The falling SmArtillery bomblets seek out individual vehicles, and set about neutralizing them with mobility-kills, combat-capability-kills and hull-kills. The armored assault falters, breaks up, and is washed away in the explosive tide.

We are whisked off in a change of course towards the gunline. A squadron of self-propelled guns sits many kilometers away behind a reverse slope; as they fire their final rounds, they power up, pull back, and move position to avoid counter-battery fire. These vehicles are uniform in appearance, with well-stowed camouflage, neat and orderly insignia and standardized antennas and weapons. A small black bull's head shows on every grey-green-brown turret. The faintest of heat hazes drifts cleanly from their purring motors. As the squadron moves off, we sweep overhead. The vehicle commanders are opening their hatches; a few look up at us. One or two wave and smile. They are all clean-cut, fit-looking and confident. Various races are apparent; both genders are present in equal proportion. They seem like nice people. This is just the kind of army you'd want to belong to, or even to be occupied by.

Now we spring higher into the air again, swirling away across the battlefield to an armored assembly area. Here, infantry carriers and tanks are forming up into their assault groupings. We watch as they cross their start line, driving fast across the rolling savannah, engaging enemy groups or bypassing them. Here is a strongpoint, with heavy stone walls and massive earthen mounds protecting a company position. Our forces deal briskly with the position. The infantry dismount from their carriers close to the objective; the tanks stay hull-down at a distance, firing onto any enemy who break loose or try to counter-attack.

Next, we see a rolling battle between armored units. It's conducted over great distances, and the greater maneuver and marksmanship skills of our forces are immediately apparent. More of the black vehicles appear, but they are overwhelmed before they can deploy. In minutes, the only moving machines are friendly.

On again, in a blur of images separated by stratospheric leaps. An infantry platoon are escorting their prisoners from a series of bunkers which they have just assaulted. They handle the situation firmly. Wrist-cuffed enemy are led up by the tough, disciplined soldiers, efficiently stripped of their weapons and kit, then searched and taken away in groups. One soldier hands personal photographs back to a prisoner. Another dresses the leg wound of an erstwhile enemy. An officer holsters her laser, gestures to a sergeant, respectfully salutes a captured enemy colonel as he is led away.

Another move, and the scene is a jungle river. Overhanging trees make a shady tunnel of the waterway; light spears down from gaps in the canopy hundreds of feet above. A patrol is wading chest deep in the water, well spread out, short-barreled rifles high up in their shoulders. Their green and brown faces turn this way and that. A few have bagged up their plaits, which flick out behind them. The air stinks of decay. Humidity turns our skin slick in seconds. Monkeys scream, and something slithers across a mud flat. The lead scout fires towards us, slightly high. The round whizzes directly overhead. A grunt behind us, and something falls through branches. There is a splash. V-shaped ripples converge.

In a field, a community elder talks to the commander of another patrol. Around him, soldiers are kidding with the young lads of the village. A game of football has been arranged. Laughing boys watch as a smiling and massively-built soldier arm-wrestles two of them simultaneously. Young girls are giggling behind their hands. A queue of mothers with babies wait their turn to see a medic. Nearby, an engineer is talking with a group of men around the well. They have stripped the village pump down and are gravely examining some components. The men seem worried, but the engineer is confident.

Faster now. Ground attack aircraft are spinning up their engines on a flight line; a crew chief accepts a data slate from a pilot, checks it, nods. He jumps down and salutes. The aircraft starts to taxi. Gleaming military police are checking ground vehicle traffic entering a headquarters. A bomb disposal technician programs his robot; infantry guard a city street perimeter as colleagues prepare to assault terrorists holed up in an apartment block. As their jetfoil circles protectively, marines and a search dog team board a river freighter, looking for drugs or weapons. A massive transport aircraft hovers, then touches down delicately on a short strip; the ramps are lowering as it sinks to earth. The pilot sees us and nods briefly, one professional to another. A weapons team are training novice riflemen on a practice range. Their students are evidently from a relatively unsophisticated army which we are aiding; they are gauche and clumsy, but the instructors are patient and encouraging.

Finally, we return to the deep wide black. A spacecraft docks with an orbiting habitat; troopers swarm into the structure. They are met with laser fire from a scruffy-looking rebel group in greasy coveralls. Within moments the troopers have ended it. The habitat is undamaged. A crying hostage is comforted by one of the troopers; another soldier looks sadly at the terrorist bodies and shakes her head.

They do seem like very nice people.

"Taurus Defense and Security. Whatever your needs, we can meet them." The voice could be no more authoritative if the god himself was speaking.

The world flickers, fades to grey, then is rapidly sucked into a single point of light as darkness falls.

△ △ △

"Very glossy, very slick. Bit too slick, d'you think?" said a voice in the gloom. Light gradually returned, and the conference room was again revealed.

Captain Andrew Macdonald sat forward in his chair and stared intently at his audience, trying to gauge their reaction. William Davidson, the gunner colonel, seemed intrigued but unsure. A couple of the other officers were smiling, criticizing points of technical detail.

The civilians were fascinated. "How much of that was real, and how much of it was generated?" the older man asked.

"Does it matter?" Macdonald replied. "The fact is, we have the capabilities to do all of it. What we don't have is the money – yet."

"And I presume that's where you want the bank's help."

△ △ △

"We can get the people, William. Many of the faithful will follow this call. Enough of the non-believers will as well. And the army is contractually obliged to release us from service with half a year's notice unless emergency threatens."

Davidson knew that Macdonald was trying hard to convince him, but it wasn't working. "That's true, but I doubt the ministry will just roll over and let a couple of thousand walk away. I'll be amazed if you raise even one battalion. There are quite a few with itchy feet, I grant you, but enough to form an effective combat unit?" He didn't like where this was heading. He'd need a deal more persuading than a stylish presentation.

But the Leo's eyes were staring at a future full of certainties. "We'll raise the people. If there aren't enough of the faithful, we'll recruit hirelings. Weapons and equipment are cheap, since the cutbacks.

"The money's not going to be a problem. You heard what the bankers want. The business plan is sound. Defense budgets are going to be hit. NipponDeutsch and ARTOK aren't very interested in the task. They both say they're stretched, for some reason. Fixed-term contract military units can fill those gaps."

Macdonald's eyes were gleaming. "But we need commanders. I need a leader for this sacred force. You have the military rank. William, the god is summoning us. Will you heed that call?"

You must be raving mad, thought Davidson.

48

Chapter 10

A Hazily Visible Structure

LOCATION: Deleted in this transcript.
CONTENTS: COMPANY SECRET

OPERATION THOUSANDEYES UNIT REPORT

DATE / TIME GROUP: Deleted in this transcript

NON-APPROVED COPY. Any use is a serious contravention. Surrender this data immediately to your nearest Company Security or Operations Protection unit.

Perception rate two to one. I am experiencing events at twice human-normal rate, the optimum sustainable surveillance mode. Position entirely concealed to flanks and rear. Front video and audio sensors exposed and covert.

This enormous machinery corridor is inert and overgrown in its lower areas. An understanding of the scale is important. The ceiling is 137 meters above my position, with no intermediate mezzanines. Unidentified structures extend for 362 meters to my rear, 4.6 kilometers to my front. *Assumption: the large device at corridor internal grid reference DELETED is another of the presumed in-system craft, but heavily obscured by plant growth.* Corridor width at this point is 74.5 meters. The nearest approximately full-height floor-to-ceiling gaps, provisionally identified by DELETED as windows, are thirty-one meters to my rear and twenty-six meters to my front, so this area became dark once the natural light faded twenty-six minutes ago.

Optics are on low-light setting.

As always, none of the machinery is active in any detected wavelength. Organic growth resembling creepers descends from any overhead or mezzanine structure. Animal movement has died down since the light faded.

I have now been following this group of subjects for five local days. Their behavior indicates that they are unaware of me. All of them are currently in my arcs. Motion detectors report no activity from any of them. Infrared observation shows that all the previously-identified subjects (*assumption: this is the entire complement of the group*) remain in their presumed sleeping area. Five hours twenty-seven minutes until daylight.

Perception rate one to one. I am now experiencing events at human-normal rate.

All silent. All alarms set. No movement anywhere.

Perception rate one to two. Preparing for rest; my awareness is effectively at half speed.

All is silent.

Perception rate one to five.

Rest mode.

#

An onshore wind bends the palm branches into curves and whitens the waves out beyond the reef. It's too blowy for a kayak or a pedalo, and I'm not good enough at windsurfing. The few people who think that they are seem to spend more time in the water than on the boards.

But it's okay, the wind never lasts long. Meanwhile, there's jangly Latino pop, cold beer and sticky cocktails. The Mai Tais nearly blow my head off. There are loungers on the beach and there's enough shade under the trees, or there's the pool or the sea when I get too hot.

The sand is gritty under my toes, and I rub some more sun cream in because I don't want to burn, not when I'm wearing something this tiny. There's a cute blond guy a few yards down the beach and I know he's noticing when I put the cream on. When

I'm finished, I stand up and head for the bar. His eyes follow me, and then he does, which is what I wanted.

And he gets to the bar and says to me –

ALARM. ACTIVE MODE.

#

Shit. Perceptions one to one. *Bloody awake.*

Datalink: inner proximity sensors quiet. Outer ring sensor group A5 detects movement.

Perceptions two to one. Motion sensors detect new subject moving towards rest area of previously-identified group. Cameras Six and Seven activated. Both show views of dormant machinery with plant growth extending to approximately one meter generally, but occasionally peaking at three meters. Nothing else yet visible.

New subject enters view field of Camera Six. Subject is translucent viscous mass, currently around four meters in length, twenty to thirty centimeters in depth, half a meter in width. The subject possesses no apparent distinct limbs or sensory organs, but flecks of assorted colors are discernible inside it. Movement resembles a very viscous liquid travelling down a slight incline. On reaching obstacles it flows up over smaller ones and around larger ones.

I watch for thirty seconds. The presumably sleeping aliens have not reacted.

The jelly-thing reaches the foot of a metal pillar supporting the platform area chosen by the octomorph subjects for their resting place. This subject is now within range of my own optics. The octomorphs rest high among an arrangement of regular shapes on the gridded platform. Earlier tentative analysis gives the structure a fifty percent probability of having previously been a lighting array.

The jelly flows to the base of the pillar and begins to creep upwards, entirely absorbing the mast into the semi-transparent gel of the creature's body. The structure remains hazily visible within it. As the lower sections emerge below the creature, they appear undamaged.

Audio to maximum. The creature is almost silent. I can hear the rustle of vegetation emerging from underneath its rear, but nothing else. However, at this amplification the movement of my own lenses is faintly audible through the bones of my skull.

Zoom to pillar structure. Mode to macro. Structure surface appears undamaged.

Zoom out.
The pillar is 5.6 meters tall. When the jelly reaches the platform, its trailing edge is around two meters clear of the ground. The subject flows onto the platform.

The sleeping octomorphs don't stir. They lie mutually entangled, limbs wound around one another in a complicated knot.

My earlier analysis was inconclusive. Is this interweaving a sexual act, a method of exchanging data, or simply mutual reassurance and a way of ensuring that no one strays away or falls off the platform?

A finger of jelly reaches out towards the nearest octomorph. I recognize it as P-4.

That's impressive. The octomorph recoils from the touch. Its optic sensory ring opens around its full circumference. P-4 disengages from its family and leaps upwards, higher into the structure. My perceptions are at five to one for emergency response. A Slow human wouldn't be moving yet, and the octo is already two meters away. The knot of bodies unravels. Figures leap in all directions, but Subject P-7 is caught by a trailing leg/arm. It clatters in a rising tone.

And that's loud. Audio down to twenty percent to protect my hearing.

P-7 continues to clatter, but the jelly flows over it and absorbs it. The sound shuts off abruptly. Once it is enveloped, motion is also damped, and dies away to zero over thirty-six seconds.

The jelly also becomes motionless.

The octo family regroup on the floor level, and choose another probable lighting pillar ten meters away. They settle down and gradually return to presumed sleep. They do not post a sentry.

Idiots. These things have already failed at being people. And they won't last long being animals, if that's the best they can do.

Perceptions one to one.

I watch for two hours. Subject P-7's form becomes more indistinct within the jelly.

Nothing moves.

Perceptions one to two.

All silent. Perceptions one to five.

Rest mode. *Now where's that blond guy?*

#

The jelly is translucent again. P-7 has vanished entirely.

The stupid bloody octo family are still asleep.

#

TRANSCRIPT ENDS.

THE MINOR WORLDS

2448 – 2449

Chapter 11

In Response To Society's Whims

"Anyone who isn't confused here doesn't really understand what is going on."
– BELFAST CITIZEN (QUOTED IN *THE TIMES*), APRIL 1970.

2448

"It was a very sad situation. Every one of them was an exemplary soldier. They were all highly motivated people – volunteers to a man and woman – and of course, the Company was very careful in selecting them. It must have paid off, because after selection and enhancement, they did tremendous work in their new units. They were a real force for peace. Tea?" Vladimir Filippovich Semyonov waved at a delicate wooden side-table. "I know it's not a popular view, but the race owes a lot to the Human Enhancement Program. All history now, of course."

The Chairman of ARTOK led David Chambers to the table, and poured two cups. He gestured at the samovar. "Do you like it? It's a nineteenth century Lisitsyn, from Tula. I was very lucky to find it." Perhaps in his late forties, he was trim and well-dressed, with a donnish manner. He moved abstractedly through his expensive surroundings. Picking up a sugar bowl, he turned it around in well-manicured hands. "Isn't it exquisite? Oh, I'm sorry, where were we?" Semyonov ushered his guest to a chair and sat opposite him, still holding the bowl. He rested the backs of his hands on his knees and smiled pleasantly, but his eyes had become dreamy.

Chambers didn't believe a word of it. The man facing him held ultimate power over a corporation which stretched from the center of Moscow to the tiniest mining stations in the asteroid belts of distant stars. He employed several million people in a 400-year-old company which possessed its own starships, habitats, naval and military units, colleges, factories, and legal systems. Along with the Euro-Japanese multiplanetary NipponDeutsch, ARTOK dominated the human race's economic structures. The 'intellectual aesthete' image fitted poorly with a man who ruled all that. Of course, Chambers was being spun; that went with being a journalist. But what was Semyonov trying to spin?

"You were telling me about the cyborgs."

The Chairman blinked, and his eyes came back into focus. "Yes, of course. It was such a shame that the Company had to close the program. But there wasn't a demand for the Enhanced anymore, such were the political realities of the day."

"Mr. Semyonov," he began, but his host set down the bowl and held up his hand, the tips of his thumb and forefinger touching each other. Eyes closed, head tilted back, he might have been listening to a violinist's diminuendo.

"Please, no formality. Call me Vladimir."

Chambers tried again. "Vladimir, tell me more about the soldiers. You say they were highly motivated – but by what?" He unrolled the slate and placed it on the table beside the bowl. Semyonov glanced at the scuffed and worn device, and the journalist thought he heard a sniff.

The Chairman seemed to be gathering his thoughts. While he waited for an answer, Chambers glanced around. The office walls showed a slowly changing series of images from across human space – landscapes, cities, orbital stations, habitats. The ARTOK company would have activities in all these places; he'd seen the logo in every scene, usually as a subtext to groups of industrious people, all of them clean, fit and happy. Now a family group appeared, beaming healthily as they stood waist deep in some luxuriant alien crop. They were faultless: a contented couple, a pretty daughter, two handsome sons. Above them, a tiny purple sun glowed in a clear blue sky.

Perfect timing. He tapped his slate, and a hologram sprouted from the device. The cyborg face was aggressive, alien. Silvery mottled skin, artificial eyes, subtler differences to the nose and ears. An expression of frightening hostility, even of rage. "What made people agree to major elective surgery when it caused them to look like this, instead of like that?" He waved at the glorious family on the wall.

Semyonov recoiled. "Hold on a moment." Abruptly the refined gentleman was replaced by an irritated industrialist. Before the man regained control of himself, Chambers was treated to a glimpse of the aggression which must have powered him to the top. "They knew what they were doing. No one lied to them. There were thousands of applications for each position, and we selected the very best. They were all professional soldiers, smart enough to realize the risks they were taking."

He didn't want to break the man's flow, just to nudge him on a little. "Risks? Do you mean the risks of combat?"

A hand was flapped dismissively. "No, no. Soldiers expect that, even want it. I'm talking about the psychological risks they accepted, the transformations of their self-image, the – disconnect? – no, the rejection they felt from their communities."

"Do you mean at the end of their service?"

The Chairman blinked at him. "End? Of course not." It sounded as if Chambers was stupid even to consider it. Had any of them reached the end of their service? "During their service – throughout it. They were hated, quite unreasonably. People rejected them as if they were evil, unnatural."

They were unnatural, weren't they? "Surely the Company supported them? Didn't their parent states protect them from that kind of prejudice?"

"I know from records of the time that the Company did its utmost to support its employees. We provided a generous pension scheme, and support with medical expenses. What happened after their service was, as you say, a matter for their home states. How they treated them, I cannot say. And, sadly, some participants were killed in the various conflicts taking place at that time. By their very nature, those persons tended to be in difficult and dangerous regions. Others will have died since. Records are patchy – the program took place a very long time ago." The little bowl rocked. Semyonov was talking faster and faster, tapping the table with each point.

Chambers tried a new tactic. "So why do you think we're so suspicious of them?" It was an easy one; Semyonov could punt it into the long grass. Get him off guard, get him relaxed – perhaps he would open up a bit. *Probably what Semyonov thinks of me, too...*

"Look, David – it turns out that there's a limit to what we, as a species, consider acceptable modifications to the human form." *Okay, not into the long grass, then.* The Chairman was going to play this one. "Have you heard of the expression 'the uncanny valley'?" Semyonov made vague fluttering gestures, as if he was drawing a human figure.

"Yes, I have. Isn't that the idea that a robot becomes more acceptable as its form approaches a lifelike human shape, but only if it gets so close to the real thing? And when it gets too close, it actually becomes repugnant?"

"Precisely." The Chairman's hands now made a churning gesture. "These constructs grossly exceed those limits. To be frank, since their memories and personalities are malleable, they have no continuous uninterrupted personality. Many people consider that uncanny."

Constructs, weapons – why couldn't the man just say "people"? Or even "cyborgs?" Since he'd started talking about their physical and mental characteristics, he seemed to have distanced himself from them. *Hang on – 'exceed', 'have'? Present tense. That's interesting.*

"I see your point. But weren't the cyborgs people who had become part machine, not machines which were beginning to look more human? Is that why the company withdrew from this market – public opposition?"

"That's a political issue. Governments legislate in response to society's mood – in response to society's whims, perhaps. But industry must follow markets. We only make the products and provide the services that we can sell. If a market goes away, we turn our attention elsewhere."

Semyonov became expansive. "It was a wonderful program, but as interest declined, the revenue stream dried up. Yet we learned valuable lessons from it. For instance, in medical technology, in optics, in truly sustainable cold sleep, in data downloading and even in reducing the size of starship drives – to name only a few."

Chambers tried to exploit the man's sudden enthusiasm. "Marvelous. Can you tell me how many cyborgs were made?"

The Chairman spread his hands apart and put his head on one side. "No, I'm sorry, that's confidential company information." He seemed to have relaxed again, now radiating honesty and decency.

"I understand. But if we can't talk about the numbers that were made, what about the numbers – how would you put it – still in service?" Semyonov smiled sadly and shook his head, eyes closed once more. The academic gentleman had returned, and regretted the unfortunate limitations of worldly commerce.

"Well, let me try this one, Vladimir. Are any of the cyborgs still alive, and if there are – can I meet them?"

Semyonov's eyes opened. "That, I'm afraid, is also something I'm not prepared to discuss at the moment." *Practically confirmation.* "What I can say is that I think the time has come to correct some historic misconceptions. The Enhanced soldiers didn't deserve the reputation which history has conferred on them. Their status and character need to be restored.

"Now, I have a proposal for you. I thought that your work with the military on Sanctuary was interesting. It did a lot of good for their army's – shall we call it tarnished? – public image after the civil war there. Ideally, I'd like you to perform a similar service for the Enhanced, if you could spare me the time. I believe that history has been unfair to them. There's a lot that we could show you, and I believe we could make it suitably rewarding."

Interesting, indeed. "Please understand me, Vladimir. After Sanctuary, I'm not keen to write any more corporate promotional material. I'll happily look at anything relevant to my areas of interest, but I can't guarantee to report what I find from one angle or another. I'm open to reasonable persuasion, but I won't set out with a conclusion in mind. And I don't want you to pay me: I sell my work, and I make a living – more or less. If I took your money, anything I wrote would be open to accusations of bias." Was he overdoing it? That had sounded a bit too holy. He dialed his journalistic principles back slightly. "But if it's acceptable, I'd be happy to write something independently. What did you have in mind?"

Semyonov stared at him. "That's quite acceptable. I'm confident that what we can show you will speak for itself. And, in addition to your interest in the Human

Enhancement Program, there's something else which I'm sure would also interest you. May I ask another thing of you?"

"Of course."

"First, allow me to invite you to go to Parnassus. The Company has a small operation there with a very specific mission. It's not directly connected to the Human Enhancement Program, but – to use your words – it's relevant. Are you aware of the phenomenon known as the scour?"

"The huge wave on Parnassus?" Chambers remembered images of vast tidal bores sweeping up river canyons, cliff faces ground away, villages perched high above raging waters. "Yes, I've heard of it. The cause isn't fully understood, I gather."

"I think you might find a visit interesting. Your contact there would be a woman named Talia Ferenc, an ARTOK company xenobiologist. She and her colleagues are doing some fascinating work, which we feel may help to explain the scour. We think there are some very interesting implications about life elsewhere, perhaps where we have not yet ventured. Will you go?"

A biologist explaining extreme tidal forces, and linked to the cyborgs? He raised his eyebrows and held the Chairman's gaze for a moment, but evidently Semyonov would give him nothing more. He'd have to make his decision based on what he had.

So: ARTOK was maintaining a very private base on a lightly-settled planet, and they had discovered something that cast light on a dangerous natural phenomenon, and somehow this was relevant to the cyborgs –

"Okay. I'll go."

Semyonov beamed in delight. "Excellent! If I cannot pay you, will you at least accept the costs of transport and accommodation?"

The journey would take three or four months, and in any event the only way to get there would be on an ARTOK starship. Why pay the man for something he was offering for free? Chambers smiled. "Transport and accommodation would be very welcome."

Chapter 12
Backing Slow Horses

"True luck consists not in holding the best of the cards at the table; luckiest is he who knows just when to rise and go home."

– JOHN MILTON HAY

The lift slid down the exterior of the building. He activated a camera. Few outsiders came here; he might sell the video, even if he didn't get a story. A sequence of the company's farming projects cycled across the car's interior walls: clifftop greenhouses on Parnassus; a dome farm in orbit around Jupiter; Orchard itself; fruit trees under glass on Sanctuary. Bigger images pulsed across the building's outer skin – maglevs, aircraft, starships; even the habs themselves. Everything was positive, exciting, optimistic, and on-message.

Not a cyborg to be seen. Funny, that.

Come to that, no images of clones either, and none of artificial intelligences. People didn't fear clones the way they'd feared the cyborgs, but they weren't trusted either. There was an occasional one here and there, the odd attempt to replicate some valuable person. But there hadn't been the widespread adoption of the technology for which ARTOK had hoped, and hence no mass production. Clones were awkward and expensive to raise, and most governments disapproved of treating humans as property. People still tended to make more people in the traditional way. In public, ARTOK claimed it had backed out of the technology, but Chambers wasn't convinced, and he wasn't disappointed by the lack of pictures. Clones made his flesh crawl. There was something eerie about lines of identical faces.

The company wasn't ever going to remind people of its role in creating AIs. That hadn't gone well either. Fear, suspicion, religious loathing – nobody had made an AI for a couple of centuries.

Cyborgs, AIs and clones – the company had backed some slow horses over the years. They weren't just a string of public relations disasters; ARTOK must have lost serious money on all of them. How the hell had it kept going back then? Any one of those commercial catastrophes should have wiped the company out.

Yet here it still was, dominating human space. If it wasn't quite as big in spacecraft as NipponDeutsch itself, it was close behind. But over the years, the Anglo-Russian company had developed a hugely profitable lead over its Euro-Japanese rival in building habitats and stations. NipponDeutsch had built the first Sanctuary colony, but they didn't come close to ARTOK in the terraforming and habitat-building work. Nobody did. Generally, if you needed habitation, you talked to ARTOK. Maybe the answer was there. Perhaps ARTOK's shady history in remodeling human beings had faded from public memory.

Naturally, ARTOK owned this entire habitat, and Semyonov was currently its absolute sovereign. The company controlled who came and went, so perhaps they would brag here about achievements that they'd keep silent about elsewhere. So, even here, why no mention of its human enhancement work? ARTOK must have total control over the news that left this hab. What were they afraid of?

For some reason they'd let him come here, and he'd been granted some of the Chairman's precious time. The puzzling bit was why he'd been told anything at all. With all modesty, the company had to know his reputation. Did Semyonov think he could just throw him a few tasty scraps and get the publicity he wanted?

Nothing Chambers had said could have worried Semyonov, or he'd never have been allowed to leave the office building, let alone the ring. They could easily make him disappear. Nonetheless, here he was, heading for a shuttle, to rendezvous with a starship bound for Parnassus. No, they had to be trying to spin him, but they also had to know that he'd resist being spun. What was the message they wanted to get out, the one that they wanted him to think he'd discovered for himself? What was the real story that lay behind it?

A voice inside him was saying that he'd just missed a chance. There were other questions he should have put to Semyonov. But he wasn't ready. If he stopped thinking about war and politics and corporate greed and exploitation, he'd have to think about why he'd fled Orchard. He wasn't ready for that.

The lift doors dissolved. A sign read *Level Zero*, and he took a walker to the rim train. The camera bobbed along behind.

△ △ △

"Your shuttle leaves from Outbound Station, dock sixteen, at thirteen fifty-three hours. Your baggage has been transferred from your hotel room, and will be waiting for you on board. Please board the rim train at your first convenience. The Company wishes you a pleasant journey." The man smiled emptily. Then his head snapped around to look at a data display, and Chambers realized that he had been talking to a simulacrum. The face was bland, and the body language was a machine's. It was another weird ARTOK take on humanity.

Chambers made his way along a platform crowded with orderly queues. He reached the right boarding gates and joined the back of the line. The camera floated discreetly beside him.

An amber light flashed. There seemed to be some hold-up. He leaned past the people in front to see. A group of figures with bandaged faces were leaving the train. The line was still blocking his view, but people were moving aside. He stepped back with them, and saw that the group passing him weren't walking, but instead were being carried on a medical transporter.

As the queue gave way, he saw with a thrill of horror that three male and two female upper bodies rose – no, grew seamlessly – from gel-filled tubs. The faces weren't bandaged; they were incomplete molds, with smooth white plastic skin. Each head's solitary feature was its mouth, silently opening and closing. The hairless, eyeless figures turned from side to side, as if searching for the source of a sound. Their torsos swayed and their arms waved as the transporter moved along. They were alive, but seemed mindless. He thought of sea-life, underwater plants with floating fronds.

The transporter and its passengers moved on, and the queue flowed back. Chambers tried to watch, but the group was hidden by the crowds. What terrified him was the crowd's indifference, as if they saw this sort of thing every day.

The line shuffled forward again. *Almost there.*

They stopped beside a stack of small cargo boxes. Behind them, someone was crying. He stared. The noise wasn't behind the stack; it was coming from one of the crates. The box was far too small to hold anything larger than a baby, but the sobs sounded adult. Whatever was inside was in deep distress. He realised that each of the boxes was just the right size to transport a human head. His stomach rose and he hesitated, but the man behind nudged him on.

The queue freed up, and he ran for the train. Nobody had given a second glance, either at the torsos growing from the tubs, or at the sobbing crate. He wanted to be out of this place right now, and away into the deep wide black.

△ △ △

Chambers boarded the train behind a noisy group who had to be students: backpacks, odd clothing choices, grumbles about lecturers and assignment deadlines. As the rim train pulled out he settled down in his seat and stared out into the black, trying to settle his nerves. *Hold it together.* Half an hour, and he'd be on the shuttle.

He felt himself being watched, and realized that he'd been gazing out at the view across the heads of a group of passengers who were now, in turn, staring back at him. With a thrill of revulsion, he saw a row of perhaps fifteen completely identical faces. This group of young men and women were identically dressed in neat work clothes. He forced a nervous smile onto his face. They turned away in unison, moving like the gears in a machine. An older woman, similarly dressed, sat with them. She gave him a cheery smile. Teacher? Supervisor? *Mother?* He was sure that his hair was standing on end.

This was just the sort of place to make cyborgs. Simulacra, human bodies grown in vats, stacks of weeping heads, clones – perhaps students like the ones he'd boarded with had built the cyborgs as part of their apprenticeships.

To his left side, under the long dome of downtown, offices and apartment buildings flashed by. To the right, outwards and below on the long docks running along the rim, a scattering of in-system craft sat on their cradles. The camera loved it, but he didn't. To an Orchard boy, the ARTOK habitat was ugly rich, flashy trash, citified. No agriculture, no parkland, no villages. Home wasn't perfect by any means, but this place depressed him. And on this little habitat, he was convinced that he could feel rotational gravity increase as the train speeded up, although a local techie had spent much of an evening's drinking trying to convince him that it couldn't be so. True or not, rural Orchard didn't feel or look like this.

The train was slowing for Outbound station, and the kids were clambering about, grabbing packs and chattering away in what seemed like three different languages. Chambers checked the bulkhead display, then pulled his bag down from the overhead locker and started towards the doors, still fighting that weird rotation. *Yeah, better gravity back home, too.*

He fumbled it, dropped the bag and swore. As one, the identical heads opposite turned towards him, then away again. The doors slid open, and he followed the crowd onto the platform. His stomach was churning.

△ △ △

He found his shuttle seat, strapped in, checked for the panic suit, the bottle jet and the sick bag. The noisy student group was settling in across the aisle, filling every inch of space with discarded outer clothes and loose baggage. Then the clones trooped past: neat, disciplined and compliant. The smiling older woman arrived. Each identical figure obediently sat where it was directed. Was that another group, further down the cabin? Where were this lot off to?

First rule of journalism? *Stories lie behind things that don't add up.*

Gas vented noisily from somewhere in the shuttle, and they started the long slide off the dock ledge. Farted backwards into space – it seemed appropriate.

A roar from the motors, a steadily building push; they were on their way. In three days, he would be climbing onboard an ARTOK starship, off to Parnassus to see something relevant to cyborgs.

Chapter 13

They Only Fade Away

"Every gun that is made, every warship launched,
every rocket fired signifies in the final sense, a
theft from those who hunger and are not fed, those
who are cold and are not clothed."

– DWIGHT D EISENHOWER.

David Chambers watched the starscape. Strange constellations whirled past the habitat wheel. *Forget them. Concentrate on the cyborgs.*

Just how serious had Semyonov been? Was he being spun? The answer to that had to be yes, all the more certainly because he couldn't yet see how. *If you can't work out who the sucker is, it's you.*

He had a couple of hypotheses. First – ARTOK was starting its own war somewhere, and they needed an army. That could be anywhere. Did Semyonov want him on Parnassus because this possible war was happening somewhere else? *No, don't kid yourself. You're not that much of a threat.*

Second theory – ARTOK's starships had got to someplace new, and they'd found something weird to deal with, out there in the deep wide black. They wanted the cyborgs to handle that new something. *Have the cyborgs somehow been dragged into this scour thing on Parnassus? Makes a kind of sense, if only I could straighten it all out.*

His screen showed a rearward view of the ARTOK hab, but his eyes kept being dragged back to the stars. The shuttle was carrying him to a starship somewhere out there in the black. It struck him that getting on any spacecraft – shuttle or starship –

was an enormous act of faith in machinery, captain, and crew. He had no real idea of where he was going, and he definitely didn't understand the technology which would take him there,

ARTOK and NipponDeutsch weren't going to be showing any kind of real profit from their starships yet. Every mission ought to be used to help build the infrastructure that the colonies needed. The tipping point ought to be coming. By now they should have been self-supporting, but they didn't appear to be.

He remembered a comment he'd heard on Sanctuary: "ARTOK and NipponDeutsch just do the minimum. They turn up somewhere, ship in some people, throw a settlement together, and then just head off deeper into the black." The starships were vital for the logistic support that they gave to the diaspora. The corporations should be putting all their efforts into developing what they'd built. But they didn't, and that left the colonies so poor that they couldn't reach their true potential. Well, now – hold onto that thought. There could be a story there as well.

But starships were obscenely expensive, and their owners would want to get every possible cent of income out of each one. It made no sense. Why keep pushing onwards?

They would have needed every cent out of the cyborgs too, it dawned on him. He stared at the starscape again. Surely, they hadn't all been killed – dismantled? *Scrapped?* Semyonov had spoken as if some of them were still alive. As if somewhere out there, the remaining cyborgs were dreaming in their extended sleep, or fighting a war.

That was the connection, of course. If you had invested fortunes in products with a rapidly diminishing appeal, wouldn't you go flat-out to maximize your returns before the whole market imploded? You'd throw your cyborgs into every war that would make you some money or avoid some greater cost, and to hell with wear and tear on people – no, on *equipment* – that you'd probably have to scrap soon, anyhow.

And there weren't so very many wars that you could use them in, were there? He thought he was up to speed with the politics of human space, but the profitable wars might be hidden deep in the details. The cyborgs could be the perfect weapon in lots of them. But there surely weren't enough of them to leave a few in every trouble spot, on the off chance of some business...

...which meant that you needed faster-than-light ships, as well. And who had those?

Precisely.

But that was circular logic. Wealthy companies needed soldiers to protect their starships, which they needed to move their soldiers around. He was getting nowhere with this.

Right. Forget the starships for now. Stick with the cyborgs.

The creatures had existed, but did they have the abilities he'd been told about? There were wild stories about them: they were monsters, they were unclean, they were demons. They were decent people tricked into a form of slavery and cynically abandoned by heartless governments. They were ruthless killers who had surrendered the right to be regarded as human. They were ordinary soldiers who had been fitted with internal radios and mechanical eyes. They moved too fast to be seen, they were super-humanly strong, they could read minds, they could fly. The technology had gone wrong and it had killed them all. They were immune to bullets; they slept for decades, waiting for war; they lived forever. Each mismatched revelation pushed the reality further away. And everybody despised them.

The cyborgs had to have been madly expensive to construct. That made them a major investment for ARTOK, and successful companies rarely left money and assets lying about unused. What had happened to them? No one seemed to know. No last stand, no apocalyptic battle. They'd just fallen out of history. *Old soldiers never die, they only fade away.*

Semyonov had been talking about them in the present tense. The man wasn't stupid. He'd been sending Chambers a message. The cyborgs were still out there, somewhere; ARTOK had sent them away, and now it was bringing them back.

Where had the monsters been? They had been *built* at huge expense, sent to fight in war after war, allowed to die or break or go insane and then just rebuilt, again and again. Then they'd gone missing from human time and space, and perhaps from the asset register as well. It somehow enraged him that the company had wasted so much money on this program. If only they'd spent a fraction of that on Orchard...

So was this anything to do with the Parnassus thing? Semyonov had said that what he would learn there was relevant to the cyborgs, but wasn't directly involved with them. That probably ruled out war. He'd been told that it had something to do with the scour, the giant waves which periodically ripped along the planet's rivers, and it might help to explain the phenomenon. He couldn't begin to see how.

ARTOK was coming under increasing pressure from a newly-crowned young Tsar who was intent on reining in the company's power. Semyonov's own position was said to be far from secure. Challengers were circling. The Chairman's motives were unknowable.

Remember the first rule of journalism – *follow the money.*

Conglomerates only made pious policy announcements if being on the moral high ground helped them to see where the cash flow was going. Semyonov hadn't quite been able to make himself admit that the cyborgs were still around. But if ARTOK had started banging on about – what was it? – "restoring the cyborgs' status and character", then someone had spotted a major financial opportunity. And for his next trick? Finding out what the hell it was.

Δ Δ Δ

He'd reached another dead end, but he'd learn more when he got to Parnassus. For now, he'd work with his theory: at least some of the cyborgs were still alive, ARTOK had a need for them once more, and it wasn't for warfare.

How many of the creatures had survived? How many had existed in the first place? He could figure this. He was an experienced military correspondent, after all – his professional resume said so.

Try wobbly logic. An infantry section – eight-ish? It had to be far, far more than that. A troop of four or five sections? No – lots more yet. *Get bolder.* A squadron or a company would be over 100 men and women, and they would continually be working flat-out. No, still too few for every story he'd heard. There had to be at least a regiment of 500-ish, and that still felt like too few. *Leave some blunder-space in the reasoning.*

Okay – *supposition.* Quite a time ago, around 1000 cyborgs had been constructed at enormous expense. Eventually he would find out *when*, and *where*, because he already knew *by whom.* The 'how many' was a real guesstimate. So how many of the 'how many' were left, and where were they?

Okay. What kind of logistics train followed the cyborgs around? They might fight light, but they wouldn't travel light. Chambers had seen enough military supply chains to know a bit about what they would need. All the obvious stuff, of course, like weapons, ammunition, food, clothing, medication, transport, and equipment for various theatres of operations. You'd need some engineering support for all this kit. But these guys were partly artificial, so they'd also need some quite sophisticated engineering support for themselves – hardware and software. What the hell did you do if a cyborg got problems with, say, its mechanical eyes? The stories suggested artificial memories, hibernation tanks, massively extended lifespans. If even a fraction of that were true, it seemed like there'd need to be a lot of technicians within a fairly short travel time. That wouldn't be an easy secret to keep. He might learn something there.

And what about Semyonov's comment that "their memories and personalities are malleable, which can also be seen as uncanny"? It seemed to confirm what he'd heard described as 'extreme psychological intervention' – forcible personality alterations. Some psychiatrists needed as well, then.

What did maintenance mean for the cyborgs? Did someone send them off to a hospital-cum-workshop somewhere, for human and machine bits to be separated, fixed and reassembled? Nasty, but straightforward for a company which routinely did disgusting things with human bodies.

Where had the ARTOK starships been, and when? Who had the contracts for shifting government and military stuff about? The Big Two, or some of the smaller companies? Surely not them. Were there also some black ops military starships? Pricey and useful, but what would ARTOK and NipponDeutsch be using them for?

He had little to no evidence for any of this. *Of course I'm paranoid. But am I paranoid enough?*

Another good question. What answers could he find on Parnassus?

$$\triangle \quad \triangle \quad \triangle$$

An Operational Readiness Audit

"Treason doth never prosper: what's the reason? Why, if it prosper, none dare call it treason." – Sir John Harington.

The unexpected craft had been hailing the ARTOK habitat wheel Forward Station Seven since it had appeared from behind the gas giant's third moon. Its course would result in a rendezvous in a little over three days. Apart from the fact that it hadn't been anticipated, there seemed to be nothing unusual about the vessel, or about its protocols.

The vessel had politely announced its presence, waited for an acknowledgement, and identified itself as an inbound ARTOK craft. Offering suitable coded identifiers, it had responded correctly when challenged. Defensive weapons systems stood down. After that, no information was received beyond an intriguingly uninformative, "Special mission. Private. For the commander's eyes only." A puzzle, but not alarming. Meanwhile, the craft rolled steadily on towards the half-completed hab, where construction work continued.

Dmitri Petruchenko studied the screen displays. "Ollie? Are they really saying nothing else?"

"You heard them. Not a squeak. Well, the usual vectors, timings, docking mechanism androgyny, delta-v blah blah blah, but nothing interesting. Not a clue who's on board, what they want, how long they're planning on being here, or what the hell they're doing in our backyard." Olivia Naismith wasn't impressed. She'd quite liked having a private solar system.

"Probably some head-office suits here to tell us how far behind the project plan we are. But you never know; with a bit of luck, they might be bringing us something we need. Like our last equipment requisition, maybe. Or some people. Engineering, agronomy, life support. I'd even take some more cooks." Petruchenko had an operation to run here.

"Optimist."

"*Optimist?* You think I want to subsist on English cooking?"

$$\triangle \quad \triangle \quad \triangle$$

"Colonel Morozov! I certainly didn't expect to see you. Welcome to ARTOK Forward Station Seven. What brings you all the way out here?" Petruchenko waved the newcomer to a chair. Two men followed the colonel into the operations room. They glanced around, dropped their carry bags, and drew up chairs for themselves.

"An operational readiness audit, I'm afraid. But not to worry, I'm sure you'll be fine." Morozov gestured at his companions. "Yevgeny Samarin and David Levitsky. They're part of my audit team." Petruchenko nodded warily; the men were studying their slates. One of them nodded at him. They looked Asiatic. Siberian, perhaps; Chukchi or Evenk? He knew little about such people. Behind Morozov, Naismith rolled her eyes.

On the habitat's suite of surveillance video screens, there was movement on the dock ledge. More of the new arrivals were unloading gear from the starship's pinnace. In groups of twos and threes, they dispersed across the habitat. Perhaps twenty people had now left the craft.

"Erm..." Baffled, Petruchenko gestured at the screen.

"I've brought some specialists with me for a look at the key areas. How's the build going?" The security colonel pointed at a view of a construction area.

Petruchenko rallied. "Well enough, given that we're short-staffed. You'll have seen that we've roofed about a quarter of the habitat, so we're airtight in this section. The barracks are up, and the defenses are live. If you hadn't squawked the right codes, you'd have seen exactly how ready we are. But our farm is behind schedule, and we need manpower and materials to fix that. That is, if we're to be ready to feed colonists as well as the military."

"And how many people are there here, now?" Morozov was peering around the screens, looking for a clue.

"Right now we're eighty-five operational heads, plus twenty-three more non-operational family members, age range seven months to eighty-three years." Petruchenko saw the raised eyebrows and explained. "We knew we were going to be here for a very long time, so we accepted family members if the administrative impact was low. There's a creche, a small school, full medical, and of course a steady job. In time, we'll fill the wheel with the colonists, and there'll be a bigger social group than in many Earth towns. The elders and toddlers are welcome."

"I see. Before we go any further, could you please call as many of your people as possible into your mess hall? Now, what about deep space observation?"

The change of tack threw Petruchenko, so Naismith cut in. "We're up and running." Dmitri was the commander; he could do the budget-fighting stuff. She was the operations officer; this was her area of expertise. "The remote imaging telescopes are watching the alien fleet. They're over twenty light years away, moving at a large fraction of light speed. You've come at an exciting time. There's an interesting looking solar system ahead of them. If the alien vessels stick to their current path, it's as good a candidate for their home system as anything we've seen before."

That gained Morozov's attention. He stared at Petruchenko. "Really? Interesting indeed. How soon could we know if that turns out to be correct?"

Petruchenko tapped a stylus against his teeth. While he pondered a politically sensible answer, Olivia Naismith carried on.

"Just as soon as they start to brake. Well, within twenty years of them starting to brake, plus, say, half a day."

"How so?"

"Let's say it *is* their home system. At their present speed, they'll need to brake for quite a while to avoid overshooting it. At this distance, they could have started their braking run twenty years ago, and we'd only now be able to observe the reduction in their speed. So, approximately twenty years from when they start to brake, and then around twelve hours or so to munch the observation data and check it often enough to be happy. We're the closest human beings to that fleet, but twenty light years isn't local. And because they keep pulling away from us, that figure increases every second." From her tone, Olivia Naismith thought this sort of stuff should be obvious.

Morozov ignored her manner and pondered this. Samarin and Levitsky, Morozov's Asiatic-looking companions, were paying attention to the conversation. Their heads were turning from speaker to speaker, like tennis spectators.

After a few moments, the security officer seemed to reach a conclusion. "Yes, I see. And why are you so sure that we're the closest to them?"

Dmitri Petruchenko decided it was time to assert himself. He leaned forward. "That definitely sounds like an operational readiness audit question! Okay, here goes. NipponDeutsch are very unlikely to be anywhere near us. Why? Since neither of us can reach the conventional velocity we'd need to tail-chase the aliens, the only way to catch up is FTL. So both companies push forward on their trail, build a station or a habitat, and then use it to observe the distant fleet in the way we're doing at the moment. Then, if we haven't seen the aliens slowing down, after a few years we leap forward again, but only to a distance where we hope we haven't overshot. In practice, because we started at separate times, that means that NipponDeutsch and ourselves are always playing leapfrog. We tend to jump past each other every five or ten years or so."

"And we're currently out front?"

"Almost definitely, sir. The last NipponDeutsch leap was to the place they've set up on Wildhunt. We went past them again eight years later, on our way here. We don't think they've come any farther forward, yet, but they're probably getting ready to. In something between another year and perhaps as much as five years, we can expect to see a NipponDeutsch DEEPSAT observation post appearing somewhere in front of us. That's why we need to move fast, and get Forward Station Seven up and running properly. Once we've got the place finished, then we can get soldiers and colonists in place. And if the aliens do start to brake because they've reached home, then we'll be able to take advantage of that. The Euro-Japanese will be nowhere near." He sat back in his chair like a satisfied exam student.

Morozov also seemed satisfied. His colleagues put their heads close together and whispered among themselves.

"Well done! A very satisfactory answer, Dmitri! Now, your next operational audit question – explain your mission to me. What two threats must you prepare for?" He waved a star globe into existence above his slate. "Come and show me on these charts."

This is easy, Petruchenko thought. *I expected an audit would be much tougher than this.* Gesturing for Naismith to join him, he approached the star globe to explain himself.

"Here's the NipponDeutsch base on Wildhunt. This is us, here. The fleet is – Olivia?"

Naismith hadn't joined him. He turned around, puzzled. She was locked in an embrace with one of the Siberians.

"Ollie, what the hell – " But it wasn't an embrace. Her legs folded beneath her as the man lowered her to the floor, pulling the knife out of her chest.

"No! What are you doing?" What he was seeing made no sense, but he didn't have a chance to understand it before an arm came around his neck and he was heaved backwards. Then sharp bright pain across his throat, and the air left him in a bubbling rush. The floor rose. He looked across at Olivia lying beside him and tried to speak as his vision faded.

△ △ △

Morozov squatted down and considered Petruchenko's eyes with gentle concern.

"You would have passed your audit. It was a very good answer." He stood up and reached for his slate. "Right. Join the others, get yourselves down to the mess hall, and finish this. Don't miss anyone. I want to be off this hab in an hour."

Samarin opened his carry bag and threw an assault rifle to Levitsky.

Two minutes later, the shooting began. Another five minutes, and Morozov heard the first of the explosions coming from the energy center. Lights began to dim; soon the emergency power would be gone.

Forward Station Seven was dying.

Chapter 14

It's Up That's Hard

"Travel and change of place impart new vigor to the mind."

– SENECA

The ekranoplan riverboat *Nizhni Novgorod* nosed in towards the dock, engine pods swiveling forward to brake the craft against the steady pressure of the tidal bore. Ropes coiled out from underwing launchers and made the boat fast to the tie-downs on the jetty, snug between a freighter and a small ferry.

Turning his back on the jetty, Chambers looked across at the western canyon walls. Here, the Jackson River cut deeply into the planet. The cliffs rose in massive slabs of ochre stone directly from the distant mudflats. He had to hold onto the rail and tilt his head far back to see their summits. The upper edges were a blade-cut against the pale blue of the sky.

Far above him, black shapes circled and swooped in the heavens. He hadn't expected there would be birds on Parnassus. Big ones, too.

The plateau had to be around 15,000 meters high, reaching well into the planet's stratosphere. In this thin atmosphere, it would resemble the edge of space. Within a few hours, he would be on his way up there. Despite the sun on his face, he shivered. How the hell did anyone survive that?

One of his cameras was in action, circling around and grabbing any images which took its fancy. He'd sort through them later, dumping the useless ones and leaving the rest until he had time to edit them properly.

He jumped. A series of loud clatters and clangs: unloading had started. The boat was still nosing into the jetty. Mobile cranes were lifting cargo containers from the open holds and placing them on the dock or onto the waiting trucks. The dockworkers scurried about in a ballet of people and vehicles.

An amplified voice carried across the dock. "Thirty minutes to the scour." A steel caisson was unfolding across the upper decks of the neighboring ferry. Once it completed its arc, the entire ferry would be under cover. Aft, a team of deckhands were clambering over the freighter, folding or dismantling equipment and fittings. The gates of a covered dock were easing open to receive it.

The far side of the canyon was in shadow. Afternoon sun threw the river into contrast with the black of that distant western wall. Chambers turned back to face the nearer shore. The few structures on the dockside were obviously temporary. High above him, on this eastern side, more substantial buildings flung the sunlight back; on the other side, all detail was lost in the gloom. That light would vanish soon, climbing up the cliff face as the sun passed beyond the canyon lip. Even from here, across two or three kilometers of water, the mudflats stank.

On this side, the concrete jetty gave onto a steep twisting road, stone-surfaced, edged with netted boulders. Further along the roadside was a tented village: a customs post, a security-police office, and a string of market stalls. Nothing was permanent. He could make out several scruffy places selling food and drink, presumably catering to the dockworkers, boat crews, and passengers. The Parnassans had a reputation for enjoying themselves, whatever the surroundings.

He looked further up. The road left the dock at a savage angle, twisting upwards for 1000 meters or so. Tunnels cut through outcrops, bridges vaulted over side valleys. Everything was massively overbuilt for such a narrow road. Above about 100 meters, he could see traces of building ruins. Below that, no sign of any permanent structures. Was this the famous scour line?

As the road reached higher, the remnants became gradually more complete until, around fifty meters higher, the first whole and undamaged building came into view. It seemed to be a pub. Awnings and sun umbrellas were flapping in a freshening wind; there must have been a spectacular view from up there. But then, everywhere around here would have a spectacular view.

Among the cluster of vehicles at the dock was an ancient wheeled bus, its rattling body panels suggesting that the engine had been left running. Mesh panels covered the body's roof and sides. Nearby, a game of some sort was going on among a group of men at a wooden trestle table. He watched; the camera got the idea and headed that way. The game involved both dice and cards, and required a good deal of shouting, plenty of gestures and a lot of laughter.

"Slapchance," said his slate. "Card and dice-based gambling game for up to seven people, widely played in..." He shut it off. Dog-tired from the journey, he wondered sourly if the group had been hired by some tourist body to provide local color for holidaymakers.

A sudden boom made him spin round. Farther down the dock, a man brought a shotgun down from his shoulder and laughed. He saw a dark figure, a winged ape, drop screaming into the water. The thing was almost man-sized, a medieval demon with leathery wings and a fanged face. What the hell was it? The gunman pumped his shotgun and fired again. Chambers watched the thing thrash around and sink.

"*Pseudopan pithecus volans*, fang-glider, carnivorous winged monkey-analogue, native to Parnassus," the slate commented.

Gangplanks rattled down onto the dock, and people started to stream off. One or two glanced down into the water where the creature had fallen. The shotgun carrier paced the dockside, looking upwards, his reloaded weapon cradled across his arms.

A few meters behind him, a woman stood by the bus, a slight figure wearing woolen headgear and long robes despite the warmth. She studied the disembarking passengers in turn, apparently dismissing each one, then seemed to notice Chambers. He straightened, slung his pack over one shoulder and picked up his bag. Was this Talia Ferenc?

The voice came again. "Twenty-five minutes to the scour." The pace of work picked up. Chambers felt a growing tension. The caisson had almost completely obscured the ferry; as he watched, the steel reached the water and dipped below it. Presumably it would reach around beneath the hull in some way. Behind, the freighter had disappeared into the dock; the gates were swinging closed. A surge of water boiled from some hidden spillway beside the nearer gate, slopping high up over the slimy timbers of a rotting quay.

He checked his watch and realized he was tapping his hand on the rail. The line was moving achingly slowly. Grabbing the camera as it floated past, he stuffed it into a pocket and joined the queue.

By the time he reached the walkway's head, a few of the vehicles had started to move off up the road, and many of the tents and stalls had been taken down. The card players weren't going anywhere yet.

The gangplank bounced under his shoes as he made his way down, uncomfortably aware of the drop to the Jackson's oily stinking water. It glopped and surged between the hull and the jetty.

He walked through a blast of warm fuel-smelly air from one of the ekranoplan's idling motors. As he drew closer to the scabbed concrete, the woman on the dock watched him attentively, as if making sure he was the one she was waiting for. She stood almost motionless, a compact and tidy figure somehow out of place in these shabby surroundings.

He was one of the last to disembark and, to the warbling of an alarm, the gangplank almost whisked his feet from under him as it recoiled onto the deck, twisting into a storage drum. A man behind him staggered, swore, and leaped for the dock. The vessel was reconfiguring itself for air-cushion flight, and all the upper deck equipment was being stowed to clean up the craft's aerodynamics. The engines were spinning up, their noise rising to a shriek.

He glanced back. Above him, in that curious glazed bulge which he'd never been able to name – flight deck? bridge? – a cluster of the boat's officers were talking urgently. One of them leaned forward to his control panel and Chambers saw his lips move. The hidden speakers boomed, now almost inaudible above the racket. "Fifteen minutes left. We leave in three minutes, whether you're ashore or not."

The engines' howl increased even more, and the motors swiveled rearwards. He turned back to the dock. The *Nizhni Novgorod* was starting to get under way. The last few boxes were hurled carelessly from the ekranoplan in the general direction of the jetty. Two made it; one hit the edge and fell into the filthy water. The waiting stevedores turned away, and headed off with their final loads towards the vehicles.

The robed woman was still watching him. Their eyes met. For want of a better idea, he waved, then instantly felt stupid. She smiled fractionally, and walked towards him. He pulled the camera out and let it go; with any luck, it wouldn't go rushing off after the *Nizhni Novgorod* but would stay within its programmed radius of him. They reached each other, and he held out his hand. She took it; her grip was light, the skin dry and soft.

"Talia Ferenc?" He was shouting above the din.

Again, he hardly understood the reply. "Yes. David Chambers?" It sounded more like "Day Shembas." Something had shifted in the local definition of English. Parnassus was isolated, so he might not be able to buy the dialect. He'd just have to get used to it.

A jeep shot past, horn blaring, two men sorting out bundles and crates on the load bed as the vehicle bounced along. A lorry followed, then a crane; the evacuation had started in earnest.

"The *Nizhni Novgorod* is departing now. You have twelve minutes to the scour. Pack up anything you want to keep. Good luck and goodbye." The ekranoplan was pulling away from the quay, turning across the Jackson, filling the dock with stifling air and noise. Chambers turned back to Ferenc. The urgency was turning to real haste, if not yet actual panic. He forced himself to relax a bit.

"I'm told you've agreed to take me up into the hills to show me something, but I admit I don't know what it is."

She smiled again, a trifle more broadly. He realized that the robes were knee length, worn over heavy trousers.

"Hills? They're rather more than hills, but yes, that's the idea. I'll explain as we go." His first impression had been right. There was something neat about her. She was small, perhaps forty, sparing in her movements, calm amid the noise and hubbub around them. A tiny cable and air hose were clipped across her shoulder and under the hood of her robes. "Time to get on the bus."

The accelerating riverboat was 100 meters away, deploying its wings to maximize the air cushion. Its deck equipment was stowed, and the keel was beginning to break clear of the water surface. Chambers noticed that whitecaps were starting to appear on the wavelets – was the wind building? Uncertain, he followed Ferenc onto the bus steps.

The gamblers, waking from a dream, grabbed their belongings and dived into an assortment of vehicles, launching themselves up the road in a commotion of revving engines, squealing tires, and scattered cards. An abandoned hand of cards fluttered in his wake, then scattered on the growing wind. Beyond the mesh-covered bus window, the entire tent village had vanished, and few other vehicles remained.

The driver was closing the doors. Metal lattices swung across the windows. Hissing and sighing, the bus crossed the end of the dock onto the road's first incline. The remaining vehicles – another jeep, and a motorbike with a huge boxy sidecar – roared past the bus, one on each side. The motorbike seemed to have four or five people and an assortment of goods wedged on it; even the rider was carrying something. Road law was evidently as casual as everything else on Parnassus. Each of the group was wearing fancy dress headgear – he could make out a three-cornered pirate hat, a spiked steel helmet, and a miter. The rider, inevitably, wore a leather flying helmet, complete with goggles. He dragged the camera out again, and let it run.

Hold on, though – there was still a stationary and silent car left on the dock, engine cover open, a panicking man giving it a despairing kick. With a final exasperated wave of his arms, the driver abandoned it and ran the length of the dock, pulling out a phone and yelling into it. His other hand struggled to keep a Roman centurion's helmet on his head. He kept yelling until the sidecar outfit executed a skidding turn and accelerated back again. The man dived on anyhow, and the whole circus turned around and headed off once more. Chambers sighed wearily and shook his head. Couldn't these people organize anything?

Away towards the center of the water, the ekranoplan was moving fast. It had turned to face back downriver, into the strengthening wind borne on the forward edge of the scour. The lift engines were howling now, plainly audible above the creaking bus, and the vessel's flight wings were fully extended. Air vortices buffeted the water surface, leaving a white trail below each wingtip. The wake was broken, as if the vessel had hopped several times before leaving the water. Several of the bus passengers were watching it; there was a cheer as the ekranoplan lurched into the air.

Despite travelling several hundred kilometers on the battered and industrial *Nizhni Novgorod*, this was the first time he had known the craft to be airborne. It supposedly had limited flight capability, but his experience of the decrepit vessel had made him doubt it. No one would trust a thing like that to fly.

As if on cue, a tumbling, rolling wall of water burst into view far down the canyon. The base was a muddy chocolate brown, but the crest was clean and white. The giant wave rolled on without breaking. Size was impossible to guess, but now the distant walls looked smaller and closer, so the swell had to be huge. The river water at its base was smooth brown silk, undisturbed; as the bore rolled closer, the constantly-renewing crest shattered repeatedly into enormous whitecaps and fountains. Chambers, watching open-mouthed, thought of an artillery fire mission he'd seen. Rummaging in his pack, he pulled out his other camera. This wasn't a scene he could afford to miss.

The scale became clear when the tiny silver and white dot of the airborne *Nizhni Novgorod* crossed over the leading edge of the wave. The ekranoplan was now a speck against the far canyon wall, but only a finger's width above the madly thrashing water. What could that be, 300 meters high? Five?

The other passengers were transfixed. The chatter fell away to silence, followed by gasps and hisses of breath as the vast wave rolled on. The locals would be used to this, wouldn't they? – so the startled ones had to be visitors like him. The *Nizhni Novgorod* vanished briefly and someone shrieked; then there was another ragged cheer as it reappeared, still climbing doggedly above the turbulent water.

"Look. Look at the dock!" A frightened voice; he looked back and down, reassured to see that they had now climbed a lot higher than the concrete jetty. The bus was negotiating one of the many hairpins, and he had to turn from side to side to get an unobstructed view.

The Jackson River was draining away from the dockside, receding and shrinking as it went, exposing the mudflats at its base. The entire caisson covering the ferry was now visible. Waterfalls poured from the corners onto the mud below. The abandoned car still sat on the dock, alone except for a couple of tent poles and a few scattered boxes.

The rolling wall of the scour sucked the water from in front of itself and heaved it upwards. Holding on tight to keep his balance against the steep incline of the road, Chambers stared further out across the vast expanse of the riverbed. Here and there black clumps poked out of the mud. Wrecks, he guessed.

The tumbling wave rolled on, moving faster than he'd first thought, filling the canyon from edge to edge and closing on the jetty, as if determined to wipe every made thing from the planet's surface.

When it hit, all the vanished water came back at once, overwhelming the jetty with a hissing roar. The caisson vanished, the freighter's covered dock vanished, the old landing stage vanished; the little car vanished. The jetty might never have been there. As if this had been a trivial thing, the massive wave rolled on along the canyon, drinking the Jackson in a continuing vast gulp and vomiting it out again.

But now it was rolling high along the canyon sides, as well as travelling onwards upriver. The tide had smashed onto the canyon road and was coming closer to the bus. The rock walls were crawling past.

The bus seemed trapped in glue as it dragged itself onwards up the slope. This felt like every nightmare cliché, but still a nightmare for all that. Chambers was on his feet, staring intently at the onrushing wave, willing the bus to climb faster, still flinching from that growling roar. If that water hit them... perhaps it would be all over quickly.

He glanced at Ferenc. She caught his eye and repeated that micro-smile. "Relax, Mr. David Chambers. We've out-climbed it. This one will peak at sixty meters, and we're well past that. It's only a little scour; bad enough, but no one's going to die this time."

He remembered what he did for a living, and got hold of himself. "Why are you so sure?" There was a lot more to this story, but he had to take it one step at a time. First rule of journalism: *be patient – don't scare the source away.*

He watched her out of the corner of his eye while he stared at the wave blasting along the canyon walls, ripping loose stones from the curbside. She'd been so infuriatingly precise about her calculation that he was almost annoyed when the thrashing white crest washed by just below them. The bus wheels could hardly have been splashed.

He tracked the wave on its way upriver, watching jets and fountains form and vanish again among the canyon walls as the wave rolled on. The roar of its passing turned into a hiss as water drained away down the slope. *Hold on, Dave, get a grip. Listen to the woman.*

"Why am I sure? I checked the road for condition when I walked down, and I saw that the surface was okay. I noticed that the bus driver had kept the engine running. I checked the forecasts, so I knew how big the scour was and when it would get here. If it's fifty-five meters at Widow's Pledge, it'll be sixty here. I kept an eye on the time, and I watched the height markers. I knew we would make it. I only go to places when I'm properly prepared, Mr. Chambers. Don't you?"

Ouch.

Hold on. "Okay. Did you just say you *walked* down?"

"Well, yes. Down is easy. It's up that's hard."

The road's steep incline swept up and up to the next tunnel, then across the canyon at the departing scour and the monstrous, endless height of the opposite cliff wall. Just as she'd predicted, water was cascading down off the rocks below them – around fifteen meters short of the marker he'd seen a few moments ago. He caught a brief glimpse of a brightly-colored shape, a solid something, flashing into view on the crest of the scour and then submerging again beneath gigatons of water. The little car? Then he thought again about walking the length of a road down such a cliff. Even downwards, it would be a massive task. Upwards didn't bear thinking about.

The road twisted sharply and crossed a gash in the cliffside. He could see vast spillways everywhere, huge pipes bored into the rock face. The bridge's parapet sidewalls were ventilated along their entire span, cut through at deck level with drains and gutter spouts. Now, as they approached another tunnel, he noticed that the roadbed was raised on piles within the bore, so that water could flow through it beneath the road.

They swept past a break in the roadside wall. Looking back from the next corner, he saw the tailboard of a lorry wedged between boulders a little way down the slope. It had left the road and only been prevented from falling for perhaps hundreds of feet by a chance impact with the rocks. As they went on, he glimpsed the wreck of a tiny car beneath its wheels. They'd collided, and the lorry had carried both off the road. Maybe no-one would die today, but people had definitely died here.

He traced the spillways down to where they disappeared into vast tanks set into the hillside. More pipes, tanks, and sluices flanked the road until it disappeared. Many led into stone-encased mounds which might have been turbine houses.

"Watch out. Fang-gliders." A shout, and all conversation stopped on the bus. The driver glanced down at the shotgun mounted on the dashboard rack.

They were approaching a tunnel with a pair of carved figures mounted on the bridgework above the entrance. Ugly ochre-colored things, they squatted on the parapet and glared down at the bus with comic menace. Gargoyles? How could they stay in place when the scour swept everything else away? Hang on – the creature which the man had shot had been that size.

The statues were alive. One of the gargoyles unfolded into an angular and scrawny ape-creature with a bat-eared face, flaring nostrils, and bulging eyes. Beneath its spindly arms, webs of skin stretched from wrists to ankles. Its partner rose too, turning side-on and showing a skeletally thin profile. The first one screamed and dropped gracelessly off the parapet as the bus passed underneath. There was a thud overhead.

The driver flicked a control, and a fizzing crack sounded above them. Something fell from the bus roof. Chambers turned to Ferenc. "I saw someone shoot one of those things down at the dock."

"Yes. They're the top native species, and nasty sods with it. Unpleasant, but not usually a threat if the vehicles are properly meshed. We learned that the hard way after a bus went off the road years ago. The little thugs will kill children if they get a chance, and they had a wonderful time with some of the crash survivors. You don't often see them this far down."

As they entered the tunnel, Chambers looked back. The surviving fang-glider crouched on the road, studying the smoking body of its companion. Then it screamed in rage at the bus.

Ferenc spoke again. "Actually, they're the reason you've been invited here. The scour is linked to them, and it tells us something important about human space."

Chapter 15
Catullus And The Plummeting Monkey

*"It can now be asserted upon convincing evidence
that savagery preceded barbarism in all the tribes
of mankind, as barbarism is known to have
preceded civilization."*
– LEWIS HENRY MORGAN, *ANCIENT SOCIETY*, 1877.

The creature rotated above the slate. It was an eight-limbed bulbous globe, radially symmetric, with a mound-like protrusion rising above the mass of its body.

"I believe that this is a sensory cluster, with a circular sight organ." Ferenc indicated the jellylike band looping around the bulge. "Okay, an eye, wrapping all the way around the body. There's something like fine musculature behind it. Nerves run to the brain from several nodes. If that's correct, it would have 360-degree vision. That's consistent with the rest of its body structure. We call them octomorphs.

"They're land-dwellers, we know that much, and the limbs can probably be used equally well as hands or legs. The mouth parts and gut suggest that it's an herbivore, and that's supported by observation, so perhaps it's evolved to browse through vegetation.

"The creature uses several limbs to feed itself while it walks on the rest. Any direction is forwards. Continuous circular vision is helpful to work out where the next mouthful is coming from, and you can keep watch for predators at the same time. Not a bad layout. The mouth's underneath it, by the way." She tapped the slate, and the image disappeared.

Chambers held on while the bus swung around a corner. They had been rattling up the steeply twisting road for nearly half an hour. He had lost count of the number of bridges, tunnels, hairpin corners, and dizzying drops on the way, and of the number of shattered buildings they had passed. At times, the road had turned so sharply he'd been unable to see where it was going next. How the hell had the Parnassans built this thing?

He was glad of the distraction. "Let me get this right. You say those things aren't from Parnassus. So where do they come from, and what have they got to do with the scour and the cyborgs, and the – what do you call them – fang-gliders?"

"I'm not permitted to tell you where the octomorphs were discovered –"

"What? Not permitted?" Suddenly, Chambers didn't know what had he got himself into.

"But they're definitely not from here." She pressed on. "The important thing is that the surveillance teams found these things living in three separate solar systems, and signs of them elsewhere. There's not the slightest chance that they evolved simultaneously around three different stars." She watched him while he thought it through.

He tried to hold the anger down. "I need to know what Semyonov's up to. First, he tells me that ARTOK has found something that's important to the whole race, and he wants me to tell the tale, but now there's a sizable chunk that I'm *not permitted* to know about. Permitted? I'm *invited* – he's not paying me. That was the crucial point of our arrangement, and now I'm bloody glad of it. You're trying to feed me a fixed-up story. Why should I listen to any more of this?"

She shrugged. "I don't know what you've been told. I've had instructions to show you certain things, but not to reveal others. The company pays *my* salary. I'll tell you what I'm instructed to tell you. It's your call whether you listen." Her face fell into shadow as they entered another tunnel.

It didn't take him long. "Okay. First, please let me know why you're only prepared to tell me some of this."

"They gave me clear instructions," she repeated. "I enjoy my job, and there isn't much alternative work for me around here. Actually, there isn't *any*, for a xenobiologist. It's an easy decision."

"So why not just leave?"

Ferenc gave a mocking laugh. "Why should I leave? I was born here, my family are here, and I like living on the Jackson River. And I told you, I enjoy my job. What's so important to me about your story that I should lose all that?"

He gave in. "Okay, fair enough. I see your point. Let's get back to these octo-creatures, then. Three planets. Do you mean to say that something took them from one system to the next? What were they, pets? Livestock? Where are the pet-owners, the farmers?" He felt quite pleased at how quickly he'd got there.

"There weren't any farmers, or none that the surveillance people could find. I doubt that there ever were any. On each of the three planets, it's obvious that these creatures used to have an advanced civilization. There are heavily-overgrown ruins, earthworks, geometrically-straight canals, broken remains of ancient machines. The buildings and artefacts suit the octomorph body shape perfectly. Chambers, we found *starships*. Wrecks, but definitely starships.

"But wherever the survey teams went, the creatures that they saw didn't take any interest in the ruins. They were made by their ancestors, but today's octomorphs don't recognize that. They've reverted to barbarism, or even worse."

He made the mistake of glancing out of the bus window. Above, below, and to either side, all he could see was air. The bus must be right on the edge of the drop. Gravel pinged underneath, and a wheel spun for a moment. He tried not to think about it. "What's worse than barbarism?"

He was thrown to one side as the bus lurched and started up another steep gradient. At least he could see the mountainside again. "They don't show any signs of intellectual activity. I've studied all the images and all the primary data. It's as if they don't see the buildings and the machines. They climb on them, they hide in them, but they treat them just like rocks or trees. It's like monkeys living in a ruined cathedral. They don't seem to have an idea what their environment was designed to do. I don't believe that the contemporary creatures are capable of reasoned thought.

"We've found the same remains of advanced technology spread across seven more planets. But on those planets, we found no trace of these creatures themselves, nor of a degraded successor race. They've completely vanished, leaving their civilization behind them. There are the same ruined buildings and machines, and plenty of other life, but no sign of the octomorphs, original or modern. Plenty of other animals, plants, insect equivalents, fungi, bacteria – that's it. Nothing that looks anything like them, let alone like a thinking species. But at some time, they'd reached at least ten stars."

Chambers looked out of the window again. Every meter of the road was bordered with spillways, water tanks, and pipes. Here and there he'd seen more of the height markers. There had been glimpses of water pouring from catch tanks in the cliff face, down spillways into other tanks further below. Plainly, drainage was a serious business here.

He dismissed the thought. "What you're telling me is that those things used to be highly developed, but that they aren't any more. That somehow, they've fallen back into savagery, and disappeared from several of their worlds."

His mind was racing. It was easy enough to say, but he recognized that the implications were immense. Humans had expanded far enough into the black to collide with something else; that something else had encountered problems which had wiped them out. The night sky had stopped being just a protecting velvet blanket 500 years ago; since then, it had been an ever-expanding frontier. Now the black seemed suddenly threatening.

Ferenc smiled at him as a teacher would smile at a clever child, but her eyes were serious. "They can't have evolved independently on several planets. We know that. Evolution is purposeful, but it's random. Similar factors might produce comparable results, but they won't get identical ones. Like kangaroos and deer." The reference escaped him. "Likewise, the octomorphs can't have spontaneously reverted to barbarism in several places over a relatively brief time. We think some of the ruins are far less than 10,000 years old, judging by likely erosion rates and by the known growth rate of indigenous plants. Over that period, you'd expect a few societies to have retained at least some of their culture and technology."

"What about a catastrophic war?" He noted sourly that war came so easily to his mind.

She stared at him. "Wars usually have winners, and no one else seems to be living there."

Chambers considered that for a moment, then rallied. "I guess you can't know much about their technology, but what if there was a mass-destruction weapon that wiped them all out?"

"They weren't wiped out. They're still on those three planets, but non-sentient. And the ecosystems of all of the planets seem to have survived."

"Okay, I give in. You must have theories about all that. What do you think happened to them?" This was a long way from what he had thought he was getting into, back when he had accepted Semyonov's invitation.

She put her head on one side and gave him a considering look. "We think they were intentionally driven back to a pre-developed state by another species. We think that they used a process which targeted the octomorphs' technology and their cognitive development, but which left the planets' ecologies undamaged. Something deliberately shut them down."

"So it *was* a weapon? Biological?" Thoughts of poisons, viruses, neurotoxins, and plague filled his mind.

"Not anything we'd recognize, if it was."

The next question hung unasked between them, as if putting it into words would make the answer real. And if the answer was real, then humanity was in trouble.

But the first rule of journalism was *get the story, no matter what.*

So he went ahead and asked it, because he knew the answer anyhow. "And since the octomorphs didn't make it here, what's all that got to do with Parnassus?" He thought of the huge waves that abraded the river banks and cut deeply into the planet's hide, and of the fang-glider in the tunnel entrance, shrieking its rage at the departing bus.

And she answered him, because she must have known that she had to. "We think that it happened here as well."

△ △ △

Poly-steel nets reached high up the road edges, holding tons of loose stone in place against the scour. The surface, scabbed and battered down at the jetty, had become progressively smoother and more regular, and now even boasted a few barriers and reflectors, and the occasional sign. They'd be at that little pub soon.

She'd flatly refused to explain what she had meant about the same catastrophe happening on Parnassus. "You'll see, that's all I'm saying. Then you can make your own mind up." She wouldn't be budged on that, so he picked up the octomorph story where they had left off. Was there a word for this? *Genocide* came closest.

"What makes you think that it was a deliberate action?"

She sighed, and the weary sound almost convinced him. "I didn't at first, not for a long while. I was part of a team working on octomorph body structures. We had some data from their starship wrecks. I noticed that the octomorph equivalent of flight helmets suggested a cranial capacity of around 1900 cubic centimeters, which is close to human.

"But the sample creatures taken by the survey teams had cranial capacities nearer to 1200, in a smaller skull case. Octomorphs seem to breed after around thirty years. Over a period of about 300 generations, their brains have become much smaller."

He must have looked blank. "Think of it like this. In the 10,000 years after agriculture was invented, human evolution speeded up. Over the same timescale, the octomorphs went a long way in the opposite direction.

"There's no known evolutionary precedent. It shouldn't happen. Evolution is about success in breeding. It's getting smarter, not dumber, that leads to success."

He thought about it. If she was right, then about the time the first human settlements experimented with growing crops and keeping livestock, these creatures had been travelling between stars, and something else had set about destroying them.

Even if human evolution had speeded up, the humanity of that time was recognizably the humanity of today. Agriculture had evolved technology even faster than it had evolved humans. Back when the octomorph civilizations fell, there had been no prospect of human space travel; by the time humans got off the planet, the octomorphs must have been witless for millennia. If that had been a deliberate action by another species, mankind might have just been lucky to escape notice.

A few pieces tumbled into place. "Where do the soldiers come into this? Where are the cyborgs now?"

"What's a cyborg? Wait, do you mean those old monster soldiers? I don't know what you're talking about." Her difficulty was honesty. Dissembling was beyond her.

"Yes, you do. Semyonov kept talking about the cyborgs in the present tense. They're still around somewhere, up to something covert. And you just said that these octomorph things breed after thirty years. You've been watching them for a very long time, and cyborgs are supposed to be able to slow their lives down, or go into standby. You're a biologist, so you might understand that; I don't. But it would be useful for watching things covertly, for a long time. Things like aliens. And you've been talking about *survey teams* and *surveillance* as if they're the same thing. They're not. You're a scientist, you do *surveys* – openly, so your results can be peer-reviewed. Soldiers and security people do *surveillance*. Covertly – they don't discuss where they've been. They *aren't permitted* to talk about it. Sound familiar? The cyborgs are in this somewhere."

Her face was stricken. "I'm not talking about this. I'm not used to this kind of attention. I'm a scientist; I'm not interested in company politics. We'd been quietly working on the octomorphs for a few years before I saw the connections with Parnassus; when I mention it, I start getting personal messages from the Chairman – me! And then you turn up and I'm supposed to tell you some of this, but not all of it. I don't like any of this stuff, and I'm no good at it. So don't push me. I'm not saying anything about those soldiers."

Time to change tack. Chambers turned to the woman and gestured at the road edge. "When did the scour last reach this high?"

She gave that micro-smile again. "Just under 200 days ago, Mr. Chambers. But that's unusual, to be fair. It's rarely more than 150 meters, although that's bad enough if you're not ready for it."

He imagined it would be, having just seen the sixty-meter version. "What happens if you're not ready?"

"Why, you die, of course." She saw his expression. "Look, think of it as evolution in action. Everyone knows that the scour is dangerous. If you live or work anywhere near it, and you don't take the trouble to find out about it, you're a damn fool. And damn fools don't tend to survive. Or deserve to."

Tough woman, then.

There was a blatting noise, and the motorbike and sidecar veered perilously past the bus again. The whole wacky hat crew were on board, looking a lot more cheerful now. Spiky Helmet and Miter waved happily as they overtook.

"What are that lot up to?"

"Them? You saw the market down on the dock? There's plenty of buying and selling whenever there's a ferry or an ekranoplan to trade with. There aren't many opportunities to get your hands on off-planet goods. If there's a scour, the market's very temporary, so most of those guys will do anything to attract attention to their stalls. Two months ago, it was circus acts. There were jugglers and acrobats everywhere. I haven't seen the hats before."

The bus had passed the hat crew ten minutes earlier, parked up on one of the hairpins. They had been standing in a line, each with a hand on his heart, staring solemnly down into the abyss. Centurion, in floods of tears, had paced up and down on the cliff edge wall waving his arms, reciting something in a highly dramatized valediction and funeral oration for his vanished car. Chambers had caught a few words through the open bus window:

"...and did not Catullus write, 'Depart from this place that pleases you, waters, destroyers of good things, and go and annoy boring people'?"

"I don't think that's quite it, actually. I'm sure what he meant was..." That was Pirate speaking, but Chambers had missed the rest as the bus took the corner.

He tried again. "So what's the highest it's reached?"

"165 years ago, the scour reached 972 meters. And before you ask, over 300 people died along the Jackson River alone, out of a local population of about seven-fifty back then. That was the first big one in human times, and the biggest so far, as it happens.

"It nearly wiped out the colony. If it wasn't for the fact that the scour doesn't hit everywhere at once, it would have finished us completely. Enough people escaped the waves where they first hit land to get the message to everyone else further up the rivers. That's when they started rethinking how we were going to live here.

"Lucky, in a way, that the monster wave happened before we'd got as far as building cities, or there could have been millions of dead. The next biggie was thirteen years after that, then thirteen years later again."

"It was a thirteen year cycle?"

"You'd think so, wouldn't you? But *seven* years later there was another one that was over 600 high. Of course, no one had done any serious building below the nine-seventy mark again, but there were still quite a few deaths around here, and a hell of a lot of damage.

"And then there are all the little ones, like today's. We might get one every couple of months, or they could come a few years apart. You just can't tell. Once the first folk figured that out, they realized that we had to put massive effort into dealing with this. And of course, we still don't know if those were the biggest possible.

"Right time to talk about it, actually. Just round the next corner you'll be able to see the *Deucalion*." She said the word as if it was a title.

"What's that?" Chambers asked.

"No, it's better that you see it first. Then you'll understand a bit more about the scour."

The bus swept round the promised corner. By now, he'd become almost used to that panicky moment when the only thing he could see through the front windscreen was sky. There'd be a brief few seconds when he had no idea at all which way they'd face next, then a stomach-churning drop, and they'd turn and climb again. Another headland would come into view, with another massive incline leading up it.

This time there was something else to see. On the far side of one more gaping gorge, wedged into a flattened valley that had to be six or 700 meters above the Jackson River, sat a ship, a cargo freighter. Chambers just stared at it, aware after a few seconds that his mouth was hanging open. Not a good look for a well-travelled sophisticate.

The vessel had probably been capable of occasional ocean voyages. It had been forced far enough and high enough into the hillside that it would never be recovered, but it appeared largely undamaged. The hull seemed practically complete from this limited view, and there were still a few cargo containers on the upper decks, hanging at crazy angles. Two or three others lay strewn about the hillside. Minor pieces of debris surrounded them.

"That happened when the seven-year wave came."

He tore his eyes away and looked at Ferenc. "How long ago was that, did you say?" He felt he was talking just to stop his brain from seizing with shock.

"In 2318. Just after the slow-liner time ended." Everyone on the bus was staring at the ship, he noticed. It wouldn't matter whether or not you were a local. You'd never take something like that for granted.

He turned back to look at the wreck. It might have been placed carefully on the only relatively flat spot on the mountainside, the bow pointing up, like a toy boat that had twirled round and settled after the bathplug had been pulled. The twin propellers hung about ten meters above the gently sloping ground; the rudder was unbent. He was no maritime expert, but he guessed it was around 100 meters long, and a couple of thousand tons, with a pair of masts and a squat superstructure aft. A deck crane of some sort still reached over one side of the vessel. A light aircraft rested on the foredeck; at this distance, he couldn't see if it had been carried as deck cargo, or if it had been another victim of some trick of the scour. The rust-streaked hull seemed unbroken. "How the hell did that happen?"

"Like I said, they thought there was a thirteen-year cycle. I guess they had planned to protect any river traffic well in advance of the next scour, but the change in the pattern just didn't give anyone the time.

"It's famous across Parnassus, of course. All but one of the crew lived through it, you know? But it must have been terrifying for them, once they heard the scour was coming and they were hours from any kind of anchorage. I've seen the vid of some interviews they gave later. Seems they argued about beaching her and getting up the cliffs, but they were nowhere near any kind of a road or path, or anything climbable.

"So they just kept going upriver as fast as they could, flinging cargo overboard to lighten the ship, hoping like hell that someone had got the sums wrong in their favor, and looking desperately for any kind of option. And all the time that bloody great wave was getting closer, ripping up the gorge behind them, a lot faster than they could ever hope to go."

The bus turned again, and the *Deucalion* disappeared once more. "That fanwing 'plane was trying to hold position over the ship to lift off the crew when the scour caught them. Mad idea, but bloody brave." Chambers realized that his heart was pounding in his chest, even though the danger was 130 years in the past.

"There's even some vid from the docking cameras. Some editor put it together afterwards, so you can see fore and aft views. Most terrifying thing I've ever seen. You see the scour coming at you till the whole sky is blocked out by the wave, then everything tilts and the ship accelerates like a missile. There's a lot of screaming and cursing on the audio, and anything not bolted down comes loose and rockets away – cargo, lifeboats, the captain's motorbike, and the one poor woman who didn't make it. As the ship fell into the void in front of the wave, she went straight up in the air and vanished. No trace, of course. The fanwing just smacked down onto the deck.

"Then they show the cliff coming at them, and you can hear the voices crying and praying. Makes my palms sweat just remembering it. But then the whole picture seems to go slow, and the ship just rises up, and it touches down as light as an arbent seed. Even the fanwing pilot survived it."

The bus lurched on, and she told him the rest. The first small settlements on Parnassus had been on the lower ground, from sea and river level up to around 1000 meters high. With so little flat land available, roads and landing strips were difficult to build, so everyone wanted to get at the rivers for transport. They knew that a water-rich planet with so many moons would have frequent and complicated tides, but in the first years no one had troubled to work out what might happen when the orbits of several moons coincided, or even when that might happen.

The tidal bore had been a profound shock to those early colonists. They soon learned that any waterside communities would be washed away, so they set about learning the celestial motions of their new solar system. Further moons were discovered, plotted, and found to be an inadequate explanation for the phenomenon. Various kinds of quasi-satellites, with deeply eccentric orbits, were regularly postulated, but no hypothesis had yet survived the unpredictable scour.

Chambers had known little about it. He'd had a vague impression that the planet had big waves now and then. Now he was here, it all seemed quite a bit more urgent... and the monstrous event he'd just witnessed was one of the smaller ones.

"Look – we're stopping."

The bus was slowing, turning creakily into the cliff edge parking area alongside the pub. A sign swung from an overhead gantry, announcing that they'd arrived at The Plummeting Monkey.

Chapter 16

Ploughing Alien Ground

*"Merchants have no country. The mere spot they
stand on does not constitute so strong an
attachment as that from which they draw their
gains."*

– THOMAS JEFFERSON.

all mesh fencing, hanging from huge poles, stretched around the parking area. Scaffolding above the building supported more. Gates swung open as they approached; the gateman was carrying a shotgun. Vehicles filled the graveled parking space.

Chambers recognized most of the vehicles from the dockside. Over there was the oddballs' sidecar outfit, shaking erratically, as if the engine wouldn't quite stop. The centurion was buying drinks for his rescuers. There was even one of the truck-mounted cranes, surrounded by a cluster of jeeps.

Inside this protected zone, the tables and benches on the tree-shaded terrace were crowded. The card-and-dice game had reconvened around a nearby table. Waiters elbowed their way through with trays of beer and food.

As soon as the bus doors opened, the passengers streamed off and headed for the terrace bar. Ferenc tapped him on the arm and indicated the main building. "It's usually a little quieter in there. Shall we get ourselves something to eat?"

There must have been a hole in the mesh fencing. In a flurry of wings, a pair of the fang-gliders flopped out of the trees and onto the grass. He watched the creatures scurry across the open space and climb onto the wall overlooking the cliff edge. Once there, they turned their heads as if geared together, and stared directly at Chambers. The smaller one spat a bloody gobbet of something onto the ground, and the pair turned away to sit motionless, staring down into the drop.

After a few seconds, one of them snatched at something on the wall, and pulled a wriggling thing out of a crack in the stones. With an efficient wrench, the fang-glider tore its prey in two and passed a still-writhing piece to its companion. He wondered if he was anthropomorphizing; was that hatred he'd seen in the thing's eyes? Were these the plummeting monkeys? Most of the customers hadn't even looked up, but one of the guards was threading his way towards the creatures, unslinging his weapon.

Chambers turned back to Ferenc. "How long will the bus wait?"

"Forty minutes or so, but don't worry. They won't leave without us."

A flat boom echoed off the cliff walls. Beyond the door, the guard pumped the shotgun and ejected a cartridge. A spindly corpse was draped over the wall, wings twitching. There was no sign of the other one, but the man aimed his weapon down over the edge and fired again. One of Chambers' cameras hovered over the scene.

A waiter, a tubby smiling man with anachronistic spectacles, brought menus and led them to a table by a window. He had been right, Chambers reflected as they settled into their chairs; the view was spectacular. 1000 meters below, the Jackson River surged and frothed in the scour's aftermath. In the early evening sun, the cliffs were redder and the shadows even deeper.

Ferenc was smiling at him – a quite generous and open smile, the more surprising given her earlier attitude. "Right, Mr. Chambers. I know you're full of questions. You can buy me a very late lunch, and I'll answer those I'm able to."

"That's a fair deal. Why don't you choose for both of us? Do you mind if I take notes?" He unfolded his slate again, setting it to record. She smiled her agreement, scanned the menu and said a few words to the waiter. Chambers noticed her accent thicken, and he found it hard to make out what she said, but what the hell; food was food. There'd be plenty of chances to check out the local delicacies later. The waiter seemed satisfied and strode rapidly away.

Right. Here goes. First rule of journalism – there's no such thing as a dumb question. "Okay. You've told me about the octomorphs. What's the connection with the scour?"

"No, not now. Food first, then we can talk."

A polite cough. The smiling waiter had returned with a tray, and started to set its contents down carefully. He distributed two glasses of dark beer, several bowls of assorted finger food, thick creamy-white bread, a water jug and tumblers, and some blindingly white cloth napkins across the table. Ferenc nodded her thanks.

He leaned back in the chair, thinking it through, and took a cautious sip of the beer. Good, actually – nutty, bitter, and with a hint of something unknown to him.

"Try something. The food's good here." She was smiling at him. "Start with this." She held out one of the bowls. "It's belly of hill-fish, fried in yak's butter and seasoned with chilies, arbent, and sesame. Spicy, but not ferocious. Like the hill-fish? Try this next. It's crispy moss with shard nuts, riverweed, and ginger. Have some bread to go with it. How's the beer?"

△ △ △

He pushed his chair back and walked out onto the terrace. A chest-height wall ran along the edge. He leaned his forearms on the stones and looked down, then left and right along the Jackson River.

Mistake. His head swirled, and the drop sucked at him like a vacuum. At this height, he might have been standing in an aircraft. Despite the food, his stomach was hollow.

Ferenc's voice came from behind him. "You're a journalist, a defense specialist, yes?" He turned around and nodded. Her face was serious. Keeping his back to the drop was just as unpleasant; the canyon gnawed at his spine.

"I'm a biologist. So neither of us is going to be an expert, are we? But have you ever seen anything like that, anywhere?" Her gesture took in the towering cliffs, the distant white wall of the mountain peaks, the shadows slashing across the valley bottom. A kilometer or more below them, the Jackson crashed and frothed. She'd said it would take days to settle. "I'm no geologist, but how the hell did that happen?"

He shrugged. "I'm sure you're going to tell me."

"No, not me. But where I'm taking you, up there in the Dead White, that's where our Parnassus research station is. It's cold there, really cold. There's around thirty of us up there now, ranging from theoretical physicists to a couple of geologists. They'll tell you all about their theories."

"And there's you."

"And there's me. Because I'm from here, and I had the bloody idea, stupid bitch that I am." Why was she so negative about it? "The astrophysicists reckon that Parnassus' moons shouldn't produce the scour by themselves. There's a maximum tide which takes place every few years, when three of the moons align. Calliope, Thalia and Euterpe, if I've got it right, not that it matters. We get big tides then, but nothing like the scour."

"So what's doing it?" He spoke over his shoulder, because he'd turned again. He couldn't make himself stand there with his back to it; he had to face it. If he stepped off here, he'd fall straight down for about fifteen seconds, and he'd hit the water like a bullet. He shuddered.

She came and joined him, leaning across the wall and staring unmoved into the void. "Something massive rips through the system, on a ragged pattern, every few years. I don't understand the mathematics well, but it's enough to drag these monster tides upriver, and it drops global sea levels significantly while it does it. But it's small enough that we can't see it, and the effects are local. We don't know what it is – it's that simple."

"I guess it's not a black hole. That would swallow the entire system. Hmm…" Later, he'd recall that as the moment when he took the bait, when the hook sank into him.

"That's what the astros say. And they can't figure out why the pattern is so unpredictable, why first it's seven years and then it's thirteen and then it's a few months, and why the size of the scour varies so much."

"Perhaps there are a couple of somethings, in varied sizes." He drummed his fingers on the top of the wall. The conversation was becoming intriguing.

She stared at him, then shrugged herself. "I don't know. Perhaps there are. You'll have to talk to them, tomorrow or perhaps the next day, when we get up there. They've got loads of theories." She straightened up abruptly. "But you can drop that *'isn't this fascinating?'* intellectual curiosity shit. This matters to me, and to a lot of other people as well. Parnassus is my home. But we've got no money, the infrastructure is crap, the wildlife is vicious, the kids leave as soon as they get a chance, and something we don't understand is trashing everything that we build. We take it seriously, even if you don't."

He opened his mouth to apologize, but she turned and walked away, straight through the restaurant and out of the other side to board the bus. Chastened, he followed her. Outside the wire, another of the flying apes gibbered at them.

He was doing this wrong. She was his source, and he'd let her mood swing around from nervous through cheerful to angry. And she was right. This wasn't a theoretical problem, another mystery of the deep wide black which might merit thirty seconds of *"and finally"* at the end of the news. Right now, something unknown to human science was hurtling outwards from Parnassus, something which might return years after he'd left, or which could even reappear while he was still here. Something big enough to lift the sea and spit it up the rivers and blast the banks clear of life.

And it wasn't a natural phenomenon for which they'd eventually find a solution; it seemed to be the deliberate action of something else unknown. Something which had destroyed thinking species before, not once, but twice. Presumably that unknown something had been here, centuries before, watching the fang-glider civilization collapse into savagery.

Chambers had been stopped at a checkpoint a few years ago, on Mars. Under one of the big domes, when the government troops had pulled out of the lawless enclave and left the locals to it. He'd tried to talk his way through the barrier, to be the first reporter on the ground, to get another breaking news story against his by-line, stupid, self-destructive sod that he was.

The kid with the old AK270 rifle might have been thirteen, and he should have been in school worrying about how he was going to fill the homework gap, or if the girl at the next table fancied him. But instead he was wondering if it was worthwhile offing this foreign journo, and Chambers saw in his eyes that he'd killed with the old weapon before.

The kid had been leaning on the bonnet of a crashed police car. Behind the shattered windscreen, a dead officer was slumped across the wheel. The back of her uniform shirt was a mass of torn and bloody cloth. The boy had nodded his head at her and grinned at Chambers. He had been playing with the safety catch.

Chambers' mouth had been dry. He hadn't thought that he'd be able to speak, but speaking was his only option. Certainly there had been nothing he could have done about it if the kid brought the weapon up to his shoulder.

He'd had a chance to talk for his life, and it had worked. But if Parnassus wanted to kill him, there wasn't a thing that he could do about it.

△ △ △

"Tell me about your home. This Orchard place. Is it any different to here?" The bus was quieter now; people were sleeping. Darkness lay across the canyon below, and lights had come on along the cliff wall. Above them, the sky was turning a richer blue, and long shadows filled every valley and hollow. They drove into one of those shadows now, and the gloomy interior of the bus darkened further.

He turned towards her, but he couldn't make her out. "Different in what way? It's a hab, not a planet. There's loads of differences."

It was as if he'd pressed a button. "Your economy. Your government. What are they like? Because we're in a mess. We can't invest in ourselves. Seventy percent of every penny that the government takes off me in tax goes straight back to Earth. Parnassus could use that money.

"Look at the state of us. Healthcare's patchy. Industry's obsolete. No infrastructure worthy of the name. Look at this road, for god's sake. No decent education past secondary school. If the kids want a degree, they leave and they don't come back. Talent outflow you wouldn't believe. That's where my second son's gone. It's a whole bloody planet, and we can't even use it."

"Have you seen what we did to Earth, *using* it?" But he knew what she meant. Orchard wasn't so very different to Parnassus; each was a bit of a backwater, under-invested, lacking in capital, struggling to make ends meet. He couldn't imagine someone immigrating to either place. Whenever he thought about the wealth of the companies, he got angry. They were sucking the life out of the minor worlds. The human communities were marginal on most of them.

She said it for him. "Please don't say the word 'environment'. Anyone on Parnassus would just love to think we even *could* exploit the planet. No fear of that for generations, if ever. We won't make those mistakes, because we can't.

"Every piece of machinery, every complex constructed device – the whole lot has to flop out of the sky in a lander once every few months, and when it's got here it has to last forever because it won't be replaced. Those ekranoplans are over 100 years old, you know. They came down in sections, and they took a lot of putting together."

A streetlight illuminated her face briefly. "And then there's the place itself. Apart from the scour, and the crappy roads which people keep driving off, those winged sods will rip your throat out if they get half a chance. This bloody planet has lots of way of killing us – that's why we party so much, and we breed with everyone we can to stop the gene pool from drying up.

"Look. I'm a little fish in a very small and isolated pond. I know what I don't know, if you follow me, and I don't know how interstellar politics works. But you've been around, Mr. Chambers. So tell me – can we make any difference to this mess we're in?"

She was right again. The little worlds, the colonies, the habitats, the moon stations: each one was desperate to break out from under Earth's control. They all wanted the same thing, to spend their own earnings the way they chose. But not one of them had a realistic idea how they'd pay for healthcare, infrastructure, education, defense, social security, or the thousand other things on which a government spent its money.

He took a deep breath. "Maybe, and maybe not. Sanctuary, Rheparion, Harmony, Indi, Second Chance, Wildhunt – and us too, on Orchard, and all the other little wheels and planetary colonies – the whole lot are facing the same problems as Parnassus. The others may not feel the pinch as strongly yet, but eventually they will, and if they're wise they know it."

Ferenc was looking at him as if he still didn't get it. "Look, what I said about my job – the whole Parnassus governments in the same position. We all love this place, even though it's falling apart. But we all work to make profits for ARTOK and for NipponDeutsch, and people are getting fed up of it. They've got a stranglehold on us.

"I love my job. I don't like all this company–secret–mystery stuff, but I don't know anything better than trying to understand these life forms that are completely unrelated to us. That's got to be the greatest challenge ever in biology.

"I like it here, and I like what I do. But we need a realignment of power. We should be taking more of our affairs into our own hands.

"Look, what if we nationalized everything? People have started talking about ideas like that. I'll bet it's the same on your Orchard. What if the governments of all the off–Earth states got together and stayed united? Wouldn't Earth have to listen?"

He'd never expected her to be such a firebrand, and that was stupid, because he'd come here full of his own questions and he hadn't given a moment's thought to the possibility that she might have her own. "Well, your government can count on quite a few friends, but they can count on a few enemies as well. If a company spent several decades investing massively in interstellar projects, they won't love the idea of everything they've worked for being nationalized, if that's what you start pushing for." Chambers pushed the point. "And if you go for secession – how are you going to make certain that your Earth-based suppliers don't just turn off the taps? If they're not seeing the money coming back, then why take the trouble?"

"Do you think that could happen? Cut us off?" Now they were between streetlights, and her face had gone into shadow again. More buildings ahead: a biggish settlement, almost a town. Presumably the Parnassans built the same things everyone else did, once you got beyond the scour line.

"There's precedent. Back in the early days of the Epsilon Indi colony, a place called Dennison State got some military support from the European Federation. A few fighter aircraft were sent in to help suppress cross-border incursions from their neighbors. The Euros couldn't keep it going, and the air force people were never taken back out again. Just abandoned on an angry planet, with no way of getting home."

" What happened to them?" She had clearly never heard the story.

"Nothing good." He'd seen the old vids. Burning buildings, uniformed bodies hanged from tree branches. Years later, broken and rusting fighter jets; work gangs of ageing once-pilots and former technicians digging ditches and ploughing alien ground.

"So you think that Earth won't loosen the reins at all?"

They all desperately needed answers. He'd seen this hunger for political progress before, on habitats and moon stations and in the colonies. It probably happened on Earth as well, but he barely knew the home planet. A holiday once, with Petra; Johannesburg and Rio de Janeiro, but little more. The political and social pressures must have been similar, though.

"Look, there isn't really an Earth, not in the way you're thinking of it." He felt under-qualified to be the spokesman for that teeming planet. "There are hundreds of nations there, and they're aligned in dozens of political structures. I know you know that, but you might not see quite how much power is exerted by the companies, mostly by ARTOK and NipponDeutsch."

She snorted. "Trust me, we know all about the strength of the companies. ARTOK almost managed to swallow our government a few years back, but we held them off. We had to make more concessions on corporation tax than we wanted, but at least they're still supplying us. Over on Harmony, they're completely under ARTOK control. The Russians have a military base on Harmony, and the Euros hate that. They'd be in there like a shot if they got the chance. I don't see that any of us get much benefit from either one."

He backpedaled. "Sorry. Of course you know all about their economic power here. But in a way, the Earth nations are in the same state. There's no effective check on the companies' activities. And if there's little enough oversight back on Earth, then there's even less control over what they do here. We all know that ARTOK and NipponDeutsch have despised each other for centuries, but they're agreed on the importance of keeping some sort of operation going in the colonies, whatever the political pressures have been back home.

"There isn't any one central body which can influence how tightly you're kept in check. The United Nations never had any real power over the situation, and it's got even less now. The Caliphate and America and China have no interest in the colonies beyond Sol. Of all the other power blocs, Russia's always in bed with ARTOK and the Euros are thoroughly dependent on NipponDeutsch, because their operations reach into so many places. There are some minor political bodies with a little bit more independence, but they aren't strong enough to face down ARTOK and ND.

"If your government wants to get out from under ARTOK, Earth's not going to be a lot of help."

Chapter 17

Left by the Previous Tenants

"Tell me thy company, and I'll tell thee what thou art."

– CERVANTES, DON QUIXOTE.

The body was curled up against a howling wind that it could no longer feel, its skin dried to a bloodless yellow parchment. Cheekbones protruded from the shrunken flesh of its face. The lips were drawn back to reveal joylessly grinning teeth. Hair and beard had turned to rigid steel; thick icicles hanging from the brows obscured the eyes. The clothes were sheets of inflexible plate.

Nailed to a post beside the body was a crudely-lettered sign: *Don't go past this point. Turn around and GO BACK. You will NOT be rescued.* The corpse had been left at the edge of the rudimentary track, in plain view of anyone foolish enough to come this way, yet it wasn't clear why anyone else might want to take this route.

Chambers wriggled deeper into his heated jacket and studied the dead man. *Why the hell hasn't someone buried him?* The man had perhaps been somewhere between thirty and fifty, probably white, presumably in good health to have got this far before the Dead White had killed him. He lay on his side in a snowdrift; perhaps he'd been there for a week or so, perhaps he'd been there for years. Chambers had no idea how long it took for aching cold to mummify a corpse.

The storm shrieked louder and drove a blast of fine gritty snow into his face. The blast felt like an industrial abrasive. Up here in HyperLand proper, in the region called the Dead White, nothing lived. No animals, no plants, no birds. The wind gusted from an unpleasant chill to a howling demon, flailing at unprotected skin, dropping the temperature from thirty or forty below to as hellish as minus seventy. All this on the very limits of the atmosphere. Semyonov's "small operation with a very specific mission" wasn't exactly accessible.

A raised voice: he turned his head to see Ferenc striding back across the snow bridge, checking a handheld instrument. The camera darted towards her. Beyond the fragile span was another device at the end of a pole, which she'd driven into the snow. They were doing the last leg on foot. No vehicle could cross this waste.

She had the helmet's faceplate raised. The corpse hadn't worn one. Perhaps the locals got used to this temperature; he hadn't. "Don't worry, I've checked. The bridge will take us. What do you think of Chilblain Charlie?" She seemed to find it amusing, waving casually at the frozen corpse.

He was damned if he was going to act horrified. He'd seen bodies before. "How long has he been there?" he yelled. Their heads were now almost touching as they bent together to avoid the wind. He searched for a clue to her feelings, but the goggles and hood prevented him from seeing her face.

He'd realized, a little guiltily, that he was using her as a windbreak, but she'd been smarter; the way they were standing, he was staring into the wind, so that the snow was still blasting into his face. She had her back to the gale, and the storm was blowing past her, straight at him.

"Maybe 100, 150 years. Kept well, hasn't he?"

△ △ △

"We're almost there. There's something I want you to see before we go into the unit." It had taken most of his second day on Parnassus to climb up the steep and winding footpath to the edge of HyperLand. Kilometers below, in a vertiginous town glued to the cliff face, they had passed the night in a small hotel. In the morning, she had given him a suit of extreme weather clothing. They had taken a jeep, a little ARTOK company vehicle. It had carried them further upwards until the road disappeared. They had left it and walked the rest of the way.

The land had been flattening out, the horizon broadening and distant summits becoming visible. Far below, the scour had turned the Jackson River into a roaring monster which would keep the ekranoplans off the water for weeks. The monstrous wave had reached the head of the river, bursting its banks and sending gigatons of water blasting upwards. The backwash was still roaring down the Jackson again, churning the river into foaming madness and ripping into the edges of the canyon, pulling apart the docks and threatening the road. For many days to come, perhaps for weeks, the water would be unusable by any vessel.

This, after all, was precisely the sort of thing he had come for. War paid well, but he needed to vary his output. Whatever the story turned out to be, the background scenes were forming in his head now. It felt like a winner.

He tried to record another piece, but the cold had his teeth chattering uncontrollably. On the playback, his voice was incomprehensible. Still, he decided, at least the vid would be usable.

So when Ferenc had spoken, it had taken him a moment to react. Then it sank in. "What is it? Another body?"

She laughed. "No, no one else has been that stupid in a long time. But it's memorable all the same. We've about half an hour to go, then we'll be there." And try as he might, she would be drawn no further.

△ △ △

The ship had hit hard, smacking against the high peak and tearing its hull into pieces. Perhaps a catastrophic loss of pressure had asphyxiated the crew, or perhaps they had died from the impact, or perhaps from some toxic release when the structure lost its integrity. After so many years, who could tell? But they were there, dead in the wreckage spread across the snowfield.

The fragmented corpse of the craft towered over them, amputated spars reaching high out of the permafrost and hinting at structural complexity further beneath. The wreck had come to rest in two major pieces. Here, the larger part seemed to be mostly habitable spaces and control systems. There, an unrecognizable convoluted mass suggested power units, engines. Protruding from the hull were control surfaces; was this thing an aircraft or a space-going vessel?

Ferenc had led him to the ridgeline and then left him to it, saying nothing. Chambers had stared and stared, then activated his cameras and started to walk down the slope towards it, realizing after a few minutes that it was much farther than he had expected. The ship was huge.

After ten more minutes, he had reached it. A gaping hole in the exterior, a chasm perhaps twenty meters across, offered him a relatively easy route into the larger fragment. He paused for a while before making his mind up, and looked at the torn decking, and then he decided not to go any further.

Sprawled in front of him on the ruptured floor, entombed in a sheet of ice, lay the frozen body of a fang-glider. The creature was wearing an aviation-type flight suit, perfectly tailored to fit its winged shape, and it had been carrying a hand tool of some sort. From the expression on its bat-eared and fanged face, the alien must have died screaming.

He became aware that Ferenc was standing beside him. "You wouldn't have believed me, would you?"

"I don't know. I've had nothing but shocks since I got off the *Novgorod*. Who found this thing?"

"A caravanserai navigator. They use yaks and camels to carry loads across the Dead White whenever there's a big scour. You've seen we can't use the rivers. Seismic shock revealed this after last year's scour. Since then, the wind has exposed a lot more of it." She had that shifty, almost embarrassed appearance about her again, he realized. Talia Ferenc was no good at lying. Something about this story was nonsense, but the basic facts were undeniable.

"Is this another company secret, then?" He was still staring at the fang-glider's body. What had happened to change a race who built this vast starship into the vicious pests that they had become?

"That's it, but I told you that I don't like all this secret stuff. It might matter to the bosses in Moscow, but it doesn't mean a thing to me. Look at the real message, why don't you?"

He saw what she meant. Here again was the monstrous intelligence which destroyed advanced societies. Something had peeled back the sky, and it was staring down at scurrying life, trying to decide whether there was another problem loose in the galaxy.

In Africa, on that trip to Earth, he'd seen a thing called a termite mound. It reached three meters above a grassy plain, and from a distance he'd thought it was a tree. But when they got closer, he'd seen a muddy tower. The guide told them it had been built by insects. One side had been cut away for the tourists, and the inside was a city.

The termites had rooms and caverns and apartments and air conditioning. They had a ruler, and social classes, and a childcare organization, and a food production and distribution network, and an irrigation system. There were workers and builders and engineers and breeders and soldiers. They had enemies and they fought wars. Tens of thousands of them lived in a closely-ordered cooperative group. And each one of them was a tiny white bug which was effectively brainless.

And, just like every other tourist, he'd marveled that the termites had such fantastic organizational skills. But they'd never seemed even slightly intelligent. He wouldn't have given it very much thought if someone had destroyed the mound. What would it matter? They were just insects. It wasn't what you'd call a society.

△ △ △

"Is this what Semyonov wants me for? Publicizing this?"

Ferenc said nothing. *Not a surprise. She's made it quite clear that she doesn't like her orders.*

They had reached the ARTOK HyperLand research station after another two hours on foot. The shelter's tiny public space was a mixture of dining room and common room. A few of the group's members had wandered in to see the new arrival. They couldn't get much company up here, and any new face was a curiosity.

ARTOK was managing the story, and Chambers wanted to be sure what the story was. Clearly, the company had been sending out covert exploration teams for a long time. They wanted to find habitable planets, and they wanted to get to them ahead of

NipponDeutsch. That made sense; the secrecy made sense, given how ARTOK made its money.

But somewhere out in the black, they had found the remains of an alien civilization which had travelled between the stars about 10,000 years ago. The eight-limbed aliens had since reverted to the intellectual level of animals, and they'd gone missing from most of the planets they'd lived on.

ARTOK had sent in a mixed team of scientists to learn what they could about this, and the team had included Ferenc. She still wouldn't say if she had seen the octomorphs' home planets in person, or had visited them virtually. But she had spotted the similarity to Parnassus, and now there was an investigation team here as well.

He stood and walked across the chilly room towards her. She remained silent, staring at him, until he reached her. "Do you see it, Mr. Chambers? Something has been wiping out civilizations for 10,000 years. That much is obvious, even if we don't know what or why."

"It doesn't matter why, does it?" It was one of the astrophysicists, a dark and heavyset man called Romanov. One or two had greeted Chambers; a few had stared and drifted off again, but Romanov gave the impression that he might want to talk. He had stayed behind with Chambers and Ferenc when the others had left. "Whatever it is, we're outgunned." This might be interesting.

"You all believe that was a deliberate act, an act of war. War makes me start asking questions about cyborgs, but none of you want to talk about that." Romanov's eyes were locked on him, but the man said nothing in reply.

The wind rattled the shelter walls, and Chambers raised his voice. "Ms. Ferenc. Somewhere out there, you'd been looking at the differences between modern animal-state octomorphs and the body size implied by their ancient flight helmets." She nodded. "There's an obvious physical relationship between the fang-gliders and the frozen corpses in the wreck. Because you just happened to be from Parnassus, you spotted the similarity to the work you'd been doing with the octomorphs. Bit convenient, all that, wasn't it?" She gave him another of her non-committal shrugs.

"The fang-gliders seem to have regressed just like the octomorphs, but this time you've found one of the smoking guns. You don't know how it happened to the octomorphs, but you know most of what happened here. The scour trashes Parnassus so thoroughly that any advanced civilization faces enormous challenges, and you're suggesting that was the cause of their society collapsing. Now it's holding humans back as well.

"That's one bit. The other bit, which you haven't found, is what caused the fang-gliders to revert biologically."

"We'll find it yet." Her voice was defiant. She was convinced that they had the explanation within reach.

"Before it finds us? I wonder. It's all about starships, isn't it? You told me that the octomorphs had them. So did the fang-gliders." Chambers looked at them. "So do we."

Ferenc stood and walked out of the room without looking at him.

He evidently wasn't the only one to have thought that.

△ △ △

Chambers took a cautious sip of the cheff, and concentrated on what Romanov was saying. "Whatever it is, the thing is under power, or at least it's under control. You're only looking at part of the evidence if you stick to thinking about a thirteen-year cycle, or a seven-year one. That's the first clue. Astronomical objects aren't erratic. Look at this."

Romanov gestured at the black sphere hanging above his slate. "Here's Parnassus, right at the center. Twenty years ago, we sowed the system with passive anomaly detectors – magnetic and gravitational – and we've used them to plot the last three scours.

"Look. 2430, 2437, and last year's. We'll get the tracks of this one soon. These tracks show the paths of the immense gravitational anomalies that went through the system each time." From three different points, red lines stabbed out across the sphere, merging to trace the same path. Each disappeared abruptly at the same spot, leaving a pulsing dot.

Romanov tugged at the neck of his insulated jacket and settled the collar. "That's at around 200 kilometers. Each time the anomalies got to here, they vanished. There's nothing remotely natural about that. Astronomical objects aren't erratic, and they don't just vanish either.

"Now watch this next bit. Here's where the anomalies came back in '37, and again last year." Red lines reappeared at two points beyond Parnassus, tracing across the black sphere to converge above the world.

"Whatever it is, it's under control, and it always disappears at the same point. And before you ask, no, we haven't been out and had a look at what goes on there. There aren't any spare ships lying around doing nothing, and this research budget doesn't stretch to any flight time. This is a shoestring operation."

Chambers took another pull at the gingery drink. He'd guessed that. He thought about Parnassus' century-old ekranoplans and crumbling roads, Epsilon Indi's horse economy, Orchard's empty seas. Why was everywhere so poor?

NipponDeutsch and ARTOK had a monopoly – a duopoly? – on the starships. They carried all the commerce that moved between the worlds. If a colony didn't make something for themselves, they paid the companies to import it. If a colony wanted to make something, they had to pay the companies to bring in the heavy equipment.

And if they made enough of whatever it was, they paid the companies to export it. The companies took money from both sides of every deal, so they had no reason to make the colonies self-sufficient. Investment in infrastructure was negligible. Investment in non-productive research would be even worse.

Why was there any investment, however shoestring, in this research project? He tried to put the timeline into human chronology. Ten millennia ago – when people were first domesticating wolves and sheep and pigs, and developing agriculture – something had destroyed the star-travelling octomorph civilization. 5000 years later, when an unknown Sumerian was writing the Epic of Gilgamesh, when vast sarsen stones were being levered on top of each other in Wiltshire, that *something* had come here to Parnassus and had done the same thing to the fang-gliders, and then it had left its weapon careering erratically through this solar system. Why? To make sure that they wouldn't recover?

Okay. Supposition time again. Suppose that ARTOK was hedging its bets, just doing some diligent business risk management. The civilization-killing whatever-it-was hadn't shown its hand for 5000 years. It might have gone away, or it might be extinct; perhaps it was a reformed character and didn't do that anymore.

But there had also been a 5000-year gap between the two bits of evidence they did have, so maybe the whatever-it-was only took action every 5000 years. That meant it was due to happen again. It made sense to keep a wary eye out. *Let's find out everything we can, in case it does come back. In the meantime – business as usual. Let's make money.*

And let's brief some journalist about what we've just found. Why had Semyonov done that?

Romanov was tidying away the paraphernalia he'd used to make the drink. It would be cold now. Chambers expected it to be disgusting, but he didn't want to offend this useful source. He took a cautious swig. Oddly, it still tasted good. The astrophysicist was watching him. The man seemed preoccupied, hesitant.

"I like this cheff." He was just carrying the conversation on, chatting idly to keep the relationship friendly, but Romanov flapped a hand at the distraction. Chambers shut up and waited for him to reach his decision. *The first rule of journalism? Don't scare away the source.*

The next reveal wasn't long in coming. "Look, I didn't say this, all right?" The man was nervous.

Chambers shook his head *no, of course not.* He did his best to radiate trustworthiness and sincerity. *Don't speak yet. He's close.*

"I'll put some data on your slate." Romanov started fiddling with the seal of his helmet, turning it over and over in his hands. "View it once, and then it'll wipe. Got it?"

Chambers nodded, still silent. *That was a promise, but whatever he says will be the delivery. Once they speak, they don't go back on it.*

"I'm giving you two words and a date, nothing more." The helmet was raised, then lowered carefully over his head and nudged into place. The faceplate stayed up. "Don't ask me any questions. Not a thing. I'll deny ever saying it."

Chambers couldn't keep nodding like an idiot. "Okay." *Nothing more. Here it comes.*

"Operation ThousandEyes. Find out what you can about it. Just don't do it here, and not where anyone can connect those words with me. Operation ThousandEyes. Got it?"

"Got it. Operation ThousandEyes, no questions." *You're agreeing to his terms. Sincere pause. Now push a little.* "And the date?"

"2437. That's when that ship came out of the ice. Ferenc was talking official Company bollocks. Not last year. 2437.

"We've been looking at this for at least thirteen years. Not one year. Thirteen. You might want to think about that." Romanov latched his faceplate closed and stepped out into the blizzard. Behind him, the door hissed into its seal.

Chapter 18
The Harmony Conflict 2449

The NFC Option
"The gentle government that promises to hold
your hand as you cross the street refuses to let go
on the other side."

– THEODORE FORSTMANN

A row of digits on a screen. A display on a slate. Not more than ten characters, and the galaxy had just changed.

She knew it was so, but it needed to be checked all the same. DEEPSAT Fourteen had given her this, and it was a reliable platform. The NipponDeutsch company's DEEPSAT optic arrays were recalibrated every thirty days, but who knew if that was enough? Any number of factors could be buggering up the data. Ad-hoc calibration took around an hour of self-checks and external reference readings, but she set it up anyway.

Meanwhile, Consuela de la Rosa sent the instructions that would swing the neighboring DEEPSATs Twelve and Thirty onto new headings. That done, she took a swig of orange juice and let her hair float free from its net. Might as well tidy herself up while she waited. No way was she reporting this before it was confirmed.

Eight minutes and twelve seconds later, DEEPSAT Twelve puffed gas from an alignment motor. Fifty-three seconds after that, DEEPSAT Thirty stopped watching an arc of the Orion Nebula and turned to study her current area of interest. Both devices got to work.

Thirty-one minutes after she had asked them for an opinion, the DEEPSATs agreed with their sister. Once the recalibration was complete, she'd call it in.

15.6 standard years and thirty-one minutes ago, a formation of eleven alien starships had begun to decelerate.

△ △ △

"What are our military options?"

"That depends on your intentions, sir." General Claus von Tschering shifted uncomfortably on the low seat. This wasn't doing his knees any good. "Do you want to continue to observe them, or to prepare to attack them, or to ensure our own defenses against an attack of theirs? I'd strongly recommend we don't even consider an attack until we know more about these aliens."

Toshio Fukuda barked a laugh. "Not them, General. The Anglo-Russians. The aliens are an asset we must exploit, not a threat we might destroy. Our predecessors were correct; these creatures possess a physics we can't equal. We can't hope to do now what they could obviously do at least 140 years ago. No, this has always been about seizing an unparalleled trading opportunity. I was referring to the steps we might take to ensure that ARTOK don't beat us to it in these last moments."

That's a relief. Von Tschering leaned back a little, but was no more comfortable. Here, on NipponDeutsch's Double Hammer habitat, his silk-robed host valued a traditional Japanese style in furnishings, clothing, and architecture. The Westphalian's tastes differed. Ignoring his creaking joints, he composed his response. At least his operations and planning team had prepared for that option.

"That's somewhat easier, but still challenging. Currently, the significant human presence that's farthest along the aliens' route is the Harmony-Parnassus system."

"Which is in ARTOK's hands," Fukuda observed.

The German stifled a sigh. It was all very well, the chief executive officer taking an interest in the company's military capability, rather than viewing it as an expensive irrelevance. But it was a shame that his interest hadn't extended beyond the obvious.

He tried again. "The enemy maintains a brigade in that system, some artillery, a few aircraft. I say a brigade, but it's very light, barely more than one and a half battalions of infantry. There's currently a capital ship there as well, the *Peter the Great*. That will stay for around a standard month before moving on again. There are also a number of lesser craft in permanent residence."

"They sound quite formidable."

At least he was paying attention. "Those forces are the only enemy assets capable of interfering with us for some years. There are several smaller outposts that are a little nearer to the aliens, but they're negligible unless the enemy reinforces them. The enemy's forces would be potent enough if they were all in one place, but they're spread over two planets. Most are on Harmony, with scarcely a platoon on Parnassus.

There's is another enemy post on an ARTOK habitat wheel around a light year further away, but I can find out little about that."

Fukuda might be no soldier, but a successful business leader could spot and seize an opportunity, Von Tschering reflected. The Japanese wasn't far behind him at all.

"That smaller forward outpost is no longer a problem to you," Fukuda said. "I've had it dealt with by a very private asset of our own. As to the others, you said they were incapable of interfering for some years? You already have a plan. I'm impressed."

"Sir, it's the role of intelligence staff to know an enemy's capabilities, and the role of operations staff to consider what can be done about them. My people have been keeping assorted options under review for a very long time." The general had noted his employer's reference to "a very private asset". He was well aware that NipponDeutsch conducted its own black operations.

"Faster-than-light drives are sizeable pieces of equipment, and expensive," Von Tschering went on. "The alien fleet doesn't possess them. Tracking these creatures means using observation devices to monitor their movement for a very extended period. ARTOK uses cheaper unmanned equipment, and makes frequent FTL visits from their outpost stations to check their data."

Without looking behind him, he raised a hand. His aide placed a slate into it. Setting it down in front of the Japanese, he waved a star sphere into existence. "We've taken a different approach. Currently, the reconnaissance party which gave us this information is around half a light year in advance of the forward ARTOK observation device. As they couriered the data to us at faster-than-light speed, our present knowledge is well ahead of the Anglo-Russians' understanding." Lights swelled and faded in the globe, illustrating his point.

Fukuda reached a hand into the sphere. "So. The alien ships commenced decelerating here. Our sharp-eyed forward post is here. ARTOK's unmanned equivalent is *here*, and it must currently be ignorant of the alien fleet's action." His gestures swept across parsecs. "Harmony and Parnassus are well to the rear, here. Our nearest forces will be even further behind?"

Von Tschering nodded. Fukuda removed his hand from the display and leaned back. "We know that 140 years ago the aliens accelerated for four years, so they might decelerate for as long. We believe that the ships only contain corpses, which their automatic devices may or may not know. Therefore, they might not decelerate at the same rate. Has your gaming included such calculations?"

The German nodded again. "It has, sir. Remember that the alien ships possess a vectored gravity device. That might not only change the direction of gravity; it might also modify the force that's experienced. That's possible, but not certain. If it *could* do that, a crew member might not feel a g-count that would otherwise kill him. Acceleration rates could be phenomenal."

"Interesting. And your conclusions?"

"Please also remember that the aliens were boarded by hostile and deadly forces. We concluded that it was a little over seventy-five percent probable that they would fly an asymmetric mission. Early acceleration would be rapid enough to stay ahead of any pursuit, but gentle enough to permit any crew members who had been left behind to rendezvous with them. We don't know why the ships then maintained a steady velocity, rather than continuing to accelerate. They may have been conserving fuel for braking.

"Deceleration into the home system would be much fiercer, letting them bring back the news of the disaster as quickly as possible. As you say, the ships may know that all the crew are dead, which would also argue for a rapid deceleration. The news is still vital, but there's no vulnerable life to protect. On the other hand, a symmetric mission, with another four years of braking, was a twenty-percent probability."

"I see. And the five-percent balance?" Fukuda waved his hand across the star sphere.

"We felt there was a three-percent chance of an entirely different profile, such as braking to rendezvous with something else. The destination could be an unknown structure, like a habitat or a smaller station, or another much bigger fleet. Then there was a possibility of just under one percent of an abandoned or random mission, due to some failure of their navigation or steering systems, perhaps caused by the attack.

"The remaining roughly one percent combined all the other weird options that the gaming teams could envisage. A Scot on the team called it the NFC option." Von Tschering waited, eyebrows raised and smiling, for the inevitable response.

"Which means?"

He shifted languages. "'Nae fucking clue,' apparently." Fukuda had enough English to acknowledge this with a wintry smile.

The Japanese unwound his folded legs and stood. Von Tschering joined him gratefully; his daily gym work didn't include yoga. He outlined his proposal as they strolled along the paneled corridor. They entered the great hall, their aides trailing them.

Screens had been pulled back to reveal the gardens. Outside, fountains tinkled, and gravel walks wound between willows that leaned across formal ponds. Above them, a strut towered up to the slender power and drive module. Against the black, stars spun behind the opposing counterweight.

Von Tschering glanced across the lawn, where his *Fallschirmjäger* command unit were exchanging glares with the corporate samurai staff group. He waved his aide away.

"It could be done, sir. And it would be deniable, but few would believe our denials." He waited while his host stepped onto a delicate bridge across a stream, then followed him. Below them, carp drifted like zeppelins.

"It will buy us time, if I understand you correctly. Will that time permit you to dislodge the Anglo-Russians from Harmony?"

"I believe that it would." Von Tschering thought he might as well try while he had the man's time. "I must land sufficient forces on Harmony to overwhelm them, and then destroy or disable their capital ship, the *Peter the Great*. Will the Company finance an additional battalion? With that, we could take the planet, and ARTOK would need at least a year, perhaps as much as eighteen months, to put together an adequate response. Their response would itself be vulnerable to the further additional forces we could introduce into theatre during that time."

Fukuda stopped in the center of the bridge and turned to face him. "The chances of success, if we do fund what you need? I am sure you can give me numbers."

That sounded positive. "Success in blinding ARTOK? If we commence immediately, more than ninety-five percent, with or without the extra unit. With them, and if we destroy the *Peter*, our chance of success in seizing Harmony is between sixty-five and seventy percent. In holding it for a year, once taken? As good as certain. They don't have the force or reach or time to retake it. Please understand that none of these are true certainties, merely probabilities. Beyond that year, I can't give you a number. It depends on how much ARTOK is willing to spend in raising a counter-attack force. Our success thereafter would be expensive, but should also be doable."

"Then let us commence."

The decisiveness was welcome, but whenever he had the opportunity, the general liked to think further ahead. "May we also discuss the star systems that are candidates for the aliens' destination? We should recall that our predecessors stumbled into a war between alien species. There may be as many as three races in conflict, and this one has, as you say, technology we lack. We *must* find out everything that we can, as soon as possible. For instance, that vectored gravity device could render all this complexity unnecessary." He waved a hand at the power module, the counterweight, and the circling stars.

The Japanese shrugged. "Later, if you would. If we destroy ARTOK in this stellar neighborhood, then we'll have plenty of time in which to work out precisely where the aliens are going, and to consider our next steps. And if we don't, the aliens won't matter."

Certainly not to us, von Tschering thought.

Chapter 19
Six Feet Under At Mach Two

"Sometimes I think war is God's way of teaching us geography."

– PAUL RODRIGUES.

Brigadier Peter Foster wriggled around inside his descent pod until he'd settled the command harness to his satisfaction. The lid sighed closed, and the pod rotated him backwards to the horizontal.

The steady *bang-bang-bang* of the firing rail was fainter with the lid shut. 'A' Company of the English Midlands were preceding his brigade headquarters out of the NipponDeutsch AstraLift starship *Sakichi Toyoda*.

The command group were podded and ready. He checked the readouts. *Thirty seconds to go.* He blanked his mind of everything except Sarah and the kids, fifteen light years away.

A clank, and the pod jerked sideways and forwards. External light vanished as he entered the magazine manifold, feet first.

Seventeen; sixteen; fifteen.

Three pod trains merged. The command group were now part of the next descent burst. A belt engaged the lugs on either side of the casing. Internal pressure changed, and the lid creaked and settled.

Ten; nine; eight.

Lateral shaking now, and his helmet settled more tightly around his skull. The assault pistol pressed against his thigh.

Forward motion again. His pod emerged from the hull, and starlight blazed above him. The firing rail shook every half- second.

He lay back and watched the stars. These last few seconds always felt like hours, peaceful hours in which he hung motionless as the galaxy turned about him. Prone in his pod on the firing rail, he could have been alone in the universe.

Three; two.

The troopers of the orbital assault regiments called themselves Pre-Packs. *Strapped into coffins, squeezed out of the ship's arse, fired straight at the planet. If the machinery screws up once, you'll be six feet under at Mach Two. No gravediggers, no padre, no weeping widow, no rifle volley, and the hole just needs to be back-filled. Slick as grease through a goose.*

One.

The readout crawled through its hundredths. He always swore that at fifty he could feel the man before him leave the rail.

The tenths slid down to zero, and the galaxy tilted.

He fell.

Δ Δ Δ

The ARTOK observation station Kazakov G-74 coasted on the extremity of the bi-solar winds. A lonely position, this; the twin star had no remotely habitable planets, and once the device had been sited, the operations crew had been happy to leave. They wouldn't be back to collect data for another six months.

Currently, the main observation telescope's mirrors were furled. The primary star was going through one of its regular flare periods, and the gouts of radiation which would have blinded Kazakov G-74 would take another ninety hours to dissipate. The ARTOK device would then unveil its apparatus and commence self-checking. Only once this was complete could it resume its search for the fleeing alien derelicts.

The NipponDeutsch corvette *Yamamoto* entered the system's contiguous space with a conventional velocity more than 200,000 kilometers an hour relative to G-74. Its eyes screwed shut, the ARTOK observation station paid it no attention. After a quick position check, *Yamamoto* released a liter of dusty water onto a convergent vector before re-engaging its superlight drive.

Once again, G-74 was alone. Eight hours and six minutes later, it was shredded into titanium mist by a shotgun blast of hypersonic ice particles.

Δ Δ Δ

Second Battalion, The Midlands, were making steady progress through the suburbs now that they had dealt with the earlier obstacles. Engineer teams were tackling booby-trapped road blocks and clearing culverts under the axis of advance. By nightfall, they should be at the city's main rail station, where the *Mare Serenitatis* armored infantry regiment would pass through them and continue the advance.

Things weren't going quite as smoothly at the second objective, but they were coming together. Foster was a little more sanguine than he had been an hour previously. The regional administrative center was the size of a large village, where a well-prepared defense had cost him three hours and much of an infantry company. The enemy had fallen back onto a hillside redoubt, and now he watched as the battalion commander's assault group crossed its start line.

"How's your Alfa Company doing, Kurt?" The brigadier raised his voice to a shout as a pair of Weasel attack drones shrieked up the valley, wings flicking from side to side as they followed the course of the stream. As they disappeared, the whoop of laser fire sounded from around the bend.

"Not bad, sir. We had a bit of a hold-up with some autoguns on the left, but Lottie's assault pioneers sorted them out." The ground shook. Dirty smoke lifted above a hillside in the middle distance. Reflexively, Foster opened his mouth to equalize pressure. The flickering image of the battalion commander vanished completely for a moment, then came back as the thunder of the artillery fire mission faded away.

"Good girl! Tell her I said so, please. What's left to do here?"

"I've Bravo and Charlie companies ready to pass through Alfa in a few minutes. The barrage will switch to depth targets, and then it's bayonets and grenades. We'll do it."

A section of friendly autoguns cantered past. "Well done, Kurt. Keep me posted." He left the command net and, climbing out of the dugout, made his way to the top of the little hillock overlooking the valley floor. A rifle section provided his personal security; three of the soldiers guarded this flank.

To his left, the logistics train was making its way forward to the city. Ammunition and fuel wagons were edging into the outskirts; without them, the attack would falter and fail within two hours. An aid station had been set up in a school. His military police unit was processing prisoners in a sports hall. Things were indeed coming together.

To his right, he could see the battle for the enemy strongpoint as a series of brief fireballs and smoke clouds. The occasional aircraft, drone or manned, flashed across the valley and released its weapons. Tiny figures scurried between earthworks. Armored vehicles moved, fired, reversed. A helidrone climbed from behind a flanking hill, and unleashed a beam of orange light on the objective. The little figures dashed forward once more.

"All right, Peter. I'm happy when you're happy." General Von Tschering materialized in front of Foster. "How's it gone?"

Foster glanced at him. "Fairly well, General. Excuse me a moment, please." He drew and fired his assault pistol. The shot passed through the general's chest.

The avatar blinked in surprise, then turned and looked behind itself. The enemy commando crumpled and fell. "Oh, I see."

Farther down the slope, a woman in ARTOK uniform stepped from an outcrop and fired a laser burst, but the brigadier had already moved. Two of his headquarters staff were running up from the dugout. Foster turned to face them. "Ask the brigade major to call end of exercise, and get hold of the security commander. That shouldn't be happening." He holstered the pistol.

The simulated ARTOK unit had reached the ridgeline and were fighting hand-to-hand with his security team. One of the riflemen was bayoneting the woman who had fired the laser. Her partner, face bleeding and unsteady on his feet, seemed to be having trouble clearing a weapon stoppage. A blast of sound, and he was thrown backwards. An infantry corporal grinned at the brigadier as he ran past him towards the skirmish.

The brigade major arrived. "Sort this out, please, Mary." Foster returned her salute and turned back to von Tschering. "It's not been bad at all, considering. I'm happy with the descent and reorganization phases." He removed his combat helmet and lit a cigar. "The assaults were a bit varied, as you'd expect, but aviation and artillery were fine."

Behind him, the exercise came to an end. The mayhem froze and the enemy avatars faded. Faint cheering rose from behind him. "I'd like another battalion, really, but I know we're strapped for assets out here." All the same, he was hoping that von Tschering had something up his sleeve.

"We shall be engaging Anglo-Russian forces. Would you be bothered if our enemies had any English units, Peter? Could you fight them?"

"Not a problem, General. Englishmen never mind fighting each other if the other blokes support the wrong team."

Firing was dying away across the valley. The Weasels returned and swept overhead. Foster watched them go; the avatar glanced up briefly before it spoke. "You're not worried about all those rumors of clone battalions, are you, Peter?" Its tone was teasing.

"Not at all, sir. Clones need to be trained, fueled, armed, transported, fed, and watered, just like anyone else. ARTOK's logistics numbers don't point to a threat of that size. If they do exist, they're in far smaller numbers, out among the frontier stations." A man of few habits, Foster enjoyed his cigar at these moments, and now he drew on it deeply.

"And the dreaded cyborgs?"

"Now you're really joking, sir. They may still exist, or they may not, but even if they do turn up I'll manage them – if you can find me that other battalion."

The avatar floated alongside him as he walked on down the slope towards the dugout. "Actually, I might have something for you. How about that mercenary unit from Sanctuary?"

Foster glanced at his commander. "The god-botherers? Do you rate them?"

Von Tschering paused before replying. "They're...quite good, but they aren't a full battalion. Maybe two rifle companies and some support. But sound enough, I think."

Foster knew his superior well enough to speak his mind. "And they have the advantage of being fairly near here, as opposed to ten light years away, I suppose."

"That's true, Peter. I can get them, at least. Perhaps you might use them for flank protection – or even headquarters security, hmm? What do you think?"

Ignoring the jibe, Foster didn't hesitate. "I'll take them, sir. They'll always come in useful." He tossed the cigar butt into a puddle as the avatar faded, and decided against saluting the empty air.

Chapter 20
Back To The Status Quo Ante

*"You will hear of wars and rumors of wars, but see
to it that you are not alarmed. These things must
happen, but the end is still to come."*

– MATTHEW 24:6.

As they moved back down towards the town, Chambers found that his slate had at last regained communication with the planet's data web.

"News alert," it said. "Euro forces strike at Russian-allied Harmony."

While he had been descending from HyperLand's wastes, the NipponDeutsch vessel *Sakichi Toyoda*, a Sumo-class heavy cargo lifter, had delivered a Euro-Japanese invasion force onto the surface of the neighboring planet of Harmony. Biko, the capital, had fallen with barely a shot being fired. Most of the nation's police force had surrendered.

A small Russian military unit was known to be on the planet, and was presumed to be preparing a counter-attack. Since Harmony's notionally parent state of South Africa couldn't learn of the invasion until a ship reached Earth system, no further response was realistically expected. The arrival of any kind of additional military force couldn't take place in less than a year. It was clear that the planet would fall to NipponDeutsch.

He smiled ruefully at the reports. Some local hack was doing exactly what he had so often done – badgering politicians for comments, begging for time and a few words from busy soldiers, staring at maps and wondering, talking their way onto transportation, pondering over weapons data, sniffing after rumors, guessing at military plans and trying to convince their cameras that they knew what the hell was going on. And that they weren't terrified.

The chargé d'affaires of the local United Nations delegation had demanded a withdrawal to the *status quo ante*, a demand which the system's senior NipponDeutsch executive had blandly turned away with the statement that his company had lawfully been transporting a large party of passengers for an unnamed military contract; no, he couldn't reveal the name of the interested party unless directed to do so by a recognized international court. He didn't believe there was such a court within twelve light years, but would of course cooperate with all local forces of law. In the meantime, if the government of Harmony had a case to make, they should take it up with whomever they felt aggrieved by.

This makes no sense, Chambers thought. *What the hell is NipponDeutsch up to? What's his name – Fukuda – must be feeling confident to do something as overt as this. The companies always like to shove each other around, but it's never led to an actual shooting war before. Why now? What has Semyonov got around here that Fukuda wants? NipponDeutsch aren't going to attack Harmony without a very good reason.*

He scoured the web for news, and for informed comment. He didn't know any of the local names, so it was tricky to decide who or what was reliable.

It struck him that the interworld media couldn't get onto this story for weeks, at least. But *he* had the knowledge, the experience, and the contacts. And here he was, right in the middle of it, stupid-silly-lucky bastard. He'd sworn to give it up, but this was too good to ignore.

Then he remembered Romanov's mysterious one-time-use data, and told the slate to produce it.

What it revealed was horrific.

△ △ △

The imagery wandered around an anonymous ARTOK habitat wheel, somewhere out in the black. You always knew ARTOK habs by the over-engineered machinery, the slab-like vehicles, the Cyrillic script on signs and displays, the occasional English language slogan, the eternal olive-green paint on metal surfaces, the dourly heroic imagery. This could have been anywhere, but it was definitely ARTOK.

Or it had been. Now it was a multiple crime scene, a massacre, a graveyard. Most of the bodies were in an assembly hall of some sort; others were strewn on stairways and in corridors, at dining tables and in beds, in vehicles and lifters. Had he been in any doubt, he could now see the ARTOK logos on their company-issue clothing. He saw all ages, from teens to elders, and winced at the violence of their deaths. Firearms, lasers, grenades. Then the camera showed the school and the nursery, and he wept.

There was little light. The energy center must have been hit. No smoke, no breeze, and no air. Shattered glaze panels showed that the hab had been vented to space. It would cost many billions to put it back into use. There was nothing to show who had done this, but who else could it be but NipponDeutsch?

The roving camera came to a halt in front of a swirl of graffiti, sprayed on the bland wall of the assembly hall. A bold black K and a cartoon eye, crossed out with two long red strokes. As the scene of destruction faded, Romanov spoke. "Who did this? Why did it happen? Why aren't we allowed to talk about it?"

Chambers tried to replay the vid, without success. Romanov had been true to his word; the data had vanished.

△ △ △

Whatever Semyonov's scheme turned out to be, it was taking him to some dangerous places. Worse: he knew that he was loving it. He might be finished with war, but war evidently wasn't finished with him. Back to his own *status quo ante.*

Once he reached the small town, Chambers talked his way onto a rockskimmer headed for the coast. Three slow days later he left Parnassus, taking passage to the neighboring planet of Harmony on the ARTOK fast packet *Michael Strogoff.*

Chapter 21
The Eigen Axis

It's a beautiful day, he realizes. The bluest of blue skies, dotted here and there with a few puffy white clouds, a light breeze, a temperature that anyone would find pleasant but not extreme. This combination is surprisingly common across the human worlds; here, as everywhere else, it gladdens the heart. Whatever is happening in life, however marginal the bank balance or the larder, however malevolent the boss, whether the barometer reads peace or war, it's one of those wonderfully uplifting days.

He's 10,000 meters above the savannah, below those wisps of cloud, floating like gossamer on the breeze, turning and twisting in each eddy current of wind. He's like a little seed, like a sycamore pod or one of the Parnassan arbent family, as he spirals and circles down, turning first this face then that to the grassy plain below.

Billy King knows he is dying.

△ △ △

Billy hangs in his straps inside the shattered landing pod, if "inside" is the right word for a grievously wounded man tied to the largest fragment of a disintegrating shell. The gale of his plummeting, unstable descent buffets him now this way, now that, bouncing his pain-wracked head against the seat's backrest, sending his arms flapping and thrashing from side to side whenever he loosens his grip on the useless glide controls. The trailing cable harness of his pilot-craft interface lashes and batters at his face. Periodically he screams in pain.

The beauty of the day has taken a while to register with Billy. His right leg is missing from the femur downwards, and a hull shard has penetrated his combat helmet above the right eye. Unaided vision is blood-filled and hazy; all his enhanced optic systems are pixelated or unserviceable. He's not certain, but there don't seem to be the standard number of fingers on his left hand any more. The ruptured cable has cost him all communications; all external data; all the descent control systems; all information about roll, pitch, and yaw. He knows the last three anyway. The Eigen axis, a measure of the erstwhile glider's combined attitude, looks strange.

Billy's in a lot of pain, and he knows he's dying. He's not a stupid man, and he's been a professional soldier for his entire adult life. He's been wounded five times – or was it six? – and pain is a familiar figure. No friend, but a lot more than an acquaintance. He knows that this time the damage will kill him, even without the fall. No nearby buddy to power him down and casevac him to safety. No adequate care for him within twenty light years, anyway. He'd have been a casket case for months, dreaming the time away on tickover while machinery kept him at minimal life status. Without all that, death is inevitable. Billy likes a gamble, but he's putting no money on this one. The bank is closed. All bets are off.

No, this time it's permanent, it's final, it's check-out time. There's no hope of regaining any kind of control over the falling eggshell. Below his remaining foot there should be a hull floor, an active shape-agile airblade with the skill and dexterity to adapt and reform itself for any combination of launch speed, atmosphere density, air conditions, and internal load. Instead, a few fragments of bracing fiber protrude from below the seat like damaged bones. The thing was designed to be tough, but it's simply not there anymore. By extrapolation, there's not going to be much else left.

The remaining hull section comprises the seat, an aerodynamic and optically-adaptive upper fuselage, the personal load carrier for his weapons and stores, and the safety kit – or it should. Billy has no confidence that anything useful is still attached behind him, and there certainly isn't much above. There's a reserve para-wing on his chest; whenever his thrashing head points briefly downwards, he sees tangled pieces of fabric flapping further and further out of the container. No help there, then. All Billy has to look forward to is impact.

He screams again, and once more, then gets hold of it and settles down to a steady, repetitive moaning. Something in him, some undamaged trace of grumpy pride, is outraged that he should be killed in such an undignified way. Of all the ways to go! No living thing can ever face death without that sense of outrage, but Billy feels that he's been dealt a particularly unreasonable exit card.

When their insertion craft was deployed from the ARTOK vessel *Peter the Great*, it emerged at an altitude of 350 kilometers above Harmony. *Peter* rarely came quite so low, but needs must. Descending steadily towards the chosen release point while *Peter* rose back to a more reassuring orbit, their SpecFor TransOrbit carrier had turned cherry red as its ablative coatings blazed in the atmospheric heat. In turn, it deployed Billy's special forces section.

The eight troopers of the Section were launched, one by one, over a drop zone around 200 kilometers in length. The little pod should have carried Billy gently down to a soft and thoroughly stealthy landing, from where he would have moved on to a lying-up point.

Should have. With a chain of these stretched across the savannah territory, they could have interdicted any Euro reconnaissance probes and figured out where the enemy's main thrust was going to come. Biko might have fallen to NipponDeutsch and the Euros, but there was still a fair chance of stopping them from building on that victory.

That was the plan, anyhow, and it might yet work. It *should* work, too, with the most technologically advanced human-machine crossbreeds in all of history, deployed with the best weapons and communications available in fifteen solar systems. But some bloody home-going NipponDeutsch pilot in a crappy old fighter (with an ethanol-avgas-blend piston engine driving a propeller, for God's sake!) had the fright of his life when Billy glided stealthily out of one of those puffy white clouds directly overhead.

Then he must have had the time of his life, wingovering and diving and chasing through that beautiful blue sky and finally letting rip with whatever he was carrying, cutting the little pod to pieces and leaving most of Billy to fall out of the sky and going back to the mess for tea.

The sheer insult. To be shot to shit by Baron von bleeding Richtofen.

△ △ △

Billy screams again. Presumably he'd blacked out for a few moments there, because he seems to have missed a bit. His body's starting to shut down the more extreme pains. Perhaps it realizes that he doesn't need any warnings of gross physical damage to protect him from further hurt.

Back at the start of the program, the medics had tried fitting the Enhanced with some form of internal pain control, an opiate type that could be released on demand and let the troopers keep going despite sickness or injury, despite broken limbs, gunshot wounds or other forms of undesired nastiness. Sounded like a great idea.

But the law of unintended consequences kicked in, and it was difficult to get the mix right, so some victims never knew about the extent of the damage and just piped in the happy juice regardless. After a few nightmarish outcomes with fatally wounded or traumatically-amputated soldiers dragging themselves towards an objective on their stumps, the idea was quietly canned as counterproductive.

Shame, in a sense; just now, Billy would give his right – well, perhaps better not pursue that thought.

But Billy's resourceful as well as tough, like most people he knocks about with. Now, just as the shattered pod flips upside down once more, and the bloody cable leaves his face alone for a moment, and his arms fly *up* to his leg-and-a-bit, and he looks straight up at the savannah which is dropping on him, and which will arrive terminally fast in around forty-five seconds –

– he thinks of a trick Kirov told him about, and he invokes neural overdrive. There's a lot of rubbish talked about overdrive, but it's mostly speeding up thinking and reaction times, and like a true squaddie, Kirov had spotted early on that you could use the kit for something it wasn't designed for but that was rather cool.

So off he goes. Physically nothing happens, but now he can think much faster, which feels like the world's going slower, and he can daydream a lot more in the time remaining to him, because it wouldn't seem right to just go without saying thanks and goodbye, so he thinks all the way back to Ulster and Granddad Victor and Gran Maggie and family mealtimes and Granddad and Dad arguing about football and the business and Mum and Aunty Jean cooking up a mountain of food and why little Billy was born William King –

– and he can remember the good stuff instead of the shit that's happening right now, learning to surf and going to school and Becky and college and holidays and the Army and the Air Wars and bombers in the warrens, then Selection and the surgery, and he can't quite understand the clarity of memory he's abruptly regained as back comes all this load of stuff that he'd forgotten forgetting –

– and is that the Lambeg drum he can hear, or is it his heart thumping out its last few beats?

– and realizing after a bunch of ops that he wasn't ever likely to get back to Craigavon, and there was really no one who mattered outside of the Section anymore, and anyhow no one who understood or could understand, but somehow Steady Freddy did and that's okay and you had to trust your partner and he did and he did and the closeness and yes call it love and it was and the rest of the Section didn't notice or didn't care because he knew and Fred knew and that was okay and one day they'd go and check out the Antrim coast together but that wouldn't happen now, and he went round it all again to make sure he'd caught every happy loving moment and then did it again faster yet and –

– and "Balls to this," says Billy, and "Be careful, Freddy," and he snaps back out of Overdrive into the now, and sees both Harmony and his death coming right at him half a second away on that beautiful blue-sky day.

Chapter 22

An Introduction from the Chairman

*"The secret of success is being able to guess what
lies beyond the next hill."*
– ARTHUR WELLESLEY, 1ST DUKE OF WELLINGTON.

"I have just about a platoon of light infantry for every line battalion that the enemy can put into the field. The Euro-Japanese have SmArtillery, I have some light field guns and mortars. They have at least fifty armored vehicles, mostly imported and a few captured and locally-made, but all capable of causing me some trouble. I have a very few autonomous vehicle-interdiction missile systems, and some commandeered old lorries, and a string of practically soft-skinned jeeps with insufficient fuel to do anything useful.

"They, on the other hand, are supported by three squadrons of admittedly modest NipponDeutsch combat aircraft, and have enough airlift capacity to move around a third of their force to anywhere they want. I have a short-range air defense unit that, young Anatoly here tells me, has enough missiles to attract hostile attention but too few to destroy it when it gets here."

Chambers watched as the colonel's adjutant, an artillery captain, grinned and shook his head in indignant rebuttal. His commanding officer slapped a beefy arm across the young officer's shoulders, and went on regardless.

"More importantly, I don't know at this moment where all my enemy are, or where they want to go next. I'm supposed to stop them doing whatever they want, and I am consequently quite busy, Mr. Chambers. So please explain to me precisely why I should bother myself with you."

Δ Δ Δ

Chambers realized that he was lucky to be tolerated. *Michael Strogoff* had achieved impressive speed from Parnassus, but by the time he had made rendezvous with *Peter the Great*, the vast ARTOK vessel had landed all of its limited complement of troops.

There had to be a reason for this war, but it escaped him at the moment. Was it something to do with this Operation ThousandEyes? ARTOK's cyborgs were still loose somewhere, as he'd suspected, looking for something sinister far out in the black, a something which had destroyed at least two alien civilizations, and was perhaps due to come back. With all that to worry about, why would NipponDeutsch take the time and trouble to invade this backwoods planet and trash that ARTOK habitat? And what the hell did that graffiti mean?

If he wanted to find out, Chambers had to find himself some transport. Getting from *Michael Strogoff* to *Peter the Great* had been relatively straightforward; ARTOK company vessels tended to cooperate. But once on the carrier, every purser and bosun had shaken their heads until *Peter's* signals officer had appeared in front of him on the ship's hangar deck.

"Are you Mr. David Chambers, sir?"

He admitted the charge, half expecting to be returned to the *Strogoff* or thrown into the brig, but the man merely passed a message to his slate. "We'll give you a lift to the surface, sir; that's an introduction from the Chairman, with an invitation to visit Colonel Korsakov. He has some news for you."

Chambers seemed to have spent longer hanging around in orbit than he had in transit between the two habitable planets of the system, but now he had a pass onto one of the ship's landers.

The descent from orbit had been one of the most terrifying journeys of his life. Strapped into the jump seat alongside the flight systems engineer, he had sweated in nauseous misery as the pilot flung the craft this way and that, pulling increasing g-force as she struggled to avoid the attentions of the Euro enemy's air defense systems.

"Try and keep the bloody thing on the planet, Katya." The engineer was laughing, but Chambers was feeling far too sick to appreciate whatever it was that he had found funny. "Oh, goody, here we go again." The flight deck came alive with warning tones; hostile fingers were raking through the sky in search of them.

By now they were plunging through low cloud, and the engines roared as the pilot tried a stall turn. The whole craft vibrated like a tuning fork, and he started to grey out as she danced the machine through a sequence of viciously uncomfortable pirouettes that had the engineer chuckling with glee. *You people are weird.* Then his vision cleared a little as the pilot brought the lander swooping down to contour around a range of rocky hills.

Trees and hillsides flashed past the flight deck's windows, and his stomach lurched as the aircraft rose, hung, and dropped again. Trying to find something to concentrate on and take his mind off this horrible experience, he twisted around and looked back down into the cargo bay.

It didn't help. The dark and smelly hold was crammed with creaking, swaying pallets of supplies. They strained against their webbing restraints, as if they were trying to spring forward and crush him against the flight deck walls. Without an external reference point, the motion was much worse.

He faced forward again. They were hurtling across the still waters of a lake, banking from one side to the other; his guts were being forced down into his boots. Then they bounced back up again.

He grabbed for the sick bag, not quite in time. Just as he was sure that he had nothing left to vomit, the warning tone cut off. Wherever it had been, the hostile missile system had lost all trace of them.

The pilot leaned back and took her hands from the controls. They settled instantly into a calmer mode of flight, and ran fast and low for another thirty minutes across a monotonous series of lakes, small islands, marshes, and woods. Crossing a clearing, they startled a herd of large animals, which fled into the trees.

"*Pseudoryx illaqueatus maximus harmonii*, herbivorous deer-analogue native to Harmony," said the slate. He was too groggy to be interested.

The lander dropped even lower, but now the motion was smooth and soothing. He was starting to doze, glad to have the nightmare part of the journey behind him, when an abrupt clank and a sudden deceleration told him that the landing gear was deploying. It forced him hard against his straps. The wind noise and air buffeting increased; and looking forward, he could see the tents and portable huts of a military camp. The warning tone returned. Missile systems were tracking them again – presumably friendly ones, now.

Despite her earlier exuberance, the pilot touched the craft down as gently as a mother's kiss. Engines whistling and hull creaking, they rolled out of their landing run and turned towards a makeshift parking area. The cargo doors unfolded while they were still moving, opening blindingly bright rectangles onto a vista of drab vehicles, tents flapping in a slight wind, some small combat aircraft, further pallets of stores. The nose dipped as they came to a standstill.

Ducking his head, Chambers moved out onto the folding steps, and discovered that the hull still held enough of the atmospheric heat to burn his hand. A military policeman was waiting for him at the foot of the stairs. The man led him to a jeep, and drove briskly across the airfield to the command post.

△　△　△

"Colonel, I'd be very pleased to cause you no bother whatsoever. Would you be so good as to look at my letters of introduction?" He extended his slate towards Korsakov. The policeman, glancing at the colonel, took it from him and handed it over to his commanding officer, who sighed as he received it. He read for a few moments, then looked up at Chambers.

"Chambers, eh? David Chambers. Sounds English to me, but you're from – Orchard? Where's that? And how would you come by an introduction from the Chairman of ARTOK? He doesn't grace field grade officers with his time. His Imperial Majesty himself apparently struggles to gain his attention. So why you?

"Even for ARTOK, sounding English isn't enough, but your Russian is elegant. And more to the point, why here?" The colonel's eyes were boring into his own, assessing him for threat or opportunity. He waved Chambers towards a folding chair. "Sergeant Gavrilov – some tea, please?" He read on, then studied the journalist again. "A very interesting read, I must say. And Chairman Vladimir Filippovich wishes you to meet my one unqualified asset and have a talk to the members of that unit. Surprising, that. A few years ago, a man would have disappeared for talking about that particular subject."

That didn't sound good. But what was that about an asset? His interest quickened. Ferenc had been right about him. However important it was to others, it only got him going if his intellectual curiosity was piqued.

"But now I am to reveal these matters to a journalist. Anatoly?" The smiling young captain turned away from his data table. "Am I deranged, dreaming, or missing the point?" The colonel rubbed his bald scalp with a large hand, then leaped to his feet. "Right. Deranged it is. We'll go and see them, and we'll have an escort, I think. I'd better take you too, young Anatoly, since Major Bulgakov seems to be back. He can have the command post. Come with me, Mr. Chambers."

A man entered, carrying a laden tray. Korsakov looked annoyed with himself. "Sorry, Sergeant Gavrilov!" The non-commissioned officer turned around and made to leave the tent again with the steaming tea, but the colonel called him back, grabbed a pair of mugs and poured a fast brew for Chambers and another for himself. They drank the tea as they headed for the jeeps, splashing their clothes and scalding their mouths.

Δ Δ Δ

The three vehicles were well spread out, trailed by an autonomous combat unit overhead. Sitting in the rear beside one of the infantrymen, Chambers had a reasonable view through the front and side screens. He kept a close eye on the taillights of the adjutant's jeep in front. Whenever it braked, his heart rate speeded up. He had little faith in the borrowed body armor.

The town seemed to have escaped the attentions of both the enemy and the defenders. The handsome official buildings that lined the avenue were undamaged, and the swaying trees hanging low over the pavements hadn't yet been cut away to clear lines of fire. But the shops were almost deserted, and he had seen few cars or pedestrians moving on the streets. Tereshchenko, the driver, kept the jeep at a steady speed, making sure his colonel wasn't bounced around unnecessarily.

They were passing straight through the commercial center of the town and heading out into the ring of suburbs. He glanced at his slate, checking where they were. This road would take them out of the city limits in another five minutes or so. As best he could tell, their destination seemed likely to be somewhere among the industrial units that ringed the city. Colonel Korsakov had mentioned a patrol base in the outskirts; it had something to do with this "one unqualified asset".

The slab-sided and squat four wheeled vehicles were quite rugged, given the colonel's description of them as soft-skinned; this one had armored doors, at least, and enough space for seven or eight soldiers. Korsakov was in front beside his driver; Chambers and the rifleman were alone in the rear. The convoy weaved through nearly empty streets, occasionally sounding sirens as they approached junctions or blind corners, reshuffling its running order every now and then. He recognized the tactic; it would conceal the vehicle that held the most senior passengers. The occasional cars they encountered either mounted the pavements or fled into side streets.

Korsakov leaned around from the front seat. "They're a long way outside the city, perhaps two days off, still milling about down on the plains. There might be the odd reconnaissance unit heading this way, but the main body are nowhere near us. I can't hold the city forever, not with so few, but they don't necessarily know that. Yet."

He pushed his combat helmet back from his forehead and wiped his brow. The air conditioning seemed to be on, but it was making trivial difference to the stuffiness inside the vehicle. "I've got to say, it took me by surprise. Not just me; our entire intelligence community had been saying for years that the Euro-Japanese wouldn't ever try it. I thought they might take a pop at something more modest, maybe seize one of the Parnassan moons. But that just sounds like excuses, doesn't it? I made the call, and I was wrong."

Chambers had had the cameras in action since they'd left the airfield, Unit One inside the jeep and Unit Two tagging along behind. He had given each one a programmed interest range; the inside machine tended to study faces, people, and voices, while the external unit was more interested in machinery and landscapes. The slate flashed up the images: here was his profile, there a tight close up of Korsakov. Beside the faces, somber vehicles snaked through empty streets. The jeeps' weapons swiveled about, looking for targets.

"Anyhow, we were on battalion exercise a couple of thousand kilometers from here; once I saw all those bloody Euro landers flopping down all over the plains outside

Biko, I knew that I'd lost the capital. This isn't Earth, Mr. Chambers; I don't have a standing army of tens of thousands, with 100,000 reservists to call on. All we can do is decide what we really want to hold on to, and that's this place. The capital's a symbol, but it can't be defended. Mabuza can. Humph. Did I just make more excuses?"

Korsakov was looking out of the window. The camera watched his hands stroke the assault rifle. It wasn't passion. This was more like a rider soothing an anxious horse, readying it to give its best. Chambers felt a growing tension.

The county town of Mabuza dominated all approaches to the region, and he reckoned that Korsakov could hold onto it, given the right kind of enemy. The high plateau offered few roads, and the town sat on a tall volcanic plug known locally as the Pietersberg. The mountain presented the defender with a choice of descents onto the plateau, but it provided an attacking enemy with an infinite number of opportunities to be ambushed, blocked, diverted, or delayed among the lava fields and stone runs clothing the volcano's walls.

Chambers turned back to the soldier beside him, listening to him talk about life in the army. Private Dmitry Leontiev was a Molokan, and he was telling Chambers about his home. He was unusual among his faith in accepting the duty of bearing arms, and uncomfortable with the consequence of being considered a heretic. Korsakov glanced back every now and then but, seeing that Leontiev was still watching the streets outside while he talked with this Englishman, he let him carry on.

A woman ran into the broad boulevard in front of them, shouting to her children to come in. Korsakov stared at her through the windscreen, and spoke into his radio handset. Unit Two watched a flock of birds take off from the top of a block of flats on their right.

"It's sad that they don't still see me as a true believer," Leontiev was saying when the bullet took the tip of his ear off. He yelped and clapped a hand to the side of his head, bringing it away covered in blood. The soldier stared at it, bewildered, as Chambers spun round and faced the front to see that the windscreen had dissolved into a web of shattered glass.

For a long moment, he didn't understand what was happening. Tereshchenko's face was a mass of blood and shattered bone, but they couldn't have crashed. Now things were pinging off the vehicle bodywork.

Korsakov punched a lever on the dashboard, and the jeep braked hard. Chambers bounced his head against the seat in front. The pain was sudden, shocking. His breath was coming faster. They began reversing at speed, the axles tramping under the unexpected load.

They were hit again, this time somewhere even more solid; the vehicle rang like a bell. Swearing, Leontiev reached forward across Tereshchenko's corpse and pressed a button in a roof panel. He left a bloody handprint on the vehicle. Outside, a pair of tiny shapes arced forwards and sideways, bouncing smoky trails up the road.

Chambers' eyes leaped from the windscreen to the doors to the smoke grenades. He heard someone cursing, then realized that it was him. The external camera accelerated past the jeep, soaring upwards above tiny vehicles in a toy town street, heading for the rooftops. Images swirled on the slate.

Korsakov was twisting around in his seat and shouting something into the radio. The jeep, still moving backwards, swerved left and right across the road, throwing them about. They came to a halt against the curb. The self-guidance mechanism must have failed, or perhaps the entire vehicle was disabled. The protective smoke was thickening, starting to fill the street.

Korsakov leaned across to check Tereshchenko. "Dead, poor sod." He tried unsuccessfully to move the body from behind the wheel, then hit the emergency lever again. The jeep groaned and shook, but it didn't move.

A massive blast. The vehicle lurched obliquely and sank to one side. Flames rose from the engine cover. Smoke flooded against the windscreen. Chambers' heart thudded; he was starting to gasp for breath.

Another volley of shots hit the bodywork. The noise was appalling, paralyzing. He couldn't think. The jeep didn't feel armored now. Every one of these shots was aimed at him in person.

"No good. They've got the range. Out, out. Debus, before they hit us again! Another missile will finish us," Korsakov bellowed. Leontiev, his ear a bloody mess, flung his door open and stepped out, firing over the vehicle at the rooftops. The Molokan was snarling something incomprehensible; it could have been prayer or curses. Gunshots and the whoop-crash of a combat laser battered at their ears.

"Come on, Mr. Chambers. I'll never get promoted if I let you get topped, not if you're a pal of Vladimir Filippovich." Korsakov tugged at his shoulder, pulling him across the seat towards the door. The air inside stank of propellants and burning jeep.

Clang. Ping. Clang. The vehicle's front was taking fire. Chambers wrenched at the handle. It didn't move. "Oh, crap! Come on, you bastard." His voice sounded thin and high. He tugged down, then up, without success. His mind flashed back to Petra, rattling at a taxi door handle and screaming.

There was no way out of this metal box. It was on fire. People were shooting at him.

Unit One stared him in the face, interested in his imminent death. These would be his last moments, right here, countless billions of kilometers from home. He'd never see Orchard's seas being filled, but he was going to join her at last.

"For Christ's sake!" Korsakov leaned over and twisted the handle. *Clang. Clang.* "Now try it."

He tugged again, and it opened just as the trailing vehicle passed them on the left, hatches wide and two of the occupants returning fire at something he couldn't see.

Chambers half-fell into the deadly street. *Oh, God.* There was the lead vehicle, the adjutant's jeep, stopped in the dead center of the road, collapsed at the front and all doors open. A figure was hanging from the driver's door, legs and feet trapped inside and head touching the pavement. Bullets bounced from the road and screamed into the sky.

The cameras were circling about. Two of Korsakov's men were running for the side of the road. One was half carrying the other, who was firing one-handed, his legs dragging uselessly behind him. Then the man carrying him stopped as if he'd been punched, fell to his knees and dropped his partner on the street, collapsed forward onto his chest, lay still.

This had gone beyond desperate. Chambers knew he'd do anything to get away, leave these men here to face whatever was waiting for them. This wasn't his war. He didn't belong here.

The third jeep staggered and exploded. It rolled onwards, blazing; more smoke billowed upwards from the open hatches, and the vehicle hit a lamppost. The doors stayed closed. A camera darted towards it. The burning machine popped and sizzled and crackled.

Something lay behind the rear of the first vehicle, as still and shapeless as a crumpled pile of washing. It had to be Anatoly, the colonel's ever-smiling young adjutant. They were all dying, one after the other. He had moments left.

"Go, lad, go!" Korsakov was pressed against the jeep, firing. Leontiev sprinted for the buildings, still swearing. Halfway across the street he staggered, screamed, ran onwards clutching at his side, made it to the protection of the buildings. Chambers didn't know what to do. He hugged the flimsy armored door. It was cold against his face, but he could feel the flames.

The wounded man lying exposed in the middle of the street was up on his elbows, rifle pointing vaguely towards the smoke, his buddy dead beside him, a vast distance separating him from the buildings and safety. His own destroyed jeep was perhaps twenty meters away, the pavement every bit as far. He'd never make it.

The soldier looked around himself for help, then locked eyes with Chambers.

The journalist hesitated behind the heavy vehicle door. He couldn't cross that murderous open space. The thinning smoke offered no cover from the enemy on the high rooftops.

What the bloody hell was Semyonov playing at? He'd been sent here and there, and he'd just gone along with it. How had "restoring the image of the Enhanced" led him into this nightmare? *Sod this.* If he was going to die in the next few minutes, he'd have some choice about how it happened. He'd had little choice about anything else lately.

"The alley, Chambers. Get to the alley!" Korsakov was yelling and pointing. He looked at the colonel, at the side street, at wounded Leontiev, at the smoke, at the flats where the enemy were, and he ran for the helpless man in the road who'd made eye contact with another human being.

I'm fifty years old. This isn't my war. I can't do this. But he weaved as he ran across the miles-wide road to the wild hope in the eyes of the man who was staring at him, and he heard the sudden increase in firing from Dmitry Leontiev, the Molokan who missed his family; and from Korsakov, the career soldier who drank tea in a hurry and didn't make excuses. As he closed in on the man, he was wondering how to pick him up; he was still carrying the slate, and he threw it down just as three more shots came through the smoke and hit the prone man in the back. His body lurched with each one; Chambers grabbed him by the shoulder straps but couldn't move him. He knew he couldn't just leave him, dead or alive, but now he was going to die here too. *We're all dying.* The camera watched him thinking about that.

But now there was someone else there beside him, bending down to scoop the man up in a practiced hold and carry him effortlessly away, and another someone firing steady bursts into the smoke, and yet another who took hold of Chambers and dragged him back to the edge of the street, where more of them were shooting towards the flats. Unit One followed them.

Each time these new ones fired, the enemy seemed to fire back less, and then they were into the alley with Korsakov and Leontiev, and he and the camera looked into the metal eyes of his rescuer and saw his multi-colored mottled skin and the cyborg face.

"Nice to see you, Sergeant Richter," said Korsakov.

Chapter 23

A Cross Country Comedy Bus

"I'd rather dig. A moving foxhole attracts the eye."
– WILLIE AND JOE, WATCHING A PASSING SHERMAN TANK, ITALY,
1943 (FROM UP FRONT BY BILL MAULDIN)

"Tell me they didn't actually build them. No, go on. Tell me I'm not seeing this." It was Kirov's voice again, this time on the common net.

"What're you on about?" Richter sounded annoyed.

"Just look at this. You won't believe it. Someone's built some."

The armored machines walked ponderously along the twisting road, turrets turning this way and that as if sniffing for prey. This was a first for Chambers as well; he'd never seen or heard of anything like this before.

The designers must have wanted them to be as beast-like as possible. Their control cabins were heads equipped with weaponry, set on thick necks. The vision slits were built to resemble eyes; air intake was positioned where a mouth might go. A ridge ran along the creatures' spines. Cooling panels? No, open hatches. There would be troops inside.

The big machines had tails, which swayed from side to side two or three meters above ground level. The legs were squat, large-footed, holding the machines' bellies about two meters clear of the roadway. They walked with a steady pace, hypnotic in their pseudo-animal stride.

"Put it on datalink, then. We're not telepathic. Let's all have a look."

"Hang on. Wait. There you go. Look at those babies."

"I don't believe it. Someone's actually bloody built some."

"That's what I said."

The volley of comments passed too quickly for him to identify individual speakers. But here he was, embedded with soldiers again. Harmony, his ARTOK sponsors facing an overwhelming NipponDeutsch-backed invasion force, and Sergeant Leon Richter's section in the middle of it all. Another planet, another war, another unit.

He tried to see what they found funny. *Strange machines. There's a couple of distinct types – two legs and four. The four-leggers must carry troops. You could fit around a company of infantry inside that many. I can see four of the small ones, and six big. And back there – a string of wheeled vehicles, a couple of them mounting decent sized turrets.*

The two-legged things have got twin-barrel guns, look like thirty or forty millimeters. They must be fire support, and those must be co-axial lasers alongside the guns on the big ones. And missile launchers. What's so bloody funny?

"God, Billy would have loved those little ones. Couldn't you just see him running about in one of them? Sorry, mate."

They'd allowed Chambers access to their common voice net, but he knew to keep quiet and let them talk.

"Hold it, everyone. Sanity check. Are we in training? Is this a simulation?" It sounded to Chambers like Arden's voice. He was getting to know them as individuals, and recognizing their voices. They were becoming people.

"No, we're here, it's real, and I don't believe it either." Barclay, one of the two women in the unit.

"Oh, goody. Playtime." That could only be Kirov, the joker.

"Well, yippee, let's have a go. Anyone got any ideas?"

Richter cut in. "Call that a contact report? Get a grip. Come on, people. Stop buggering about and skip the comedy. They'll be halfway here in a few minutes, and then they'll debus. Won't be funny then. Orders in two minutes."

"Ooh, Mister Grumpy."

"Shut it, Kirov. Chambers – you're out. This could be when you find yourself on your own. Stay still, be quiet, don't attract attention. If you don't hear from us after thirty minutes, make up your own mind what to do."

The common net went abruptly silent. He was alone.

△ △ △

"Legger. Public transport vehicle in use in the marsh areas of Harmony." The slate showed a similarly-configured device, painted a jolly yellow. It was wading through swampland, climbing out of the water and across the rocky beach of an islet. Its control cabin bore a cheery face, and it was wagging its tail.

The vehicles in front of him were sandy brown now, but he wouldn't be surprised to see them change color in a different setting. *Okay. So they're based on a neighborhood cross-country comedy bus. Someone's taken a few and added weapons and armor, and recruited them into the local forces.*

Now the invaders had them, and here they were, pushing forward from the plateau to investigate the road up to Mabuza and start to take the town.

△ △ △

The mountain road snaked around the flanks of the Pietersberg, cutting through the volcano's residue of lava flows and stone runs. These armored vehicles had come into view about a kilometer away, around the curve of the hillside.

Chambers and the troopers had been tucked away in a side valley carved by a little stream, talking while the soldiers ate and drank. He'd been keeping track of Sergeant Leon Richter's unit for several days now, meeting up with them whenever his slate picked up a message. *Be at this grid reference in two hours' time. Bring fresh food – bread, hot meals, fruit. Get enough to give all of us a decent meal.* That was typical, so he'd gone there in the borrowed jeep and done as requested.

He'd arrived to find them waiting for him, cleaning weapons and changing clothes, brewing up. He parked the jeep where he was told to, out of sight of the road. Barclay threw a camouflage web over it, making the vehicle almost invisible.

Arden had left as soon as he'd eaten the meal Chambers had brought, walking off with hardly a word; Kirov, the joker of the pack, strolled in a few moments later. The food had earned him some thanks, a few tall tales he could use for background, and permission to keep a camera running while they talked. It took a while for him to realize that Kirov had would have been aiming a weapon at him as he approached, making sure that he had come alone.

As soon as each trooper had eaten, they picked up their packs and left, heading off silently in different directions. Eventually he was left alone with Kirov. The man was easy company: amusing, relaxed, apparently as interested in Chambers as he was intrigued by the troopers.

They swapped stories for a while, talking in Russian. He'd noticed that the troopers' default language was English, but the man said his family had Ukrainian connections. Yet there were no intimate family tales, no nostalgia for the old country. It puzzled him for a while; every squaddie he'd ever met wanted to talk about home. Was this something to do with the altered memories he'd been told about?

Then he got it, and felt stupid. Kirov had to be closing on 200 years old. He wouldn't be leaving the army to get any civvy job. The family would be long dead. His future didn't hold dreams of retirement, of watching the kids grow up, or of bouncing grandkids on his knee. There weren't going to be any nights in smoky halls with beery mates; no regimental reunions in smart suits and faded berets and ancient shiny medals; no respectful salutes from fresh-faced recruits.

All he had to look forward to was a dusty death on some alien battlefield. If he was lucky, he might be forgotten. But his memory would be despised, and he knew it. Chambers reckoned that if it had been him, he'd have wanted to lose his memory too.

Then Kirov stood up, pulled on his pack, and checked over his weapon. "Time to go, David Petrovich. Thanks for the food. Leon says you're to stay here for a while. You don't want to be where we're going. We'll be in touch, I guess."

Chapter 24
Interesting Schutzes

*"The thing about an ambush is – you sit there,
armed to the teeth, fat, dumb and happy. And you
wait for the idiots to walk right onto your sights.
But sometimes the idiots have the cheek to attack
you. If the enemy don't cooperate, an ambush is a
dangerous place to wait for someone."*
– INFANTRY PLATOON COMMANDER, TIBET CAMPAIGN.

Four days earlier, he'd been amazed to be alive.

"Here's your slate, Mr. Chambers." It was battered and stained. "I guess you weren't carrying it when that happened." There was a long gouge scored into the device. A bullet had ripped across it.

He took it out of the colonel's hands, rolled it up and stuffed it into his backpack. "No, I just dumped it." He could find nothing intelligent to say.

What did a slate matter when there was a street full of dead people, and a dozen more bodies in the flats or lying here in these alleys, where they'd been hunted down by the cyborgs? He could imagine their fear. He'd felt it himself, only a little while ago.

Right up until that moment, they'd been watching the kill zone and waiting for the imminently dead prey. He knew that a classic ambush could fail if the victims counter-assaulted immediately; that couldn't have happened here, with the attackers unreachable on top of the flats, and the targets robbed of cover in the empty boulevard. They'd been impregnable, but then it had all gone wrong.

The cameras had caught it, but only just. Circling above the building, the airborne Unit Two had seen the fast and silent stealthy things dropping onto the roof with lift packs. They had appeared from nowhere to attack the ambush, shooting with inhuman accuracy, moving too quickly to hit. The Euro soldiers operating the missile system had died at their controls.

A few of the enemy reconnaissance troops had run down to the streets, crossing the little square, covering each other's withdrawal with textbook fire and maneuver. But the cyborgs had outflanked them, outrun them, outshot them.

Yet one had broken clear. He must have been the fastest runner. A lone enemy commando had managed to evade the cyborgs and run for his mates and their vehicles.

Δ   Δ   Δ

The man was running down the street, body armor bouncing, helmet lost. His breath came in gasps. The rifle was slowing him down, but he held tightly onto it. Every few meters he threw a glance behind him. His face was tight and his eyes were frightened. Looking back, he lost his balance and stumbled, bouncing off a wall before he got himself under control again. Unit Two must have been overhead, to give the slate this image.

He had almost reached the vehicles. The little buggies had been tucked into the corner of the yard against the walls, out of sight of the enemy. His unit had travelled light and fast, in classic recce troop style, leaving only two men with their wagons while they moved in to their objective on foot. Perhaps he was wondering why no one at the rendezvous answered his radio calls.

The man was thinking only of making distance, not of avoiding detection, so he ran straight around the corner without first checking to see if it was safe. Then the camera watched him come to a stop in the middle of the empty space. Perhaps his heart rose up in hope when he saw the vehicles.

He hesitated, and Unit Two watched his mouth and eyes open wide when he saw the dead man at the wheel of the first wagon, and the second driver lying with his throat cut at the edge of the yard. His thoughts were plain on his face. There would be no exfiltration from this failed mission.

Then something appallingly fast and silent rose from behind a pile of crates and leaped at him, and the camera watched as a hand seized him by his hair and a bayonet slashed across his throat. He might have realized what this thing called Arden was, as it took the last seconds from his life.

The camera hovered above the body, recording the flow of blood and the choking hissing noise of a man dying, and the sudden drumming of heels against the packed earth. That done, Unit Two turned and followed Arden across the yard.

When he finally checked the images on his slate, days later, it took Chambers some time to realize which device had captured the scenes, and at first he couldn't understand why Unit Two had paid so much attention to people. But then he grasped that it had stayed true to its instincts. The camera had judged Arden to be machinery.

△ △ △

The bodies had been spread over no more than 200 meters. Here was one, sprawled in the narrow passageway a few meters from the combat laser he'd thrown down. There was a second, lying against a bloodstained wall with a single gunshot wound to the eye and a gaping hole in the chest.

The quick reaction force had arrived; Chambers couldn't see what was left for them to do. The Russians had sealed off the street anyway, attended to his cuts and bruises, and taken away the dead bodies. Then Chambers sat on the pavement and slumped against the wall.

His ears were ringing from the gunfire and the missile explosion; his nose had been bleeding; his forehead ached where it had been slammed against the vehicle seat; at some point, gravel and dirt had been ground into his hands. His ripped trousers showed a bloody knee, he had wrenched his back, and his cheek was burned raw. The last might have happened when he took cover against the burning jeep; most of the rest was a mystery. On balance, he felt lucky.

Korsakov and Leontiev had taken off after the cyborgs, despite lagging far behind them. Chambers knew he couldn't stay here. Camera Unit One was bobbing around the cordon, annoying the soldiers. He recalled it, and asked the nearest soldier if he knew where Korsakov had gone.

The man shrugged. "He's the colonel. He goes where he pleases. Hang on – aren't you the guy who went for Piotr Vasiliev? That was well done. Wait here. I'll ask." He headed off towards his sergeant.

Vasiliev? Had that been the name of the man in the street? Moments later, the squaddie was back with directions.

△ △ △

The yard was busy with soldiers. More jeeps and lorries had arrived, spilling out troops who had spread across the streets, established a perimeter, and cleared the area. Richter and two of his cyborg troopers were still here: the one called Arden, who'd killed three people right here in this little yard, and a blazingly angry man called Irwin. Chambers had tried talking to them. Arden had been civil, but distant. Irwin had been terrifying, possessed by a rage so intense that he had moved to an entirely different and uncompromising mental state. The journalist got the message, and backed off. The two troopers had ignored him then, and had carried on tinkering with a lift pack.

The sergeant and a corporal from a military intelligence unit were studying the bodies and their weapons and equipment, looking for information about the enemy. A couple of local policemen had also turned up, their jolly blue and white vehicle out of place among all the drab jeeps. Chambers had long since realized that war and peace didn't sit on opposite sides of some neat border. You weren't necessarily in one state or the other. And policemen habitually took an interest in killings.

Twenty minutes ago, these people had been within a moment of killing him, and now most of them were dead, and somehow, they weren't enemy any longer. He bent down over the body of the last runner, wondering who this stranger was, and where he'd come from, and why he'd wanted to kill David Chambers. A neatly bagged plait trailed from under the man's combat helmet.

Chambers straightened up again, dizzy with a mix of recognition, post-terror euphoria, and the guilt of living, and then the shock of seeing the bull's-head emblem stenciled onto the body of his enemy's buggy. He studied the nearer vehicle and its dead driver, seeing another plait.

Korsakov watched him from across the yard. "It's not pretty, is it? There's precious little heroism in that, cutting the throat of a man who couldn't see you because you moved too fast." He pointed at the body in the corner of the yard. Chambers stared at him, puzzled by his tone.

"No, don't go thinking it was unfair or evil. Trooper Arden there did just what he was supposed to do, and so did all his mates. Don't waste your sympathy on these men. Their friends tried to kill us all, and we've butchered them instead.

"Taking you out for a drive today has cost me ten good people – ten! Anatoly was my wife's cousin's boy, just twenty-three. Lev Tereshchenko was my driver for four years. Believe it or not, he played the flute. I'm no judge, but it sounded fine to me. And I held Corporal Ivanchuk's brand-new baby only six weeks back. All of them were real people I knew well, Mr. Chambers. I'm not simply going to shrug that off. None of them are just numbers."

His eyes were burning. "Why the hell are you so bloody important to the Chairman, that he's determined to put you together with Sergeant Richter and his men?"

And why was he? "I know these people, Colonel Korsakov. Do you?"

"What are you getting at? They're Eurostate reconnaissance troops, and they were brought here by NipponDeutsch. Oh, I see; the plait. He's one of those so-called believers, is he? What of it?"

"I reckon these guys will all turn out to be believers."

"You'd better tell me what you know about them. I've not seen them on Harmony before. I've heard the name, and the thing about the plait, but that's it."

Korsakov walked across the yard to the slumped corpse of the sentry. They bent over it. Flies were settling on the hideous wound in the man's throat. The colonel found the plait bagged and tangled in the man's helmet straps.

"Okay, looks like you're right." He let the man's almost severed head drop back. Chambers winced. "So where does that take us? Who are they?"

"I think they're religious mercenaries. They think of themselves almost as holy warriors, fighting the good fight. They're very secretive about their religion, and they won't talk about their god, but I know some of them think they're obliged to follow the god's orders without question. They'll die for their faith."

"What – like suicide bombers, do you mean?" Korsakov's tone was contemptuous. "Does anyone still do that these days, on the big sophisticated planets? We're a little too backward for that sort of thing in these parts."

That didn't seem to fit with Chambers' recollections of the devout but affable men he'd met on Sanctuary. "No, I've never heard of them doing that. I think they've come here because of your Sergeant Richter and his troopers. They know about them, and they want to kill them."

Korsakov gave a short, barking laugh. "Them and about 10,000 others, Mr. Chambers. There's quite a queue of Euros lining up for a crack at us, and once they get onto the plateau in enough numbers, they'll have their chance. Tell me something I don't know."

"No, not like that either. It's not you they're after, it's the cyborgs." He realized he'd blundered when Korsakov's face froze. Across the yard Richter turned away from the intelligence corporal and stared, then strode towards him. Irwin and Arden also spun around, as if driven by the gears of a single motor. He stood there, waiting for it to happen, whatever it was that the cyborg wanted to do. There was self-evidently no point in running.

But Richter just stood in front of him. "Tell me more about these people. And don't call us cyborgs. It's offensive."

Chambers let his breath out in a rush. "I'm sorry, I didn't know."

"Now you do. Go on, tell me." Was that accent German? What was a German doing, serving with a Russian unit against the Euros? And why the accent? Chambers had bought himself formal Russian fluency long before coming to the Parnassus-Harmony system, back when he'd had that curious invitation to meet Chairman Vladimir Filippovich Semyonov. The language felt comfortable in his mouth, and he never found himself struggling for a word. He knew that he spoke it well; he'd always bought his languages from the same supplier. He'd taken Korsakov's remark as a reflection of a sensible purchase, not as a compliment to someone else's recorded skill. If you still had your native accent when you spoke another language, did it mean that you'd bought unwisely? Or that you had learned it a very long time ago, by a far more primitive means?

He let it go. How was the man going to react to this? "These guys have sworn to – well, they say *eradicate* you all. Not the colonel's regular guys" – this was getting awkward – "but people like you." He gave it up. "Dammit, Sergeant, I don't know how to refer to you. You just saved my life, so I'm grateful, and I've just offended you, and I know you could kill me in a blink of an eye, so I'm scared. Why the hell would I want to piss you off? Just tell me what to say."

The man was swaying silently from one side to the other, like a tree in the wind. The other two troopers were doing the same thing. Was this laughter? "Fair enough. We like to be known as Enhanced, and it's important to us that you don't treat us like machines." Chambers nodded energetic agreement.

"But listen, these *schutzes* are interesting," Richter went on. "I've seen these plaits before, on a few foreign squaddies. So where are they from, and what have they got against us personally?"

"They're from Sanctuary. Do you know it?"

"I've never been there, but I've heard of it. What's special about the place?" The sergeant's eyes weren't metal, he realized, but they were clearly artificial, with the lens the most machine-like part. Right now, they were locked on his own eyes. It was as if a weapon was tracking him. Of course it was.

"It's pretty underdeveloped." *Wasn't everywhere?* "They're still recovering from a major war that took place there some years ago. It left the locals very hostile to the military." That was putting it mildly. "But there are a lot of these 'believers' in their forces, and they've been putting together a mercenary unit for a while now, doing off-planet work, gradually building up their contracts. Funny strategy; some of the locals like them for it, because it gives some employment and it brings in hard currency. But a lot of folks say that it shows that you can't trust soldiers, because they'll fight for anyone who pays them. Anyhow, I guess they persuaded the Euros to put one of their units into the invasion force. Cheaper than dragging a regular unit out from Earth system."

"How do you know so much about them?"

"I'm a journalist, a defense specialist. A few years back I was actually working there for the government." Putting it like that felt like a betrayal. It seemed like a lot more than a few years since Petra had died. It was a lifetime, and it was yesterday. Calling it a few years made those years seem trivial.

Chapter 25

Maskirovka

*"Timeo Danaos et dona ferentes." (I fear the
Greeks, even bearing gifts.)*

– AENEID II, 49 (VIRGIL).

But now perhaps he'd found a way to get himself killed. The moment he'd heard about the invasion, Chambers knew that the cyborgs would be close. He wondered how the hell he'd track them down, and how he could persuade them to talk to him once he did. Now he'd met them, and he owed them his life, and now he knew that they weren't to be called cyborgs, and he knew these few by name, and he had been embedded into their operation. *Not bad for a few days' work, Dave.*

Three weeks ago, the Euros had materialized in the system, landed, and advanced in strength from Biko towards Mabuza County. *Blitzkrieg* was reborn. Their reconnaissance drones and ground attack aircraft had made short work of the few air defense systems that Korsakov had unmasked.

However, the Russian had played a clever game of blocking and delaying tactics, never quite bringing the Euros to battle but never quite breaking contact either. He challenged the forward Euro units with slowly-yielding vehicle-mounted infantry, and tempted them into pursuits which led onto minefields or into the arcs of autoguns and robotic interdiction systems. But whenever the Euro main body committed itself and deployed, Korsakov's men abandoned their defenses and ran, falling back onto alternate positions or handing over the battle to fresher units.

The Euro *blitzkrieg* was never allowed to develop as its commanders wished; their ARTOK enemies were every bit as adept at fast-moving mobile warfare, and they were falling back onto their own supply lines. The Euro advance frequently stalled for want of fuel or ammunition; Korsakov's men were losing ground, but were never short of resources. Mobile warfare, Chambers had learned – from these very men who were now advancing on him in their armored monsters – was a matter of time and space. If you didn't have one, you needed the other. You used what time you had to build your defenses, or to mass your attack. You sacrificed your space to fall back and robbed your enemy of his time, delaying him while you prepared your own space in which to bring him to battle. Korsakov was using the cunning art which the Russians called *maskirovka:* the business of tricking your enemy in many layers, from troop-level camouflage through tactical deception to strategic misdirection.

But then the tide of battle had started to turn the Euros' way. The *Peter the Great* had vanished from orbit-facing radars. Video had revealed a monstrous fireball. With the capital in Euro hands, no detailed knowledge of the enemy's dispositions, and their only significant space-going asset destroyed, Korsakov's little force was on its own.

The next blow came when the Russians' intelligence satellites suffered some sort of terminal systems failure. The intelligence people talked about electromagnetic pulse from the ship-killing weapon, although the technicians were at a loss to explain what had happened. All their imagery had been wiped from the datanet; they were blind. The NipponDeutsch-backed invaders must have carried out a cyber-attack of some kind; the sats were still there, but silent.

Just the moment for David Chambers to rock up.

The scour had missed him by meters on Parnassus, but Chambers had crossed the solar system and left it millions of kilometers behind. He had boarded the ARTOK capital ship, and left it in orbit only days before its destruction. Then the ambush in the streets of Mabuza, when bullets had cut the air just centimeters away. However fast he ran, death was closing in on him. But he'd wanted that, hadn't he?

△ △ △

Harmony was a beautiful place, he realized, or at least this mountainside was. The sun warm on his back, the sky almost cloudless; up here on the high edge of the valley in the foothills of the Pietersberg, he lay among the rocks in a deep and peaceful silence. Insects murmured among the hillside vegetation, and a soft wind brought him strange but pleasant scents.

And somewhere below him, Richter and his Enhanced troopers were making ready to go about their business of killing around 100 strangers. He'd been staring down at the valley from a break in the ridgeline. The troopers had vanished to hunt the armored vehicles a while ago. That must have been fifteen minutes by now, he decided. He wriggled back a few meters, so he didn't break the skyline, and came up into a crouch; then he shuffled farther back again and stood.

Birds squawked and shrieked above him, and something took off with a whirr like a helicopter. He swore, and flung himself down on his belly, but no lasers whoop-crashed, and no needlers screamed. The common net stayed silent. He seemed to have got away with it, but he couldn't believe that he hadn't been seen.

Now, which way had they gone? A stream bed ran down the hillside; dry at this time of year but heavily overgrown, the gully offered a concealed route towards the valley floor. He clambered into it, taking a camera with him. It wasn't quite as dry as he'd hoped, but it gave him some cover. He slithered down a leafy tunnel.

The hillside was steep enough to threaten a tumble, and he chided himself for forgetting the simple truth that water always takes the most direct route in a descent. Within twenty meters he was holding tightly onto branches and concentrating on where he put his feet, afraid of slipping and breaking a leg, or of making so much noise that Richter – or even worse, Irwin – heard him and came to see what the din was. They'd talked a few times by now, but he still feared Irwin's rage.

When *Peter the Great* had entered the orbit of Harmony in response to the invasion force delivered by the *Sakichi Toyoda*, it had deployed a special forces vessel, which had in turn released a string of one-man descent pods carrying the troopers of Richter's section. He'd thought that they'd been stationed here for a long time, perhaps for years, but apparently they had turned up only weeks before him.

The "one unqualified asset" was a recent arrival. In that arrival one of their number, Billy King, had encountered an elderly but still capable Euro combat aircraft. The old fighter's weapons had shattered the trooper's descent pod even before the impact itself had killed him. Richter had told him that the dead man had been Irwin's lover. Chambers felt that he understood that loss.

When it was there, his own grief still felt overwhelming, as if nothing could ever ease it. But now there were more days in which he didn't think of her at all, and then the grief was compounded by guilt when she came dancing back into his thoughts. He didn't want to get over it, and it seemed like a betrayal whenever he coped for a while.

Sweat was pouring down his face. He needed a rest. Anyway, he should check how far he'd got. It wouldn't be smart to break cover right between the opposing forces. He couldn't expect Richter to come to his rescue a second time.

He'd come back home from Sanctuary, back to Petra; it had been wonderful again, for a few months. Then they'd argued once more, because they always managed to, and she'd gone, but he knew that it would come right again within a few days, because it always did.

Creeping up the wall of the streambed, he peered cautiously over the lip, between a couple of thorn bushes with viciously spiny leaves, and forced himself not to move. His mind snapped back to the here and now. The camera, still following him, started to rise, and he hastily brought it back to ground level.

More by dumb luck than by any kind of judgement, he had emerged with a grandstand view of the valley road barely fifteen meters below. A few paces further on, the stream left its sloping bed as a waterfall; in this dry season, it was little more than a tap left running, but in the wet it would be a torrent. Had he gone any further forward, he would have fallen down the slope onto the road. He lay still, wondering where the armored walking machines had got to.

At that moment the lead vehicle emerged below him, rounding the tip of this protruding finger of hillside. He looked straight down onto the top of its control cabin, a little behind the main gun. A man's head and shoulders protruded from a small cupola. Molded sat-dish ears sat high up at the rear of the turret-head, passing so close beneath that he felt he could reach out and touch them. The soldier stared through a pair of binoculars, occasionally glancing down at the route the vehicle was taking.

The rest of the machine's body followed. Hatches were folded open along its upper back, giving him a clear view down into the hull where at least ten men sat, rifles across their laps. They faced outwards: he could make out weapons ports along the vehicle's flanks. If one of them glanced up...

The machine hissed as it moved; air or hydraulics powering the limbs, he guessed. A deep bass hum came from the hull, where cooling vents suggested there would be an engine. The ponderous feet crunched down heavily with each step.

Finally, the tail swept past, now raised up high above the road level. As it approached, he saw the little surveillance camera mounted on its tip. Motionless, he tried to shrink in on himself even further, but it moved on without showing any interest in him. His own camera trembled, as if eager to start work.

The first of the two-legger vehicles jogged by. Its head swiveled this way and that, a pair of cannon protruding from the mouth. A bull's head was stenciled on the side of the machine. The vehicle commander sat counterbalanced against the machine's movement, motionless in a stabilized turret. There would only be space for one other crewman.

The convoy flowed past, on legs and wheels. The narrowness of the road kept them in line, their turrets sweeping through broad arcs on either side. A pair of combat drones hovered above the vehicles, trying to see as far as possible both forward and to the flanks. Any higher, and they might attract the attention of Russian air defenses. Here, above this twisting road, their flight was a risk worth taking.

And was this risk worth him taking it? He hardly cared any more. One day, a little while after she'd left, the village copper had come to the apartment in Bytham where they lived, his Dad's old place with the nearly-wonderful view over the empty sea bed, and had given him the news which he already knew, the news which should have stopped the world from turning. He'd never be able to make it up with her.

Trapped inside that burning jeep in Mabuza, he'd felt a shadow fall across the street. Death had been stretching its cold fingers towards him. Perhaps it had been Korsakov's bitterness at losing so many men, men he commanded and liked and laughed with and led. Perhaps it had been Irwin's blazing rage at the loss of his lover. Whatever had caused this, Chambers couldn't hold it down any longer. Such a useless, meaningless thing. For five years he'd been running away from the stupid banality of Petra's death. He had never let himself face it.

But now he found that he cared after all. He cared enough to grieve, and he sat on an alien hillside in a war zone with a battle imminent and he gulped for air as a sob rose in him. His shoulders shook and his chest heaved. He heard himself make little gasping sounds as he wept harder and harder, no longer trying to control the noise. David Chambers wailed in his grief and waited for someone to kill him.

Eventually he became quieter, and found that he was lying on his side in the mud. Tears and filth stained his face. He dragged his fingers across his cheeks, rubbed his eyes with the heels of his hands and tugged at his hair.

"Unknown animals," his slate observed, vibrating an alarm. He silenced it again.

Two weeks later, after the funeral, he'd taken passage to Earth, looking for wars and a way to get himself killed. It had never quite happened. Now, after five years, he lay still, listening and watching, waiting for Richter to do whatever he intended. He might live another few minutes, or he might not. A hundred different possible deaths could result from the mass of weapons in front of him. It didn't seem to matter.

But for some reason the back of his neck was prickling.

Chapter 26

If A Machine Man Honors The God

"Everything under heaven is in utter chaos; the situation is excellent."

– MAO ZEDONG

nside the vehicle, they were still grousing. "This is just crap. The infantry are sitting ducks in those things. The little fire support ones are okay, but the big ones are bloody useless death traps. They should be going up here on foot."

Drovan traversed his weapons again; not that he had a target. A four-legger paced a few meters in front of them, obscuring his arc. The gunner hated this. They were vulnerable, crawling along in this armored queue, and it put him on edge.

"Drovan, you're an audio loop. I don't like it any more than you do, but give it a rest." The woman's voice was clear in his headset.

The gunner looked up at his sergeant. Carmalette was only half listening, trying to peer past the hull obstructing their view forward. He'd guessed that she felt no better about it, but she was the boss and he had no one else to tell. "Why are they so bloody high off the ground? What's wrong with wheels, anyhow? Crap design."

"They're what the locals had, as well you know. That's what they've got, and at least we're on wheels, so shut it." She'd plainly had enough, so he took the point and fell silent.

Harvetz gave a mocking laugh. "Sounds like you're finally appreciating my driving, Drovan. I never thought I'd see the day." He edged the little scout car around a pothole left by the foot of one of the despised troop carriers. "They aren't doing the road much good, either."

"Now don't go off on one, Harvetz, but it's all your bloody priest's fault." The commander winced, but Drovan continued. "We were making good money for a couple of years, and then we had to leave it all behind to go on this bleeding crusade. Do you believe all that shit about cyborgs? I think he's losing it."

The driver's troubled answer surprised Drovan. The gunner hadn't really wanted to wind up Harvetz, but he'd had enough of this campaign. "Look, you two don't get it, but that's your problem. You know how much the god means to me. I thought I'd follow the Adept wherever he led me, but I'm not sure what we're doing here. There may have been cyborgs here once, and there might even be some now."

Harvetz's voice slowed as he picked their way across the broken and shifting surface of a stone run. Gravel pinged from under the tires; the car slithered to one side and then steadied again. "But they're not doing me any harm, and if I ever meet one I'll judge him on his actions, not on his existence. Perhaps even a machine man can honor the god."

Drovan swallowed a sarcastic comment. "Well, okay, if you say so. I suppose we signed up for this, but it doesn't feel right, does it?"

Carmalette sighed. "I'll tell you what doesn't feel right: this deployment. If we make contact, we've got no room to maneuver here. I'd have us well forward – a couple of kilometers, say. And I've not got enough data share from the drones, so keep watching the high ground as well, Drovan."

"You got it."

"What's up this time?" Harvetz stopped the vehicle as Drovan slewed the turret around to the left side, elevating his weapons to cover further up the hillside. "You're right, we're too close together. Every time someone in front slows down, we come to a bloody stop. Boss, when we get going again, I want to leave a bigger spacing."

"Works for me, Harvetz."

Chapter 27
The Undefeated Sun

"No plan ever survives contact with the enemy."
– GENERALFELDMARSCHALL HELMUTH GRAF VON MOLTKE, 1800-
1891.

"Contact. Enemy front!" Harvetz was the first to see the troop carrier fall. The vehicle's right front leg began to crumple. Inertia carried it forward a few more meters before it began to roll over. A rear leg waved in the air, grasping for contact.

The main armament had been turning to compensate for the roll, and now it began to elevate as well. Too slow. The gun barrel drove into the stony earth, buckling under the impact.

Harvetz fired smoke grenades to the front. He braked hard and accelerated rearwards, weaving the car between rocks and bushes, braking again. Another troop carrier was coming up the road behind them, taking fire from the rear and the left. He spun the steering wheel to the right. They left the road forwards, bouncing down the slope in a rush to leave the killing zone.

"Missile came from high and left. Engage when you've got a target." Carmalette was reading the battle, looking for a way to carry the fight back to the enemy. They had to assault the ambush or break free. The alternative was to stay and be destroyed.

Drovan was being thrown about in his cupola, traversing the armament, looking for targets and swearing. From his own controls, Harvetz saw that the vehicle's combat workstation had considered the contact and identified a possible missile launch position 307 meters forward and left, higher up the slope. He heard the gunner instruct the main armament to fire canister. The cloth-ripping sound of a three-round volley meant that 7500 flechette were going back at the enemy.

Harvetz was looking for routes out. *Ahh, possible.* Among the rocks downslope, a pair of the two-legged fire support vehicles had squatted down and were similarly firing bursts over the embattled convoy and onto the hillside. The combined effect of their quick-firing thirty millimeter cannon and of Drovan's single-barreled seventy millimeter might put sufficient pressure on the enemy to let the infantry debus from the dying carriers and break out from the killing zone. Best he got there sharpish to give some help.

△ △ △

Chambers couldn't move any farther forward without being exposed to fire from both sides. Up here on the hillside he was well concealed, but as soon as he stood up or crawled forward he'd be a target. A perfect moment, then, for the cameras. He got Unit Two out of his pack and powered it up.

△ △ △

Farther up the hillside, the cyborg's missile launcher wasn't responding to its programming. Surprisingly, the enemy scout car had been quick to return fire, far quicker than those stupid walking machines, and had loosed a volley of probably-canister back at the autonomous weapon. Thousands of metal fragments had shredded it. *Could have been worse*, thought Fred Irwin, 200 meters to the right. *Could have been this one.*

He had two missile reloads left, and then he'd be basic dumb infantry again.

Better deal with that scout car first. You're a bit slick, you are. Can't have that, sunshine.

He took hold of the controls of his combat workstation.

△ △ △

There was an explosion, which Harvetz felt more than heard. The vehicle was thrown to one side, and the turret spun on its mounting ring. Above and behind him, Carmalette and Drovan screamed. Harvetz, ears ringing from the shock, had his hands and feet thrown from the controls. Brakes released, the scout car rolled backwards away from the sheltering rocks.

Another blast. The hull rippled and twisted as a second missile slammed into the rear of the vehicle. He knew immediately that the scout car had suffered both combat-capability and mobility kills. A highly skilled driver, he understood every detail of his vehicle systems. He knew what was coming next.

Fire suppression systems would pump propellant gas into foam reservoirs to flood the motor compartments and the ammunition magazines. "Vehicle on Fire" warning messages, accompanied by the unit call sign and a location symbol, would be appearing on the company tactical datanet. Inside the car, power supply would disconnect from all non-essential systems. Air conditioning was shutting down to suffocate the fire; shutters were dropping across the motor compartment vents; local alarms were activating at all the crew positions.

Harvetz needed none of this. Fire is the armored vehicle crewman's greatest fear. Almost before the dying weapons carrier had rolled to a halt, he was disconnecting his crash web and opening the driver's hatch. He could hear screaming above him. After a panicky few seconds when his right foot was trapped by the twisted controls, he freed it and then found that the seat wouldn't raise. Scrambling on top of it, he pulled himself up and out, sprawling onto the decking. It was hot.

Fire suppression or not, smoke was rising from the vents beside his face. He rolled across the roasting engine cover, hearing pops and creaks beneath him, then off the edge of the deck, to land with a bone-jarring thud alongside the undamaged front wheel. Machine gun fire pinged off the far side of the armor.

Only then did he pay any attention to anything else. The two fire-support vehicles were still under fire from the hillside. As he looked around him, one of the two-legged machines exploded, its body blasted away from the propulsion unit and the legs. The other rose and made a run for it, trotting awkwardly around the rocks and then turning to descend further into the valley. It promptly drew fire from several enemy positions. As it fled, a missile took one of its legs off; the crippled machine somersaulted and then cartwheeled down the hill.

Where were his crewmates? Still lying on the ground, he peered up at the turret. If the hatches had been open, he would have been able to see them from here. There was no sign of them. He stood up, opened a locker on the vehicle's flank, and pulled a crowbar from inside.

△ △ △

It had taken little more than ten savage minutes, Chambers thought, numbed. He couldn't believe he still lived. Once again, so many others had died around him, and he'd not been scratched. Had he really wanted to do this again?

Black smoke rose from the burning vehicles and drifted across the valley road. Destroyed carriers knelt or lay where they had been hit, hatches ripped open, weapons silent. Most of the convoy's wheeled vehicles were motionless: bent, crippled, turrets askew on their mountings, armament twisted or ruptured. The bodies of perhaps twenty men and women were spread across the hillside. Many more must have died before they had left their vehicles.

Here and there, Richter's men could briefly be seen, darting from place to place, assessing their work. Autoguns tracked and swiveled, looking for hostiles.

"Unknown animals," his slate repeated. "Potentially dangerous."

Sodding stupid thing. Known and unknown dangerous people bloody everywhere.

Chambers wanted to get closer. He left the cameras running and asked the slate to find Richter. Instantly, a data message flashed back.

Not now. We're not done.

Chastened, he turned his attention away from the slate and back to the scene before him. Far down the hill, a scout car was burning strongly; a man was prizing at a turret hatch with a crowbar. He pointed Unit One at the activity, and it darted away.

△ △ △

Harvetz was crying with the effort and with the heat in his hands. The crowbar was wedged tightly under the twisted hatch, but however much force he put into it, he couldn't make it move. The wagon was brewing up, that much was certain; the ammunition was going to cook off, and the batteries and the high-pressure hydraulics would let go any time now. Harvetz didn't dare think about what it would be like inside the scout car. He couldn't stand up straight on this hillside, so he couldn't get enough weight on the bloody crowbar, so he'd never get the others out.

He prayed. The words of the Yasht, spoken first in Persia over 3000 years ago and again in Rome 800 years later, came back to him unbidden, flowing naturally from his heart to his mouth and up to the god. *Lord of wide pastures, sleepless, and ever awake; I invoke you for assistance: may you join me in aid. The god is strong, praiseworthy and splendid, master of nations, worthy to be worshipped, worthy to be prayed to.* He prayed as he struggled, and the rhythm of his prayers was the rhythm of his arms as he tugged at the stubborn unyielding bar. The crackling within the engine compartment grew louder.

Some kind of camera floated in front of him as his soul poured forth.

Invincible god, I, Yeoman Darius Harvetz, willingly and deservedly have fulfilled my vow. As you slew the bull, let me defeat this stubborn steel.

He had to make it move. He was snarling his prayers, needing the bastard god to come to his bloody aid, needing to be repaid in this moment *right now* for a lifetime's devotion to the invincible and undefeated sun.

If not now, when?

He was shouting the prayer now, roaring in anger at his god.

He is good,

Heave.

...strong, supernatural,

Heave.

...foremost, merciful,

Heave.

...incomparable, high-dwelling, a mighty strong warrior.

Heave. Each word was an oath and a prayer and a bone-cracking, muscle-tearing wrench.

A blue and orange flame licked out from under the engine compartment cover.

Bathed in blood. The ordeal of heat.

A hand reached across and seized the crowbar. "Come on, son, let's shift the bloody thing, shall we?"

The newcomer added his own strength to Darius Harvetz's stubborn efforts. Together they dug deep, and the crowbar bit into the latch, and the latch parted.

They sprawled on the ground, but Harvetz sprang up again, up onto the decking to reach down into the ruined turret and to put his hands under the arms of the unconscious Drovan. The other climbed up alongside him and again the hands helped him, and they lifted the gunner up and out, and they lowered him down onto the ground, and the newcomer shouted to him to drag Drovan to safety.

Harvetz wrestled the unbeliever Drovan onto his shoulders and staggered away across the hillside and dropped him down and turned around to go back again, in time to hear Farzana Carmalette's screams from the commander's cupola as the oxygen-fed flames leaped up high, and the cyborg on the decking reached to pull her out and the ammunition exploded and consumed them both in the light and heat of the undefeated sun.

Chapter 28

What If Your Prayers Were Answered?

*"At the Day of Judgment, we shall not be asked
what we have read, but what we have done."*

– THOMAS A KEMPIS, 1380-1471.

*B*oot down, *steady yourself, get your balance, push,* Harvetz thought. *Readjust the weight on your shoulders.* His mouth was dry and his chest ached from drawing breath. All that he could see in front of him was his own right leg.

Just swing the left leg past the right and repeat the whole business. He could still taste the smoke. *Maybe it takes all the strength you have just to keep going, but you can't stop.* He *wouldn't, would he?*

He was knackered. The hill was too steep, and every step was the hardest work he had ever done. The ammunition had mostly cooked itself by now, and only the occasional round flew screaming off into the sky. He'd thought that they would die there, taking those first few steps away from the burning wagon through the firestorm of random pyrotechnics and flechette, but somehow none of it had hit him, so he was climbing stubbornly on up the hill.

But did any of the rounds hit Drovan? Don't even think that.

They called it the Pietersberg, this bloody thing, and it went on up forever. Harvetz's breath sucked hot in his chest, his neck and shoulders and back and legs were killing him, sweat was running down him, and he didn't dare stop.

Why am I doing this for an unbeliever?

Drovan was a leaden burden across his shoulders and back, dreadfully silent now. Harvetz didn't want to think about what carrying him like this was doing to his burns, and he didn't want to think the words *dead weight*.

Because he's a man, that's why. And you wouldn't be, if you weren't prepared to do this.

Left arm around Drovan's thigh, right arm across his arm, right hand holding on tight to the poor bastard's jacket. It was forcing his head downwards so that all he could see was his own boots, and he didn't want to stop for a breather, in case he never started going again. Drovan might be an unbeliever, but he was going to get some help.

And you didn't do it for Farzana, so you've got to do it for him. She was beautiful, and now she's gone.

Darius Harvetz was going to go on, staggering up the Pietersberg's lower slopes, back to the road that he'd driven off when the missiles came swooping in and trashed the carriers, leaving him with the dead vehicle and the ashes of Farzana Carmalette and the cyborg. His pistol was back down there on the ground somewhere, and he'd no idea what had happened to his belt kit.

It had seemed like seconds, bouncing down that hillside while Drovan cracked round after round back at the enemy and Farzana tried to find a way for them to get out of the killing area and start rolling up the ambush from its flank. Now it was hours, or forever, and all he could think of was getting Drovan to some help, and the only possible help was up there on the road where the enemy was.

He went on and on up the slope that the cyborg must have run down, heading up for help, and he didn't dare to pray for it. What the hell would he do if his prayers were answered again?

△ △ △

The road hugged the flank of the mountain, but its shoulder was broad and set it back a little from the beginning of the downward slope, so when Harvetz crested the rise and saw the vehicle tracks in front of him, it came as a slight surprise. Nothing else seemed to be going right, but the wagons were a little bit closer than he'd first expected.

His downward-staring eyes saw only the carriers' massive footprints, and the muddy tracks of wheeled vehicles like his own. Darius Harvetz knew everything about every combat vehicle in use in any operational theatre in which he'd served. These tracks belonged to their own machines. Their ruined machines.

Help was near, wasn't it?

Drovan's weight pressed him down. He couldn't raise his head, but he trudged on towards the wrecked column, towards the Adept's carrier. The cyborgs would be there, but he had nowhere else to go. Enemy or not, they'd help him, wouldn't they? Their mate had done.

It was much easier to move along the flat ground.

Drovan hadn't stirred or made a sound in a while.

Chapter 29
The God's Duty

*"We are but of yesterday, yet your whole world is
full of us"*

– TERTULLIAN, 197 AD

"Freddy is down. Gone. Final. No hope."

"Where? What happened? Have we got a hot one still?"

"That burning gun wagon. He went in. Look. Data now."

"Shit, no."

David Chambers was back on the common radio net, and could hear the troopers talking it through. All resistance had ceased, but they stayed focused, searching for hostile activity. Then Unit One had shown him the man's desperate battle to open the vehicle hatch, and the other camera had picked up something else.

From the hillside above the road, Fred Irwin had come running as only the Enhanced could run, leaning back against the slope, leaping downhill faster than the spreading stone slide he had started. Irwin had sprung across the road, past the tangled wreckage of the troop carriers and fire support vehicles, and farther on down the slope to the tumbled rocks where the enemy vehicles had set up their failed fire base. Irwin must have fired the missiles that destroyed the vehicle. Then he'd run all that way to help the driver try to rescue his mates, and they had got one out, and then the vehicle had exploded.

Now the camera brought him images of the enemy driver bent over his buddy on the ground, and Chambers knew him. Back on Sanctuary, he'd chatted with this man, trying as usual to uncover the humans behind the uniforms. This one, like Lev

Tereshchenko, was a man of faith – but no Molokan. His name was – what was it again? No, gone. His slate would have it. Yet he remembered an easy wit, a happy nature, and a clear boundary. *This much of me is okay for casual conversation, for your human-interest stuff. But all that bit of me is private, and it includes my faith.*

The casualty was desperately burned, clothes smoking, hair gone, skin charred, and the driver was injection-spraying him with something. Behind them the wreck still gushed flames and smoke, and the occasional round of ammunition was still cooking off in the fire, and tracers flashed skywards in fireworks or spun away like deadly skimming stones. And somewhere in that mess were the remains of Steady Freddy Irwin and of the unknown enemy vehicle commander.

A few weeks ago, Chambers would have doubted that any man would take a risk like that for someone he didn't know. But that was before the ambush in the suburbs of Mabuza, and still he didn't think that he could have done what Irwin had just done. Chambers had gone to help a man who'd been, if not a friend or even known to him, at least in some way part of the same endeavor. And anyway, the man Vasiliev had looked him in the eye. You couldn't look straight back at a man and then abandon him like that. But Irwin had tried to kill those people, those strangers, and then he'd gone to their aid, and he'd died trying to help them. Where was the sense in that?

And here was this man from Sanctuary, who had been willing to throw away his own life for his mate, and whose enemy had given it back, and he was bending to lift the injured man again and struggling up the hill with him over his shoulders once more as the ammunition whooshed and screamed and whistled through the air.

His slate finally spoke. "Darius Harvetz. Soldier, armed forces of Sanctuary. Rank of Yeoman. See attached interviews."

"Look in, folks. White flag, third carrier back." That was Barclay.

He tasked a camera.

△ △ △

Macdonald wearily raised the commander's hatch, placed his pistol on the top decking, and pulled himself out.

The road twisted about the mountain's rocky flanks for hundreds of meters to his front, before vanishing round an outcrop. To his left, brush-covered ground tumbled steeply from the scarps and cliffs where the cyborg abominations had sited their missiles to such devastating effect. Somewhere above him, there would be more of the enemy. To his right and below, the gradient lessened as the cliffs collapsed into rock piles, stone runs, and scree.

His carrier was kneeling in the center of the road, the turret facing rearwards in surrender. The tail lay flat on the road in defeat. Through the single open top hatch on the hull, he could see that the vehicle's belly doors hung open. That was good; his dog could leave when it wished.

The air stank of burning. In these metal sarcophagi, the faithful dead lay waiting the god's pleasure. On his own vehicle, the white flag fashioned from a crewman's undershirt flapped mockingly from the antenna.

Roscoe Reilly, the gunner, was standing below him in the road, hands deep in his pockets. He took off his combat jacket and threw it on the ground, then started to walk away.

The driver, Peter Whitman, was sitting cross-legged on top of the hull, head in his hands. A hired man, not a believer, he raised his head and stared angrily at Adept Macdonald. Whitman's eyes were red-rimmed with smoke and tiredness, but there was no mistaking his rage. He spat on the turret's top armor.

"Call yourself a leader? Do you see what you led us to? Your bloody god might forgive you for this fuckup, but *they* won't." He waved at the string of wrecked and burning vehicles.

Macdonald had no interest in Whitman's insubordinate blasphemy. An unbeliever would do what unbelievers did. He straightened, and picked his pistol up.

In front of the vehicle stood three cyborgs.

The god was calling him to his duty.

△ △ △

The enemy officer was clambering down a ladder from the vehicle's turret-cabin to the body's upper deck. Richter called to him. "Let's get this clear. Are you surrendering, or are you calling truce? Think carefully before you answer." He wasn't going to have the man put one over on him.

The commander stepped down onto the hull. Despite his defeat, he managed to raise some disdain. "I do not negotiate with filth like you. Take me to the Russian commander, or to some other human being, machine-man, and he may receive my surrender. See that you treat my *human* men well." The crewman sitting on the turret above looked down and shook his head.

"Human men? You're a charmer, aren't you? I noticed a few human women among your troops. Or don't they count?" Barclay matched his contempt. Behind her floated one of Chambers' cameras, seizing the scene for his next report. Richter ignored it.

The officer was wearing vehicle crewman's overalls with a combat helmet and a pouched belt. An old-fashioned sheathed bayonet was clipped to the belt, and he tapped a pistol against his thigh. Keegan raised her rifle and stepped forward.

"You. Drop your sidearm and get down off there. You'll go where we say, when we say." The man didn't move. "Come on, get on with it."

He paid her no attention. She raised her voice. "Can you hear me? Drop the weapon and come down, or I'll drop you." He was staring over her head as if the troopers weren't there.

"Come on, man, you're getting nowhere with this." Richter turned his attention to the driver above. "You there; don't move, but talk to him. Keegan – put him in the ground if that sidearm isn't on the deck in five seconds."

Now the driver was straightening up too, ignoring the troopers, staring across them. Richter made to climb the ladder, but stopped at the enemy crewman's words.

"What the hell is that?"

Something flickered at the corner of Richter's eye. He turned.

△ △ △

No Matter What

In a trickle of movement, then a flow, then a torrent, animals were streaming down the hillside towards Chambers.

"Rabbit-analogue, *Pseudolepus minor harmonii*, first identified in 2362, native to this planet. Fox-type canid resembling *Pseudovulpes aliena harmonii*. Deer-analogue..." the slate explained. He wasn't listening.

The hillside was alive with running, panicking creatures. A tide of native life poured from the rocks, the scrub, and the bushes, sweeping past him down the hill. Leaping over abandoned weapons and machines, ignoring the dead and wounded. Herbivore ran with hunter, fleeing from whatever was behind them. Birds leaped into the sky in clouds. Tens – no, 100 or more – the animals stampeded, separately and together.

What the hell?

Then he saw what they were running from.

△ △ △

Chambers needed to make himself breathe, but if he did, the monsters would see him. The nightmares were stalking past him with the lazily powerful stride which said *carnivore* to any mammal. Six of them? Seven?

Way bigger than a horse, bigger than a bear, more savage than anything he'd ever seen before. A huge body mounted on six long legs, a wide and focused hunter's gaze. The middle and rear legs placed their feet flat on the ground, clawed toes spreading out under their weight, but the front ones had *hands* which brushed lightly across the surface. A flat snout, a deep lower jaw with flesh-ripping teeth, an armored cap on the head which became a mantle, reaching down towards the back and protecting the neck. Long neck, a dangerously calculating intelligence in forward-mounted eyes, weight evenly spread across that complicated gait, a counterbalancing tail. Muscles moved beneath the skin like cables under tarpaulins.

Chambers must be okay here, because he was still alive. If they noticed him –

"Alert! Presumed dangerous predators, not native to this planet, not known. Alert!"

–and one did, turning its head to stare straight into his eyes. That vast jaw unhinged itself, and he was staring directly into its fang-rimmed gaping mouth. But a second later the beast snapped its gaze away again, dismissing him as unworthy of attention, ignoring him. The pack paced steadily past him, eyes fixed on some other more valuable prize, leaving him still needing that terrified breath.

He couldn't move for several seconds.

△ △ △

Chambers couldn't decide which was more dangerous – going onwards after Richter and his people, or heading back towards his jeep so he could get the hell out of here. If he went after Richter, he'd be following those creatures down the hill, and they might be more interested in him next time. Somehow getting himself killed had lost a lot of its attraction, now that he had the chance to avoid it.

On the other hand, while he couldn't imagine the troopers needing any help from him in dealing with the nightmares, at least he ought to let them know about them. Anything less felt too much like running away, and he didn't think he could do that.

He needed to get this story, too. Chambers summoned the cameras and changed their instructions. He didn't need them blundering into those things and alerting them to his presence, like his bloody slate.

Oh, shit; here we go. Like Korsakov: no more excuses. It was, after all, the first rule of journalism: *get the story, no matter what.*

He keyed the transmit button. "Richter?"

Chapter 30

I Know You

"The picture we frame of the past... grows every day less similar to the original experience which it purports to describe."

– *GEORGE SANTAYANA*, THE LIFE OF REASON.

Weapon raised, Leon Richter faced his front. Where was it? He scanned again. *There.* A head – broad, armored, grey-green – appeared for a moment behind one of the wrecked vehicles, 107 meters away by the roadside.

Engage neural overdrive. Activate targeting systems. For a moment, he had thought he'd seen a combat helmet, but the recalled image seemed to be an animal, and not one his database could identify. But he knew that he knew it, somewhere deep within.

Another alert. Now he had two targets, but the first had vanished again, and his systems offered unreliable estimations. Then another target, and then again. The graphics appeared among the column of wrecked vehicles. A pack of large and unknown animals had arrived from nowhere, stalking between the wrecks, spread out like a patrol in hostile territory, moving in short tactical bounds as if covering each other.

His organic memory couldn't yet have been completely overwritten, because something ancient and dreadful was stirring. An image that was a 140 years old, from an encounter in a derelict spacecraft orbiting a gas giant planet around a distant star. The scenes had the vague certainty of natural memory, and he knew them for truth.

He searched the ground to his front, waiting for one of the creatures to reappear. *Front and right. Closing rapidly, behind that wrecked carrier.* Reflexively, he checked for the range. Thirty-six meters.

Smile for the camera, please. He compared the image and the memory.

A perfect match.

I know you.

Somewhere deep down, way down in the cellular depths where that memory had been buried, he had always known that one day this moment would come. Whatever ARTOK had done to him, they hadn't wiped this. This was why NipponDeutsch had killed Lisl and Max, why he'd run, why he'd defected, why – he couldn't remember anything else. But *this* was why.

Richter studied the creature in his sights. These were the killers, the cause of the massacre on those alien starships, the creatures no one on the *Amaterasu* could explain.

Hello again, you murderous bastards.

△ △ △

His radio crackled.

"Richter? There's a pack of animals –"

"I know, Chambers. They're here. They're all over us, but they're not attacking. Stay still. Get inside one of the vehicles if you can. Don't attract their attention."

Richter had sights on one of the monsters, a little smaller than the others but still massive. The journalist would have to sit and wait for the moment. His eye display gave him a tactical map: Kirov – there. Keegan: still watching his back, and keeping an eye on the enemy officer above her. Barclay, beside the wagon's hull. Arden – there. Yu Ling – there. *That's all of us, now.*

He keyed the switch and spoke to his troopers.

△ △ △

"Contact. Dangerous creatures, aggressive and hostile." Richter's voice was calm.

"Listen in. All round defense, centered on that carrier. Fire in self-defense only. These things are organized and dangerous, so keep sights on them, but don't fire unless you're attacked. Don't take them for granted. I've seen what they can do, and I reckon they'll move quickly. Be very careful. Something else commands them, and we don't know what."

Arden looked across at Kirov as Richter's voice cut off. He went onto the private net. "What was that all about? He's seen them before?"

"Dunno, Steve. But *watch the bastards* is good enough for me. Where are Carol and Angie?"

"Up by that command carrier, where Richter is."

"Got you."

△ △ △

Richter held his sights on the animal, waiting for it to reveal whatever it was going to do. He was in no doubt; these were the creatures whose handiwork he had seen all those years ago, in the starship's silent hull. Where the massacre had taken place. It was coming back to him, piece by bloody piece.

He relaxed his hands. The fog was lifting away from his mind; he could see the butchered aliens in the derelict ship, and the corpse of one of their killers. Again he felt the tug of that twisted gravity, and the confidence, born of free-soloing in the Chiemgau mountains, that told him that he could do this. Again, he knew the rising panic he had felt when Pedersen told him the ships were starting to move.

And that had led him on the long road back to Charon, to Earth, to Russia, to the moment of taking ARTOK's pay, to Enhancement, to countless wars across mankind's little corner of the galaxy, to Operation ThousandEyes, to personal discontinuity.

His mind was awash with an unexpected flood of rediscovered organic memories. The sight of these lizard-things was unleashing so much: a split second in mid-air; nano-boots in a kitbag; a crappy little barracks; Hans Becker crying; the lunacy of the psycho drive; flickers of soft X-rays; gravity shifts; Krause dead, halfway up the wall; alien bodies massacred. Climbing up the barrack walls from the seventh floor; the Frauenkirche; the monk; the hammer and the nails.

Here I am fighting Euros, he thought, *but I said I'd never take up arms against my own people. How the hell did that happen? Why didn't I think about that before?*

And why wasn't his rifle up in the aim? Richter had never in his life lost focus on his weapon. He checked it.

Safety catch. Selection lever. Ammunition block. Ejection port. Body lock. Stabilization system. Target designator – and then he saw the hand that was going through the automatic motions. Silver-flecked skin? People didn't have skin like that.

He concentrated on that weird skin, and it came closer, sliding smoothly in until he could see the pores. People didn't have eyes that could do that.

Normal people didn't have brains with inbuilt processors, and they couldn't speed up their perceptions and slow them down again. They didn't have backups. Normal people couldn't talk silently to each other, or hear a pin drop down the street, or run faster than a car, almost as fast as a bullet. They didn't sleep for years, like someone in a bloody fairy-tale.

The self-realization felt like a blow to the chest: why the hell had he let ARTOK do this to him? He didn't remember much about it. Just a cup of coffee, the Russian dacha, and a woman's voice. "Take your time, Herr Richter. Go and climb Mount Elbrus. We'll think of something, between us." And then this.

This isn't the time. Leon Richter might die here if he lost himself in dreams. He struggled to concentrate on the here and now.

The creatures were clambering across the vehicles, sniffing at bodies, scratching at equipment with huge clawed hands. *These aren't just brainless animals. This is tactical intelligence gathering. All those years ago, we were right about them.*

Chapter 31
Backwards Fast

A few hundred meters away, something was going on around the Adept's carrier. With Drovan's weight forcing his head down, Harvetz couldn't make it out, but at the base of the vehicle's legs he could see more of the cyborgs, the Adept and his dog and, a little further off – some animals?

This couldn't be good. He staggered into cover behind the nearest vehicle. Taking great care, he lowered Drovan to the ground. His back was killing him; it was hard to stand.

Harvetz leaned against the wagon, and recognized it. He shuddered. It was one of the little four-wheeled jeeps, well armored and equipped with twin lasers and a quick-firing thirty millimeter. The upper armor had taken two or three hits from the enemy's micro-missiles, and the crew had abandoned it. Their bodies lay nearby. Harvetz recognized the torn corpse of the commander: Danny Pietro, a friend and co-communicant.

Someone was coming along the track towards him. An older man, not in uniform.

Harvetz drew Drovan's pistol from his belt and tossed it onto the seat. He forced strength on himself and lifted the silent man once more, laying him down on the rear bench.

He slid into the seat and tried the engine.

△ △ △

"I know you. You're that journalist."

"And you're Darius Harvetz."

"Come on, get in." The man signaled him into the vehicle. Chambers didn't like getting in. The vehicle had taken a couple of hits, not enough to destroy it, but he was thinking of people firing at him in the middle of an empty street. Harvetz had got it working well enough to move. The rear doors were twisted open, and there was the man he'd been carrying, lying on the back deck: maybe alive, maybe not.

His brain felt dull. "Where are we going?"

"That's my Adept, over there with the cyborgs. My mate here needs help. I've got nowhere else to go."

Δ Δ Δ

The creatures had surrounded the Euro commander's four-legged carrier, Chambers saw, facing outwards. The ring of Enhanced troopers was barely visible as their cam skin adapted to the background. A very thin defensive line, but a weapon covering each direction. And in the shadows of the vehicle, a couple of the recent enemy and a large dog. The Euro officer seemed familiar – it was Harvetz's priest, of course. What had he called him? Adept.

If there was any safety to be had here, it could only be found in the center of that ring, because between *here* and *there*, the monsters were circling.

Harvetz pulled the battered jeep to a halt about fifty meters short, as gently as possible, then carefully selected reverse and held the vehicle still. Their way forward was blocked by wreckage, and by the monsters.

The six-legged centaur-lizard-things paced and stalked about, slithering across each other like snakes, then turning around and snarling the ancient warning of the as-yet-undecided carnivore. There was no doubt that was what they were. Wherever they came from, this body language must be universal. Huge jaws spread wide, drool splashed, claws were flourished. The animals were circling the carrier, looking for gaps, working out what it was that they had trapped.

"What the hell are they?" Harvetz whispered.

"I don't know. My slate says they're not native to Harmony."

"I'm guessing that doesn't much matter. Still look capable of killing us all. I don't see us getting help for my mate while they're here, and I can't see them just pissing off."

One of the creatures turned and saw them. A brown and green colored thing, it made a coughing sound, lifted a razor-tipped hand, gestured to another beast. A grey animal stopped its own pacing and turned to face them.

Chambers felt something pushed into his hand. A pistol.

"It's cocked, and it's set for three-round bursts. Careful, safety catch is off." Harvetz was speaking very softly, keeping his eyes on the animals. "If they rush us, aim for the mass of the body. There'll be a red dot where it's pointed. Use both hands, left one holding your right wrist. It's stabilized; don't fight it. The ammunition is standard, non-explosive, and you'll only get about ten bursts. Shift targets after each burst. Got that?"

"I think so. What will you be doing?"

"Driving backwards, very bloody fast."

Chapter 32

Tauroctony

*"When Gilgamesh upset the goddess Ishtar, she
convinced her father Anu to send the Bull of
Heaven to destroy the crops and kill the people of
earth. But Gilgamesh slew the Bull, which enraged
the gods."*

– *THE* EPIC OF GILGAMESH.

"Be still, Enkidu. Everything's okay. Good dog. Well done." The great mastiff leaned against him, wagging its stump of a tail and trembling. Macdonald scratched it behind the ear. The dog relaxed, and sat.

One of his weapons-carrier jeeps was approaching, slowing as the driver saw the lizards. The driver was Trooper Harvetz, and the passenger was somehow familiar. Adept Macdonald ignored them, looking at the creatures. Groping for the bayonet at his side, he unbuckled the scabbard and moaned softly.

The dog watched his hand stroking the hilt of the weapon.

Δ Δ Δ

The monsters turned around as one, and started moving away. The enemy officer stepped forward and followed them, drawing his bayonet. His dog sprang to its feet.

"Hey, you. What are you playing at?" Keegan shouted.

The officer started to trot, holding the bayonet lightly in his hand, eyes locked on the alien creatures. His dog loped beside him, nudging against his hip.

"You, get back here!" Richter was shouting after him.

The man was running now. The mastiff gathered pace and surged alongside him.

One of the beasts had halted and was looking back at him over its shoulder, raising its head, exposing the neck.

They hit the alien together, the soldier surging high to land well up onto its broad back, and the dog leaping at its throat. The man seized the animal by its snout with his left hand, grasping at the tough cartilage of its lips with his fingers, pulling the head back and up, driving his knee into its back and raising the bayonet in his right hand to drive it into the creature's throat, laughing and crying at once.

A massive arm tore him from the creature's back and flung him to the ground. The animal leaped at the mastiff, and the dog howled.

△ △ △

"That's the Adept. Give me that. I've got to go to him." Harvetz reached for the pistol.

"You're nuts. Those things will rip you to pieces, and you'll have to get through the whole lot to get to him. Stay in the jeep!" The driver was tugging at the pistol, but Chambers wasn't about to release it. "He's brought it on himself."

But they couldn't just watch the creature tear the man apart.

Harvetz released his grip, then reached across as the reporter relaxed, punched Chambers awkwardly in the stomach and grabbed the pistol as he doubled over. "Sorry, mate."

△ △ △

"Steady. Hold your fire. Weapons tight. This isn't our fight. Ammunition states?" Richter knew he couldn't afford to lose control of this. They owed the enemy officer nothing; if he chose to attack the lizards, he'd have to take the consequences.

△ △ △

Harvetz jumped down from the jeep. Even at this distance, he could hear Macdonald's breath grating; something had to be badly broken in his chest. Blood poured from his left hand. His chest armor had deep parallel gouges from top to bottom. But the Adept made it to his feet, grunting and leaning to one side, and staggered forward again. "Enkidu. Hold on. Good dog!"

The dog was thrashing around, whining, unable to stand, spine broken and entrails flooding from the gash in its belly. It couldn't last long.

Harvetz realized what the priest was trying to do, and knew that Adept Macdonald was insane. He was re-enacting the Tauroctony, the holiest rite in their faith. This was how the god had slain the bull of heaven.

Macdonald lurched forward again, the blade held poised for a downward slash. The dog howled, weaker now, and crawled a few meters to its front.

The centaur-lizard watched him come.

Δ Δ Δ

Harvetz ran forward and brought the pistol up into the aim. The other creatures were circling, watching him warily.

The Adept's in trouble. I've got to do this. But before he could fire at the creature that was attacking Macdonald, a brown and green monster turned towards him.

If I'm down, there's no one else.

He fired. The animal stumbled. He fired more bursts. It kept coming, but more weakly.

Another burst. It reared up, then fell.

Chambers was standing up in the jeep, unarmed and defenseless. He would have to take his chances. Beyond this lizard corpse, the Adept was in even greater danger.

Δ Δ Δ

"Oh, shit. They're going for Chambers and the other guy. Richter, are we involved yet?" Keegan was tracking one of the nearer lizards with her weapon. The thing knew it, and rose massively onto its hind legs.

Richter checked his sights. *Range:* 22.5 meters.

"We're involved." The journalist had gone for Vasiliev, the Russian lying in the road, hadn't he?

Δ Δ Δ

"Come back, man. It'll kill you!"

Harvetz didn't have a clear shot, but he was up and running. Beyond him, the lizard slashed at Macdonald twice more with its huge clawed hand. The priest screeched and staggered back, legs obviously weakening. He came at it again, but he could barely raise the bayonet. There was no force in the blow that glanced off the monster's thick hide. Macdonald sprawled across its broad back, scratching and gouging at it.

The creature grunted and whipped its chest-thick tail around him, held him pinned against its side. Its jaws closed massively around Macdonald's arm, and bit down hard.

Δ Δ Δ

"Oh, God, God, God." Chambers didn't know who was shouting, but it might even be him. Harvetz had nearly got there, and he was dodging around trying to get a shot at the monster without hitting his dying priest. The other creatures watched the slaughter impassively.

The alien released Macdonald, and spat out his severed arm. The screaming man lurched, off balance, and tried to scuttle away from the lizard. Vomit rose in Chambers' throat as the lopsided figure stumbled, fell, and struggled to rise.

Harvetz got a clear view and fired a shot, with no apparent effect. *Miss.*

The creature ignored him and sprang after the Adept, ramming him squarely in the back with its blunt head. Blood still trailing from its jaws, it seized him again and rose to balance on hind legs and tail, forelegs raised and arms spread wide. It stood around four meters tall. Macdonald hung from its jaws like a dog's toy. It shook him from side to side, then flung the man to the ground and fell on him, hand claws first.

It trampled the body into the muddy earth, and watched until Macdonald had stopped moving. The dog was yelping and whimpering as it tried to get to the ruined corpse of its master, and the lizard opened its mouth wide as the dog snarled at it weakly. The thing snapped its jaws closed and the headless dog collapsed, and the lizard spat.

And then all four of the remaining horrors turned, and stared at Harvetz and Chambers.

△ △ △

The creatures were a vision from hell, four vast leathery shapes, all claws and fangs and roaring aggression and hate. Their leader rose again into that towering posture, looming over the humans. Those others stood on four legs, upper bodies vertical, swaying like wrestlers or boxers making ready for combat. One even slapped its ghastly hands together as if gleefully anticipating mayhem. Tails writhed, jaws gaped wide.

Chambers had been scared before, but now he felt the ancient terror of the prey. His breath was coming in shallow gasps and he could feel his legs trembling. Running was pointless. He'd collapse from pure fear if he turned his back on them, but facing them was facing death.

Harvetz must have been equally frightened, but he was still functioning. He stood like a weapons student on a range, feet apart, shoulders square to the target, arms reaching out in an A-frame to give a firm grip to the pistol, left hand supporting the right as he'd told Chambers to do. A red dot showed that the weapon was aligned on the center of the lead animal's chest, twenty-five meters away.

The beast's torso rose and fell as it breathed. Chambers saw that its arms and hands were weaving complex shapes in the air, shapes which the others watched. It abandoned its waving and dropped to its feet. The creatures slithered towards them, following the big one, swaggering their power in the roll of their muscles and the cough and grunt of their breathing, snorting contempt at the feeble humans.

△ △ △

Darius Harvetz wasn't going to pray to anyone anymore. What if he got another answer? But he was going to avenge his Adept, who'd been a suicidal bloody fool though he was still Leo and he was still the commander as well, and the thing had killed him, just played with him, just ripped him to pieces. That wasn't right; the god would never sanction that, would he?

He'd need to be quick changing targets.

Harvetz kept the dot right in the middle of the thing's chest and let the target image flood his mind. It wasn't much of a distance. He gently squeezed the trigger.

△ △ △

The monsters were well spread out, presenting too many targets. They were staring straight at the troopers, facing them down, daring them to attack. Yu Ling's needler screamed once, a long burst, and the nearest creature fell in a mist of blood and bone. It triggered a whirlwind response. The others charged, moving terrifyingly fast.

"Ammunition!" The needler spun down to useless silence as a coordinated volley came from Arden and Kirov.

△ △ △

Afterwards, Chambers would find it difficult to disentangle the sequence of those events. One of the creatures raised a clawed hand, someone shouted "Look out!" and a weapon boomed. The animal stumbled and dropped, writhing, and then the other aliens were surging forward and he knew that he couldn't face them, so he turned to run. This wasn't like the streets of Mabuza, where the enemy might hit him or might not. Here, that way was death and this way wasn't, not straight away. He really didn't have a choice.

And as he backed away, making ready to run, he heard the dreadful click of Harvetz's pistol as the firing pin drove into the empty housing where the ammunition had been.

△ △ △

The Euro guy's pistol had a stoppage, or perhaps he was out of rounds, Arden saw. He was standing there like a marksman, and that took balls, but now he had a lost look on his face. It was all happening bloody fast, but he and Kirov and Richter were there, and Yu Ling and Carol Keegan and Angie Barclay. So here was the bloody reporter running like a bunny, and who could blame him when he didn't even carry a weapon? Not Stevie Arden, who'd never been more than an arm's reach from a rifle for most of his life.

Pavel Kirov was standing like a tree in a storm, not budging whatever happened, and there wasn't a joke to be heard. His weapon was up in the shoulder and he was cracking away, getting fire down into the monsters and hitting them, and Arden's mind went back 138 years to a muddy planet and charging horses and Brown Horse Bloke with a saber and *where the hell did that come from?*

Now there was only one of the beasts on its feet, the others were dead or dying, the beast was on them all and it swiped at Pavel and missed because they were all in neural overdrive and moving far too fast for it, and then it spun around and kicked backwards at Chambers who wasn't and it *got him...*

△ △ △

...and that huge foot came back at him and it was inevitable and he couldn't get out of its way and it smacked into him and sent him flying and he couldn't look at the flapping fabric of his jacket, certain that he would see his guts spilling out. The thing had claws like huge knives, wide-gaping jaws, blades on its feet. He couldn't breathe. His legs were buckling. He was falling, starting to black out, terrified that they'd think he'd died and they'd just leave him there where that nightmare could rip him apart...

△ △ △

Bloody hell, you idiot. It's got you, and now we've got to pull you out of there, thought Kirov. The reporter would have to take his chances just now, till they'd killed this thing. The last one was easily the biggest, and the animal wasn't going down fast enough, even with the killing power of the ten millimeter rounds.

The thing was like the crocodile-snake monster from Lake Somin that his grandmother had terrified him with. Dad said it was just a catfish, but Gran said that it came up out of the lake and ate bad boys, and if he didn't behave... *What the hell was he dreaming about?*

Kirov knew that he was hitting it. It had to be bleeding internally, but it didn't know how to die. The others had gone down, sure enough, but the Euro had hit this one with the first and last shot from his crewman's pistol, and it hadn't even flinched. There couldn't be much zip in those rounds. But the ten mils from his CLAW close-combat light assault weapon weren't having much more effect, the laser was low on power and Yu Ling's needler had an empty cassette, and the beast was on him...

...but Stevie was with them, and he had the AAR anti-armor rifle with the explosive-tipped rounds, and Richter was back over there with another one, and those should do it...

△ △ △

"Arden. No rounds!"

The creature was upon them as Arden dropped the useless empty AAR and went for his pistol.

Oh, shit. I'm going to be too slow again. Sorry, Molly.

"Richter. I'm on it!" His weapon boomed.

△ △ △

Units One and Two returned and circled to float by a prone man. Their programming permitted considerable autonomy so, after the man proved to be inactive and nothing else seemed to be happening, they separated and concentrated on the things which interested them. Unit One looked for humans-with-equipment activity, audio impressions, vox-pop clips, and other fundamentals of reportage.

Unit Two was programmed to get background shots. A wide view of the wrecked convoy, smoke drifting across the vehicles and rolling down the hillside. A long shot showing a four-legged carrier, belly doors hanging open and flames licking out. Another carrier, doors also open, human figures dead around it. The wreckage of a wheeled Euro gun carrier.

Unit One: a close-up of a Euro body, sprawled on the roadside. Carcasses of massive six-legged lizard-like aliens. A jeep with a badly burned man in the back, moaning in pain.

The audio: a light wind, crackling flames, voices.

△ △ △

"The reporter's alive. Come on, let's get him in that wagon." Richter bent over the man's body. He had to get the survivors away from here, and fast. Euro reinforcements would be arriving soon.

"There's another Euro here; alive, just." Keegan's voice.

"Stevie too, maybe." Kirov was working desperately to stabilize Arden, Barclay seeing to Yu Ling's torn and bloodied arm, Keegan helping the Euros with their injured mate on the jeep's rear deck.

"He's still conscious." Richter concentrated on stopping the bleeding of Chambers' chest wounds.

"...Orchard..."

"What did he say?" Richter tossed a bloody dressing to one side.

"It sounded like 'go to Orchard.' Does that make any sense to you?" Barclay's voice.

"Are you calling in the lander?" That was Kirov, focused, not a joke to be heard.

"Where did those things come from? Anyone got any backup data?" Yu Ling, over the top of Barclay's head, studying the rip in his armor and wondering about an animal which could cause that.

"Where the hell's Orchard?"

△ △ △

"Here it comes. How far back are the NipponDeutsch recce?" Richter reckoned they had five minutes before they were overrun.

That left him with a problem. Even if they survived another contact, he wasn't prepared to stay on Harmony to fight or die for the company that had stolen his mind.

But he had to get treatment for his injured people, and he couldn't trust anyone else, so that meant they needed the TransOrbit carrier's medical pod. Could they overcome the four crew on board?

Two dead: Fred and Billy, down and not coming back. Stevie Arden wounded badly, powered down. Yu Ling, one arm out of action. Chambers – ribs broken, lost some blood, out of it for now and no kind of fighter anyway. Keegan, Barclay, Kirov and himself. Four weapons walking. A bit tight on numbers.

He studied the two Euro drivers. They might do. *Harvetz* and *Whitman*, their jackets read. One of Chambers' bloody cameras was bobbing about, getting in people's faces.

"You two. I could do with you coming with us. We need extra hands to take on some Russians and then get off the planet. Or do you want to stay here?"

The man called Harvetz spoke first. "I'm here because my Adept called me. But that's over now. I'll come if you'll help me take care of Drovan." He gestured at the wounded man beside Chambers on the vehicle deck. "We were on hire. The Euros won't be interested in looking after him."

Whitman shook his head. "I'll stay and take my chances. I don't fancy yours."

Richter considered it. Yes, seizing the carrier could be doable with five, once they'd got on board. Probably best to take the injured Euro; he'd never make it if he was left.

A descending dot became a shape, gained definition, became a lander from the SpecFor TransOrbit carrier. It touched down on a broader patch of the hillside road, raised a dust storm and opened its hatches.

Oh, crap. Here we go again. Bloody aircraft. Puke time.

The carrier crew would let them on board, no trouble there. He had the numbers to seize control, just, or at least to exert massive influence on what happened next. But then where? *Peter the Great* was gone, but ARTOK had two other starships in this system. Perhaps Chambers might be right about this Orchard place. Perhaps they could get there. Too much of the perhaps, but there was some kind of hope.

His proximity alarms yowled. An armored shape nosed around a distant corner.

Vehicle armament boomed.

"Come on! Get the wounded on board!"

Δ Δ Δ

Unit Two watched the TransOrbit carrier's takeoff. As it climbed, the carrier received a cascade of fire from the advancing Euro reinforcements. Some damage was caused, but structural integrity seemed unaffected.

The camera rose at speed and entered the craft's loading hatch, seconds before it closed.

ORCHARD 2450

Chapter 33
Moving Faster By Standing Still

"Business is good, the Universe is expanding."

– TONY FOLLARI

Chambers was touring around Orchard on a rent-a-bike, and he could see that there was money about. Lots of it. Orchard had never been as prosperous as this before. Busy roads, full employment, people spending money, new trains – full seas! The economy was booming.

A lot of this cash had to be coming from agriculture. No surprise there; after all, that was why Orchard had been created. *The clue's in the name, Dave.* But growing food for Tau Ceti's moon stations and orbitals hadn't brought in this much money back in his dad's time, so what had changed?

Since he'd come back home, his days had been full. Full of pain and recuperation and healing, full of fear. Fear of the security policeman he thought of as Blank Face, fear of arrest and a trip back to some deniable dungeon. Fear of the creature which had back-kicked its massive claws deeply into his chest.

Now it seemed as if the days had been too full of fear for him to think, or at least to think properly. Back on Parnassus, hadn't the woman Talia Ferenc told him about her homeland's poverty? Hadn't they spent hours talking about this in a rackety bus creaking up the twisting canyonside roads, as the sky above them darkened to violet? And then Romanov, who'd handed him the one-time-use video at the research station up in the Dead White – *this is a shoestring operation. Parnassus' crumbling roads, Epsilon Indi's horse economy, the empty seas on Orchard. Everywhere was so bloody poor.*

But it wasn't, was it? Orchard was making money. What the hell had changed in the last few years?

△ △ △

As the autonomous bike carried him onto the main road out of Penty, heading for home, a name came to him. Zulfikar. Zulfikar Someone-or-other. He'd been a – center? A face surfaced from the depths of memory. Long hair, dark glossy beard, cheery smile. No, not a center. Second row; a big guy, like most second rows. Back in the day, Chambers had been a center himself, playing for the village rugby team every weekend, a regular pair of boots for the College side, even trying out for the Orchard Seconds one year. He didn't play any more – he hadn't for years – but he remembered Zulfikar.

The man had been a civil servant, hadn't he? Hang on a minute... Was that why his memory had served up the name? Chambers couldn't go near his regular contacts, that much was obvious. If Zulfikar Whatsit was still around, perhaps he could look him up for a beer and a catch-up. He needed to start somewhere, and a man in the service of the government might know a thing or two.

Zulfikar Abdul Rahman. *Got him.*

The rugby scene on Orchard was big, but Orchard itself wasn't. Sooner or later you met everyone, and then you kept on meeting them. Zulf – that's what they called him, Zulf the Wolf – had played for Penty, and in one bruising encounter he'd knocked the wind out of Chambers, very nearly snapping one of his ribs. It hadn't been malicious, just a hard coming together on the field of play, but it had taken Chambers out of the game. In the bar afterwards, it had seemed as if Zulf was trying to drown him in beer. The huge second row was genuinely horrified that he'd hurt him. *Nice guy.* The memory cheered him, perversely enough. Years later, and his ribs were creaking again.

He took over control from the bike, and abandoned himself to the enjoyment of movement. With the windscreens adjusted, the flow of air was pleasant rather than battering, and he got into the thrill of banking the machine into corners and powering it along the straights. He glanced at the displays. A screen indicated that they were moving at around fifty meters per second. It felt ferociously quick, until it occurred to him that Orchard itself was spinning about fifteen times as fast. He would have been moving faster if he'd been standing still.

Lost in thought, he hadn't noticed that night had rolled over him. The bike was approaching Bridgford, still moving quickly. He realized where he was, and his heart stuttered again. The road was as straight as an arrow, becoming the village street for a while and then going right out the far side and over that railway crossing before leaving the houses behind. As they entered the village, a cat sprang from a wall and leapt into his path. Even before he had made out the shape, he felt the handlebars twitch and crash straps tighten around him. The bike slowed sharply, flicked left-right-left, then continued at a much lower speed.

"Do you wish to resume control?" it asked.

"No thanks, I'm good. You do it." His heart thudded in his chest. His reactions had been so far behind the machine that his body hadn't even had time to panic until the danger was long gone. He glanced back. The cat sat contemptuously on top of a gate post on the opposite side of the street, washing its paws.

That was strange. "Wait a minute." The bike took him literally and stopped.

"No, I meant – oh, forget it. Just hold on here." A pair of prop stands glided down to support the machine. The cat sat there, a black shape barely visible against the night. In case he'd been imagining it, he faced the front again. The road ahead was as clear as day.

If you came from Orchard, you always knew where the terminator line was, and it was nowhere near them. They must have crossed it twenty or so minutes ago, but there was daylight ahead of them. How could he not have noticed the transition? It was disorienting for a second – literally; he didn't know how he could be facing that way, and seeing what he saw – and then he realized there was night to either side of him as well.

It was the bike's screen. The machine was giving him a human-eye-adjusted view of the road ahead, replacing the darkness with data gleaned from its machine senses. He leaned out and looked forward. A darkened street replaced the sunlit view. He leaned back in – daylight again. "Why did you do that?" he asked it.

"You instructed me to stop."

"No, I mean why did you give me this image? The view ahead? Why not just put some lights on?"

"That option is available if you prefer. As a default, most riders prefer the daytime image. Emergency response times are usually improved. My collision avoidance systems require neither." *Usually?* It had sounded a little judgmental, even haughty. "Most hirers also prefer the daytime image when the cycle is moving autonomously."

"I'll bet they do." He thought about travelling at those speeds on an unlit country road, the machine's brain in control, unable to see where you were being taken. Steep banking, sharp braking, all in complete darkness. Not nice.

The bike was quite a little gadget, that was clear. There had been nothing like this on the taxi ranks when he'd left, just tatty old chugbuckets that got you where you wanted five times out of ten.

This was one of the most overt examples of public spending that he'd found. The machines were municipally owned, and in his experience Orchard governments never spent a penny that they didn't expect to see coming back as a euro. This kind of investment had to mean that his home's economy had turned a corner.

They set off, the bike in control once more. This time, streetlights rippled on ahead of them, and shut down again behind. He leaned out to look, and felt the machine bank in compensation. A beam of white light speared forwards from the bike, even though the screen still showed everything in the perfect clarity of Orchard's noon. Was the bike taking the piss?

They slowed as they entered the village, and stopped at the foot of the apartment stairs. "Pick me up here in the morning," he said.

"At what time?"

"Nine." He stood on the step and watched as the bike purred away into the night, its lights derisively turned off.

Chapter 34

If You Were The Data

"Only the shallow know themselves."

– OSCAR WILDE.

The truth was always buried. Facts hid behind recollections and reasons. Throughout his career, Chambers had oversimplified so many things with the best journalistic intentions, wanting to do justice to the real facts. He knew his greatest sin was that he'd tried to present those facts as if they were linear, sequential, things wired in series. Yet although facts might be obscure, they were absolute; events had an objective truth. Things had *happened*, even if you couldn't quite establish what or why.

But recollections were parallel-wired, independent. One person's memories were completely different to another's. The recollections of mind-wiped cyborgs would be utterly unreliable. Reasons were always slippery, and knowing them rarely helped. People always claimed to have a valid reason for their actions. What reasons could a 200-year-old man give?

And what reasons did the companies have for spending trillions in setting up bases and outstations, then leaving them to struggle in near-poverty?

Enough. What had he learned about the cyborgs?

One. Arden, Richter and the rest were bloody ancient, even if they didn't always act like it. Relativity, extensive medical resources, and the frozen sleep that the Enhanced called "the dreamtime" meant that the cyborgs hadn't aged a fraction as much as they should have done. If there had been a start to all this, it had happened a long time ago. Those scary stories from history had been right: the beasts hadn't gone, they'd just been lying very low. That's all that people would hear; how could he persuade them otherwise?

Two. If the cyborgs weren't human, he was a bug-eyed monster. They looked scary, they moved so fast that you could hardly see them, they could kill you in strange ways, they had improbable abilities which said *monster* or *magic* or *demon*. But they laughed, they worried, they loved, they feared; they played and they joked and they raged. They behaved well, or not so well, or badly. They didn't seem to cry, but he knew they grieved. The cyborgs were human, all right, and that made them no better or worse than anyone else. Just like everyone else. Shame that nobody seemed to believe that.

Three. The police spook he called Blank Face might have been right. Maybe the Enhanced weren't the race's only hope, or whatever he had sneeringly called them. Semyonov had some idea of using the soldiers out in the deep wide black, but Chambers couldn't see why. This little knot of planets where humanity lived didn't matter much to the universe; there were plenty of other lumps of rock and water spinning around balls of gas. Billions of human lives meant even less. What help would cyborgs be? The policeman might have been right, for all the wrong reasons.

So he knew three things about the cyborgs: they were human, they were ancient, and they weren't going to save the world.

△ △ △

But he knew some other stuff as well.

He knew that the monstrous lizard-creatures back on Parnassus weren't native to that planet. His slate hadn't recognized them, and the waves of fleeing animals evidently hadn't known them either. The creatures were savage, merciless, and intelligent; but they didn't wear clothes, or carry things, or use devices. So where the hell had they come from, and how? Richter's avatar had said, "I've met one of those lizard-things before, a long time back." Then it had told him about its fragmentary memories of a massacre of alien beings, and a fleet of derelict starships which had started to move.

It didn't matter what the avatar's real motives were. If it was genuinely what it claimed to be, then the being was an ally and he could take the risk of trusting it. But if it was somehow operated by Orchard's security apparatus, then all they were going to find out from him was the same thing that he had been trying to tell them all along. There was a menace out there, and it was coming for the human race.

Whatever its motivations, the avatar was in a mess. It was plainly psychologically damaged, and above all, it wanted to find its physical self. Chambers had spent fruitless hours turning it over in his head without arriving at any different conclusion. He felt certain now that this was a genuine life form, not merely some manifestation of clever programming. A clump of cells, reaching some critical mass of neural complexity in the development of early biological life, must ultimately have led to consciousness. Something in the downloading process had had the same effect, even if the ARTOK designers had never intended it. Your memories made you into a person. What had happened to you in the past affected how you behaved in the present.

Your memories controlled who you were. If you had someone else's memories, you'd act like them, you'd think like them, you'd remember what had happened to them. You'd know the people they knew and you'd feel about those people the same way that they had. Didn't all that make you a person? In this process of downloading, the man had made another self. Once that thought had occurred, he hadn't been able to shake it. If it was true of the avatar, and if that made the avatar a person, then it had to be true of him, too. What had happened to Petra *had* affected everything that he'd done since then. It had chased him away from Orchard, driven him out into the galaxy, made him run away and hide himself in his work.

△ △ △

What kind of a nightmare must that have been, to connect yourself to a memory-recording device, planning to back up all your experiences, and then to find that you were part of the data? If you copied yourself, then each of the selves was going to feel as if it was the real you. But once it was done, the original fleshy part of you would walk away from the process and have a cup of tea, or share a joke, or go to sleep, or eat a meal or perhaps take part in some combat operation and get killed. You wouldn't give the data another thought, once you'd done the routine and necessary chore.

But what if *you* were the part that came to awareness inside the recording device, inside the data? If you split yourself, something like that would happen. In your head, inside yourself – in your *soul* – you'd feel like you were still you. But you had no form, no flesh. Perhaps you would never die, but at what a cost! You couldn't move, or speak, or eat, or sleep.

Richter's avatar would know that he'd never again climb his beloved mountains, never again hang above some aching void in icy frigid air, never again scramble up a tower of rocks as if he was flying. He wouldn't taste the chill sharp buzz of a beer with his mates, and laugh with them in some bar; he wouldn't have the wild thrill of motion he got when he rode a bike, or feel the joyous pump of blood in the veins and breath in the lungs as he ran in the rain and the sun, or flirt with a pretty girl, or use a rifle, or work out...

Your bodily awareness was such a part of being yourself that Chambers couldn't begin to imagine what that might feel like. The physical Richter, that self-contained man, was forbidding enough. This sad, lost creature was doubly sinister, the ghost of a demon.

Chapter 35
Frightening But Not Illegal

*"Sharing a landmass doesn't mean we have a
common identity."*
– UNATTRIBUTED, BELIEVED TO REFER TO 1970S NORTHERN
IRELAND.

"David, how are you? Wonderful to see you. How long has it been – ten, fifteen years? No, that's not possible. You're looking in decent shape, mind, I've got to say it."

"Not true, but it's kind of you to say so, Zulf. Now, you *are* looking well. Still playing rugby?"

It was quite possible. The full beard had flecks of grey in it, and the long hair – oiled and possibly scented now, but also graying – started a little further back than Chambers remembered. But Zulfikar Abdul Rahman was still big, still well-muscled, still trim and fit. And something else, which was either a recent development, or which Chambers hadn't known about back then: he was prosperous. The light blue robe was expensive, open at the neck to show a creamy white collarless shirt, and his shoes were a pair of very soft and elegant not-quite slippers. Understated, but clearly doing well. Chambers felt decidedly scruffy beside him. A waiter was hovering close by; he imagined the man's disdain for his polished but scuffed old boots, faded trousers and battered jacket. At least he'd shaved. The avatar would have been pleased.

"Not for a while now, but I'm doing a bit of coaching. Penty's got a good youth side these days, and I lend a hand with the Under Sixteen team. We're chasing the top slot in the league, but I don't think we'll crack it this year. Maybe next. What about you? Still involved?"

Chambers shook his head. "No, not for a few years, I'm afraid." He didn't know how to go on; for a long moment, he couldn't find the words he needed to bridge the gap of fifteen years – Zulfikar had been spot on – and pick up their acquaintanceship again. There was a pause, and the big man smiled at him quizzically, then led the way to a quiet corner table surrounded by leather sofas. Penty's Lowland Country Club catered to the well-heeled. The waiter glided after them.

"What do you fancy? A beer? They keep some very nice Solo, and the White Sun is as good as you'll find it." Leather creaked as Zulf sank deeply into the couch; Chambers perched on the edge of his seat squab. The waiter took their orders and padded away again. Another silence descended.

He took a breath. This wasn't getting him anywhere. "It's great to see you again, Zulfikar. Thanks for agreeing to meet me. I've been away a long time, and I'm only just back, so I'm trying to pick up with a few folks again. It's amazing how much the place has changed. It's really looking good these days." *Slow down, now. Don't babble.*

Zulfikar nodded agreement but only offered, "Things are going well, that's true."

"Tell me, are you still working for the government? "

The big man laughed comfortably. "No, I've been out of that around ten years now. Government money hasn't kept pace with the private sector, you know?"

Chambers' hopes crashed. He'd wanted to pump the man for any information he could get about what was happening in local politics. "So what are you up to instead?" He wasn't particularly interested, but you never knew. Perhaps he could pick up a name or two to follow up.

"You remember I was in the Ports and Transport Department?" Chambers nodded, trying not to reveal his disappointment. Back in his rugby playing days, he hadn't been in journalism long enough to acquire the useful habit of squirreling away every possible detail about everyone he had any dealings with. He'd never known exactly where Zulfikar had worked, and it didn't seem important. He was just another bloke on the rugby circuit.

"Well, I saw an opportunity I couldn't ignore, did some research and handed in my notice. I started up a little brokerage handling in-system load space, then after a while I got into groupage loads, and eventually we made the move into out-systems stuff as well." *God, this sounded dull.* "I've started to get interested in local rail freight, lately. Now we're handling all kinds of load-haulers, pretty much everywhere. Not passengers, though. Just goods. I prefer cargoes that don't talk back.

"What about you, David? What have you been up to since we last met? I mean, I used to see a lot of your stuff, of course, but a few years ago you dropped out of sight."

A broad mirror-screen wrapped around the near-empty room, showing sports highlights and news feeds. Considering the question, he glanced up at it and watched a batsman striking a long drive towards mid-off. The view of the pitch faded, replaced by the avatar's face. He felt as if he was being haunted.

Chambers took a deep breath, realizing that he must seem like a broken man who was trying to hold himself together. Perhaps he wouldn't get anywhere, but it was time to shape up, or this wealthy man would soon be wondering why he had bothered wasting his time on such an obvious loser.

"Well, when I first left, I wanted a change from the usual local sport-social-politics stuff. To be honest, I was doing okay, but I was after the big time. I went to Sol system and tried to get myself into the defense correspondent game, covering some of the conflicts that were happening back then. And they're still happening." He thought of burning villages, missiles streaking from the decks of naval vessels, the stench of mass graves, autonomous aircraft laying cluster munitions, feral children carrying stolen weapons, political extermination squads, combat teams fighting room-to-room along the main corridor of a habitat. And the cyborgs.

He risked a glance back at the screen. The avatar was barely perceptible, little more than a pattern imagined in flame or clouds. Either the other customers hadn't noticed, or else some more of Richter's ancient technology was involved.

The beer arrived. They reached for the glasses in almost perfect unison, as if they'd rehearsed it, and then both laughed. That helped him, a bit.

Ignoring the watcher, he started again. After all these years, it was still hard to say. "I came back to Orchard, after a while, and I thought I'd settle down here again. But my – I had to go away again. Back to Earth. I've been in the roving reporter business ever since."

Zulfikar had lowered his beer, and was studying him carefully. He'd noticed the correction, and must have been wondering about it. He might even have remembered the story. "Always in the defense and security game, though, I believe?"

"Yes, always that. I seem to have a knack for going where I can scare the shit out of myself." They laughed again, and Chambers began to relax a little. It was beginning to dawn on him that a well-connected and wealthy man with wide-ranging interests in transport and logistics could be the very person to tell him all about Orchard's newly busy industries, and the throwaway comment about rail freight had just resurfaced. Jackpot on the first attempt? He'd been about to dismiss him as a dead end, a nostalgic irrelevance.

"So what brings you back here this time?" The killer question. He'd have to give a plausible response if he was going to learn anything from Zulf, but he couldn't tell him the whole truth, old rugby buddy or not. It would have to be sanitized, to say the least.

He took a sip at the White Sun beer. "You're right – it's decent stuff, isn't it? What brought me back? Look, Zulf, I got myself into some trouble out there, and – what's the phrase? – I had to get the hell out of town. I managed to scare myself properly, this time. Running for home seemed like the only real option I had, so here I am." It Csounded weak, even to him.

"What kind of trouble?"

"Nothing illegal, don't worry." He believed that was true, but Blank Face might disagree. "What happened was that I ran into some frightening characters far out in the black. Frightening, but very unusual and interesting, and I knew there was a story there."

"Let me guess – they didn't want you nosing around?"

"Spot on. I got the story, but they made it clear that if I published. I'd be dead. Melodramatic, but I believed them, so I ran for it." That would have to do, and it wasn't very far from the truth, if you camouflaged terrifying aliens as 'frightening characters'.

"And are you going to publish? I mean, you're here, they're presumably still *there*. What can they do about it?"

"Perhaps nothing, perhaps a lot." That last bit was true. "They might still be there, or they might not be. I'm not sure what to do, to be honest. I plan on just thinking about it for a while." He hadn't thought this through; Zulf was getting interested now, and his next words confirmed it.

"Look, David. I might be able to help. From time to time I need some security myself. In business, you come up against the occasional very determined opponent, every now and then. I have a couple of people who – well, they help me out with that sort of thing. Would you like me to see if they can watch your back?"

This was getting complicated. He wanted information from Zulf, not protection. Didn't he?

"That's a kind offer, Zulfikar. I mean that, but I don't see why you'd want to do it. I mean, I turn up after an absence of years with a tale about being in deep shit, and you offer me this kind of support. Aren't you worried that I'll drop you in it?"

The trader smiled, as if the idea of tackling unknown opponents appealed to a whimsical sense of humor. "No, David. I'm very confident in my people, and I've got to say that this appeals to me. Life's been a little boring lately. It feels like we've gone almost as far with the business as we can. I seemed to enjoy building the thing up more than running it, you know?

"So I could do with a distraction. And if your frightening-but-not-illegal friends are heading for Orchard, or even here already, then I ought to be able to find out about it. We've got excellent management information on everything that moves in the system, and though I don't do passenger transport, I'm on good terms with the people who do. If your friends are here, we'll find them."

How the hell did he get out of this? Now he'd let himself convince Zulf that he was on the run from some band of interplanetary gangsters. As he sat there irresolute, the avatar spoke from the screen, and Zulfikar's head lifted at the sound of the scratchy voice.

"Tell him, Chambers. Tell him why you're really here."

Chapter 36
Counter Penetration

*"Nothing focuses the mind better than the
constant sight of a competitor who wants to wipe
you off the map."*
– WAYNE CALLOWAY, 1935-1998, PEPSICO CHIEF EXECUTIVE.

"Let's get this straight. You came to me wanting information, but now it's starting to turn into a selling job. Let me see what's on the table, what you're offering. Am I buying? I don't know." Zulfikar Abdul Rahman was pacing about, one hand deep in the folds of that elegant robe, the other teasing at a curl in his beard. "Right. Over to you, David."

After the avatar had made itself known, Zulfikar and Chambers had left the country club. The avatar had vanished, returning when they arrived at the offices of the Chief Executive of Rahman Logistics.

Chambers had rehearsed the story a dozen times, trying different approaches. But now that he had to say it, none of them seemed even faintly convincing. *What the hell. Zulf probably heard crap sales pitches every day. Just tell the man.*

So he did. "This is the avatar of Leon Richter, a soldier born in Germany 165 years ago. It's more than any phone agent, but I'll come to that. His memories are patchy, but he's remembering more and more each day. In 2310, aged twenty-five, Leon Richter travelled on one of the experimental NipponDeutsch FTL missions as military security.

"The spacecraft was called the *Amaterasu Ōmikami*. They encountered a derelict fleet of eleven alien vessels. On board one of them were hundreds of corpses of primate-like aliens, and one corpse of a different kind, a ferocious six-limbed carnivore. The alien ships started to move, and Richter fled."

The moment Chambers began to speak, Zulfikar stopped pacing about and sat down. He leaned forward, resting his outstretched hands on the desktop, eyes locked on the journalist.

"The NipponDeutsch operations team believed that the carnivores were intelligent, but not tool users. They judged that they must have been under the control of a third species. The operations team had no theory about what those might be, but nothing else explained what they had found. I'll come back to the third group of creatures in a moment.

"The alien fleet kept moving, and the NipponDeutsch crew returned to Earth with their prototype starship. The entire crew were abducted, probably by NipponDeutsch security, and at least two of them were killed. Richter, however, defected to ARTOK with his information. At some point since then, he's been forced to undergo their human enhancement process. He can't remember this occurring, but his memories are fragmentary. I believe that this version of him is an independent personality, a being brought into existence by the memory downloads used by ARTOK to preserve operational data. And remember that his physical original is now, therefore, a cyborg."

The avatar stirred at Chambers' use of the word, but it remained silent. It appeared to be sitting at an invisible desk, feet pulled back under a seat, chin resting on clenched hands, leaning forward on its elbows and concentrating.

"Earlier this year, I was asked by Vladimir Filippovich Semyonov to visit Parnassus, where ARTOK has a research station." Zulfikar's eyebrows rose at the name. "Semyonov claimed that he wanted me to help rehabilitate the reputation of the enhanced soldiers, and that this research station was connected in some way to the human enhancement program. I wasn't prepared to do anything he asked without question, but I agreed to go and have a look.

"ARTOK's researchers have found evidence that over a period of 10,000 years, at least two advanced alien societies which existed in this area of the galaxy have reverted to – I can't find a word for this. It's as if their evolution has been reversed. It's worse than savagery. Each species seems to have lost their reason, their intellect. They live among the remains of their societies like monkeys in a ruined cathedral, as one of the researchers put it."

He took a sip of water, anticipating a challenge. But the avatar had faded to transparency, and the businessman remained silent. He put the glass down. "Have you heard of the animals on Parnassus known as fang-gliders?"

Zulfikar frowned for a second, then nodded. "A kind of flying monkey-thing, yes?"

"Yes. They're one of the species which has reverted. Zulfikar, I've seen the evidence. This is real! In the Parnassus ice zone, high up in the mountains, I was shown the wreckage of an ancient starship that was crewed by their ancestors. There are frozen corpses up there, 5000-year-old bodies of fang-gliders in flight suits and crew helmets. Their descendants have much smaller brains, no technology, and they eat carrion... and they let humans take their planet away from them.

"I've seen another example. Octopus-shaped creatures from a planet that wasn't identified. The same thing seems to have happened there, much longer ago. I was given the data covertly, and a lot of it had been redacted. But I know that ARTOK has been running something they called Operation ThousandEyes, which seems to have involved positioning enhanced soldiers in military starships across part of this arm of the galaxy."

He paused, struck by a sudden thought. Saying the words aloud had just made him realize what that graffiti meant. A bold black K and a cartoon eye? *K-eye. ThousandEyes.* And the two long red strokes crossing it out? Something like "this is our turf. Don't try that around here." If there could have been any doubt about who was responsible, he had the answer now. And NipponDeutsch wanted ARTOK to understand the message.

Zulfikar Rahman was waiting for him to go on. Chambers gathered himself together. "The soldiers' mission was to watch for signs of alien activity. They're perfect for that assignment, and nobody wants them anywhere else. We believe that Richter himself might have been involved. That could account for some of his lost memories."

The avatar cut in. "Operation ThousandEyes means something to me, definitely. I have no picture of what it is, but I know it exists." The voice was firm and clear, human-normal, and the image had strengthened. "And yes, it could explain some of my memory gaps."

Zulfikar came out from behind the desk. His hands went back into the folds of his robe. "So ARTOK has been looking for aliens out in the black. And a couple of alien species ran into trouble back when – what? – when humans were hunter-gatherers?" He nodded at the avatar. "And the cyborgs still exist.

"David, all this is interesting – and I mean that – but it doesn't explain why you feel personally threatened, or what any of this has to do with Orchard. I'm not surprised that the Parnassus flying-monkey things regressed. It's a miracle they developed at all, with those monster waves wrecking the planet."

That gave Chambers the cue he needed. "Zulf, the evidence is piling up that those waves aren't natural. I was shown data which demonstrates that there's an artificial cause, a kind of weapon.

"You remember I mentioned that there had to be a third species of unknown beings, which NipponDeutsch concluded were behind the massacre on the alien fleet? Well, I think that third species caused the scour wave on Parnassus, and destroyed the octomorph civilization. And sooner or later, they're going to come after us."

△ △ △

They sat at a small dining table on the balcony, watching the terminator line rolling towards them. Chambers' slate lay amongst the plates and cutlery. The meal had been pleasant but not showy; decent food, served by human staff in comfortable surroundings. It had made him raise his private estimate of Zulfikar's wealth. The avatar, which had disappeared again while the meal was being served, had rejoined them once the waiters had left.

"Look. If Richter and the others met those creatures 140 years ago, it means that the companies have been keeping the threat a secret all that time. Why would they do that? They've got more interest than anyone in being able to operate safely out in the black." Zulfikar's voice was low, in the quiet of the late afternoon.

"Zulf, I don't know. This Operation ThousandEyes has been puzzling me. ARTOK realized that there was something threatening out there in the black, so it put out a chain of scouts. But what where they going to do? Richter, what would you do?"

The avatar had shrunk itself to the size of a doll. Now it straightened up and stood, expanding to human size, feet floating above the floor. Its eyeless stare was locked on Chambers. The scratchy voice was steady.

"If you know your enemy is looking for you, and if you're spread too thin to have your main force standing shoulder to shoulder along your perimeter, you need fast-moving light reconnaissance units well spread out. That way you can see when he advances. They need to be backed up by hard-hitting battle forces, which you can call on when you know which way he's coming. You sacrifice some space while you use the time to assemble your force. It's called counter-penetration.

"Operation ThousandEyes looks a bit like that, but I don't know where the big combat forces can be, or who they are. ARTOK and NipponDeutsch have each got a sizeable military, but they're spread all over the place. They can't be concentrated into powerful units quickly enough, and neither of them are configured for force-on-force engagements out in the black. They're all about border control, counter-insurgency, trade protection, a bit of saber-rattling when the other company gets too pushy. They lack too many vital elements to be an effective defense against a large attacking force." It flared to near-solidity, then shrank and faded. Its transparent face hung over the table.

"So far, it's all in here, isn't it?" Zulfikar waved at the slate. "If I'm to believe that there's a mysterious species of aliens which have a pathological loathing for developed species, then you have to show me convincing evidence. Personally, I'm not quite there yet. I'm still on the brink.

"Yes, I've seen these octo-whatsits, and the fang-glider starship, and the lizard-things – but there are strange creatures all over the worlds. You could have created those images easily enough yourself, given a bit of time. Look at what the entertainment industry can do."

Zulfikar's right hand emerged from his robe, to strike out the score on the fingers of the left.

"There are still bits missing. First, like we keep saying, why have the companies been keeping this secret? What made Semyonov himself decide that this was the right time to let you in on some of it?

"Next – and this one's been bothering me since you first mentioned it – what happened to that alien fleet? You said it started to move. Where did it go? 140 years have gone by, and no one's mentioned it?

"Where did those lizard-things come from, and how does it fit in with the war on Harmony? Is anyone interested in the wreckage and the lizard bodies that must be lying all over that mountainside?

"When you got back here, you were all arrested. The others have vanished, but you were released with a warning to keep well away from politics. The police aren't interested in your story, except to threaten you with death if you spread it. What the hell is that all about?

"And you say you can't understand what's been happening lately to make Orchard become so prosperous, but you feel that it's somehow linked to the police's complete indifference. Since I've been making some money here, I'm particularly interested in that claim.

"Finally, you tell me that the cyborgs, far from being monsters from ancient history, are actually the best weapon we have to fight all these aliens. *That's* going to be a tough sell.

"Have I missed anything?" Zulfikar was smiling fiercely, with such intensity that Chambers stupidly wondered if that was how the nickname had started. "Because I've got to say that this is either the scariest thing that I've ever heard, or else it's the biggest load of bollocks that I've ever heard.

"So am I buying? No. Not yet. But I'm not walking away yet, either. You, there. Richter? Should I call you that? You're quiet. How would you convince me?"

The avatar gained depth and definition once again. Chambers felt he was seeing a kind of body language develop. "I think you should be convincing us that it's *not* so. Neither of us understands what's going on here, but it all feels wrong. Chambers has been trying to get the police to listen since they took him. They won't. For a while I didn't see what he was on about. I didn't get this thing about all the new money and what it might mean, but I see it now.

"Forget the police for the moment. Let's start with the money. Chambers tells me he's also seen a one-time-use video of a destroyed ARTOK habitat. No one else could do that but NipponDeutsch. Why would they do that? What would they have to gain? And, since you're in business here, why don't you tell us about where all this place's new wealth has sprung from? What's changed while Chambers has been gone, that the companies are battling each other, and yet they're spending big bucks back here?"

The avatar was right, of course. It was the first rule of journalism: *follow the money.*

"You might not want to hear this, but I genuinely don't know what triggered it. I'm not going to turn down business, because since I started out the orders have come pouring in. As I said, I spotted an opportunity to move small loads on and off Orchard in a cost-effective way, and one thing led to another.

"Soon I was recruiting people, and leasing vehicles and rail cars, and then I was moving into in-system freight haulers. Mostly fruit, vegetables, oils, dairy, and other foodstuffs, but also engineering supplies, machine tools, and spares. I was shipping it all out to the transfer point to meet a starship and go on out of the system. The big operators were shipping full loads only, which meant they waited until somebody had built one up. I was putting together lots of the smaller players' part loads, so I was moving quicker than anyone else. It felt as if I was printing money for a while, but I was only doing something no one else had thought of. I'd no idea that people ate so much!" He smiled contentedly.

"What I do know is that the increase in government spending is very easily explained: more revenue from income and corporation taxes, and increased borrowing made available to the government by banks, which are happy to lend as long as they see the tax revenue going up to pay it back. The borrowing pays for the infrastructure projects, like the new trains and rail lines."

"And the seas?" Chambers could see the pattern; it made sense, so far.

"And the seas. But the tax income is the thing. Better infrastructure means more business wants to be here. More business means more work, more work means more tax revenue. The government paid off the mortgage on the habitat three years back. That's where your scary security police have come from – the government's not going to let anyone rain on this parade."

"Okay, I see that. Go on. Tell me about new business."

"There are plenty of young operations like mine around Orchard these days. Oh, not so very many hauling freight, but enough to service a growing market. There are lots of start-ups and fresh players in the logistics and service industries, and ARTOK is all over the habitat. It's not obvious to everyone, perhaps, but they're here all right. Sometimes it's hard to know if you're talking to the government or talking to ARTOK, they seem so aligned.

"I'm subcontracting from them – selling them local transport services, filling space on their starships for shipping foodstuffs out to Centauri, Cygni, Epsilon Indi, and the rest. I've even bought a small farm and started growing and shipping some of my own produce. So life here is okay, at the moment."

Zulfikar smiled that wolf-smile again. "But you're looking at one part of it wrong – the police must be very interested in your story, or they wouldn't be threatening you. Well, you've got my attention. Because if this is true, we all need to know. We'd have to get the worlds interested, and start them doing something about it. But if it isn't true, then I don't want to be getting on the wrong side of the administration. Or losing business. Or pissing off ARTOK.

"Frankly, meeting you again is very pleasant, but this story could be a risky thing for me. I need to know why I should take that risk."

Chapter 37
Ice Cream and Threats

"Temporary madness may be necessary in some cases, to cleanse and renovate the mind; just as a fit of illness is to carry off the humours of the body."
– AUGUSTUS WILLIAM HARE AND JULIUS CHARLES HARE, GUESSES AT TRUTH, 1838.

David Chambers sat on the top of Moonbarrow Hill, staring down at the seashore, studying the shapes of the ripples and dimples on the surface of the water. When he'd been a kid, this had just been a grass-covered mound behind the village, and when you sat up here you faced the other way. It was the houses that you looked at, the houses and the road and the railway track, and you followed the line out of the village and on up the curve. There had been no sea, back then. But now there *was* a sea, so he turned his back on the village and looked at the water instead.

What the hell were Semyonov and Fukuda up to?

There's a small ARTOK operation on Parnassus. It's not directly connected to the Human Enhancement Program, but it's relevant.

Chambers, we found octomorph starships. Wrecks, but starships. We think that it happened here as well.

NipponDeutsch's early FTL missions. A derelict fleet full of alien corpses, killed by the centaur-lizards.

Find out what you can about Operation ThousandEyes.

A multiple crime scene, a massacre, a graveyard; a hab vented to space. A bold black K and a cartoon eye, crossed out. "Who did this? Why did it happen? Why aren't we allowed to talk about it?"

You will not persuade people that these ancient bogey-men are our only hope against some ridiculous alien you've dreamed up.

The companies had known about the lizards for over a century. They had known that something else controlled the lizards, and that those beings had ruined at least two advanced species, and massacred hundreds of a third species.

Why the hell hadn't the companies done something with that knowledge? Why was there now a secret war between them? Why wouldn't ARTOK want everyone to know that NipponDeutsch had destroyed one of their habitats and massacred the population? Surely that scandal would cause massive damage to their Euro-Japanese rivals? But here comes the great David Chambers bearing that news, and the chief of the security police on his ARTOK-aligned home world just didn't seem to care.

He stayed there for a long while, engrossed in the shifting blues, catching reflected sparkles of light on the water and looking for patterns. Perhaps it was his age, he thought glumly, or something to do with the water surface, but his vision seemed a bit less sharp than he recalled from the memories. Looking across the width of the habitat from Moonbarrow's summit, you could easily see the far wall and the hills below it, but now the villages on the other shore were just a little hazy. In his mind's eye, the view had always been pin-sharp in Orchard's clear air.

△ △ △

Another day, and Chambers was feeling a little better, but still low. He was scared and suspicious, and his ribs ached, although the scar was fading to a baby-smooth pink line up his chest that contrasted oddly with the grey hair and the waning tan.

Two nights ago, as he had been getting ready for bed, Blank Face had appeared on his slate, smiling benignly at him. He'd been holding a finger up to his lips. No audio, no text, just that empty meaningless smile, the eyes locked on his own. Quite the opposite of audio, in fact; as the image had appeared, the music Chambers had been listening to faded down to silence, while a flat, anechoic deadness swallowed the remaining sounds of the street outside. It was a dulling sensation, a little like being underwater. In an undramatic way, it had fixed his attention on the silent screen, and on the man's face.

Breaking away from that hypnotic smirk, he'd got up and walked out of the lounge. As he entered the kitchen, the window's polarity had shifted to become a screen on which Blank Face still smiled at him. The policeman winked conspiratorially and vanished.

The message was quite clear. He was being watched, and he was expected to remain silent. Yet somehow the clear warning had given his weak resolve a boost, and he'd woken this morning with a marginally more positive outlook. The policeman's threat had made it plain that there was indeed something hidden.

For all the confidence that he'd earlier shown to the avatar, he hadn't been at all sure that he wanted to pick a fight with Orchard's scary new security organization. It was just too big and too capable, but the threat that was lurking out there in the black was even more overwhelmingly powerful. What could he do? Even if he could manage to tell the story, what could humanity do about whatever was out there? There was no prospect that people would unite in the face of this threat. A few people would get it, but most would simply laugh it off, or ignore it, or decide it was someone else's problem.

Yet, somewhere inside him, he could feel the stirrings of the story. He had to tell it, not for some fool idea of journalistic integrity so much as for the knowledge that he was more terrified by the thought of *not* telling it.

△ △ △

After Blank Face's unsettling appearance, Chambers had thought that would have been the end of it. But yesterday, as he'd been walking along the shore drinking coffee, the interrogator had returned. The promenade was edged with a row of benches, positioned to provide a view across the new bay. Here and there people were sitting, or strolling, or skating, or biking. Everything was reassuringly peaceful. The newly-comfortable world just kept on turning smoothly. As he'd slouched along, head down and one hand bent round his cup, the other deep in a pocket, a figure rose and approached him. The man was eating an ice cream.

He'd tried to ignore his unwanted companion, but the policeman had fallen into step at his side. "Hello again, David. You're getting about a bit, aren't you? All over the habitat. Now, let's recap, shall we?"

He took Chambers' arm in a friendly way as they walked, two pals enjoying the morning air. On the road, a car started up and cruised slowly alongside them. The interrogator glanced at it briefly, then returned his attention to the ice cream. It was almost finished.

"I think it's just fine that you're so busy. Come and go as you like – I said I'd take a chance on you. Sightsee, chat to people, admire stuff. It's a wonderful world, isn't it? You'll want to start writing and reporting again, I expect. That should be fine, too, if you're wise.

"Stick to sport, the arts, music. People always need humor; why not try that? There are lots of *inoffensive* things you could do. Do them." He licked the cone clean, and tugged Chambers to a halt. He turned, so that they faced each other.

"Now, I'm keen that you understand this next bit. *Stay out of politics.* I'm starting to get the idea that you're up to something, trying to out-maneuver me, trying to slip through any cracks in my advice. Don't.

"Your strange friends are nothing more than dreams. If they really did exist, I'd know where they were, and nobody else would. And if I thought you were trying to cause me trouble, one of them would cease to exist each time I became worried by you.

"Perhaps – let's say – there was somebody called Pavel Kirov. Ridiculous, I know, but let's pretend. Let's pretend that he was there, and then you worried me, and then he wasn't there. He's become a memory. *Less* than a memory." He released Chambers, and holding the empty cone over a bin, crushed it to dust.

He brushed his hands clean. "But he doesn't exist. Nor do the rest. Neither will you, if you don't listen. You've dropped out of view on Orchard once before; no one will be surprised if you do it again. Only next time you won't be coming back."

Alongside them, the car halted. A pair of uniformed policemen were sitting on their bikes at the end of the promenade, where the walkway joined the village street. Chambers glanced at them.

Blank Face laughed. "Forget it. People like that exist to control people like them." He waved a hand in the general direction of the shoppers on the street. "People like me exist to control people like you. We work to different rules." He walked to the waiting car, climbed in, and was driven away.

Oddly, Chambers felt hopeful. *You will not destabilize our world? Sod you.* The defiance was feeble, but it was also heartening. He didn't want to break cover and attract Blank Face's attention once again. But he could do this: the Orchard story *would* come good, and he might even live through it. He walked back to his new best buddy, the supercilious bike.

So long as he didn't touch politics, he'd hoped that the police wouldn't care about him nosing around in local economics. He'd obviously been wrong; there had to be a connection between the security interest, all this sudden wealth, the huge upsurge in production, the new seas, and whatever had happened to Richter and Arden and the others. If they were connected, then of course the spooks would be interested. And that had to take him right back to whatever they'd found out in the deep wide black.

"Take me home," he told the bike.

Chapter 38
Interest Criteria

"Anger is never without reason, but seldom with a good one."

– BENJAMIN FRANKLIN, 1706-1790.

Chambers studied the alien that had almost killed him. The commanding lizard – it had to be, the other ones had clearly been following its lead – was staring straight into camera Unit One. When was this? He didn't remember giving the camera any such instruction.

Drool was splashing on the ground. The beast's huge jaw dropped open and shifted down and rearwards, a move he doubted any Earth creature could make. The beast must have been watching prey. This readiness to pounce would be a universal carnivore behavior.

But instead, it was studying Unit One. After a moment, it raised one of those bayonet claws and batted the little machine away. The camera turned slightly as it pulled back, and showed Chambers a view of himself, huddled in the ditch. Oblivious to the danger, he was facing away from the alien. Weeks later, light years away, the lizard was dead and Chambers was recuperating well, but the blood went chilly in his veins. He'd never known this was happening.

On the vid's audio track, he heard an engine, recognized the sound of the armored walking machines, and placed the scene in his mind's eye. He had been hiding in the gully while Richter's team prepared their ambush, looking down as the armored column passed beneath him.

The camera turned back to the lizard. The thing stared at Chambers' still-vulnerable back, and abruptly slithered away into the undergrowth. Once again, he forgot to breathe. The lizard had been behind him, observing him, assessing what he was doing and what the combat vehicles might do. It had been watching him, and thinking about what it was seeing, and he hadn't known it was there.

An animal would have seized the chance, and he would have been dead. The lizard-creature had encountered something new to it, and had decided to learn more. Then it had stepped away from a situation which it didn't fully understand, from an opportunity which a mere carnivore would have exploited immediately. The savage intelligence chilled him.

△ △ △

Now he saw another view of his own body, this time bleeding on the medevac platform. This time, he was just another battle casualty to Unit One. Plenty of war reporters had got a little too close to the action; the machine was bound to pay attention to the injury and possible death of its operator. One of its interest criteria was *injured subject*, and he qualified.

Now he could look dispassionately at his blood soaking into the jacket, the gouge carved through his body armor, the heaving of his damaged chest. A needle arched above him; swabs and clamps waited to pounce. Unconscious, ribs broken, his chest ripped open by ten-inch claws. The camera watched him as if those were the only problems he faced.

He knew he was lucky that the troopers had even bothered to drag him away from the lizard, but the wounds had been the least of his problems. As well as managing to keep breathing, he had urgently needed to get away from this planet where the invading NipponDeutsch forces cared nothing about him, and where the outnumbered defenders at best thought him an inconvenience. If he'd stayed on Harmony, sooner or later he would have ended up in somebody's jail, and then death would have been a real possibility. Reporters weren't ever truly welcome in war zones. Governments became even keener to control the news.

But now that he'd stayed alive, and now that he'd found somewhere to run to, this government didn't give a damn about his story. No, worse than that. If he spoke out, he'd be eliminated. He'd been spun, all right, and now he was being sidelined.

Somewhere in his reports and videos, he might find the answer. What the hell had Semyonov been up to?

△ △ △

"They knew what they were doing. No one lied to them. They realized the risks they were taking." Semyonov's voice; firm, self-certain. He wasn't used to disagreement.

"They were psychologically very far removed from any definition of humanity... they have no continuous and uninterrupted personality... there is a limit to what we, as a species, consider acceptable modifications to the human form..."

No, that wasn't it. It hadn't been words. He'd seen something on the ARTOK habitat.

... images of ARTOK projects projected on the walls...

... a simulacrum's head snapping around to face a data display...

... bodies growing in gel-filled tubs...

... something sobbing inside a crate...

All wrong. Weird, unnerving, but not what he was thinking about.

... a group with identical faces, men and women around twenty years old, moving like the gears in a machine... each figure sitting where it was directed...

Where were this lot off to?

Clones.

That was it.

△ △ △

So Bloody Orchard

It had been such a stupid simple thing, and so Orchard. Petra had been staying with a friend, letting her anger with him cool like it had cooled so many times. She wasn't even in Bytham, but further up the curve at Bridgford, and they'd been sharing a taxi to work one morning, Petra and her childhood friend Paola. *Petra and Paola*; they used to sing it like a little jingle.

He could hear her voice as clearly as if she was there with him.

△ △ △

The autotaxi had slowed down to cross the tracks on the outskirts of the village, just in front of the station. There weren't so many places where you had to do that, but Orchard village stations almost always had road crossings nearby. Then an automatic load hauler had turned onto the narrow village road, dragging a cargo pod towards the railhead like they did a hundred times a day.

Their taxi had given way, because their stupid machine brains weren't bright enough to know that people were more important than loads of vegetables, and it had backed up to a wider point; backed up until it was straddling the tracks again, and another taxi had pulled up close behind it.

She'd not noticed at first, she was so busy laughing with Paola. They laughed a lot; he remembered how excluded he used to feel. But at some point, she'd noticed that they weren't going anywhere, and then she'd noticed that they were still sitting across the railway tracks.

△ △ △

Their idiot taxi had just locked up, right there in the middle of the tracks, its brain frozen solid with conflicting demands. They weren't terribly bright; they didn't usually need to be. There were only so many places to go on Orchard, and it wasn't too hard for a taxi brain to know all the likely variations.

She'd looked up along the tracks and seen the train while it was still about a kilometer away. They'd tried the doors, rattling the handles and pressing the window buttons. But the doors were locked shut, because all the taxi's meagre brain space had been given over to solving this conundrum, and it must have thought that it was about to move off again.

Paola had been screaming, but Petra had tried to solve it. Dave-O would know what to do. He was good at solving problems. Her phone agent was fast and determined, and she would have known that it still had priority access to him. However angry he was, he'd never cancel that.

△ △ △

Chambers heard her shouting for him and came into the lounge at a run. Her phone agent was there in the center of the room, and Petra was leaning forward out of a seat, eyes wide with fright. She was rattling something, shaking something that the phone agent wasn't showing him, throwing her entire bodyweight into fighting whatever it was.

"Dave-O! What do we do? The bloody doors are jammed. What do we *do*?" Behind her voice he could hear someone crying, and realized that it was Paola.

"Where are you? What's happening?" He hadn't spoken to her properly for days, and here she was in trouble. "What do you want me to do?"

"Dave-O. The doors are..."

She turned to look over her shoulder behind her, at something out of his sight. Her hair flicked around her face as she screamed. The phone agent froze in place.

The image hung there in mid-air in the middle of the lounge, then broke into fragments which faded away, one after another, until all he could see was a lock of her hair. A moment of her scream, not more than a second, repeated and repeated in a loop, fading to silence.

△ △ △

The train's control unit had tried quite hard to avoid the collision, but its distance judgement had been just a little out, and it had come to a careful halt two meters past the crossing.

So stupid, so avoidable in any well-resourced habitat where the road and rail network was up to the job. So bloody Orchard.

If, back then, the government had spent a fraction of what they were spending now on infrastructure ... He couldn't complete the thought.

Chapter 39

Frosty Windows

"Zulf. You said, 'I'd no idea that people ate so much.' That's what you said. Do you remember?"

"Yes, I think so. Something like that, at any rate. Why?"

"How much *do* people eat?" Chambers flicked a finger against his slate. "In kilograms, or pallets, or shiploads, I mean? Whatever units are best."

"I'm not with you." Zulfikar looked at him. "What are you getting at?"

Chambers realized that he was getting frustrated, which wouldn't help. He made himself slow down, and tried again. "You said that things really took off once you started the business. Mostly fruit and vegetables and other foodstuffs, you said. If you're moving that much food, who's eating it?"

"I haven't a bloody clue! I sell space for loads, and I move thousands of tons. I'm not some kind of dietician. How the hell do I know who's eating it? What's this about?"

"It's about where all that food is going. It could tell us something about what the companies are up to. Where is it all routed to?" *The first rule of journalism: governments lie. But what are they lying about?* "Where's the money coming from, and where are your loads going?"

Zulfikar was silent for a moment. "I send it to the transfer point, mostly. Some of it stays in the system, but most it goes out to the point, and then it goes down-route. Centauri, Cygni, Epsilon Indi, just as I said. Some of it goes to the Parnassus–Harmony system, I suppose. Is that any help?"

Chambers wasn't sure. "I think I'm on to something. But what I need to know is how much goes where, once it has left the system. How would I do that?"

"I don't think you can. All that information will be held by ARTOK. Their Orchard operation is more like an enclave. Physically private, and locked down tightly. If you think Orchard security is a little heavy, you should see theirs. I don't see how you can get your answer."

"I do." The avatar's voice crackled from the air, but there was no image accompanying it. "Point me there, and I'll find it out."

Zulfikar shrugged. "How would you be able to do that?"

"Because of what I am now. I wouldn't expect you to understand, but Chambers is right about this much. I've discovered that I can move around the data world easily, like you can feel your way around your house in the dark. I can't see much detail, but I can tell what things are by their shapes and by where I am. Some things are easy enough to make out."

"Like what?"

"Like this: Rahman Logistics didn't turn a profit until it had been trading for three years. Your capital was practically gone before it all came good, and you played things close with your taxes for a year or two. You're planning to delay the payments on the new orbital tugs you've ordered once you've paid the deposits, because your supplier messed you around on the last leasing agreement. And your largest customer, ARTOK, wants to buy you out, and you're thinking about letting them. You don't know why they want to, but the money's very tempting. Believe me yet?" The image returned in full strength.

Zulfikar stared at the avatar, then laughed. "I paid a lot of money for my data security structures. I suppose you could tell me exactly how much. So, data man, you can get into very secure and private records. But are you able to get through ARTOK's defenses?"

"I think I am. When I'm looking at data, I can see into a lot of it, like peering through frosty windows. If I try hard enough, I can make out all the details, but very slowly. It's like turning heavy pages, covered in blurred writing. ARTOK's stuff should be hard, but not impossible. I reckon I'm in with a chance.

"If there's a physical disconnect between the Orchard dataweb and ARTOK's structures, I'll need help bridging that gap. But get me anywhere near ARTOK's enclave and point me at their systems, and I'll get you the data."

Chapter 40
Data From Noise

*"Our main business is not to see what lies dimly at
a distance, but to do what lies clearly at hand."*

– THOMAS CARLYLE

"It's there, all right. On the other side of that access cover there's a fiber splice. It must be one of the oldest pieces of kit in the whole of Orchard, and it looks like it. It's been there since the place was built."

The weaselly little man on the car's rear seat was wriggling around, consulting a slate he was holding below the window sill. Keeping his hand low, he wagged a finger towards the corridor bulkhead. Chambers stared, but failed to see anything significant.

"Got it," the avatar's voice whispered in his ear. Once again, the being was invisible.

The Nepalese security man turned around from the car's front seat. "Sir. There it is. Underneath the light tubing, there is a run of trunking. Please look where it bends. The connection is next to that."

Chambers spotted it. The panel was two meters above the corridor floor. Half covered by overlapping layers of ancient paper posters, it was etched with specifications and logos, and completely anonymous.

"Don't stare at it! I don't want to be seen anywhere near here." Chambers glanced at their guide. The man was sweating. The car windows had polarized; from outside, they would be completely black.

"There aren't many places where the ARTOK grid is accessible from the Orchard dataweb. That's one of the service access points. I think it's the best chance you've got. I don't know what the hell you're trying to do, but that's the link you're looking for.

"Now let's get away. I'm a dead man if ARTOK security find out I'm here. Your boss isn't paying me anything like enough for this."

"I'm gone," a voice whispered, and Chambers felt something leave. The security man faced front again, and the silent car moved off along the corridor.

Δ Δ Δ

The avatar of Leon Richter hung motionless in a vast and simplified world. Zeroes and ones, on and off, positive and negative, true and false; around it, meaningless walls of data stretched to infinity. The blocks of information reached in monotonous waves upwards, downwards and from side to side. The avatar's horizons were unlimited spans of bits and bytes. For all its earlier confidence, this massive volume was daunting.

The avatar had come to awareness in Orchard's dataweb. The storage medium was colossal; it knew Orchard to be the physical size of a German *landkreis* or an English rural county, and the data requirements of a million people, thousands of businesses, and the habitat itself were huge. The information world of Orchard was terrifying.

The avatar didn't understand its own existence, but its former experience and training as a soldier had taught it how to fear for its life. This time, it wasn't running from an ambush after walking into an enemy's killing zone, or curling up in a fire trench while a storm of artillery filled the air overhead with jagged steel. Nothing so overt. On Orchard, it had been leading the existence of a fugitive in enemy territory, slipping between checkpoints, dodging patrols and searching for the dead ground beneath observation towers. The habitat felt like a vast occupied land, with a million hostile eyes searching for it.

But ARTOK's data expanse dwarfed little Orchard's domestic concerns. Mere agricultural yields, logistics information, and banking data occupied much of the Orchard web. This ARTOK configuration seemed big enough to contain all human knowledge since the creation of writing. It was an impassable chaos of structure. The avatar could see no way of moving through it.

But it had a job to do. Chambers needed this information. This might be the missing piece that would tell them what ARTOK was up to, but it had even more to do. Somewhere in this mass of data, there might be something which would reveal what had happened to Leon Richter and the others.

Dusty memories were stirring. Nearly a century and a half earlier, *Jäger* Leon Richter had been in the Sarawak jungle. Wiry little Ibans had shown him how to move in that hostile environment; which plants might harm him, which might be eaten, and which provided shelter.

They had studied tactical movement, patrolling, attack, and ambush; and they had practiced tracking, avoiding or killing enemy scouts, and disrupting larger units. Richter had learned why you carried short-barreled rifles and flechette guns, and why ancient shotguns were much deadlier than modern laser weapons in secondary jungle. A soldier should fear claymores in clearings, and *pangi* sticks in streambeds. A patrolling unit should always reverse direction and ambush its own trail before settling down for the night.

Much of what he had learned had consisted of the same lesson in different forms: how to filter data from noise. The avatar of Leon Richter recalled that lesson as it stared at the ARTOK data structures. Without care, this vast mass of information would overwhelm it; it couldn't organize this chaos into meaningful structure. There were threats here; the avatar needed to ambush its own trail.

There were walls, blocks, cones, and pyramids. Formless piles loomed above deep chasms. Shapes were stacked on shapes, reaching far beyond perception. Waves of transformation shimmered through the structure as ones became zeroes, as charges reversed.

Abruptly, the avatar felt a hint of uneasiness. Something was moving through the datascape. A formless and threatening presence, a flickering roll of change, was advancing on it, interrogating the data as it came. Whatever it was, the avatar of Leon Richter had no desire to meet it.

The avatar's perceptions shifted for a moment as the forms around it switched position. The threat was closing in. Data was resolving itself into new shapes, like a rockfall in...

... mountains.

And Leon Richter had been at home in mountains since he was a teenager. You might meet wolves or lynxes or bears in the mountains, but he had long known what to do if he did.

Now the avatar understood how to perceive this world, and how to survive in it.

Chapter 41

Ekishi

*"Weapons are an important factor in war, but not
the decisive one; it is man and not materials that
counts."*

– MAO ZEDONG.

The avatar of Leon Richter flickered into existence in David Chambers' kitchen, while he was scribbling notes on his slate. "Are you ready for this, Chambers?" The scratchy voice had returned. "I think I'll need to keep a closer eye on you from now on. In the last three days, someone's been tinkering with the software of the emergency safety pod in your apartment. I've fixed it, but don't go in there, not for any reason."

"What? The safety pod? No one on Orchard believes we'll ever need those. We're not going to have an atmosphere breach." Then he thought of the wrecked ARTOK hab. "Anyhow, I just keep beer and old junk in mine."

"I know. The door auto controls and the atmosphere maintenance system were jiggered. You'd be locked in, and the air would gradually go. That was a deliberate attempt to kill you. Don't go in there. Forget your beer."

"So Blank Face is going to be overt about it, is he?" Chambers had suspected that this moment would come.

"Funny you should mention him. There's something more, which I know you're going to be interested in."

"What? Something else to do with Blank Face?"

"He's supposed to be working for the Orchard government, isn't he? But his loyalty lies elsewhere." The avatar's tone was contemptuous.

"Do you mean ARTOK? I could have guessed that." It didn't surprise Chambers. Zulf had said as much about Orchard's public servants. "Half of our establishment is in ARTOK's pocket."

"Well, ARTOK might think so, and he's definitely taking money from them, but he's working even deeper than that. It explains what's happened to my people, and why he wants to silence you." The avatar's audio quality was getting worse, as if rage was making it harder to speak.

"God. What the hell is it?"

"Look at this." The avatar gestured a screen into existence. It showed Blank Face talking to somebody out of view. The audio quality was little better than the avatar's, but Chambers would have recognized the interrogator's voice anywhere.

"...the man is getting to be a pest. He dropped out of sight for years, so no one will be surprised if he does it again. I can deal with that. He's just another journalist. But the government isn't the problem, it's ARTOK. They're outraged about their habitat wheel. As I'm your *ekishi*, believe me when I say that they'll make us pay at some point, but right now they don't want the exposure any more than we do..." The image faded out.

Chambers looked at the avatar. "Who was he talking to? And what was that – *ekishi?*"

"I found this in Orchard's security files. Much of it was deleted, but this bit might have been missed. It was on a security camera in the government offices. I can't see who he met, but I think he's working for NipponDeutsch. And *ekishi* is a Japanese expression for a trusted messenger." The avatar's voice was calmer now. "It makes sense. It would explain a lot."

Chambers started pacing about his kitchen. "Well, it puts a new light on things. We're seeing hints about where they're shipping all that food. And if an Orchard security policeman is pocketing ARTOK money, but taking orders from NipponDeutsch, then there's something very dirty going on. That could be a reason for doing away with anyone who knows what's behind the NipponDeutsch invasion of Harmony.

"Right, I think we've got enough to start telling people about this. Richter, Zulfikar tells me that the *Kiev* will reach Orchard in a week or so. If I can put the story together, could you find a way to get it onboard?"

Chapter 42
Going Off Route

Zulfikar Abdul Rahman grabbed Chambers' arm and pulled him aside as the auto tug dragged its trailers towards the loading doors. A sign warned of hard vacuum beyond. "So what exactly are you proposing?" The businessman had to shout to make himself heard.

The loading docks clanged and roared with activity. They walked on, along endless racking aisles and pod stacks. This was nothing like the docks Chambers remembered; they had been dirty, broken-down, decrepit and usually half-deserted. This operation was new, slick, well-equipped and thoroughly active.

Rahman Logistics was evidently a major player. Zulfikar was constantly greeted by busy-looking people. The avatar faded in and out of visibility as its mood dictated.

Chambers tried to pitch his voice to be discreet. "Richter tells me you've a load leaving for Earth on the *Kiev*, when she docks sometime next week. We'd like to put a package on it."

Walking a few meters behind them were the minders, an Asian man and a white woman, each with an air of expensive and dangerous competence. Zulfikar's escorts had been everywhere with him for the last few days. They had seemed no more than professionally curious about the sketched outline of the avatar, certainly not alarmed. In turn, Richter's avatar had circled around them like a bloodstock buyer studying a possible purchase, then nodded something like approval.

A woman called down to them from a high gantry. Zulfikar waved back at her, smiling, and shouted an enquiry about her family. She laughed and raised both thumbs, then stepped through a doorway and out of sight. He turned his attention back to Chambers. "Okay, I'm getting used to you two knowing about things it should be impossible for you to know. What would this package be? A dead alien? A cyborg? A miracle weapon? Let me guess – whatever it is, you don't want it on the manifest."

The avatar's head bloomed into near-solidity in front of them. Its body had disappeared. "This thing won't be on any manifest, and it won't be found either. You won't notice it, the *Kiev* won't notice it, and it won't weigh anything, cost anything, or break anything. Now, Rahman, yes or no?"

Zulfikar turned to face Chambers. "Your partner needs to learn a lot about negotiations. Tell me why I should do this, please. The business is doing well, the habitat's pleasant, and I'm comfortable. I'm a little bored, perhaps, but I'm not on the point of pissing off ARTOK just for a laugh."

"I don't think that's likely, Zulf. Richter's right; ARTOK would never know about it. But let's leave it for the moment. I want to talk to you about something else."

"Mixing with you two is interesting. By the way, when did you start calling your odd partner 'Richter'? Does that mean you're satisfied that it's a person? Or have you given up on finding the real man?"

The avatar's face blazed like a sun, throwing brilliant beams of white light across the entire dock and casting the far sides of the towers of goods into deep shadow. The security woman was instantly at Zulfikar's side, a hand inside her short jacket.

"Don't even think about that, either of you. I *will* find myself, and as for whether I'm human, which of us seems to give a damn about the threat we face? I'll get this message out to the entire human race, with you or without you. And if you shirk that duty, what does that make *you*? Human, or something else?"

The golden orb circled around them, Richter's enraged features faintly visible through the glare. It accelerated away down the dock, gaining height as it went, and vanished through the bulkhead into the hard vacuum beyond. They watched it go, hands up to protect their sight. Purple after-images danced in Chambers' eyes. His heart thudded from the confrontation.

Along the dock, people were staring at them. Zulfikar took Chambers by the sleeve, and together they stumbled, half-blind, along a goods aisle and through a doorway. The minders trotted with them effortlessly, the woman alongside them and the man following. Their hands were empty, but for a second each had been pointing a weapon at the blazing avatar. Neither had seemed surprised by the incident.

They emerged in a corridor of offices; they could have belonged to any sort of business. Zulfikar led Chambers into an unoccupied room. The Nepalese bodyguard swept his eyes around the little office, nodded at Zulfikar, then stepped outside to join his partner.

"He's not going to remain covert very long if he keeps doing that, is he?" But Zulfikar's voice sounded shaken. "Go on. What did you want to talk about?"

Chambers had almost forgotten, and took a moment to collect himself. "You know we've been all over the data. For the last few days Richter and I have been talking about what he found, and what it tells us. I'm not going to apologize; we needed to be sure who we're dealing with.

"Richter turned up references to ARTOK places called Forward Station One, Two and Three, and so on. I've never heard of them, and they don't seem to match with anywhere. They're far beyond human space, way out in the black. I'm guessing that the mysterious ARTOK hab that NipponDeutsch destroyed was one of them.

"Zulfikar, you're using ARTOK load space on *Kiev* or the *Boyar Duma* or whatever to shift huge amounts of food, machinery and parts. But you've also put loads onto the NipponDeutsch ships *Sakichi Toyoda* and *Guderian*. When did NipponDeutsch and ARTOK get so friendly that they're going to the same places with each other's cargoes? Zulf, they're at war with each other on Harmony, and we know that NipponDeutsch has destroyed at least one ARTOK hab. Maybe they've returned the favor. It makes no sense.

"If you study the coordinates of the ARTOK habs, you'll see they're spread out in a jagged line. Remember the ancient alien fleet? It went somewhere, and I think both companies have been following it. It's like some kind of hostile truce."

Zulfikar leaned against a desk, and stared at him. Chambers went on.

"What it adds up to is this: you're hauling Orchard foodstuffs, and the bills of lading add up to very substantial quantities. The amount of food you've been moving exceeds the population ARTOK claims to be sending it to, by quite a margin, and it's going to covert places far out in the black. Zulfikar, over the past year, Orchard has fed nearly 100,000 people who shouldn't exist. But I know ARTOK can breed clones, and God knows what NipponDeutsch can do."

Zulfikar's eyes were boring into him. "Do you realize what you're saying?"

He thought of Blank Face, and his warnings to stay out of politics. "Yes, I do. I know exactly what I'm saying. And I want everyone else to know about it."

Chapter 43
The Incomparable Mullah Nasruddin

*"The great and honorable Nasruddin never
showed his face at his own banquet."*
– "THE SECOND BANQUET," FROM THE OUTRAGEOUS WISDOM OF
NASRUDDIN.

They hung on the underside of the world. The craters of inverted hills swam by overhead, surrounded by hectares of machinery, pipe work and ducting; that smooth flat mound had to be the sea bed.

The Incomparable Mullah Nasruddin was actually a fair-sized vessel, just not quite what Chambers had been expecting. There was accommodation for seven or eight in reasonable comfort, if not in any kind of luxury. There was also a considerable amount of load space, which he couldn't figure out at all. His host just laughed.

"It isn't a yacht, it's light haulage. I'm doing all right, but I'm not in that league. You and your electric buddy have made yourselves so at home in my accounts that you ought to know that. And this thing isn't mine, it's on lease."

He straightened the cuffs of his neat coverall, and tinkered with the ponytail which had so alarmed Chambers. For a moment, he'd thought it was a plait, which took him back to the street in Mabuza and brought the fear pouring in again. "I can't afford to have an asset on the books that doesn't work for a living. So I use all the space and delta-V that I've got to haul loads. Hold on now."

A rumble grew from deep in the structure. *The Incomparable Mullah Nasruddin* edged into the black.

△ △ △

"He started his braking run above and beyond Rostam. An eyeballs-out dive through the ecliptic, fast loop around the planet, dodge the Twins, and straight through the Bowling Alley. So smooth it glistens. Got to say it: ARTOKkers can do the deed." Chambers hardly understood a word, but Zulfikar Abdul Rahman's pilot was evidently an enthusiast.

The *Kiev* was invisible to the naked eye. At maximum magnification, the vessel was just distinguishable from billions of hard points of light. Orchard was far behind them now, a silver ring against the black. On the flight deck of the *Mullah Nasruddin*, Zulfikar studied the displays. "Is she still on schedule for docking, Andy? I don't want to be hanging around."

"He'll be there, boss. You have to say 'he'; it's a Russian ship. Large as life, turning and burning. Snd so will we. Synchronized and slick."

Zulfikar slipped out of the seat and glided through the bulkhead aperture. Chambers followed, bashing his hip against the rim. In the living space, the security woman Arnott alternated between studying the environment status displays and watching the external monitors. She rested silently against a wall, knees bent, ready to launch herself. Chambers had seen her in the same position two hours before. She seemed incapable of boredom. No weapons were in evidence, but he had little doubt there was something lethal within easy reach. Rai, the Nepalese security man, was off-shift and resting, so she had the space to herself.

Reaching the office space, Zulfikar closed the privacy door behind them. He didn't waste any time. "The *Kiev* will be there, David. Are you sure you want to do this?"

"What else can we do? We've got to get the message out, and I can't see any other way. Anyway, I should be the one asking you that. Have I shown you enough to convince you?"

They had spent hours studying Chambers' slate, and the avatar's data. At first, Zulfikar had been doubtful, almost scornful. But Chambers had worn him down, and gradually his attitude had shifted. *Why wouldn't ARTOK and NipponDeutsch want us to know about those lizards? When were these covert stations established? How has Orchard gained 100,000 new customers out in the black? What have the companies found out there?*

And, since the avatar's latest discoveries in the ARTOK dataweb:

What have we learned about the Orchard security police? Who are they working for? The Orchard Government, ARTOK, or NipponDeutsch?

"You realize they might kill us if this doesn't work? Or even if it does?" Chambers nodded. He was sure of that. "But you're right, David. We've got to do it. Your package is the best shot we've got."

Chapter 44
Without Loss Or Corruption

He never gave commandment for their death...
...Since you from the Polack wars, and you from England
Are here arrived, give order that these bodies
High on a stage be placed to the view
And let me speak to the yet unknowing world
How these things came about.

– HAMLET, ACT V, SCENE II.

"Couriers to the mailroom, please." It was always the first pipe when a ship went contiguous, which meant that the couriers had less time than anyone else to get over the nausea and to stop throwing up. The anti-nausea drug regimens made for sleepiness; the people who audited the data transfers had to be highly alert to validate the departure of the mails, so they had to do without. But ARTOK courier Marianna Park had never evaded the queasiness.

The diplomatic courier needed to be the first to reach the mailroom. It would take the ARTOK starship *Kiev* weeks to lose enough of his speed to dock with the Transfer Point. Park had learned early in her career that Russian vessels were presumed to be male. While his 12,000-plus tons of cargo could be of no use to his customers for a long time yet, his data package had economic and political value. Knowing about gluts and scarcities could make or lose fortunes. Marianna Park had a job to do.

Earth's sun was a hard-bright point in the black, indistinguishable from a billion billion others. In this intense and lonely cold, the clockwork whirling of the great galaxies above and below the lens seemed like an optimistic myth.

The Orchard governmental communications took priority even over the company's own data; that was the official position, and Park had to ensure that it was observed. There was always only so much bandwidth, and ARTOK had its own commercial relationships to consider; centuries of careful growth could be wrecked by a reckless release of critical information. Its own welfare was of paramount importance to the company, so she followed firmly-established procedures.

She would release a package of heavily encrypted information on arrival into the system's contiguous space, and many of the package's contents would only be made public after careful analysis in Moscow. Time was rarely pressing for the purely commercial data; the information could be sifted through, weighed and considered, and an approved version put on general release long before the ship itself docked.

317 separate stellar observations were carried out by the *Kiev's* onboard navigational devices to eliminate the various potential errors which might result from reflected sunlight, aberrations in the optical instruments, false returns from gas vented from the attitudinal thrusters, or a hundred other potential causes. Once she was satisfied that the *Kiev* knew where it was, Park authorized the signaling package to shake hands with the ARTOK deep-space array on Luna.

The response was rapid, taking slightly more than twenty-five hours for receipt of the handshake and the first packets of data. Acknowledgement was sent immediately. Information began to flow. The *Kiev* hurtled on.

The data was extensive and complex, as usual. Standardized protocols separated the elements into their appropriate groups and diverted the data to its expected recipient systems. The process was well established; it had multiple redundancy, as befitted a risk-averse mega-corporation, and so it worked perfectly every time. Corporate, client, general commercial and governmental information transited smoothly between the solar systems without data loss or corruption.

But this time something highly unusual happened.

Chapter 45
The Type For Violence
Orchard, Sunday 25th December 2450

The batsman went onto his back foot and drove hard for deep square leg. The Penty crowd loved it, shouting and singing as the ball slipped neatly past the fielder and away for a useful four. The Ancaster First Eleven's fielding was getting ragged. Cricket continued below the whirling stars much as it had done for centuries.

Chambers sat back and sipped his redbush tea. It was hard to be certain, but they thought today would be the day. In a swirl of robes, Zulfikar entered the lounge and made himself comfortable on the settee. Rai followed, carrying a cup of cheff, which he handed to his principal before settling down on a corner stool, as unremarkably at ease as a man sunning himself on a park bench in his lunch break. He sipped at a glass of water and glanced at the match.

"Are we kidding ourselves? Does it need to be coordinated like this? What does it matter if it happens here today, and on Earth yesterday, and on Parnassus tomorrow?" Zulfikar was sniffing at the cheff as he spoke. "By the way, I think this stuff could be huge."

"It's all about the impact. Getting the message out here doesn't mean much if Earth and everywhere else don't know a thing about it. If it happens everywhere at the same time, it's that much harder to stop it spreading, or to deny it." It didn't matter, and he thought they both knew it. Getting the story out to the whole human race – that was what mattered. They were talking more to stop themselves thinking about what might go wrong, than to tell each other anything new. They'd been over this a hundred times.

"What day is it on Earth?"

"December the twenty-fifth, Christian festival of Christmas."

Zulfikar stared upwards, calculating something. "You're joking. Rai? What is the date in your home?"

The man raised his head and smiled, still radiating calm. "The same day in the month of Thin lā, sir, 1570, according to the Nepal Samvat calendar." Zulfikar nodded acknowledgement.

"What's on your mind?" Chambers couldn't see where he was going with this.

"You told me enough about those mercenaries to interest me, so I've been reading about them, and thinking a lot about their beliefs. I worked it out after we put the package on the *Kiev*, and I couldn't get over the coincidence. In Rome, this day was the festival of *Sol Invictus*, the Undefeated Sun, and today is Sunday."

The door to the apartment swung back with a thud, and Chambers leaped to his feet, but Rai was already there. The Nepalese had left his chair and crossed the room before Chambers could take even a step forward. He was standing with his hands crossed in front of him, blocking the entry of a dark-suited man. Blank Face.

Behind him were two uniformed cops, visors down but still transparent. One was removing a device from the lock on the door frame. Blank Face placed his hand against Rai's chest and pushed. He swayed, but didn't move. The policeman's eyes narrowed.

"Right then, sir. Let's move aside, shall we, or do I have to get physical about this?" The cop behind him raised a weapon, an unpleasant looking collection of coils and rods; the absence of any kind of barrel gave it a peculiar menace. Rai glanced at it but remained motionless.

"Thank you, Mr. Rai, it's all right. I'll deal with this." Chambers didn't know what he was going to do but, short of violence, he didn't see how the security man could help.

Rai stepped aside and allowed Blank Face and his officers to pass. The policeman looked at him, at the seated Zulfikar, and then back at Chambers.

"So, David, you've found yourself some friends. Mr. Rahman: I'm disappointed to see you in this man's company. Girindra Rai: I don't like you, and I admit that I didn't expect to find you here, either. Be so good as to remove *all* your weapons, extremely slowly, and place them on the carpet. Then step away, also slowly, and turn your back on us."

A roar of approval came from the screen; voices called out "howzat!"

Rai gave a curt nod and, unbuttoning his jacket, divested himself steadily of a transparent ceramic pistol, a telescopic metal tube about twenty centimeters in length, a dagger apparently made from glass, a coil of wire, a kukri, and what appeared to be two slabs of soft green clay. A pair of small pistols were added, one from each sock. Chambers and the uniformed officers were hypnotized by the growing pile of potential mayhem. The match played on, ignored, as Rai put his fingers into his mouth and very carefully tugged out a tooth. He placed the gleamingly white object on top of the pile of weapons.

"The collar, Rai?" Blank Face wasn't satisfied.

The Nepalese stared at him for a moment, then raised both hands to his neck and pulled a length of smooth springy steel from the neckline of his jacket. He flexed it, and placed a razor-edged miniature sword on top of the pile.

Rai turned his back on the police officers and walked towards the wall. "Do not touch those items, sirs. You might hurt yourself quite severely." He stood unmoving, facing the lounge window. Beyond him the sea lapped at the shoreline; children's voices rose from the strip of beach.

The cops kept their gaze fixed on Rai as he disarmed himself. Blank Face ignored them. "Right then, David. I've had enough of you prowling around the world, poking your nose into things that don't concern you. It's time you dropped out of sight again; I did warn you repeatedly. You're coming with us. Mr. Rahman, I strongly advise you to leave this business well alone. Whatever this man has told you is unreliable."

"And if I do not?" Zulfikar rose to his feet, dominating the room by sheer mass. He stepped towards the agent.

Blank Face held his ground. "What if your bankers heard serious allegations about your personal character? What if your government haulage contracts dried up? If undesirable things were to happen to your lines of credit? Licenses might be delayed. Visas and work permits for any foreign hires among your staff could be denied or revoked. The revenue department might become anxious about overdue taxes. Safety and regulatory compliance inspections might start to dig very deeply indeed. Rahman Logistics could find its trading and operating environment very hostile. Do I make myself clear?"

"So, *there* you are. I wondered when some sleazy spook would turn up." Chambers noticed that the big man was rocking on the balls of his feet. Rai, his back turned, remained almost motionless, his head tilted.

One of the uniforms crossed towards Chambers, leaving his partner by the door, and took him by the arm. Blank Face ran his gaze up and down Zulfikar, carefully noting his hands and eyes. "Rahman, Rai – stay still. David, come along."

"I'm not moving." He wanted to be firm, but it just sounded petulant, like a child refusing to go to bed when the adults wanted to talk.

"Don't be a fool. You can't prevent this; you're not the type for violence. I don't think you are, either, Mr. Rahman. Bring him."

The cop tightened his grip. There was a blur of movement and two faint popping sounds, almost close enough to sound like a single noise. The man holding Chambers' arm dragged on it and fell to his knees, then released him and collapsed. Across the room the second officer was falling against the door frame and sliding down it like a drunk, a hand pawing at his neck. He slumped to the floor, twitching and shaking.

Rai was standing with his arms outstretched, pointing at each man. There was something wrong with his hands. Chambers stared at him, uncomprehending, and realized that both of his middle fingers were missing beyond the knuckle. Small mechanisms protruded from the truncated digits. There was very little blood.

"Stop right there. Someone explain to me why I shouldn't kill him." Blank Face must have reached inside his jacket; the weapon was a twin of the device carried by the uniformed cop. It was pressing against Zulfikar's face; the flesh was pushed hard against the cheekbone. They were standing in the exact center of the lounge. The trader's nostrils were flaring and his eyes were boring back into the policeman's.

Blank Face's voice was tense. "Rahman, you're a fool too, which I didn't expect. Killing police officers is very stupid indeed. There's no way back from this. Rai – do nothing more, or I will kill your employer now. You know what this is."

The Nepalese lowered his arms. "I do. Sir, please be still. It's a neural tangle. The device disturbs physiological functions at a very basic level."

"Well put, Rai. Now, I'm known to be here, and others are on their way. Everyone calm down, and we'll all live through this. Unlike my officers, you bloody fool. Stay *still*, David." Chambers found that he had stepped forward. His hand was raised, stroking the empty air. He lowered it.

Rai raised his own empty hands, palms out, and moved quickly to the man who had been holding Chambers. Blank Face snarled, and ground the weapon into Zulfikar's cheek.

"They're not dead, and they won't be if I do *this*." Rai pulled at the tiny dart in the man's neck, reversed it, and drove it sharply back into the skin. "Regrettably I *am* the type for violence, but the nerve agent in these devices will only be fatal if the dart remains in the skin for a sustained period. Excuse the lecture, but the chemical agent's inhibition of acetyl cholinesterase is reversed by the biperiden-atropine mix in the auto-injector at the opposite end of the dart."

He straightened up and repeated the process with the other officer. "They will unfortunately be quite unwell for a little while, but they will recover in full." The shaking and trembling did seem to calm quite quickly.

The policeman grunted and nodded at the wall; Rai stood and returned to his previous position, back turned once more. Chambers felt a familiar and unwelcome tension at the violence. *A body lying in a street, a severed throat, a blazing vehicle, a lopsided screaming man.* He was still trying to grasp the speed with which the balance of power had shifted when he noticed the faint pattern of hazing in the air by the door.

"I know why you did this, and I know *what* you all did, you stupid idiot. I know what your precious companies were up to." He'd thought that he'd have to act it out, but now he found that the rage was sincere. Why hadn't they *seen*?

The policeman stared at him, nonplussed. "What are you talking about? You don't have the beginnings of a clue about anything, as far as I can see. Reporter? You? You've been too busy trailing around the galaxy after your pet monsters to notice the important things on Orchard. We're making money and we're improving the quality of life for millions. I would have thought someone with a tragic story like yours would want to see our world improved. You could tell that good news story, but for some reason people like you don't seem to like it."

Chambers' anger was intense enough to make speech difficult. "No. You're the one who's been chasing after monsters, literally. Your ARTOK boss, Semyonov, sent me to make friends with cyborgs, just in case he needed to make people accept them. Meanwhile, ARTOK and NipponDeutsch have had a cozy agreement for a century and a half to keep us all in the dark while they have a go at trading with aliens – aliens who might want to wipe out the entire human race." He saw that the agent's mouth had dropped open in surprise. "Are you all mad? Who said you could speak for the rest of us? Did you all have any idea about how dangerous this could be? And you did it all for profit, for your bottom line. How *dare* you think you have the right to do that?" His voice was shaking, but this time it was fury, not fear.

The tangle remained pressed into Zulfikar's cheek; Blank Face shook his head. "You're a complete fool, Chambers. I've tolerated you for long enough. No more. You've just committed suicide, and condemned these men with you. Girindra Rai will be no loss to humanity, but if Rahman here had been prepared to keep his mouth shut, I might have been minded to let him live. Now? No. *No one* may say those things, or hear them, and expect to survive."

It felt personal now. This undercover vermin was standing on the very spot where *she* had left him, and was threatening his life while doing it. It felt like a desecration.

Blank Face might not use the weapon on Zulfikar just yet; he'd have little fear of Chambers, but Rai was a threat to him. So he'd try to keep the situation under control until his reinforcements arrived. Then they'd be overwhelmed and they'd disappear back into the underground corridors, and this time he'd never emerge.

But behind Blank Face, the shape was becoming more defined as the air coalesced into the avatar's misty image. Chambers realized that they could still do it, still get the words out where they needed to be and survive, if he could only make the being understand. "How long do you think you can keep a lid on it? Once people understand what you've been doing, you're finished. They'll only have to hear about it, and it'll all unravel." Would the avatar get that?

"Long enough, Chambers, long enough. People aren't going to hear about it, not from you at any rate. You'll be history before any of this comes out, and by then we'll all be too used to the jobs and the money and the development to want to stop it. That's what you'd bring down – some economic success for this mediaeval backwater at last." The avatar nodded its translucent head, and its hands made a *keep it going* gesture.

"But he's right, isn't he?" Zulfikar's words were distorted by the pressure against his cheek, but he'd got it too, and his voice was angry. "It had to be trade. You did it, all of you; you all had some mad idea that the trading power of ARTOK and NipponDeutsch would just be irresistibly attractive to these aliens you've found, somewhere out in the black.

"You've been pushing out there for decades, trying to find their home world, and we've all been too distracted by our economy to notice. But now you've got hold of something, and you're using Orchard as a stepping stone to get there, and I've been busy supplying your push out into the black, pumping out food and machinery and supplies and giving you somewhere to build your ships. I'm through with making money from this."

Chambers let the contempt flood back into his voice. "And that's where ARTOK makes its specialist contribution, with all the farmed people it's sending out from its corporate habitats. They're the cannon fodder – workers and colonists, aren't they?" The policeman's eyes were flicking from side to side under the verbal onslaught. If they kept it going, maybe they could keep him off balance.

"And that accounts for the flight time that's missing from the logs of ARTOK ships. Your masters have been breeding those people for your new stepping stone colonies, haven't they? There's an old and ugly word for that. It's called slavery. Sleepy little Orchard is feeding your slaves. Making money out of this makes us slavers, too.

"Well, I've met some of those aliens you're trying to befriend, and they're dangerous murderous carnivores, and they're controlled by something even worse. Now they're going to come after us. And now that you've found the aliens' home, ARTOK and NipponDeutsch are going to sort out who gets to trade with them. Hence the secret war."

"Right, that's enough. Another word from any of you and you'll learn what a tangle feels like." The policeman swung it between his three targets. "Rai understands what this can do. You two don't want to know."

"I know what it can do, too." Blank Face spun around as the avatar's voice came from behind him. Chambers leaped forward, but Rai sprang past him, one hand going for the policeman's throat and the other for his wrist; the tangle fell to the floor. The bodyguard's foot kicked it aside.

"Get back from there, you bastard, get away!" Chambers found that he was shouting. "You cheapskate bastards killed my wife!" He tried to push Rai to one side so he could reach the policeman, but the Nepalese fended him off.

"No, sir. This is for me to do. But please remove the tangle." Chambers took the thing very gingerly and carried it away from the struggling men and into the kitchen.

The agent spoke as Rai loosened his grip. "So what is it? Am I your hostage now?" His voice was hoarse from Rai's crushing grip on his throat. "When the others get here, they won't worry about me. If you resist, they'll kill you, whether I get killed or not." He twisted to look at the avatar. "What is this thing?"

"Never mind what I am, Colonel Morozov." The man flinched. "It's what you are that matters. You're an agent of a deeply black Orchard government body that exists to control and eliminate political opposition." Morozov stared at the avatar as it floated in front of his face.

"But you're worse than that, Colonel Morozov. You're not just an agent of the state of Orchard at all, are you? You seem like one, but you're deeply enmeshed with the ARTOK company's security organization. Drawing two salaries, are you? Where does your loyalty lie? To be honest, that wasn't a hard conclusion to reach.

"But if you're an ARTOK man, why wouldn't you want the worlds to know about the NipponDeutsch attack on Harmony, or the destruction of an ARTOK hab? You ought to be desperate for that information to get out, but you'd like to hush it up.

"Then we found references to you which used the word *ekishi*, and we didn't know what that was. In Japan, that word once meant a trusted messenger for the government, someone who carries vital information and who must never be hindered. You're working for NipponDeutsch, aren't you? Triple agent, Colonel? How do you juggle all that?" The avatar's voice dripped contempt.

"You abducted and probably killed the foreign soldiers who fled here from your secret corporate war on Harmony. Orchard might not care about that, and ARTOK might not want those people dead, but NipponDeutsch would.

"But that's only the tip of the iceberg. You, the Orchard government, perhaps other governments, and both the ARTOK and NipponDeutsch companies – you're all involved in slavery, covert misuse of public money, maltreatment of prisoners, and illegal detention. You've personally threatened to kill David Chambers here if he continues investigating what the companies are doing. You're part of an interplanetary conspiracy to pursue a foreign policy that isn't supported by any elected government anywhere. You've decided to chase a fleeing alien species all the way to its home world. They might very well think that's a declaration of war."

Blank Face got it, nearly. "You're talking for the record, aren't you? Okay, so you've now got a card to play, all of you. I remember telling you a while ago that you had strange friends, David – cyborgs, mercenaries, and pagans, I think I said. You haven't got any better. Well, you and your odd pals have got a stake in the game, now. A recording like that could be worth something, I suppose, if you've had the wit to send it off securely to somewhere. What are you planning on doing with it? Let me guess – you want something, or else you'll release it? Open the bidding, then."

He must have been surprised by the laughter. Richter's avatar spoke for them all. "Now you're missing the point. It's already been released. You see the camera?" It gestured at the shelf in the corner, where Chambers' slate rested among a mixed pile of recording and data equipment. Rai forced Morozov's head round to Camera Unit

One. "Never mind what I am, but believe me when I say that I can influence equipment and data. Look at the match. Go on, turn around."

The mystified Blank Face studied the screen. On the big screens around the Penty ground, instead of the close-ups and slow-mo replays of the Twenty20 match, he could see his own face as he talked to Chambers and Zulfikar. People were looking up at it; the game had halted.

And Colonel Morozov heard the words, "*aliens – carnivores – people aren't going to hear about it – economic success – I might have let him live – cannon fodder – slavery –*" and he heard his own deeply covert name, and he heard all the level-voiced accusations of the avatar. He saw the crowd staring up at the huge images, and he saw the batsman taking off his gloves as he watched as well, and he heard the commentators fall silent, and he saw the confusion spread across the faces of the crowd, and he saw it followed by the anger.

Chambers picked it up. "Don't make another dumb mistake, Colonel. You can't even stop this by arresting the whole crowd. It's currently showing on every vid screen and slate in the system. Every single place where people see images, they're seeing this. Every bar and restaurant and college and school and anywhere people get onto the dataweb, there's nothing else showing but this, right now.

"And it's on every navigation screen. Whenever a ship arrives anywhere, they're seeing this all over their docks and bridges, and every passenger's screen and slate.

"Once all this is done, there's another statement telling the whole story about the aliens, and who this avatar is, and what we think you've done with the original man and his colleagues, and why you've done it. The story goes back two centuries, and people are going to watch it.

"The message has gone to Earth, and to Parnassus, and to Second Chance, and to Harmony and Epsilon Indi and Rheparion and all the rest.

"I think people need to know that humanity has met hostile aliens. What they do about it is up to them, not me; and it's certainly not up to you."

Chapter 46
Outside The Circle Of Firelight

*"Eventually, he is able to look at the stars and
moon at night."*

– THE ALLEGORY OF THE CAVE *(PLATO)*.

Chambers knew how it was going to work; the avatar had grossly oversimplified the process so that he could understand. The data stream had a complex series of self-check protocols, so it would take a very long time to satisfy itself that the package had been transmitted and received without error. But after a few seconds the routines would be complete, and the process could begin.

From the deep-space array, the signal would be re-transferred into the ARTOK base-to-space routine and general communication systems, the navigation and telemetry structures and the maintenance systems-checking network, and then it would piggyback onto the commercial services system.

A copy would infiltrate into the Greater Luna dataweb. From there it would spread across all the lunar surface and low-orbital systems. Even the most intensely secured commercial networks would receive it within fractions of a second.

In moments, it would expand onto L5. Duplicates of the data would make their way into the webs of Mars, the Jovian and Saturnian moons, and thousands of navigation and communication networks across the entire system.

The endless stream of data flowing between Earth and its moon would give the package a smooth and fast highway straight into the teeming mass of information that comprised humanity's oldest web. After five hours, a copy of the package would reach the Pluto-Charon pair.

By that time, the process would effectively have been completed within Sol system.

△ △ △

He learned later that the process hadn't quite been simultaneous. Interstellar ship movements were fast enough, but not quite frequent enough, for that. But over a period of around fifteen days, the data package spread throughout human space.

Jamming systems, virus checkers, and firewalls were simply bypassed. In all cases, the message was the same. Whether it was experienced on a private slate or on a public information screen, or in a bar as it overrode a sports channel; whether it appeared on commercial data access points or in public address screens; whether intruding into navigation systems or messaging services or entertainment channels: an unchanging message was presented to billions. It was always presented in the most prominent local language, although invariably it would be paralleled in an appropriate minority tongue on a nearby screen. Changing channels didn't help – it was everywhere.

There was a man, dressed in anonymously military clothing, looking trustworthy and unthreatening; an ordinary, pleasant-seeming and confident man who walked out of the screens and displays and looked at the viewer with frank urgency. It was clearly not an advertisement or a publicity stunt.

"My name is Leon Richter. I have something very important to tell you, and you must listen to it."

△ △ △

David Chambers noticed a tiny splash, and a faint plop. Concentric ripples expanded, and he wondered what could have fallen into his tea. Forgetting the slate and the story that just wouldn't come right, he frowned at the cup. Tea had stained the table top. It was quiet on the balcony, and the nearest overhead objects were more than 100 kilometers above him. He had no idea what could have caused it.

Then he felt something land softly in his hair, and a circular mark appeared on the table, and then another. There was a momentary sensation of cold wetness on his bare forearm, and on his shoulders, and more of the little marks appeared briefly before vanishing again. Another plop, and the tea rippled again.

Then it came faster and faster. He stood, and turned his face up to the sky, and let the soft rain hit him on the face and trickle down his arms, and he felt stupid. Of course, it was always going to happen once the seas had been filled, and once the mirrored sun had warmed the water for long enough. This was why there had been the haziness in the air.

All of Orchard had known that this would happen, everyone but him. His mind had been full of monsters and aliens and abduction and corporate exploitation and greed, and whether he could do anything about it. In the meantime, the seas had been filled and the fish had been introduced into the water, and the boats had started to travel up and down the curve. People were swimming, and boating, and soon they'd be fishing. Now it was raining, and his dad's world had been finished. Life was good.

No, sod it, it isn't. Don't be distracted by the bread and circuses. Don't lose the rage. Too much of it still wasn't anything like right. It wasn't enough that there was talk of congressional commissions and parliamentary enquiries and judicial reviews. That was just kicking it into the long grass. Morozov and a few of his cronies might have been flushed out from under the stones, and there was noise about a trading alliance between the small worlds, and Zulfikar had taken off for Parnassus looking into opportunities to invest in cheff, and the Euros and the Russians had at least reached a cease-fire agreement on Harmony – but it wasn't enough.

There was no sign yet of Richter and his men and women; they'd believed him, and he'd brought them here to Orchard. Each of those people was an embarrassment to ARTOK and to NipponDeutsch, and although the commercial mega-states had gone quiet for a while, surely there were still deeply black programs lurking out of sight. The avatar had hurt the companies badly, but they'd be back.

Every day, another former corporate apparatchik popped up with yet another revelation about the decades of pursuit of the alien fleet, or about farm-bred slaves from covert habitats, or about battles between company starships in secretly colonized solar systems. The result was a kind of indignation fatigue; people were beginning to long for the good old days of domestic political corruption. Hostile aliens, particularly carnivorous aliens that wanted to destroy humanity, were too much of a problem for the ordinary bloke to think about. It was all very nasty, but it was a long way away, and surely someone important was doing something about it.

But his story still wouldn't come good. This was supposed to be what a journalist would die for, the ultimate story, and he nearly *had* died for it. So why did he feel this way? Had everyone who'd been right there at one of Arden's hinges of history felt the same way when they realized it? *Why me? What can I do? I'm just an ordinary bloke.*

But so what? Human history was mostly just ordinary people doing what seemed right. Ordinary people were also capable of hatred and suspicion, foul acts and irrational fears. People could act like monsters, like the terrifying creatures they had imagined just outside the circle of firelight. They were capable of exploiting, dehumanizing, enslaving, killing and maiming; of rape and murder. That's what ordinary people did.

But ordinary people did other things as well. They put themselves in harm's way for each other, they took each other's grief and pain onto their own shoulders. Whether that grief and pain came from another ordinary person, just like them, or whether it stemmed from the blind and random workings of the universe. He thought of Harvetz, going back into the blazing carrier to rescue Drovan the atheist, a man whose view of the universe was far removed from his own. He didn't do that for fear of his god. He didn't even like the other man much. Chambers was sure that if he'd asked Harvetz why he did it, he wouldn't have had an answer. No god, no reward, no praise.

And Steady Freddy Irwin, destroying that armored vehicle, then dying while he tried to rescue the crew. You just did it, because that's what people did. Was that a religion? Did Freddy have a god? Chambers hadn't a clue, but he didn't think it mattered.

And Macdonald, the crusading mercenary. Harvetz had called him Leo, Adept. Another ordinary man. If non-believers were such a threat, what did that say about this mysterious religion? How did that work – believing something you couldn't see or hear, rather than the evidence of your senses? Well, the Leo might know the truth by now.

And the people Macdonald had despised, the cyborgs; perhaps he had been right and they were a wrong turn, a dead end in human development, but they were still people. Kirov and Arden and Richter and the others had proved that often enough. David Chambers picked up the cup and took a sip of the diluted tea. It was almost cold.

Where did this take him? What good did it do? *Don't create saints.* Remember the first rule of journalism: *be skeptical.* But no, wasn't the first rule of journalism *choose your saints carefully? Don't idealize them.*

What mattered was that he should make up his own mind, urgently. Surely this was the biggest story of all time. Speaking the words that Chambers had written, the avatar had told humanity, "we are not alone". Put like that, it was the biggest cliché he'd ever committed, but there was more: out there, out in the deep wide black that spacers talked about, there was something else coming our way, something that seemed unknowably different, something particularly nasty.

The first rule of journalism? *Get your readers' attention.*

He smiled ruefully, put his cup down and stood up, a little less painfully now. *Gotcha.* It was the oldest story of all. There was a monster after all, just outside the circle of firelight.

Time to go tell people about it.

POSTSCRIPT

The God

Readers may have wondered about the identity of the god. It's a strange way to address the supreme being, but that is how the worshippers of the god choose to refer to their maker. This anonymity confused and intrigued me for quite a while.

You may not yet be familiar with the very private group who call themselves simply "believers," but if not – you soon will be. I first came across them when I was embedded with the armed forces of the small planet of Sanctuary. That world's sad and bloody history had fascinated me for some time, and when I was offered an opportunity to become a press officer for their military directorate, I seized it at once. Many of their male soldiers turned out to be believers, though at first all I noticed was the plaits, which I innocently assumed were just the current fashion.

After the Orchard business, it was a long time before I had the chance to learn more about the believers. With all due respect to them, it didn't seem quite as important right then. You may feel differently, if you are of that faith.

It would be unreasonable for me to attempt to give a proper account of their practices and beliefs, and in any event, these things are kept very private. I recently spent some time on Sanctuary in the learned company of Heliodromos Aloysius Clarke, the Rector of the State Seminary. Heliodromos Clarke helped me to understand a great deal about his co-communicants and their faith, without either patronizing or preaching. I am grateful to him. Any errors in this account are mine, not his, and I trust that he and his co-communicants will excuse them.

The god is, of course, Mithras. He has been worshipped in many places over many thousands of years, and for much of that time there seems to have been debate about the correct form that the worship should take. But there also seems to be general agreement that the faith grew from Persian roots and blossomed in the Roman Empire during the reign of Nero.

The rise of Christianity tended to overshadow the worship of Mithras (sometimes called Mithra), and Heliodromos Clarke was unwilling to talk about what had become of the faith in the years since then. But it is now on the rise once more, and I believe that we will see much more of the believers in the years to come.

In Roman times, many of the followers of the faith were soldiers, but it was widespread and classless. Worship involved many secret ceremonies, and members progressed through a series of levels that depended on their performance in several tests. Worshippers met in temples known as *Mithraea*, which were designed to resemble the cave birthplace of the god, and a communal meal would be taken there.

These ancient temples can still be found in various places on Earth – in London, in the disputed North Humberland region of the British Isles, in Syria, and in North Africa, for example. More modern ones exist – there is one under a bar intriguingly called the Bull's Head in Copernicus, on Luna – and at many other places across the worlds. Sanctuary, naturally, has hundreds.

The worshippers believe that the god killed a divine bull, and that blood from the dying animal's body fertilized the earth. Heliodromos Clarke showed me a statue called a Tauroctony, which is apparently a typical devotional scene in both ancient and modern Mithraea. I'm not ashamed to say that I gasped out loud when I saw it. The scene shows the god astride the bull's back, his left hand in its gaping mouth, driving a knife or short sword into the animal's neck. A dog is also attacking the bull, biting at its throat. I began to grasp what had motivated Adept Macdonald.

Examples of the Tauroctony statue can be found at the Boston Museum of Fine Arts, Estados Unidos de America; in the Vatican Museum, Rome, Europe; and of course, at the State Seminary on Sanctuary. The Bull's Head pub even has an animated virtual Tauroctony that appears in many forms, in an unpredictable pattern.

The Heliodromos was intrigued and saddened by my story of the encounter on the slopes of the Pietersberg. He knew about the Sacred Battalion, of course, but would say little about them, and I got the distinct impression that he deeply disapproved of Macdonald's actions and behavior.

The only substantive comment he made concerned the name of the Adept's dog, Enkidu. The ancient king Gilgamesh, who ruled in the city of Uruk around 2700 BC, had a constant and dearly-loved companion, a wild man also called Enkidu, who helped Gilgamesh to kill the Bull of Heaven. Heliodromos Clarke wouldn't be drawn on whether Gilgamesh and Mithras were one and the same.

My thanks go to the Heliodromos for his help.

A Word on Cheff

People have enthusiastically consumed tea and coffee for centuries, and little has ever challenged the pre-eminence of these two drinks. Each has its advocates, rituals and hierarchies, and neither will ever seriously threaten the other. Just as there are some people who own both dogs and cats, many folks are enthusiastic consumers of both beverages, but – as with the pet owners – each has its own band of fanatical devotees of the one, who would never demean themselves by association with the other.

Yet both might find themselves under pressure from a newcomer. Cheff is a fast-growing craze which is rapidly spreading out from its beginnings on the so-called "Minor Worlds". This gingery-tasting drink originated on Parnassus, and it is still created there in the small cliff-side factories which cling to the precipices above the scour line.

It is made from the fermented sap of an airborne plant known locally as arbent. Arbent is a motile growth, which reaches out from the face of the rocks until it overbalances and tears itself free from its thin roots. The plant then falls freely down the cliff face until it encounters an updraft that may carry it to a new rooting place. There it exchanges genetic material with its new neighbors, and these random pollinations encourage strong and healthy growth.

If this does not happen, however, a strong-smelling sap is produced that is attractive to birds. Consequently, the plant's genetic material travels widely, and this determined plant has a third trick – the seeds pass through the birds' digestive systems and are often excreted in midair, to float down to a new and distant location to try again.

The sap of the second-stage arbent is the basis for this delicate and tasty drink. Once fermented, cheff is made and enjoyed hot or cold, seems either to stimulate or to relax depending on the drinker's mood, and can be kept ready prepared for many days before its flavor spoils. Consequently, it has become very popular with soldiers, campers, prospectors, explorers, and others who appreciate a convenient and easily made drink.

Cheff is becoming more available all the time. I tried it first on Parnassus, and liked it immediately. You'll be able to get it quite easily on Parnassus, on Sanctuary, on Epsilon Indi, on Rheparion, and on Second Chance. In Sol system, its sole importers are Rahman Food Chain Inc., and it is currently only retailed at branches of Imperial Teas. I know they have outlets in Friendship City on Luna; at Second Street, Waterfall on L5; at the Upwelling on Titan; and on Steep Hill, Lincoln, Europe. I do recommend it.

DAVID CHAMBERS, BYTHAM, ORCHARD

THIRD QUARTER, 2451

Thank you for reading ThousandEyes, book 2 of The Deep Wide Black Series. If you enjoyed this book please leave a review at your favorite retailer.

Would you like to know when the next book in The Formist Series comes out?

Sign up here: www.castrumpress.com/subscribe.
Subscribers get lower prices on new releases.

ABOUT THE AUTHOR

Prior to his SF novel series set in the galaxy of The Deep Wide Black, JCH Rigby (Charlie) wrote well-received short stories and professionally-performed plays, on subjects as diverse as a comedy about a medieval bishop who takes up piracy, and a satirical near-future in which motorbikes are forbidden until a covert brotherhood of bikers reclaim their ancient freedoms.

In the 1990s he published and edited the Science Fiction and Fantasy Magazine Far Point. Later, he developed "Nano Futures," mini short stories which distil SF tropes into 100 words.

After Ampleforth and Oxford, Charlie served with the Royal Air Force Regiment in Cold War West Germany, in Northern Ireland, in Cyprus and in the Falkland Islands. When his first military exercise was launched, he watched from underneath his steel helmet as a squadron of Vulcan bombers scrambled from a Cambridgeshire runway. There and then, he knew he'd made the right career choice. The "big boys' toy box" thrills continued with Scorpion and Spartan light armored vehicles, cross-country motorbikes, helicopters, Hercules transport aircraft and a huge range of things which went bang, generally when they were intended to. Much of the rest of his service seemed to involve carrying heavy things while running, generally in bad weather.

He subsequently worked in the print industry and in publishing. Born in Newcastle, he lives in Grantham, Lincolnshire, with his extremely tolerant wife and the world's fastest Labrador retriever. Father to three daughters, he is joyously surrounded by smart and wonderful women.

BOOKS BY JCH RIGBY

<u>THE DEEP WIDE BLACK SERIES</u>
Cyborg, book 1
ThousandEyes, book 2

<u>ANTHOLOGIES</u>
Future Days: A Science Fiction Short Story Collection

CONNECT WITH JCH RIGBY

Find me on my author page: www.castrumpress.com/jch-rigby

CASTRUM PRESS PRESENTS

FUTURE DAYS

A Science Fiction Short Story Collection

Hitch a thrilling ride into the future days of humanity.

Featuring:
USA TODAY bestselling author Christopher Nuttall
Amazon #1 bestselling author Rick Partlow
Amazon #1 bestselling author PP Corcoran
Irish Writers' Centre Novel Fair Award Winner R. B. Kelly

Visit: www.castrumpress.com/SciFi-Fantasy-books/Future-Days-Anthology

www.ingramcontent.com/pod-product-compliance
Lightning Source LLC
Chambersburg PA
CBHW050516190726
48284CB00003B/833